Patrick Redmond was born in Essex in 1966. After
school in Essex and the Channel Islands he completed a Law
degree at Leicester University and then a Masters at University
of British Columbia in Vancouver. He spent ten years working in
the City of London specialising in Commercial and EU law,
before leaving to become a full time writer.

His novels have hit the bestseller lists in the UK, Germany
and Italy, and have been translated into fifteen languages.
Patrick lives in West London.

www.patrickredmondbooks.com
@PRedmondAuthor

Praise for Patrick Redmond

'Assured writing sets up evil to overcome the weak in
this deft, Hitchcockian portrayal of a malevolent
microcosm of warped power'
Publishing News

'A highly successful thriller: a page-turner, certainly, but
also original, well-constructed and intelligent'
Spectator

'The ghastliness of the English class system lies at the heart
of Redmond's creepy psychological thriller . . .
Du Maurier meets Patrick Hamilton'
Guardian

Novels by Patrick Redmond

The Wishing Game
The Puppet Show
Apple of My Eye
All She Ever Wanted

THE
REPLACEMENT

Patrick Redmond

sphere

SPHERE

First published in Great Britain in 2014 by Sphere
This paperback edition published in 2015 by Sphere

1 3 5 7 9 10 8 6 4 2

A CIP catalogue record for this book
is available from the British Library.

ISBN 978-0-7515-5891-3

Typeset in Sabon by M Rules
Printed and bound in Great Britain by
Clays Ltd, St Ives plc

Papers used by Sphere are from well-managed forests
and other responsible sources.

MIX
Paper from
responsible sources
FSC www.fsc.org   FSC® C104740

Sphere
An imprint of
Little, Brown Book Group
Carmelite House
50 Victoria Embankment
London EC4Y 0DZ

An Hachette UK Company
www.hachette.co.uk

www.littlebrown.co.uk

To Graham

PROLOGUE

Oxfordshire, December 2013

The house was silent. All the noise came from outside. They waited at the end of the drive with their cameras, their microphones and their endless questions, like vampires ready to suck out her last drop of life.

Caroline stood in the living room, watching them through a crack in the curtains that she never opened any more. The weather was dry and mild for the time of year. It was the sort of morning she would once have spent in her garden, planting and weeding, making her home as beautiful without as it was within. Keeping up appearances, only there was no longer any point. Not now everyone knew.

She told herself to stay strong. That it would soon be over. That her story was just one in an endless procession of nine-day wonders for the media to chew over then spit out, leaving her to try and rebuild her life from the scraps that remained.

The morning post lay on a side table, as substantial as the previous day's had been. She flicked through the envelopes. Most were handwritten. She knew what they would say. The same messages of hate she had received yesterday and would receive tomorrow too.

She focused on one that had been typed. It looked official; a circular or notice of some sort. She tore it open, grateful for anything that reminded her of normality.

But it wasn't a circular. Just a single sheet of paper, covered in angry scrawl:

This is all your fault. You make me sick. How can you call yourself a mother after what you've done? You're an insult to all the millions of women out there who can't have children of their own. I don't know how you can look at yourself in the mirror. I really don't.

How could you not know? That's what I don't understand. You MUST have known. They were your children. You were closer to them than anyone. What sort of woman are you? How could you possibly not know …

She didn't read any more. Just threw it and all the others into the bin.

A grand piano stood in the centre of the room. Once her sons had sat together on its stool performing duets for their grandparents. She remembered them laughing as they made mistake after mistake while their grandparents pretended not to notice; she had tried not to laugh herself and her husband had muttered about the fortune he was wasting on music lessons. It had been a happy time. There had been so many happy times watching them grow up.

The piano was covered in framed photographs. In one she and her husband looked young and in love on their wedding day. In another she sat in a hospital bed, proudly holding twin babies in her arms. But most were of the boys themselves; as

2

toddlers opening Christmas presents, playing cricket in the back garden, posing on the slopes during a skiing holiday, looking serious in their new school uniforms and later in their graduation robes. The entire history of her family captured in a series of simple images.

One in particular held her gaze, taken at a charity lunch back in August. She and her husband stood together outside the village hall, bathed in sunshine and with their sons on either side. It hurt to look at it now. To remember the last time they had all been together.

Before the sky collapsed on top of them.

PART 1

ONE

Oxfordshire: August 2013

'Smug bitch,' muttered Doug Cooper.

'Shush,' hissed his wife, Moira.

'Why? You think it too.'

It was Sunday. Another sunny day in what was proving a glorious summer. In the Fleckney Village Hall, the Ladies Charity Committee was holding its annual lunch. Chairwoman Caroline Randall stood at a podium, making a speech about how much money they'd raised and how many worthy causes they'd sponsored.

'Bloody farce,' continued Doug. 'The bill for this meal has got to be at least as much as you Do-gooding Dolittles have made.'

'We're not Dolittles. We make a difference. Besides, we're not using charity money to pay for it.'

'Tell me about it. Eighty quid a head. Charity really does begin at home.'

Caroline was drawing to a close. 'I don't want to keep you from your desserts any longer but I'd like to end by sharing one final piece of good news. My husband, Robert, has promised to donate a thousand pounds to the famine relief fund . . . '

People began to applaud. Caroline held up her hand for silence.

'And, better still, both my sons have agreed to match that sum.'

The applause resumed, now even louder. 'Big deal,' said Doug. 'A whole week's interest on their trust funds.'

'Be quiet!'

'So, in summing up, I'd like to thank my fellow committee members for their hard work.' Caroline raised her glass. 'And here's to an even better next year.'

The applause reached its peak. As the caterers served the next course Caroline moved between the tables, exchanging greetings with the guests. 'Here comes Her Majesty,' Doug whispered. 'Don't forget to curtsy.'

'Shut up.'

Caroline reached their table and bestowed dazzling smiles on each of them. She was a tall, elegant woman in her early fifties, beautiful in a cool, refined way and so perfectly groomed she could have stepped straight out of a fashion magazine. 'Moira! Doug! I'm so glad you could both come.'

'We wouldn't have missed it for anything,' Moira told her.

'Absolutely,' agreed Doug. 'And congratulations on such a successful year.'

'Thank you. It's been hard work but I think it was worth it.'

'Undoubtedly so,' said Moira. 'The committee is lucky to have you.'

'Well, I do my best. Are you enjoying the meal?'

'Very much.' Doug patted his stomach. 'Worth every penny.'

Moira nodded. 'It's lovely that both your sons are here.'

'Isn't it. I told them there was no need but they insisted.'

Caroline noticed the empty seat next to Doug and frowned. 'I thought Ryan was coming.'

'Um . . .' Moira struggled to think of an excuse. Their son Ryan had returned from a party early that morning, only to retire to bed and scream 'Sod off!' whenever they knocked on his door and suggested it was time to change. 'He's got a stomach bug.'

'Poor thing. He's at college now, isn't he?'

'Yes. Downton College. Art and crafts. It's in Oxford.'

'Oxford? How nice. James was there too. Of course he was at the university.'

'Of course. And how is Robert finding retirement?'

'Loving it. We both are. It's wonderful to have time to enjoy life while we're still young enough to do so. Well, I'll leave you to your desserts. Thanks again for coming. It wouldn't have been the same without you.'

Caroline returned to her own table. Her husband rose as she approached, pulling out her chair in readiness. He was in his late fifties and tall and handsome like his wife. Her sons also rose; both were in their late twenties and as good-looking as their parents. James was fair like his mother, Thomas dark like his father. James said something and they all began to laugh. They looked like the perfect family, radiating health, wealth and happiness. But that was only to be expected. When it came to Caroline, only perfection would do.

'Smug bitch,' muttered Moira.

Doug began to chuckle, almost choking on his dessert as a result.

A visit to her sister Caroline always left Helen Jones feeling inadequate.

She was standing in the kitchen, listening to Caroline describe the charity lunch she had just hosted while they waited for the kettle to boil. The kitchen was immaculate: every surface spotless and the utensils colour-coordinated with the decor. It was like standing in a showroom. Helen kept expecting people with brochures to appear and ask if the washing machine was included in the purchase price.

'Sounds like it was a big success,' she said.

'No thanks to the caterers. Any slower and they'd have been dead.' Caroline loaded a tray with coffee and biscuits and carried it through the French windows out into the garden.

'Isn't Bob joining us?' asked Helen as she followed behind.

'He'd love to but he has to work. He's a freelance consultant now.'

'So much for retirement being the easy option.' Helen glanced up at Robert's study. He was standing at the window. She waved to him. He waved back.

The garden was immaculate too. One acre of perfectly mown grass, decorated with flowerbeds, leading down to the river and the small rowboat moored there. Helen's daughter Vanessa sat at a table, laughing with James and Thomas. 'What are you three plotting?' Helen asked.

'We're giving Jimmy grief about his new girlfriend,' explained Vanessa. She was a year younger than the twins: a plump girl whose homely features were made attractive by a very lively expression.

'Is this Kate?'

Thomas nodded. 'Miss Uberbitch herself.' He and Vanessa continued to laugh while James tried, unsuccessfully, to look annoyed. Helen had a sudden memory of sitting at the same table, watching the three of them playing pirates on the river. It had been fifteen years ago but seemed like yesterday. The realisation made her feel sad, as if half her life had passed without her even noticing.

'So what's Kate like?' she asked.

'A very nice girl,' said Caroline.

'That's not what you said when you met her, Mum,' said Thomas.

James turned to Caroline. 'Why? What did you say?'

'Exactly what I've just said. She's a very nice girl. Your brother's trying to be funny; though, as we all know, comedy has never been his forte.'

Thomas looked sheepish. 'Well, I like her,' said James defiantly.

'And that's good enough for us,' Caroline told him.

'Exactly,' agreed Vanessa. 'If the bitch makes you happy then we're happy too.'

Caroline glared at Vanessa who smiled sweetly at her. Helen decided to change the subject. 'How are things at work?' she asked James.

'He's doing extremely well,' answered Caroline. 'He's being seconded to one of his firm's biggest clients. They asked for him specifically.'

'It's not definite, Mum. It may not happen.'

'Of course it'll happen. You're the best lawyer in your department.'

'Which is a polite way of saying he's the biggest crook there,' said Vanessa.

Both boys laughed. 'Tom's doing well too,' said James. 'He's just been given a major client account.'

'And what about you, Nessa?' asked Caroline. 'Your mother tells me you're starting a new job tomorrow.'

'Yeah. I'm receptionist for a local newspaper in Barnet.'

'Barnet? That's a nice area. Is it permanent?'

'No. I'm just covering maternity leave.'

'Oh.'

'*Oh?*'

'You're twenty-six. You can't temp for ever.'

'Why not? I enjoy it.'

'But it's not a career.'

'Who says I want a career? You never had one. You stopped working the second Tweedledum and Tweedledee were born.'

It was Helen's turn to glare at her daughter, who responded by lighting a cigarette. 'Which one am I?' asked James.

'I dunno. The one who pretended he'd given up smoking whenever he went home, only to light up as soon as he was out of the door.'

'They've both given up,' said Caroline firmly. A pause. 'Haven't you?'

'Absolutely,' said James.

'Absolutely,' echoed Thomas.

Vanessa mimed a growing nose. 'You should give up too,' Caroline told her.

'I know. I'm a disgrace. I'm surprised you let me through the door.'

'We did think about barricading it,' said James, 'but you'd only force a window.'

Vanessa and the boys began to plan their next get-together in London while Caroline told Helen about a recent trip she and Robert had made to Barcelona. As she listened, Helen watched a narrowboat glide down the river, sending ripples to make the rowboat rock. Turning, she gazed up at the house: four storeys of beautiful white Georgian stone. Caroline was always complaining that maintaining it was a full-time job. Perhaps it was, but when Helen compared it to her own two-bedroom semi and her civil service job she couldn't help but feel envious.

Robert was back at his study window. Again she waved. Again he waved back.

*

'You shouldn't tease your aunt like that,' she told Vanessa as they drove away.

'Why not? She asks for it.'

Helen guided the car through Fleckney. Its streets were lined with houses that were more like mansions, all with ornate gates and long, well-tended drives. A place that oozed wealth and privilege and stood in stark contrast to her own home town of Skipworth ten miles away.

'Anyway,' continued Vanessa, 'the twins thought it was funny.'

'That's not the point. You're a guest in her house.'

'I notice Uncle Bob didn't grace us with his presence. Aren't you supposed to make guests feel welcome?'

'He was busy.'

'Was he hell. He just couldn't be bothered making small talk with a pair of nobodies.'

'Nessa!'

'Get real, Mum. He's a total snob. They both are.'

'I think you're being very unfair. They were very good to us when your father lost his job.'

'*Good?* Uncle Bob lent us less money than he'd spend on champagne in a fortnight and kept rubbing Dad's nose in it long after he'd paid it back. Arsehole.'

'Vanessa, that's enough.'

Silence. Helen focused on the traffic. A car braked sharply in front of her. Muttering, she steered around it.

'Sorry, Mum. You know me and my big gob.'

They stopped at a set of lights. Helen sighed. 'I know Caroline can be trying but it's not been easy for her, having to bring up the boys on her own with Robert being away so much. And Robert's not the easiest of men . . .'

'Amen to that.'

The traffic began to move. Helen shook her head. 'He does have his good points but ... well ... he's not ...'

'Dad?'

'No. Nobody could ever have as many good points as your dad.'

Another silence. Companionable this time. Vanessa touched her mother's arm. Helen took her hand and squeezed it. 'Are you driving back to town tonight?' she asked.

'No. I'll go early tomorrow.'

'Won't you be tired? New job and all.'

'I'll be fine. Let's go to the pub tonight. Get totally pissed like us working-class spongers do.'

'Nessa!'

'Love you, Mum.'

'Love you too, baby. Love you too.'

An hour later Caroline stood in the drive with Robert, watching James's new Porsche race towards the gate. Thomas waved from the passenger window. She waved back, while feeling anxiety consume her. James loved fast cars and she lived in constant dread of a phone call telling her he'd been involved in an accident.

'I wish he'd bought something less powerful,' she told her husband.

'Why? He's a good driver.'

'But it's dangerous.'

'You worry too much.'

'I'm his mother. That's my job.'

'And he's a grown man with a job of his own. They're not your babies any more, no matter how hard you pretend they are.'

'I don't pretend that.'

He rolled his eyes.

'You might have made an effort.'

'I was busy.'

'She's my sister. I'm very fond of her.'

'No, you're not. She's just someone you use to feel better about yourself.'

He entered the house. She followed him in. 'Why did you say that?'

'Because it's true.'

'It isn't.'

He didn't answer. Just took his car keys from the hall table. 'Where are you going?' she asked.

'For a drive.'

'What about supper?'

'I'm not hungry.'

'Where will you go?'

'I don't know.'

'I could come with you. We could drive to Findal. The scenery is beautiful.'

He shook his head.

'Or we could go for a walk by the river. It's lovely this time of day ...'

'For Christ's sake! If I wanted company I'd ask for it.' He made as if to leave then turned back. 'Don't take any notice of me. My head's aching and driving always helps it clear. You put your feet up. You deserve it after all your hard work.'

'Very well. Enjoy yourself.'

'I won't be long.'

'Be as long as you want. I don't mind.'

He headed outside. She remained where she was. The house, so full of voices an hour ago, now seemed eerily silent.

She went to the kitchen, switched on the radio and began to

wash the coffee cups, using noise and action as shields to keep the feelings of emptiness at bay.

'Thank God that's over,' said Thomas.

'I enjoyed it,' James told him.

'Liar. You were as bored as I was.'

'But not as bored as Dad. I had to keep nudging him during Mum's speech. Otherwise he'd have nodded off.'

The car inched its way over the Hammersmith flyover. James revved the engine in frustration. 'Nessa's a liar too, implying we're still smoking.'

'I know. Shame on her.' Thomas produced a packet of cigarettes, lit two and gave one to his brother. James took a drag, sighed contentedly and blew smoke out of the window. 'We must give up,' he said.

'We'll make it our New Year's resolution.'

'But that's months away.'

'Exactly.'

The car came to a complete standstill. Thomas groaned. 'Told you we should have left earlier.'

'How? We couldn't just leave after lunch.' James shook his head. 'It's weird having Dad around all the time. I'm so used to his flying visits. Like that summer when we were seventeen. Back from one business trip only to jet off on the next.'

'That was the summer he promised to teach us to drive. No wonder we both failed our tests.' Thomas flicked through a pile of CDs and frowned. 'Celine Dion?'

'It's Kate's.'

'That figures.'

'Don't start.'

'I'm not. I think she's great.'

'Who's the liar now?'

'You are. Pretending it's a big romance when anyone can see it's pure rebound.'

'Rubbish.'

'So you don't think about Becky any more?'

'No. Not much.'

'Told you.'

'Oh shut up.'

'You could call her.'

'Why?'

'Because you had something special. Everyone could see it.'

'She couldn't. She was the one who ended it, remember.'

'Maybe she regrets it.'

'And maybe she doesn't. Just drop it, will you. Some things aren't meant to be.' James sat back in his seat and took another drag on his cigarette. The traffic remained at a standstill. Thomas resumed his examination of the CDs, eventually putting on Nirvana. 'Good album,' observed James.

'The best. Nothing can top it except *Celine Dion's Greatest Hits*.'

'I'm warning you ...'

'What? It's a masterpiece. All deaf people agree.'

James felt his lips start to twitch. Thomas began to hum the tune of 'My Heart Will Go On' while nudging his brother's arm. James nudged him back and they began to jostle, both dissolving into laughter, failing to notice the traffic was moving again and having to be hooted by the driver of the car behind.

After dropping Thomas at his Chelsea flat, James returned to his own in Notting Hill.

It was on the top floor of a portered block with three good-sized bedrooms, two bathrooms, a modern kitchen and a large living room with views of the street below. The decor was simple:

functional furniture and Turner prints on the wall. A style Kate had dubbed 'can't-be-arsed chic'. He knew he should make more of an effort, but interior design had never been his forte.

He sat in the living room, reviewing a share purchase agreement, covering its pages in handwritten amendments while wishing he was doing something else. Sometimes it seemed all he ever did was work. But it was the life he had chosen and there was no point resenting it now.

His mother phoned, checking he was home safely. 'I was worried when you didn't call,' she said.

'I was going to. I needed to finish some work first.'

'Thanks for coming today. It really made the occasion.'

'You don't need to thank me.'

'Do you honestly think it went well?'

'Yes.'

'The food was nice? My speech wasn't too long?'

'Everything was perfect. I had loads of people coming up to me afterwards saying how much they enjoyed it. You were great, Mum. I was proud of you.'

'Thanks, sweetheart. That means a lot. What are you working on?'

'Stuff for a meeting tomorrow.'

'Well, I'm sure you'll do brilliantly. You always do. I'm proud of you too and so is Dad. It means the world to him that you're following in his footsteps.'

He sighed. 'Pretty big footsteps.'

'You can fill them. You'll be an even bigger success than he was.'

'God, don't let him hear you say that.'

'Why not? He'd agree. He's gone for a drive. He wanted me to go too but I wasn't in the mood.'

'It must be nice having him around.'

'Lovely, but I still miss you.'

'Hey, I'm not that far away, and I'll be home again before you know it.'

'Promise?'

'Scout's honour.'

'You were never a scout.'

'More's the pity; otherwise I'd be able to tie every knot known to man and build a nuclear missile out of toilet rolls.'

She laughed. 'Will you call Tom?' he asked.

'He's going out tonight.'

'He didn't tell me that.'

'I'm sure he said he was. Anyway, there's no point now. I only wanted to check you were both safe. I won't disturb you any more. Don't work too late.'

'I won't. And don't worry about lunch. You were a star.'

He disconnected the call. Instantly the phone rang again with a message from Kate, asking if he was back and if he wanted her to come over. She had some new ideas on decorating.

Becky had wanted to help him decorate too. He remembered the two of them walking around the flat together on the day he bought it. She was like a child at Christmas, full of ideas for colour schemes, none of which he liked but all of which he agreed to. He would have agreed to anything that would make her happy.

But that was in the past now.

Though he didn't want company, he phoned Kate back and told her to come over. She arrived ten minutes later, bursting with ideas she wanted to share. He agreed to them all, wanting to make her happy too.

As James listened to Kate's plans, a bored Thomas sat in front of his television, flicking through the channels.

His flat was in a side street off the Kings Road. Through an open window he could hear people heading out to enjoy all the fun that Chelsea had to offer. His sense of boredom increased. Reaching for his phone, he dialled the number of an old school friend who lived nearby.

'Nick! Hi, it's Tom.'

'Tom! How you doing?'

'Just back from a weekend with the parents.' He gave a groan. 'Want a drink tonight?'

'Definitely. Where?'

'What about that place in Sloane Square?'

'Wouldn't the pub on Kensington High Street be better for Jimmy? Less far for him to travel.'

'Jimmy's not coming. It's just me.'

'Oh.'

'Is that all right?'

'Um ... sure. Let's go to Sloane Square, then.' A pause. 'I've got some things I need to sort out but I could meet you for last orders.'

'Last orders?'

'Yeah. Better not to drink too much. We've got work tomorrow.'

'I suppose so. Look, if it's just going to be one drink maybe we should meet up another time.'

'It makes sense. Let's get together in the week when Jimmy can come too.'

'Sure. It wouldn't be the same without Jimmy.'

Putting down the phone, he continued flicking through the channels, eventually setting on a comedy. It wasn't particularly funny but he made himself laugh anyway.

TWO

Emma Ames was enjoying her day.

She worked as a receptionist for the *Barnet Chronicle*. Her fellow receptionist was on maternity leave, requiring Emma to supervise a succession of temps. The last one had been incompetent and humourless, but Vanessa Jones was both capable and funny. In the three days since Vanessa had started they seemed to have spent their whole time laughing.

It was Wednesday afternoon. Emma complained to Vanessa about her boyfriend who had yet to see any of the flats she had found for them to rent. 'He shows no interest at all. You don't think he's going off me, do you?'

'Of course not. You know what men are like. My cousin Jimmy has the most gorgeous flat in Notting Hill and he furnishes it like a student squat.'

'Is this the lawyer cousin with the stuck-up girlfriend?'

'Yes, and his brother Tom is as bad. If I had a flat in Chelsea I'd be spending my whole life in IKEA, but as long as Tom has his TV, his iPod and the phone number for Domino's he's happy as a pig in shit.'

Two couriers arrived with deliveries. Vanessa dealt efficiently with both of them, watched by a reassured Emma who was going to be on holiday for the next few days. 'What are you doing this evening?' she asked Vanessa once the desk was quiet again.

'Nothing. Why?'

'I'm seeing a flat and could use a second opinion. Will you come?'

'Sure. We can grab a drink afterwards.'

Emma beamed. 'I know just the place. It's out in the country. That's the great thing about Barnet. You're only a few minutes away from open spaces.'

Vanessa beamed too. 'Great.'

An hour later they stood outside a grotty block of flats just off Barnet High Street. 'It's gorgeous inside,' said Emma, trying to sound positive. 'That's what the letting agents told me.'

'Well, they're hardly going to tell you it's a dump, are they? The first rule of successful selling is lie your arse off.'

A hatchback pulled up with the logo HARVEY LETTINGS AGENCY emblazoned on its side. 'Driving a white car,' observed Vanessa. 'Evil wearing the mask of innocence.'

As Emma struggled to keep her laughter under control, a cheerful-looking man of about thirty hurried towards them. 'Miss Ames?'

'That's me,' Emma told him. 'This is my friend, Vanessa.'

'Pleased to meet you both. I'm Stuart Godwin. Shall we go in?'

He led them into the building. The flat was on the second floor. It was small but bright and beautifully furnished, just as Emma had been told. 'It's a popular block,' said Stuart. 'It's quiet but only two minutes from the High Street. Do you work in Barnet?'

'Yes. My boyfriend works in Southgate but it's not a big drive.'

'Not at all. I live there, actually.'

'Where?'

'Near the Asda superstore.' He patted his stomach. 'I owe my lean physique to their microwave meals.'

Emma laughed, expecting Vanessa to do likewise, only Vanessa's attention was elsewhere. She was staring warily at Stuart.

'Nessa?'

No answer. Vanessa continued to stare.

'Nessa?'

'What?' The tone was sharp.

'Do you like it?'

'Like what?'

'The flat, of course.'

'Yes. Very nice. You should grab it.'

'I second that,' said Stuart. He grinned at Vanessa, who turned away as if alarmed. For a moment he looked confused. Quickly, he turned his attention back to Emma, handing her his card. 'Call me if you have any more questions, and if you want another look around that's absolutely fine.'

'You don't want me to sign in blood now?'

'No way. We can't risk getting stains on the carpet.' Stuart gestured to the door. 'Shall we go down?'

They made their way outside. 'Are you OK?' Emma asked Vanessa as they watched Stuart drive away. 'You seem ... a bit ...'

'I have to go.'

'*Go?* But I thought we were having a drink.'

'Not tonight. I have to be somewhere. I'd forgotten all about it.'

'Oh. OK.'

Vanessa walked away, leaving a baffled Emma behind.

Once the viewing was done, Stuart drove to Henning Hall.

It was an old people's home, just outside Amersham: a large, red-brick Victorian house with twenty-five residents. Though the decor was shabby, it had good-sized gardens and attractive views from the windows and did at least have the air of being a private house rather than an institution.

His grandmother's room was on the ground floor. She was a tiny, bird-like woman of eighty-five with skin as thin as rice paper and a voice as soft as a whisper. She was telling him a story about her fellow residents, only she constantly lost the thread and had to start again. He kept nodding and smiling, trying to feign interest while feeling a mixture of affection and exasperation.

The story staggered to its conclusion. 'So they're looking after you properly,' he said brightly.

A nod.

'And there's nothing you need?'

'No.'

'Because if there is, all you have to do is say.'

She started another story, even more jumbled than the last. 'Do you like the flowers?' he asked quickly, gesturing to a vase full of lilies.

'They're lovely.'

'I'll bring you some more next week. Would you like lilies again?'

She shook her head.

'Roses?'

'I'd like to go home.'

His heart sank. Taking her hand, he gave it a gentle squeeze. 'Gran, we talked about this. This is your home now.'

'No, it's not.'

'But you like it here. You said last time how nice everyone is. And it's true. They are nice. You don't think I'd let you stay anywhere that wasn't nice, do you?'

She stared at him reproachfully. He began to feel guilty while resenting her for making him feel like that. It wasn't his fault. He was doing the best he could.

He started to describe his own day, trying to make it as entertaining as possible. Briefly, the look of reproach remained. Then it faded, replaced by a faraway expression. He knew she wasn't listening but kept on talking anyway. From the corridor outside he heard laughter. It sounded mocking, even though he knew it wasn't.

His mobile buzzed: a text message from his boss, asking if he could manage an early morning viewing. He began to compose a reply.

'It's lovely to see you, John,' said his grandmother suddenly, calling him by his father's name, 'but isn't Mary coming?'

'I'm not, John, Gran. I'm Stuart.'

She looked blank.

'Your grandson.'

She shook her head. He realised there was no point trying to convince her. More and more her mind kept wandering. It was a rare visit now when she didn't question his identity. Though it broke his heart to see her decline, a part of him was glad of it.

'Are you tired?' he asked.

'Yes.'

'Then I'll let you rest. I'll come and see you again soon, OK?'

She closed her eyes while people continued to laugh outside. He kissed her cheek, then crept from the room as quietly as possible.

Two women stood in the corridor, joking as they prepared cups of tea. One was about forty, the other considerably younger. 'Do you mind keeping the noise down?' he said. 'This isn't a youth hostel.'

'We're not doing any harm,' the younger woman told him.

'You're disturbing people trying to sleep.'

'We're just having a laugh.'

'Yeah, 'cause old age is really funny, isn't it? You're supposed to be caring for these people.'

'Oh, get off your high horse. At least we *do* care about them which is more than most of you so-called loved ones do.'

The older woman looked horrified. 'Jennifer!'

'What? It's the truth. You said so yourself.'

He glared at her. She glared back. 'You don't know anything,' he told her. 'Not a thing.'

Then he turned and made his way outside.

Ten minutes later he sat on a bench in the garden, smoking a cigarette.

He heard footsteps approach, then the sound of someone clearing their throat. The younger woman stood nearby, staring solemnly at him.

Before producing a white handkerchief and waving it like a flag.

He started to laugh. Seeing this, she did the same.

'Can I scrounge one?' she asked.

He held out the pack. She sat down, took one and let him light it. 'I'm really sorry,' she told him. 'I had no right to say that.'

'Forget it. I was being a jerk.'

'No, you weren't. Karen told me you're here every weekend and at least one evening a week too. If only there were more people like you.'

'Is it that bad?'

'For some people it is. Karen says there's one man who's got loads of family nearby but none of them can be bothered to come and see him except for about an hour at Christmas.'

'Maybe they just can't face it. It's hard seeing someone you love decline.'

'It doesn't stop *you* coming.'

'That's different. I'm all the family Gran's got. If I didn't come she'd be all alone and I couldn't bear the thought of that.'

'She's a lovely lady. That's what Karen says. I haven't got to know her yet.'

'You're new, then?'

'Yes. I'm helping out for a month before I go back to college.'

'What are you studying?'

'Hotel management.' She rolled her eyes. 'Three years learning how to stop guests nicking towels.'

Again he laughed. 'I used to be a secretary,' she told him, 'but when your boss can type faster than you can it's definitely time to make a change. I'm Jennifer, by the way.'

'And I'm Stuart.' He offered her his hand. Smiling, she shook it. She was about twenty-five with shoulder-length red hair.

'You're not from round here,' she said. 'Judging by that accent.'

'No. I'm from Birmingham originally. Sutton Coldfield to be precise. Gran was in a home there but it closed down and there weren't any others in the area I liked that were in my price range.'

'Well, you've made a good choice with this one. My parents are friends with the owners. They're decent people.'

'Thanks, Jennifer.'

'Jen.'

'OK. Thanks, Jen.'

'No problem, Stuart.'

'Stu.'

'No problem, Stu.' A pause. 'Is that what your gran calls you?'

He shook his head.

'What then?'

'Stuey. When she knows who I am.'

'It must hurt when she doesn't.'

'Yeah, but it's probably for the best.'

'Why do you say that?'

'Because if she remembers me she has to remember other stuff too.'

He waited for the inevitable question, only it never came. He was grateful for that.

'I must go,' she told him. 'Thanks for the smoke.'

'My pleasure.'

'Bye, Stu.'

'Bye, Jen.'

She rose to her feet. He lit another cigarette. She made a tutting sound.

'What?'

'Disgusting habit.'

'Hypocrite.'

'Oh, please! I only had one to make you feel less of an outcast.' The evening sun caught in her hair, making it shine. She had a warm, open face. The sort of face he knew his grandmother would like.

'Would you like a drink some time?' he asked.

Her face lit up. He felt his own do the same.

*

Later, after battling the traffic, he arrived home.

His flat was on the ground floor of an ugly modern block just off Southgate High Street. As he parked his car he wondered, for the millionth time, what had possessed him to buy in this dreary place that had no real identity of its own and was simply a location you passed through on the way to somewhere else.

The bulb in the hallway had blown so he had to grope in the dark trying to fit his key in the lock. After two minutes of fumbling and cursing he finally succeeded.

The flat was small: one bedroom, kitchen, living room, bathroom, and low ceilings. House music pounded overhead. His upstairs neighbours were a young couple who couldn't go five minutes without an argument, and their baby who couldn't go five seconds without screaming. Not that he blamed the baby. If his parents had played house music all the time he would have screamed too.

He checked the fridge. Its fruit and vegetable drawers were conspicuously empty. On its door was an article explaining the benefits of fruit smoothies. A work colleague had given it to him, together with a lecture about his unhealthy diet. He kept meaning to improve it but on this particular evening opted for pizza instead, only to realise, once it was heated, that he wasn't hungry. That was the problem with all the trips to Amersham. By the time he returned home he was usually too tired to eat. There were many times when he felt like not going, yet he always did, knowing that soon the day would come when he would never need to go again.

Only he didn't want to think about that.

He began to eat, waiting in vain for his appetite to return while thinking of how busy the following day would be. Nine hours of back-to-back viewings with clients who often just seemed to want to find fault with the properties on offer, assuming they bothered to turn up at all. It was hard to keep smiling but he made himself do it. Commission was an important part of his salary and, for now at least, he needed all the money he could get.

The phone in the living room was ringing. By the time he reached it the call had gone to message. As he reached for the receiver he recognised the voice and pulled back his hand.

'Stuart, it's Uncle Gordon. I just wanted to let you know you might get a call from Adam next week. He'll be in town for a job interview. It's with a PR company. A very good one so keep your fingers crossed for him. Anyway, I hope things are good with you.' A pause. 'And with your gran. I know it must be a struggle and I'd be pleased to help if I can. I don't like to think of you carrying that burden on your own.' Another pause. 'Anyway, do give us a call. Let us know your news.'

The line went dead. The message counter began to flash. Quickly, he pressed the delete button.

In your dreams.

He knew he was being a fool. Cutting off his nose to spite his face. But it was his face to spite.

After putting the rest of the pizza in the bin he ran himself a bath. He stood watching the tub fill with water while overhead music continued to pound, the couple to shout and the baby, clearly not wanting to feel left out, turned its screams to the max.

As Stuart soaked in his bath, Vanessa sat chain-smoking in her flat. The ashtray was overflowing and the room was thick with smoke. Her head was spinning, but nicotine was not the cause.

She decided to call her mother. The one person she trusted above all. Stubbing out her cigarette, she reached for the telephone, only for an alarm to start ringing inside her brain.

You can't tell her. You can't tell anyone.
Think what you'll be starting if you do.

She pulled back her hand, reaching for another cigarette instead.

THREE

The following morning Thomas sat at his desk, staring out of the window.

Carter Bruce was located just behind Oxford Street. It was a small accountancy firm with a client portfolio of privately owned businesses and the self-employed. From his window Thomas could see tourists poring over guide books. He wondered what outings they were planning and wished he could go too.

Papers covered his desk, all sent in by a website designer who wanted to know what savings he would make if he incorporated. Thomas's impulse was to tell him that as his earnings were completely eclipsed by his overheads he would be better just throwing in the towel and declaring bankruptcy. But that was not the Carter Bruce way. 'Our motto is that there's no problem we can't fix,' the senior partner was always saying at their weekly meetings. Thomas thought a better motto would be 'We're so desperate for business we'll promise you the earth as long as you pay our bills,' but he was discreet enough to keep such thoughts to himself.

Not that he would have to for much longer. The job was only a stepping stone to a high-powered position in industry.

Often, when boredom overwhelmed him, he would fantasise about running the financial heart of a multinational, bellowing orders to his underlings and threatening to fire lawyers when they didn't give him the level of service he required.

Lawyers like his brother and that bitch of a girlfriend, Kate.

There was a knock on his door. A blonde girl of about twenty entered. 'Mr Randall?' she asked shyly.

'Are you the temp?' He struggled to recall her name.

'Alice. Yes. I've done your letters.'

He gestured to a space on his desk. 'How are you getting on?'

'OK, I think. At least no one's screamed at me yet.'

'Give it time. The day is still young.' He smiled to show he was joking.

'I don't know how you keep all that financial stuff in your head. I get confused just typing it.'

'So these letters are full of mistakes, are they?'

'No!' She looked horrified. 'At least I don't think so.'

'I'm sure they're fine. It isn't as complicated as it sounds. One of the tricks of the trade is knowing how to blind your clients with science.'

She laughed. It was an appealing sound. She was delicately pretty with a sweet expression and looked like Kate's younger sister. Only there was nothing sweet about Kate. He often joked with friends that the only way to give Kate an orgasm was to read aloud from the *Financial Times*.

He wondered what it took with Alice.

She remained where she was. He raised an eyebrow and saw her blush.

'Was there anything else?' he asked.

'No. Unless there's anything else you need me to do.'

'No, that's all. Thanks, Alice.'

She left the office. He turned his attention to the letter, trying to ignore the fire that had started in his groin.

His phone rang. He picked it up. 'Thomas Randall speaking.'

'Tom, it's Mum.'

'Hi, Mum.' He tried to keep the surprise out of his voice.

'I'm in town, shopping for a silver wedding present for the Bishops, and wondered if you were free for lunch.'

He wanted to say no. The last thing he needed was to play gooseberry while she and his brother had a love-in. But filial duty proved too strong. 'Yes. OK.'

'I'm sure we can find somewhere near your office. It's so good for restaurants.'

'A bit of a walk for Jimmy, though.'

'I haven't asked Jimmy. I wanted it to be just the two of us. We didn't get the chance to have a proper chat at the weekend and I'd love to hear all your news.'

'Why not come by the office? I'll book somewhere. I know just the place.'

'Lovely.' She sounded delighted. As he put down the phone he felt delighted too.

Until suspicions began to crowd his mind.

Can't Jimmy make it? Is that why she's calling me?

And then an email arrived from his brother. *Hi, Tom. I'm bored. Are you free for lunch?*

The suspicions lifted. Smiling, he typed a reply. *Sorry. Prior engagement.*

Half an hour later his mother was in reception. As he went to meet her he passed the secretarial bay. Alice was sitting at her desk, reading a magazine. She looked up as he went by. Again he raised an eyebrow. Again she blushed.

Feeling ten feet tall, he continued on his way.

*

They sat together in a bistro near Bond Street. He devoured a Thai curry while she picked at a salad. 'Are you sure that's enough for you?' he asked.

She nodded. 'I need to watch my figure.'

'No, you don't. You look great.'

'So do you. I love that haircut.'

'You don't think it's too short?'

'No. It shows off your handsome face.'

A woman on the next table smiled. He felt embarrassed. 'Mum . . .'

'It's true. You *are* handsome.' She sipped her wine and looked conspiratorial. 'Are there any young ladies I should know about?'

'If only. I'm too busy working.'

'That's no excuse. It doesn't stop your brother and it shouldn't stop you.'

'But you hate all Jimmy's girlfriends.'

'Naturally. No girl will ever be good enough for one of my boys.'

Again the woman on the next table smiled. Again he felt embarrassed. Embarrassed but pleased. It was a nice feeling.

'I don't blame you for hating Kate,' he told her. 'She's a bitch.'

His mother tried to look disapproving.

'It's true. Talk about control freak. None of our friends can stand her. They complain about her all the time.'

'That's very wicked,' she told him in a tone that suggested she thought it no such thing. A waiter appeared, asking if they wanted anything. Though he knew he shouldn't drink at lunchtime, he ordered a gin and tonic.

'How did the present-buying go?' he asked.

'I haven't started yet. I wanted to pick your brains. You're so good at presents.'

Again he felt pleased. 'How much do you want to spend?'

'Not much. Your father would never forgive me. He can't stand the Bishops.'

'But he plays golf with John Bishop all the time.'

'Only because John is lousy at it. You know how competitive your father is.'

'But you like them, don't you? Susan is one of your best friends.'

'Yes, poor thing.' She lowered her voice even though the next table was now empty. 'She thinks John's having an affair. Whenever we meet, it's all she talks about.'

'Who'd have an affair with him? All *he* ever talks about is share prices.'

'That's what I told her, though not quite so bluntly. An affair is supposed to put some excitement in your life, not make it twice as boring as it was before . . .'

They began an enjoyable gossip about their Fleckney neighbours. The waiter collected their plates and asked if they wanted dessert. 'Go on,' his mother told him. 'They do sticky toffee pudding and it's always been your favourite.'

He placed his order. When it arrived she watched him eat it, smiling and shaking her head. 'You've spilled some on your shirt.'

'Damn.' He tried to wipe it away.

'Don't worry. It hardly shows.' Another shake of the head. 'Do you remember our holiday in Mauritius when you were ten? The hotel had a wonderful dessert trolley and you and Jimmy insisted on trying every one. I thought you were both going to explode.'

'That was a great holiday. We learned how to water-ski.'

'You were very good.'

'Well, Jimmy was.'

'You both were. I remember watching you from the beach and boasting to all the other guests that those two brave boys were my sons.'

'Did Dad try it? I don't remember.'

'No. He was either on the phone to the office or on the golf course. Typical.'

They both laughed. The waiter brought another glass of wine for her and another gin and tonic for him. She gave a contented sigh. 'This is a lovely place. Thanks for bringing me here.'

'My pleasure.'

'I'm happy to pay. You don't have to.'

'Absolutely not. If I can't treat my mother who can I treat?'

'Well, I feel very spoiled.'

'You deserve it.'

'Try telling your brother that. His idea of treating me is a stale turkey sandwich at one of those ghastly City wine bars.'

'Those places are a complete rip-off. Ten quid for a microwave lasagne with salmonella thrown in for free.'

'Don't remind me. The last time I had lunch with him I felt queasy all the way home.' Again she laughed. 'Thank God he was busy today.'

He laughed too.

Then realised what she had said.

He saw her eyes widen. Clearly, she had realised too.

'So much for wanting to hear my news,' he said quietly.

'But I did want to.'

'Just not as much as you wanted to hear his.'

She assumed the overly defiant expression of someone trying to mask guilt. He took another bite of his dessert but his appetite was gone and he pushed his plate away.

'You're twenty-seven,' she told him. 'You're too old for this.'

'And when I was eight? Was I too old for it then?'

'What do you mean?'

'That some things never change.'

Silence. Her look of defiance remained, as unconvincing as before.

'Why is it, Mum? Why am I always second best?'

'You're not. Thomas, stop this.'

'I understand it with Dad. Jimmy's the confident one. The athletic one. The sort of son Dad always wanted. I used to think that was the reason for you too but it's not. On the few occasions Jimmy's ever stumbled, you've always rushed to pick him up while I'm just left to flounder.'

The bill arrived. He paid with a credit card. 'You didn't have to do that,' she told him. 'I could have paid.'

'Why? It's only lunch. I'd buy you the world if I thought it would make any difference, only it wouldn't. Jimmy could buy you the cheapest piece of crap around and you'd still like it better.'

The defiance faded, replaced by hurt. She blinked, as if fighting back tears. Though he knew he was being manipulated, he began to feel ashamed. Like love and jealousy, old habits died hard.

He forced a laugh. 'God, listen to me. Two drinks and I start spouting rubbish.'

'It *is* rubbish. I love you, Tommy. You know that, don't you?'

He nodded. She reached across the table and squeezed his hand. He squeezed back. The action felt forced and artificial: the story of their relationship summed up in a single gesture.

'I'd better get back,' he said. 'Good luck with the shopping. I'm sure you'll find just the right thing.'

They walked out into the street. He kissed her cheek then strode quickly away.

Caroline remained where she was, blocking the path of people trying to pass. One man glared at her as he did so. She glared back, projecting onto him all the hate she felt for herself.

It's not my fault. I'm not the one to blame.

I never meant it to be like this.

She remembered the day the doctor told her she was expecting twins; how she had rushed home to tell her friends the exciting news. All had been thrilled except one who had warned that it could prove a greater undertaking than she realised. 'I don't just mean the extra work. It's the fact of having two babies itself. Your attention is constantly being pulled in different directions. When you're tending to one you're always half-watching the other and that can slow the bonding process.'

She had dismissed the words, too caught up in the moment to allow anything to dampen her joy. And when, finally, she had brought her sons home and gazed down on them in their cot it had seemed that her life was as close to perfect as it could possibly be.

Until she realised that James was the one who always drew her eyes.

Perhaps it was because he was the one who resembled her more. Perhaps because he cried less and always seemed happier to see her. Perhaps because he slept on the right side of the cot. She couldn't say with certainty. All she knew was that when she experienced the first rush of motherly love, an emotion a hundred times more powerful than any she had ever known, he was the one on which it focused.

She had done everything for Thomas, just as she did for his

brother: washed and changed him, fed him from her body, lavished him with kisses and cuddles, all the time waiting for that same feeling to develop. Knowing that it would come one day. That it was just a question of being patient.

For twenty-seven years.

But I do love him. I do. If something were to happen . . .

She tried to imagine losing him. Only she couldn't. All she could picture was losing James. She knew how that loss would feel; like someone tearing out her heart and burning it in front of her eyes. Her life would end with his. It was as simple as that.

And it's not my fault.

The self-hatred remained. She began to walk, striding as fast as she could, as if trying to outrun its shadow.

An hour later she felt herself again.

After buying a present for the Bishops she entered a men's clothes shop. A salesman showed her their range of tailored shirts. 'They're for my son,' she explained.

'What sort of shirts does he like?'

'Ones that do him no favours. This lunchtime being a case in point.'

She continued her inspection, eventually picking half a dozen. The salesman calculated the total cost and winced. 'Maternal love isn't cheap.'

'Nothing but the best will do for my Thomas.'

'He's lucky to have a mother like you.'

'Yes, he is. Not that he deserves me.' And it was true. Not after the way he had spoken to her at lunchtime. Not after the accusations he had made and the way he had made her feel.

She arranged for the shirts to be delivered to his office, together with a handwritten note: *Now you don't have to worry about the stain. I recommend the red one. It will go perfectly with your tie.* She imagined his face when he saw what she had done for him. How he would regret his words.

Money and guilt could cure all.

That evening James played squash with his brother.

It was a weekly ritual, an enjoyable way of burning off calories before putting them back on with an equally enjoyable session in the pub. Normally they would just knock the ball back and forth while chatting about life but on this particular evening Thomas had insisted on playing a proper match.

They had been playing for an hour. Each had won a game and they now battled their way through the decider. The score was level. James prepared to serve, knowing that only two more points would mean victory. He slammed the ball against the far wall and the rally commenced. It lasted almost a minute until finally Thomas failed to hit his return before the ball bounced twice.

James picked it up, ready to serve again.

'What are you doing?' Thomas demanded. 'The rally wasn't over.'

He wiped sweat from his eyes. 'It double-bounced.'

'Crap.'

'It did. I saw it.'

'You're a fucking liar!'

'Hey, calm down. It's only a game.'

'Yeah, and games have rules so why not try sticking to them, or is cheating the only way you know how to win?'

James's first instinct was to continue arguing but Thomas looked so angry that he decided against. Holding up his hands in a gesture of submission, he threw his brother the ball. 'OK, then. I'm sorry. You win the rally and it's your serve.'

Thomas served immediately, giving him no time to prepare. James lunged for the ball, just managing to hit a weak return before stumbling and falling. Thomas pushed past him, hitting his own return with such force that the ball flew back and caught James hard in the ribs. Letting out a yell, he dropped his racket.

'Point to me,' Thomas told him.

He climbed to his feet, rubbing his side. 'I'm fine,' he said sarcastically. 'Thanks for asking.'

'It was nothing. Don't be such a drama queen. Ready?'

He nodded. Again Thomas served. This time his return was a good one. Another rally started, as intense as the last. Over a dozen shots neither gave an inch until finally Thomas mis-hit, setting James up for the winner. For a moment he was determined to take it but then, knowing how much victory would mean to his brother, he faked another fall, missing the ball completely.

Letting out a whoop, Thomas punched the air.

Climbing to his feet, James began to applaud. 'Good game,' he said sportingly.

'Shame about the cheating.'

'I was not cheating!'

'Whatever.' Thomas pushed past him, heading for the showers. Swallowing down his anger, James followed him out.

The changing rooms were crowded, the air full of the smell of sweat and the buzz of conversation. Two young Americans stood nearby, talking about business deals in excessively loud voices, each boasting about bonuses they were going to receive. As he towelled himself down, Thomas kept glaring at them. 'What's the matter with you?' James asked him. 'You've been in a foul mood all evening.'

'Nothing.'

'Is this to do with Mum? I know you had lunch with her today.'

'And how *exactly* do you know that?'

'I spoke to her this afternoon.'

'And not this morning?'

'No.'

Thomas continued to dry himself. James watched him, wondering if he knew the truth. He hoped not.

The Americans were still talking too loudly, now complaining about the London transport system. 'It sucks. Every day there are delays. This shit would never happen in New York.' A middle-aged man changing nearby rolled his eyes at James. Smiling, he returned the gesture.

And then heard Thomas say, 'If it's so bad in this country then why not do us all a favour and fuck off home?'

The changing room fell silent. The Americans stared at Thomas. 'You got a problem?' demanded one of them, a tall thickset man with the overdeveloped physique of someone who spent every spare moment in the gym.

'No, he doesn't,' said James quickly. 'He didn't mean anything.'

The American ignored him. 'You gonna apologise?' he demanded.

Thomas shook his head. His gaze was defiant but James saw his Adam's apple twitch and knew he was already regretting his words.

'Steady on, chaps,' said the middle-aged man. 'No need for this.'

'Butt out,' snapped the American, still glaring at Thomas. All the other occupants of the changing room were now watching, their expressions a mixture of alarm and anticipation.

'Or do I have to kick your ass first?'

Thomas swallowed. James willed him to say he was sorry and have done with it. Though it would be humiliating, he had only himself to blame.

And then he saw the look in his brother's eyes. Like that of a cornered animal. It was a look he had seen before, many years ago, in another changing room during their first term at boarding school.

Something triggered in him. The instinct to protect at all costs. Just as it had all those years ago.

'You can try,' he said, positioning himself between Thomas and the American, 'but you'll have to go through me.'

'Can't he speak for himself?'

'He doesn't need to. He's my twin and we speak for each other. A bit like you and your boyfriend, really.'

'Are you calling me a fag?'

'Absolutely not. The expression I'd use is Muscle Mary.'

Someone laughed. The American began to look uncomfortable. 'Fuck you!'

'No thanks. I appreciate the offer but you're not my type.'

Another person started to laugh. Then another.

'You really should lay off the steroids. They're already causing your balls to shrivel up and if ten years of kickboxing has taught me anything it's that you should only ever aim for a target you can actually see.'

The laughter grew, as did the American's discomfort. He tried to outstare James, who flexed his right leg as if warming up.

The stare faltered. Grabbing his jacket, the American headed for the door, shouting the words 'Shithole country' as he went. His friend hurried after him, a chorus of laughter following them both on their way.

Five minutes later James stood in the lobby of the gym, talking on his mobile.

Thomas appeared beside him as he finished the call. 'Who was that?'

'Kate. She wanted to know what I was doing for the rest of the evening.'

'What did you tell her?'

'That I'm spending it in the pub with my idiot brother.'

'You didn't need to do that.'

'Yes, I did. You hate Kate.'

Thomas shook his head. 'You should have let him hit me. I deserved it.'

'You're telling me.'

They stared at each other. The middle-aged man emerged from the changing room. 'Your brother's got guts,' he told Thomas as he passed by. 'You're lucky to have him.'

'I know.' A pause. 'Thanks, Jimmy.'

He felt embarrassed. 'Shut up.'

'Why? It's true. Go and see Kate if you want. I don't mind.'

'No chance. You don't get out of buying me drinks that easily.'

Thomas's face lit up.

'Just promise me you won't pick any more fights.'

'What does it matter if I do? I've got a champion kickboxer in my corner.'

'Did you like my leg flex?'

'Yeah, it was cool. Which Michael Jackson video did you nick it from?'

'"Bad".'

'That figures. You'd look great in eyeliner and a leather jumpsuit.'

They made for the pub, all the earlier tension forgotten.

'Are you mad?' demanded Kate. 'You could have been hurt.'

James, now full of lager, was back at his flat. 'No, I wouldn't. I know his type. All mouth and trousers.'

'Sounds like someone else we know.'

'And who would that be?'

'The Pope's mother. Who do you think?'

'He's my brother! What am I supposed to do? Just stand there and let some jerk thump him?'

She didn't answer.

'Fine. Remind me not to stick up for you if ever anyone has a go.'

'You'll never need to. Unlike your precious Thomas, I know how to act like a grown-up.'

'Well, three cheers for you.'

'I'm not arguing with you when you're drunk. I'm going to make some coffee.' Turning, she headed for the kitchen.

He followed her down the corridor. 'If my being drunk is so objectionable then why did you insist on coming over?'

'So you want me to leave? Right, I'll get my bag.'

'I didn't say that.'

'Sounded like it.'

'Oh, for God's sake.' He took a deep breath. 'Look, I'm glad you're here. Just lay off Tom, OK? You're always having digs at him.'

'*Me?* I think you've got that the wrong way round. Every time I see him he says something spiteful.'

'That's not true.'

'Yes, it is.' She filled the kettle. 'From the moment we got together he's been trying to split us up.'

'Why would he want to do that?'

'Because he's scared of losing you.'

'Rubbish.'

'Think about it, Jimmy. All his friends were your friends first. They like you because you're you and they tolerate him because he's your brother. Without you to lean on he'd be nothing.'

'People like him. So would you if you gave him a chance.'

'I would, if only he'd give me one.'

The kettle boiled. She turned away, pouring water into mugs. 'He won't split us up,' James told her.

She continued making the coffee.

'He won't, Katie. Honestly.'

'Do you promise?'

Something in her tone caught his attention. A vulnerability that bore no relation to the confident young woman she normally was. Reaching out, he turned her to face him. Her expression was anxious. He felt protective, just as he had in the changing rooms. Pulling her towards him, he gave her a hug.

'Yes,' he whispered.

She hugged him back, inadvertently pressing on the bruise the squash ball had left. He winced. 'Are you OK?' she asked.

'Fine. Just took a tumble on the court.'

'Is it really painful?'

'Agony. You can kiss it better later if you like.'

'So you want me to stay the night?'

'Very much.'

'Good.'

They kissed each other. 'I'm sorry about before,' she said. 'It's just ...'

He covered her mouth with his fingers. 'You don't have to explain. I understand. But we've got something good and no one is going to spoil it.'

She smiled at him. He smiled back, catching their reflection in the kitchen window. They made a handsome couple. The sort who looked right together.

Just as he and Becky had.

He wondered what she was doing now. Who she was with. Whether she was thinking about him.

Not that it mattered.

'I'll talk to Tom,' he told Kate. 'Tell him to make more of an effort.'

'Do you think he'll listen?'

'He will if he wants me to save his arse again.'

'While you're at it, maybe you could talk to your mother too.'

'Let's not run before we can walk.'

She laughed. He did too.

Midnight.

Thomas sat alone in his flat. The room was dark, the only light coming from the pornography playing on his computer screen.

The shirts his mother had bought him lay scattered across the floor. He kicked one across the room. If his mother could see it she'd have been horrified. Not that there was much chance of that. The last time he had played host to his parents had been a year ago and only because both of James's spare rooms had been occupied by visiting friends.

He remembered serving them drinks in the room in which he now sat, talking about his job while his father looked bored and his mother kept interrupting with stories of how well James was doing, of what a star James was, while expecting him to applaud like the supporting player he had always been.

Any port in a storm. Even his.

He didn't want to feel like this. James had been a wonderful brother. He couldn't have asked for better. The one person who had always been there for him and whom he loved more than anyone else in the world.

Even though he often dreamed of how perfect his life would have been if he had never had a brother at all.

But they were just dreams. They didn't mean anything. What happened in his head stayed in his head.

Or so he told himself.

The screen went blank. He pressed replay. The film began to run again while on the camera behind his eyes the dream of a perfect life was replayed too.

FOUR

Saturday evening.

Stuart sat with Jennifer in the window of an Italian restaurant on Southgate High Street, eating plates of pasta and sharing a bottle of wine. The place was packed, full of people radiating weekend cheer. He was feeling cheerful himself. 'I didn't think you'd meet me,' he told her.

'Why not?'

'Because I called you on Thursday. Don't dating experts say you should never admit to being free if you're called after Wednesday?'

'Luckily for you, George Clooney had just cancelled our weekend in Cannes.'

'Bastard.'

'You're telling me. That's the last time I sit through one of his worthy films.'

He laughed. She was wearing a light blue dress and looked very pretty. Clearly, she had made a huge effort. He felt his shirt bulging out of his waist and tried surreptitiously to tuck it back in. Unsuccessfully. He saw her notice and smile.

'Besides,' she said, 'I had to find out if you're still a hardened criminal.'

He groaned. 'What's Gran been saying?'

'She told me about you letting down the tyres of your neighbour's car.'

'Oh, come on. I was only seven. Anyway, he asked for it. He kept threatening to shoot our dog.'

'What sort of dog?'

'A little bit of everything and lots of fleas. We rescued her from a dog shelter.'

'What was her name?'

'Skippy.'

'*Skippy?*'

'Blame my sister. She loved *Skippy the Bush Kangaroo* reruns.'

'Do you mind me asking your gran about you?'

'Not at all. It's nice for her to have someone else to talk to.' He refilled her wine glass. 'So what were you like as a child?'

'An angel.'

'That explains why George Clooney blew you out. He only likes bad girls.' He sipped his wine. 'So where did you grow up?'

'Hallett. It's a village near Watford. My parents own a pub. I used to help out there in the holidays. That's how I became interested in catering.'

'So do you want to end up running your own hotel?'

'I think what I'd really like is to have my own restaurant.'

'What sort?'

'Nothing fancy. Just comfort food, really.'

'Sounds great.'

'Well, we can dream.'

'It doesn't have to stay a dream. I'm sure you'll make it happen.'

Smiling, she continued eating her food. He glanced out at the street, watching groups of people milling about. One man caught his eye. Feeling suddenly nervous, he looked away. For the last couple of days he had had the odd sensation of being followed. But that was probably just tiredness.

He glanced back at Jennifer, relieved to see she hadn't noticed. 'Are you close to your family?' he asked.

'Very, though when we were kids my sister and I fought all the time.'

'What's she doing now?'

'She still lives in Hallett, is married to an electrician and has two little boys. What about you and your sister? Were you close as kids?'

He didn't answer; just poked at his food.

'Do you mind me asking about her?'

'No. It's fine and yes, we were.'

She nodded. He could tell what she wanted to know but was reluctant to ask.

'She and my parents were killed in a car accident when I was thirteen.'

She gasped. 'It's OK,' he said quickly. 'It was a long time ago.'

'I shouldn't have asked. It's none of my business.'

'Yes, it is. I asked about your family. You have every right to ask about mine.'

'So what happened to you?'

'I went to live with my uncle and his family. Only that didn't work out so I spent the last few years with foster parents.'

'Just the one set?'

'Three.'

'Oh, Stu . . .'

He continued to play with his food. 'But they were all local so at least I could stay in the same school. The person who really suffered was Gran. Even then her health wasn't good and she'd been living most of the time with us. Once my parents were dead she had to go into a home. That's why I'm glad her memory's going. What happened to our family broke her heart. At least now she doesn't have to deal with that.'

'But you do.'

'Well, you know what they say. What doesn't kill you makes you stronger.'

'Not that strong.'

He looked up. Her eyes were full of pity. He knew she meant well but still he hated it: afraid of the effect it might have on him.

She seemed to sense it. Excusing herself, she made her way to the ladies. He remained where he was, staring down at his plate. The sauce was as red as blood. He remembered kids at school talking about the accident, speculating as to how much blood there had been. The ones who hadn't been his friends and thought that even the worst of tragedies was simply an excuse for fun.

A lump came into his throat. Angrily, he swallowed it down. He had dealt with his loss and moved on. Stronger indeed.

A waitress approached, asking if everything was all right with his food. He made a joke about needing to watch his waistline, taking refuge in humour, just as he had done so many times since he was thirteen. It had worked in the past and it worked now. By the time Jennifer returned he was all smiles.

'So that's my life story,' he said cheerfully. 'What shall we talk about now? Fashion? Politics? Global warming?'

'We don't have to talk at all if you don't want to.'

'God, am I that boring?'

'No. That's the last thing you are.'

The waitress cleared their plates. 'Would you like coffee?' Stuart asked Jennifer.

'Yes.'

'Me too.'

They stared at each other. The concern was still in her face. He found himself no longer resenting it. Instead he worried that he had spoiled her evening. He hoped he hadn't. He hoped so very much.

'I guess the question is where,' he said.

'I guess so.'

'We could go back to mine, though we'd have to listen to house music.'

She nodded.

'So maybe we should stay here.'

'Yes, maybe we should.'

He nodded too, anxious that he might have given the wrong impression. He wasn't looking for anything else. Just being with her was enough.

'Funny thing is,' she told him. 'I like house music.'

'But you probably hate instant coffee.'

'Actually, I never drink anything else.'

He smiled at her. She smiled back.

'I'll get the bill,' he said.

Sunday lunchtime.

Jennifer was serving behind the bar of her parents' pub with her sister, Debbie.

It was called the Crown, dated back to the Tudor era, had large gardens at its rear and was packed with people wanting to take advantage of the good weather.

Jennifer's mother rushed by, carrying plates of food. 'I thought we were here for lunch,' Jennifer called after her.

'Not on your life. When I'm two barmaids down it's all hands to the pump.'

'We could get social services on you.'

'Aren't you a bit old for that?' asked a young man waiting to be served.

'Absolutely not.' She gestured to Debbie. 'She's fourteen and I'm ten. Years of abuse have aged us prematurely.'

The man laughed. Debbie gave another customer his change while glancing out into the garden. 'Do you think the boys are all right?'

'Yes. They're with Geoff.'

'That won't stop them fighting. That's all they do at the moment.'

Jennifer took another drinks order while explaining there was a twenty-minute wait for food. 'Well, that's all we ever did at their age. Remember some of the fights we had? It's a miracle one of us wasn't killed.'

'Sounds like a happy family,' said the young man.

'Absolutely. We make the Waltons look dysfunctional.' She took his drinks order. 'Are you having food?'

'Yes. What roasts do you do?'

'Turkey or beef.'

'Beef, please.'

'We've just run out,' said her mother as she rushed back to the kitchen.

'Then I guess it'll be turkey.'

She laughed. 'You don't mind the wait?'

He shook his head. She gave him his change. 'We'll bring it to your table.'

'I look forward to it,' he said before walking away.

'Someone's pulled,' observed Debbie.

'Shut up!'

'Why? He's cute. But is he as cute as Stuart?'

Jennifer took another order, relieved to see that the scrum at the bar was thinning. Perhaps she would get some lunch after all.

'Is he?'

'Give it a rest. It was only a date.'

'Some date. You've been in a dream since you got here.'

She served her final orders, chatting with the customers, all of them regulars she had known for years. Debbie stared at her expectantly. 'So, tell me everything.'

'He's nice.' She gave the last customer his change.

'More than nice.' Debbie gave her a wry smile. 'Little sister's growing up.'

'And big sister is being a patronising cow.'

'Big sister is offended.'

'Yeah, well, big sister can bite me.'

Their mother emerged from the kitchen, carrying more food. 'Do you need a hand in there, Mum?' Jennifer asked.

'Certainly not. Your dad's having a row with Chef so I'd keep well clear.'

Debbie poured two glasses of wine and gave one to Jennifer. 'So, when am I going to meet him?'

'I've only just met him myself.'

'What does that matter? When it feels right it feels right, and this feels right, doesn't it?'

She felt herself blush. 'It probably won't come to anything.'

'Why won't it? You're lovely. Barry certainly thinks so.'

'Who?'

Debbie gestured to the man who was waiting for his turkey

56

roast. He was about her age and looked a bit like George Clooney. The sort of man she always went for.

Stuart was having a picnic lunch with his grandmother on the lawn of the home. She was glad the weather was good for them. She hoped they were having a nice time.

And that he was thinking about her.

It was frightening to feel this way. To be so totally smitten. Her friends were always falling for guys and she was always teasing them about it, so sure it could never happen to her.

She knew she was being stupid. It had just been one night. It wasn't going to lead anywhere. In truth she hoped it didn't. She enjoyed her independence and needed the ties of a relationship like she needed a hole in the head.

A text message arrived on her mobile. She opened it, trying not to hope it was from him:

Hi. Lovely day here. Gran and I enjoying ourselves. Hope you're OK and having fun with the family.

It was a nice message. Friendly. And that was all.

But that was good. It really was.

She decided to brave the kitchen and see if she could calm things down between her father and the chef.

Then another text arrived.

Missing you.

She couldn't help it. She let out a whoop.

Debbie grabbed the phone. Laughing, Jennifer tried to grab it back while customers looked on in amusement. Barry was one of them. 'She's just met the man of her dreams,' Debbie explained.

Some people clapped. Barry good-naturedly raised his glass. Again she felt herself blush. 'What's his name?' asked one of the regulars.

'Stuart,' answered Debbie. 'Apparently he's got a lovely smile.'

'Shut up!'

'Oh dear. Am I embarrassing you? Well, now you know how it feels. The first time I brought a boy home you told him I had herpes!'

An old man choked on his drink. 'I don't, though,' said Debbie quickly, giving Jennifer the phone back. 'Go and call him back. I can deal with this lot.'

'I can't call him. He's busy.'

'Well, text him then, or stop your nephews from killing each other. You're no use here, are you?'

She went to join her brother-in-law and nephews, texting Stuart as she did so.

Tuesday morning.

Grabbing a quick break between viewings, Stuart sat at his desk, checking the property list on the website was up to date while listening to Pam Morris, the property manager, tell him about her weekend.

'I thought you were supposed to be updating the staff page,' he told her. 'I'm still not on it.'

'I'm doing it this afternoon.'

'Well, no rush. I've only been here three months.'

Brian Scott, his boss, arrived. 'Hi, team. Are we winning?'

Stuart nodded while inwardly gritting his teeth. Brian used this catchphrase every time he returned to the office – even, on one famous occasion, when he'd only been to the toilet. From behind Brian's back, Pam pretended to gag.

'How did the date go?' Brian asked.

'How did you know about that?'

Brian gestured towards Pam who stopped making faces and developed a sudden fascination for paperwork. 'Well? Are you seeing her again?'

'I don't know. Maybe.' Actually they were meeting the following evening but that was no one else's business. Quickly, he changed the subject. 'Good news. I've let the flat in Tooley Road. Full rent, and a six-week deposit.'

Brian looked delighted. He was a cheerful man in his late forties with a huge belly. 'Well, that calls for a celebratory Danish,' he announced. Pam, who was always nagging them both about their diets, made a tutting sound.

Stuart's phone began to ring. Laughing, he picked up the receiver. 'Hello. Stuart Godwin speaking.'

'Hi, Stuart. It's Adam.'

He stopped laughing. 'Hello, Adam.'

'I think Dad told you I was going to call. I'm in town and wondered if you fancied a drink tonight.'

'Tonight? That might be difficult ...'

'Or any night this week.'

'Um ...'

'Or I could come by your office. I'm really flexible.'

He knew he was trapped. 'OK, let's make it tonight.'

'I'll come to your flat. I know where it is. I'm staying with friends of Mum and Dad in Russell Square so it's direct on the Piccadilly Line.'

'Sure. Come round about eight. I should be home by then.'

'Who's Adam?' Pam asked as he put down the phone.

He mimed a growing nose.

'I'm just asking.'

'My cousin.'

'I didn't know you had a cousin.'

'We're not close.'

'Why not?'

'We just don't have much in common.'

'But still. You are family. That means something, doesn't it?'

'You'd think so, wouldn't you?'

She gave him a quizzical look. Ignoring it, he focused on the day ahead.

Back in the office after her few days away, Emma Ames kept dipping into the box of handmade chocolates on her desk. 'You really didn't need to,' she told Vanessa.

'Yes, I did. I feel awful about last week.'

'I'm the one who should feel bad. I just wish you'd told me.'

'Why? It was ages ago. I'd forgotten all about it until I saw Stuart.'

'It wasn't him, though, was it?'

'No, it was some jerk in Hackney. I can't even remember his name now or the company he worked for.'

'You should have made a complaint. He was supposed to be showing you a flat and he makes a pass at you. That's terrible.'

'Well, I was younger then. We were alone in the flat and I got scared and ... well, Stuart looked really like him and it just took me back.' Vanessa shook her head. 'It's so stupid. If a guy tried that now I'd kick his balls into touch and sue his arse off too.'

'I'm glad it wasn't Stuart. He seemed nice.'

'Yeah, he did. But how can he be? He's an estate agent. It's like my cousin, James. I keep telling him he's far too nice to be a lawyer.' Vanessa grinned. 'What do you call fifty lawyers at the bottom of the ocean?'

'What?'

'A good start.'

Emma laughed.

'How old do you think he is?' Vanessa asked.

'Your cousin?'

'Stuart.'

'Thirty.'

'Did he tell you that?'

'No. I'm just guessing.'

'I think he's younger.'

Emma nodded, not particularly interested in the conversation, but happy they were friends again.

Nine in the evening.

Stuart was playing pool with his cousin in a Southgate pub.

'I like your flat,' Adam told him.

He lined up his shot. 'Why? It's a dump.'

'No, it's not. It's ... well, it's got potential.'

'Yeah, the potential for me to kill my neighbours.'

Adam grinned. He was a fresh-faced twenty-four-year-old with the excessive confidence of an indulged only child. 'When I get this job I'm going to buy a flat.'

'I'm glad the interview went well.'

'It should have done. I knew all about their clients.'

'And presumably they knew that Uncle Gordon is friends with the MD.'

Adam looked indignant. 'They're not going to give me the job because of that.'

Stuart hit his shot, failing to pot. 'Where do you want to buy a flat?'

'Fulham. Some of my friends live there.'

'It's an expensive area.'

Adam potted a ball. 'Mum and Dad said they'd help with the deposit.'

'That's good.'

'They want to help you, too.'

Stuart sipped his pint, gazing over at the corner of the room where a group of youths sat watching a cricket match on a giant screen. A fielder dropped an easy catch, prompting a chorus of groans.

'Did you hear what I said?' Adam asked.

He nodded.

'So, why not let them? They've got money. You haven't.'

'I've got enough.'

'Nursing homes aren't cheap.'

'Is that a fact?' He gestured to the table.

Adam failed to take the hint. 'I saw a documentary about it. Some of them are terrible. People get treated really badly. With Mum and Dad's help you could send your gran somewhere decent.'

Stuart tried to drown his irritation with a mouthful of beer. 'The place she's at is very decent and they treat her well.'

'How do you know? You're not there all the time.'

'I trust the staff.'

'I'm sure they're all smiles when you're there, but what about when you're not?'

He exhaled. 'Look, are you going to take your shot?'

'No need to get annoyed. I'm just saying ...'

'Well, don't. Gran's the only family I've got. There's no way I'd ever leave her with people I wasn't one hundred per cent sure about.'

'We're your family too. Mum, Dad and me.'

'I know. What I meant was she's the only one of my dad's family left.'

'I remember your dad. He liked doing up old cars, didn't he? Mum says he always reeked of oil.'

'*Does* she?'

'She doesn't mean it in a bad way. She liked your dad. We all did.'

He pointed to the youths. 'Come on, Adam. They're waiting for a game.'

'No, they're not. They're watching the match.'

'Yes, they are. They told me while you were in the gents.' It was a lie but he was becoming ever more desperate to bring this unwanted reunion to a close.

Adam potted another ball. Then another. 'Looks like I'm going to win.'

'Yes, you're much better than me.'

'Don't feel bad about it. Remember, I've got a snooker table at home so I get more practice than you.'

'Not the one you had when you were a kid.'

'No. We had to get rid of that one.'

'Oh yes. So you did. It got broken, didn't it?'

Adam began to look uncomfortable, while missing an easy pot.

'Bad luck,' Stuart told him.

'Doesn't matter. It's only a game.' A pause. 'Like when we were kids.'

'Yeah, like when we were kids. That was a fun game, wasn't it?' He took his shot while Adam chalked his cue, staring down at the table.

'I was only ten, Stuart.'

'And I was only thirteen and had just lost my entire family. But you're right. I was older so I should have known better.'

Adam put down his cue. 'Why are you being like this?'

'Like what? We're just having a catch-up. That's what you wanted, isn't it?'

'I didn't want this.'

'Then I apologise. Let's pretend all that stuff never happened. That's what you really want, isn't it? And what Adam wants, Adam gets.'

He saw Adam swallow. 'But I didn't want . . . '

'Yes, you did, and so did your mother. I was lucky I didn't end up in a young offenders institution after what you did to me.'

'If that was true then why would she and Dad be trying to help you now?'

'Guilt.'

They stared at each other, while on the screen a wicket fell, causing all the youths to cheer.

'Why are you really here, Adam?'

'I wanted to see you.'

'No. You're here because Uncle Gordon told you to check up on me and you didn't want to risk pissing him off by refusing. Otherwise he might not help with a deposit and your friends in Fulham might not talk to you any more.'

'You don't know anything about my friends.'

'They're willing to spend time with you. That tells me all I need to know.'

Adam flushed. 'At least they're not losers like you.'

He began to clap. 'Bravo. Telling the truth at last. That's quite a rarity for you.'

'I don't know why I bothered coming. Mum told me it would be a waste of time. That you'd still be the whining baby you always were.'

'And you're still the vicious little shit you always will be.' He smiled. 'Oh, I am enjoying our reunion. Why don't you set up the balls for another game while I get us some more drinks?'

Adam reached for his jacket. 'In your dreams.'

'No. In my nightmares. That's the only part of my life where you and your parents ever feature.'

Adam tried to push past. Stuart grabbed his arm.

'And tell your dad to stop calling me. Tell him that hell will freeze over before I'd ever accept his help.'

Pulling himself free, Adam marched out of the pub. Stuart remained where he was, staring at the pool table. A few balls were still in play. He hit some shots, missing the pockets, while in the background the match continued.

Wednesday lunchtime.

When Stuart returned to the office after a morning of viewings, Pam told him, 'Someone's been asking about you'.

He searched through a pile of files, pulling out those he would need for the afternoon. One was missing. Muttering, he tried another pile.

'I was in the Royal Oak with Graham from Heathdene Lettings.'

'Shit! Do you know where the Forest Drive file is?'

Pam brought it over. 'And this girl started asking all sorts of questions.'

'Thanks. Sorry, who are you talking about?'

'A girl in the pub. She came over, saying she really liked my top and asking where I'd got it. It's that red one from Jaeger.'

'Yeah. Look, I've got to go . . .'

'Anyway, she said she might get one for her birthday. We got chatting about birthdays and she was complaining that because hers is on New Year's Eve she only ever gets one set of presents for Christmas and birthday combined. I told her I worked with someone whose birthday was on the same day and then she started asking all sorts of questions.'

His curiosity was piqued. 'Like what?'

'How old you were. What your family were like. Where you were born ...'

'Where I was *born*. Why did she want to know that?'

'I don't know. I didn't really think about it at the time but I was quite pissed. It's Graham's fault. He kept buying me drinks while trying to find out what our monthly sales figures are like. His are really good, apparently ...'

'Who was this girl?'

'She didn't tell me her name. At least I don't think she did.'

Though wanting to ask more questions, he realised he was running late. Feeling more than a little unsettled, he left the office.

The following lunchtime, after another successful date with Jennifer the previous evening, Stuart walked along Barnet High Street.

It was crowded. People stood in groups, passing the time of day. All of them seemed leisurely in their movements. That was the thing he liked about Barnet. Though situated on the outskirts of London, it felt more like a country town than a suburb. It was a relaxing place to be.

Only he wasn't finding it relaxing that day.

The sense of being followed was still there. Once he had dismissed it as a symptom of overwork. Now he was sure it wasn't.

He pretended to examine deals in a travel agency window. A part of him was genuinely interested in what they had to offer. He longed for a break and the chance to unwind. But he couldn't. Not when his grandmother needed him.

He waited for a couple of minutes, trying to act relaxed while feeling eyes boring into his back like rays of heat. Then suddenly he turned.

A girl stood about ten yards away, holding a load of sandwiches. He shouted 'Boo!' and she jumped, dropping them onto the pavement; then, bending down, tried hastily to pick them up.

He walked towards her. 'Why are you following me?' he demanded.

'I'm not.' She continued gathering the sandwiches.

Crouching down, he handed her one. 'So why all the questions?'

'What questions?'

'In the pub the other night, grilling my colleague. It was you, wasn't it?'

She shook her head. Her eyes remained focused on the ground.

'When I met you for the flat viewing you looked like you'd seen a ghost. Why is that? Do you know me from somewhere?'

She reached for the last sandwich. He pulled it away from her. At last she looked up into his face, her eyes widening as if she couldn't believe what she was seeing.

A chill swept through him. 'What is it?' he whispered. 'What's going on?'

'Nothing.' She rose to her feet.

He rose too, grabbing her arm. 'Tell me!'

She tried to pull away. He retained his hold. A middle-aged woman frowned at them. 'Is everything all right here?'

'Everything's fine. This has nothing to do with you.'

'I'm asking the young lady. Are you all right, dear? Is this man bothering you? Do you want me to get someone?'

Quickly, he released his grip. The girl took a step back while the woman glared at him. Other people were stopping to watch too.

'I'm fine,' said the girl suddenly. 'Really I am.'

'Well, if you're sure,' said the woman.

'I am. Thank you.'

She turned to go. He called out her name and she turned back.

'I'm sorry, Stuart. This isn't your fault. None of it.'

'What isn't?'

Shaking her head, she hurried away. Aware that he was still being watched, he let her go.

'You've done *what?*'

That evening, back at her flat, Vanessa argued with her mother on the telephone. 'I've quit. It's no big deal. I'll just get another job.'

'Assuming anyone will hire you. You can't just walk out on people like that.'

'I had my reasons.'

'What reasons?'

'I just didn't like it there. That's all.'

'You're lying.'

'I'm not!'

'Nessa, this is me, OK? I *know* when something is wrong. You haven't been returning my calls and when I finally manage to make contact you don't sound like yourself at all. Are you in trouble?'

'No! Mum, just mind your own business.'

'You're my daughter. That makes it my business. I'm sorry if I seem like an interfering old bag but I love you and if there's something wrong then I want to help. I don't care what it is. There's nothing you can't tell me.'

Vanessa didn't answer. Her head was aching. She wished she had never picked up the phone. She wished she had never taken the job.

She wished she wished she wished ...

'Nessa?'

'You have to promise you won't tell anyone.'

'Tell them *what*?'

Once again the alarm sounded in her brain. As loud as before.

But even if I keep quiet he's still going to be there. He'll always be there.

'I'm not in trouble, Mum. It's not me.'

'Is it one of your friends?'

'No.'

'Then is it one of the twins?'

She didn't answer.

'It is, isn't it? Which one? Is it Jimmy or Tom?'

'Both.'

'*Both?* What are you talking about?'

'What if they're not twins, Mum? What if they never were ... ?'

FIVE

The following Monday.

Home after a meeting of her charity committee, Caroline drank coffee in her living room with her friend Susan Bishop.

The house was quiet, the only sound that of her cleaner vacuuming an upstairs room. Robert had locked himself away in his office, finishing his latest consultancy project. 'It's ironic,' she told Susan. 'Now he's retired he's more in demand than ever.'

Susan nodded. She was a petite, pretty, nervous woman in her early forties whose husband John was a successful merchant banker. 'It's nice that he's keeping busy.'

'And what about John? Is he busy too?'

'Well, that's what he says.'

'You still think he's fooling around?'

'It's stupid, I know. He just seems so restless around the house, always acting like he wishes he was somewhere else.'

'That doesn't mean he wishes he was with *someone* else.

You know what men are like. Totally work-obsessed. Robert's the same, even now.'

'It's more than that. He keeps talking about his new secretary. She's very attractive, apparently. And young.'

'You're young and attractive. John is lucky to have you.'

'But John's attractive too. I don't mean looks. I know he's not handsome, but ... well, he's successful and wealthy. That's all that matters to some women.'

'Have you met this secretary?'

'No.'

'Maybe you should. It might help put your mind at rest.'

'But what if it doesn't?'

Silence. Susan sipped her coffee. Caroline looked around the room, spotting dust on a windowsill and making a mental note to reprimand the cleaner.

'Those are lovely,' said Susan eventually, gesturing to a vase full of roses.

'Aren't they? Thomas sent them to me.' They had arrived at the weekend, together with a note thanking her for the shirts. It had taken him a week but better late than never.

'How is he?'

'Fine. James is too. If he carries on doing as well as he is he'll be the youngest partner his firm has ever had.'

'He looks so like you.'

'Thank you.' She tried not to sound smug.

'I envy you. Two lovely sons and a lovely husband too. All I have is John. That's why I get scared when I think I might lose him.'

'I'm sure you've got nothing to worry about.'

'I just wish ... ' Susan stopped, looking embarrassed.

'What?'

'That we had a relationship like you and Robert do. You're

so solid as a couple. And Robert's such a lovely man. Far more of a catch than John. I'm sure there are loads of women who'd love to have an affair with him.'

Caroline nodded, while inside she felt the faintest of chills.

'Not that he ever would. You can see by the way he looks at you how much he loves you. I wish John still looked at me like that.'

Another nod. She wished it too, only not for Susan and John.

'I'm dreading the day John retires. He'll be so bored. If things are bad now, God knows what they'll be like then.'

'Retirement doesn't have to be the end. He could still work, like Robert.'

'Yes, like Robert. Only Robert doesn't need to. I'm sure he enjoys being retired. I can't imagine him ever being bored.'

'No,' she said softly. 'He's never bored.'

'That's the terrible thing for women like us who've never had careers of our own. Our husband is our whole world. Lose him and we lose everything.'

'I'd still have my sons.'

'They're grown up now.'

'But they'll always be my sons.'

'Will they? You said James has a new girlfriend. Perhaps, soon, he'll be starting a family of his own.'

'Not with her. It's not serious.'

'But he will. They both will. It's only a matter of time. What is it my mother used to say? A daughter is yours for all of your life but a son is your son until he takes a wife.'

The chill returned, stronger than before. She sipped her own coffee. It tasted bitter, even though it was made just the way she liked.

'That won't happen to me,' she said firmly.

'I hope not, but even if it does you'll still have Robert. Whatever happens you'll always have him. That's why I envy you. You don't ever need to be scared like I am.'

Susan swallowed, looking close to tears. Caroline patted her friend's arm, acting the good Samaritan while trying to push her own fears to one side.

Tuesday morning.

Thomas stood in his boss's office, trying to look enthusiastic about his latest assignment.

'This is an important job. Our newsletter makes a public statement about the quality of the service we offer. It's amazing how many new instructions it can lead to. That's why it can't just be written by anyone.'

He nodded, knowing full well that no one ever read the newsletter. It could have been written by a monkey for all the difference it made. 'The problem is,' he told his boss, 'I may not be able to do it this week. Walker Electronics want a meeting on Friday and there'll be a ton of paperwork to review before then.'

'And why would that affect you?'

'Because I'll be servicing them. With your supervision, of course.'

'Actually. I'm giving that account to Maureen Wells.'

'Maureen?' He tried to control his indignation. 'But she's more junior than me.'

'And has a lighter workload.'

'No, she doesn't. She told me yesterday she was swamped. But mine's not that heavy. I could do both. I mean ...'

'No. Maureen will do it.' His boss's tone was firm. 'Anyway, as I said, the newsletter is an important job. This way you'll have time to do it properly.'

He swallowed down his frustration. 'OK.'

'At least you'll have a good secretary to help you. Not like that useless temp. What was her name?'

'Alice.'

'Yes, Alice. Sweet girl but no brain. Her typing was even worse than mine.'

Thomas forced himself to laugh while inside he was seething.

'How is your father enjoying retirement?'

'What retirement? He spends all his time working.'

'That sounds like Robert. Always the dynamo. Give him my regards, won't you?'

'Of course.'

'Well, bye then. And I'm happy to know I've got my best man on the job.'

'Yeah, your best man.'

He walked slowly back to his office. Maureen stood in the secretarial bay, supervising changes to a letter of advice. She gave him a wave as he passed. Her expression seemed smug but perhaps that was just his imagination.

He sat at his desk, staring into space. A print of the Eiffel Tower hung on the far wall. James was in Paris for the day, handholding important clients through a major acquisition. A partner was supposed to have gone with him but in the end James had gone alone. Not that it mattered. James was as good as a partner already.

A sense of worthlessness swept over him. He tried to push it away. One day soon he would be the success story of the family. Soon, when he had his big job in industry and was calling all the shots, getting his menials to write stupid newsletters that no one in a million years would ever read.

And it would happen. He knew it would happen.

But still the sense of worthlessness persisted.

He knew a way to feel strong, though. A way to feel ten feet tall.

Picking up his mobile, he searched for a number.

That evening he showed Alice around his Chelsea flat. 'It's beautiful,' she told him. 'I wish I lived somewhere as lovely as this.'

He nodded, pleased by her reaction but not surprised by it. She lived in a shared flat in some ugly modern development in Peckham. At least she said it was ugly. He had never been to Peckham and had no desire to do so.

'I guess I'm lucky,' he said.

'You deserve it, though. You work really hard.'

'You work hard too.'

'But I'm not clever like you. I didn't understand a word of the letters I typed. That's why I made so many mistakes.'

'You didn't make many. My boss said he thought you were very good.'

She looked delighted. It was easy to make her happy. He liked that.

'Thanks for the meal,' she said. He had taken her to a bistro on the Kings Road, a place he often went to where the staff all knew his name and made a fuss of him.

'I'm glad you enjoyed it.' He gestured to the kitchen. 'Coffee?'

'I'd love one.' A pause. 'Only, it's getting late.'

'Don't worry. I'll pay for a taxi home.'

'You don't need to. I can catch the bus.'

'No way. I wouldn't be much of a gentleman if I let you do that.'

Her face continued to shine. She looked very pretty. Sweet

and eager. Desire surged through him. 'I'm glad you were free tonight,' he told her.

'I didn't think you'd call me.'

'Why wouldn't I? You're gorgeous.'

She blushed. 'So are you.'

His desire intensified. They stared at each other. The blush remained on her cheeks. 'Do you really want coffee?' he asked.

A giggle. He saw her wet her lips.

'Me neither,' he said and pulled her towards him.

The following morning James called him while he was walking into the office.

'How was Paris?' he asked.

'Exhausting.'

Thomas laughed, feeling pretty exhausted himself.

'You sound in a good mood. What's up?'

'Nothing.'

'I know that voice. You got lucky, didn't you? Who was she?'

'No one special,' he said, and it was true. It had just been a bit of fun. An enjoyable experience he didn't plan on repeating.

'Are you still OK for dinner on Friday evening?'

'Yeah, sure.' He walked into his office reception, waving to the receptionist.

'And you're to be nice to Kate, OK?'

'I'm always nice to Kate.'

'I mean it, Tom.'

'Yes, Dad.'

'Talking about Dad, he's in town on Friday and wants to meet us for lunch.'

'Oh, shit.'

'My thoughts entirely. Two hours at his awful club being told that however well we do we'll never match up to him.'

'Even God would struggle to match up to Dad.'

They both laughed. 'Have you spoken to Nessa recently?' James asked.

'No. Why?'

'I want to invite her on Friday. I've left messages but she hasn't got back to me.'

'She's probably just busy.'

'I guess. Listen, if you want to bring this girl then feel free. I'd like to meet her.'

'There's no point. It was a one-off.'

'Well, it's up to you. Talk later, OK?'

'OK.'

Thomas reached his office and sat down at his desk. His notes for the newsletter lay scattered across it, the sight killing his good mood as effectively as poisoned gas.

Friday morning.

Robert Randall sat in the office of Clive Allen, Head of the Commercial Law Department at Walker Scott Gregory. It was on the fifteenth floor of a modern skyscraper with panoramic views of the City. Papers covered every surface. The sight of them irritated Robert. When it had been his office he had kept it neat.

'You've done a great job,' Clive was saying. 'And we're very grateful.'

He nodded, feeling impatient. 'So what's the next project?'

'That's the thing. We won't be needing your help any more.'

He sat forward in his chair. 'What?'

'We've decided to use other consultants in future.'

'Which consultants?'

'Tony Gregg and his team.'

'Tony Gregg? The man's an idiot! He couldn't structure a deal if his life depended on it.'

'We've found him very capable.'

Robert snorted. 'More fool you.'

'You're entitled to your opinion.'

'It's a fact. He doesn't have half my experience.'

'Maybe not, but at least he's not under the delusion that he's still in charge of this department.'

'What's that supposed to mean?'

Clive sighed. 'Look, Bob, I don't see what the problem is. You're retired. The years at the coalface are over. You should be enjoying yourself.'

'Don't patronise me.'

'I'm not.'

'You *need* my help. You said so yourself.'

'I never said that. You did.'

'Well, it's true. I *made* this fucking department. None of you would have jobs if it wasn't for me.'

'Actually, none of us would have jobs if it wasn't for professional insurance. Don't you remember the Whicker deal fiasco?'

'That wasn't my fault. The client was a cunt. Anyway, I did a good job.'

'And the Levitt merger? Was that a good job too?'

'That could have happened to anyone.'

'Could it? You made one wrong decision after another. We tried to tell you but you wouldn't listen. As Head of Department I suppose you didn't have to. But I'm in charge now and I have decided that in future we'll be using Tony Gregg.'

They stared at each other. Robert fought an urge to punch Clive in the mouth. Instead he reached into his pocket and pulled out a packet of cigars.

'There's no smoking in the office.'

'So who's going to stop me? You?' He gave a contemptuous laugh.

'Security. But if you don't mind the humiliation of being escorted from the premises then please light up.'

He put his cigars away. Clive nodded approvingly. Robert's desire to punch him grew ever stronger.

'I've given this firm everything. Why are you doing this to me?'

'Do you remember Malcolm Barrow?'

'Of course I do. What a bloody stupid question.'

'That's right. Of course you do. He was Head of Department before you.'

'And?'

'And then he retired. He was looking forward to it, so he said. He was going to travel and take an architecture course. Only he didn't. Instead he kept coming back to the office, acting like he was still in charge, throwing his weight around, finding fault with everyone. He ended up becoming a huge joke. People used to snigger at him behind his back. You used to call him the Ghost of Christmas Past and said that if you ever acted like that you hoped someone would shoot you.'

Robert swallowed. In his head was the image of a lost old man marching into people's offices, trying desperately to still feel important. A man he had laughed at and despised. He tried to picture that man only it was himself that he saw.

'Do they snigger at me?'

'Not yet. But they will, Bob, and that's why we need to end this now. I know it's hard to leave it behind. I'm sure when my time comes I'll find it hard too. But the fact is, your time *has* come and for your own sake you need to accept it.'

They continued to stare at each other. Clive's expression

was sympathetic, almost pitying. Robert hated it more than he could say.

'Is it really so bad, Bob? You've got pots of money, a lovely home and family. Your boy James is at Saunders Allbright, isn't he? You must be proud. It's a good firm.'

'Not as good as this one.'

'The point I'm making is you can do anything you want.'

'But I want to be here,' he said, before he could stop himself.

'Not any more. I'm sorry, Bob. I really am. You had a great career. You did great things. But it's over now. It has to be, don't you see that?'

'I need a smoke. I'm going outside.'

Clive rose to his feet. 'I'll see you out.'

'No. Stay where you are. I can find my own way. After all, I've spent more years here than you have.'

He walked down the corridor, past the secretarial bays and the offices where lawyers worked at their desks. The air was thick with the smell of printers and dusty documents and the constant hum of computers. A wave of loss swept over him, so powerful he thought he might cry.

One junior lawyer stood in a doorway, talking into a Dictaphone. He saw a pair of eyes widen in recognition, a momentary standing to attention followed by an almost instant realisation that there was no need. Not for the Ghost of Christmas Past.

'Hello, Mr Randall. How are you?'

'Couldn't be better.' He put on his most dazzling smile. 'Just telling Clive he'll have to find someone else to do his consulting. I'm too busy doing other things.'

The young man nodded. He was about James's age and looked like him too. One day both of them would be ghosts, only that day was so far away neither of them believed it would ever come.

He continued on his way, keeping the smile fixed upon his face.

Early afternoon.

Caroline stood in her garden, telling the gardener about the changes she wanted made to the flowerbeds. He stared sullenly at her. 'Sounds like a load of unnecessary hassle to me.'

'But not to me.'

He continued to look sullen. She wished she could find someone else but even in a place as wealthy as Fleckney good gardeners were like gold dust, and she simply couldn't manage all the work on her own. From the house she heard the telephone. Leaving the gardener to his muttering she went to answer it.

'Hi, Mum. It's me.'

'Jimmy!' Her spirits soared. 'How was lunch with Dad?'

'That's why I'm calling. I didn't hear from him.'

'You *didn't*?'

'I wondered if I'd put the wrong date in the diary.'

'No, it was today.'

'Oh, well. You know Dad. He probably got caught up reminiscing with people at the office and had lunch with them instead.'

'Yes, that's probably what happened. I'm sorry.'

'Hey, it's not your fault. I'm frantic anyway, so it was a blessing in disguise. Mum, have you spoken to Nessa recently?'

'No, though Aunt Helen told me she's quit her job.'

'Blimey. What did Helen say?'

'Not much. She didn't want to talk about it. It's annoying because at our last committee meeting one of the women mentioned that her nephew is being seconded from Leeds to

Watford. He's looking for a place to rent but doesn't want to live anywhere too built up. I suggested Barnet and promised I'd get Nessa to recommend a good letting agency.'

'Well, you don't need her for that. They'll all be online.'

'Oh.'

He laughed. 'I'll check them out for you. I know what you're like with computers.'

'Thanks, Jimmy. You're an angel.'

'No problem.' In the background she heard someone call his name. 'Mum, I've got a meeting. I'll call you over the weekend, and tell Dad I'm sorry I missed him.'

She put down the phone, feeling suddenly anxious. Robert had left for town that morning, booking a table at his club for lunch before he did. She had heard him do it.

Or had that just been a performance for her benefit?

The gardener banged on the window. Not wanting to risk his quitting, she went to see what the problem was.

That evening James hosted his dinner party.

He had wanted to hold it on Saturday but Friday was the only evening that everyone could manage. Instead of spending a leisurely afternoon cooking, he had spent a frantic fifteen minutes in Marks and Spencer, buying as many microwaveable dishes as he could find, accompanied by an irritable Kate who kept saying they should have hired caterers. 'It looks so tacky, serving everyone chicken tikka masala.'

'Why? People like chicken tikka masala. Just relax. It'll be a good evening.'

And it was true. Or at least it wasn't going to be ruined by the food.

Thomas had been drinking constantly since his arrival while firing questions at Kate's friends: a recently married pair of merchant bankers called Wendy and Horatio. 'So, you work at the same bank?' he asked.

Wendy nodded. 'In the same department, actually.'

Thomas beamed at her. 'That's great news.'

'Is it?'

'You know what they say: the family that arranges mezzanine finance together stays together.'

Wendy gave a nervous laugh. 'You're on good form tonight, Tom,' said Kate archly.

'And you're looking very lovely, if I may say so.'

'Thank you.' Her tone was crisp.

'No, really you do. It's probably because you're in casual clothes rather than one of those terrifying work suits.'

'And what's terrifying about them, exactly?'

'What *isn't*? They radiate this aura of "obey my every command". Which label do you favour? The Donna Karan dominatrix line?'

Horatio burst out laughing, choking on his wine. Kate looked furious. 'I'm going to fetch the main course,' announced James, gesturing for Thomas to follow him.

'I told you to be nice,' he said, once they were in the kitchen.

'Oh come on. I'm paying Kate compliments and showing an interest in her friends. What more do you want?'

'A bit of sincerity wouldn't hurt.'

'Do you know what Horatio's brother is called? Lysander. *Lysander!* Who calls their kids Horatio and Lysander? Imagine what dinner is like at their house. They probably spend all their time talking in ancient Greek.'

James frowned, trying to project anger.

'And Kate's black suit wouldn't look out of place in an S&M parlour.'

'I like that suit.'

'I bet you do. I bet she wears it in bed, sitting astride you, making you recite the Companies Act and whipping you if you get a single clause wrong.'

Laughter got the better of James. Worried the others might hear, he pushed the door closed and struggled to regain his composure. 'Look, I know Wendy and Horatio aren't the most exciting people in the world ...'

'Too right. Aunt Helen's goldfish has more personality.'

'But Kate's very fond of them and for her sake I want this evening to go well, so ease up on the jokes, OK?'

'What's it worth?'

'I'm serious. Please, Tom. For me.'

'OK. I'm sorry. It's just been a shit week and it's left me feeling wired.'

'That's because you read too much into things. So you had to draft your newsletter. Big deal. I have to draft ours.'

'Really?'

'Yes. We all have to do crappy jobs sometimes. It doesn't mean anything.' He gave his brother an affectionate punch on the arm. 'Look, Kate's away tomorrow night so why don't we get together. Just the two of us.'

'I'd like that.'

'So would I. Now help me carry this stuff through ...'

They returned to the living room with the food. Thomas helped serve it, asking Wendy and Horatio about their new house in Clapham, this time sounding genuinely interested while being watched by a suspicious-looking Kate. Wendy described the trouble they'd been having with the builders who were converting their loft. 'If we'd known it was going to be this much of a headache we'd never have bothered.'

'My neighbours had the same problem,' Thomas told her. 'Their new bathroom was only supposed to take a week but ended up taking six. However, it looks fantastic now and I'm sure your conversion will too.'

Wendy and Horatio both looked pleased. James grinned at Kate who responded with a tight-lipped smile. He made a face at her, trying to get her to relax.

'Why don't I put on some music,' he suggested.

She nodded. He made his way to the stereo. 'Any requests?'

'Coldplay?' suggested Horatio.

'Celine Dion,' suggested Wendy.

'Oh God, please no!' cried Thomas. 'Anything but that.'

Horatio nodded. 'That's music for people who don't like music.'

'I like Celine Dion,' said Kate.

'I rest my case,' said Thomas with a laugh. The sound was warm and friendly and devoid of malice. Wendy and Horatio laughed too, as did James.

While noticing Kate's eyes narrow.

Feeling uneasy, he returned to the table.

Wendy asked Thomas about his flat. 'You live in Chelsea, don't you?'

'Yes. Just off the Kings Road.'

'We wanted to buy there but it was out of our price range.'

'Yes, it's not cheap.'

'It was for you,' said Kate suddenly.

Thomas looked surprised. 'It cost a bomb.'

'It didn't cost him a penny,' Kate explained to Wendy. 'His grandparents died and left him enough money to buy it outright.'

'That was nice,' said Wendy, who then looked mortified. 'I don't mean your grandparents dying. I just . . . '

'No, you're right,' agreed Kate. 'It *was* nice for him. He'd never be able to afford a place like that on his own.'

Thomas put down his fork. 'What's that supposed to mean?'

'Nothing. I'm just stating a fact.'

'Well, the same is true for me,' said James quickly. 'That's how I bought this place. I couldn't have afforded it on my wages.'

'But you *will* be able to,' said Kate. 'In a few years.'

'So will I,' Thomas told her.

Kate gave him the sweetest of smiles. 'If you say so.'

'It's true.'

'Of course. With your newsletter-writing skills the sky's the limit.'

'And what's wrong with writing a newsletter? Jimmy does it. Are you trying to suggest he's a loser too?'

'*Jimmy* does?' Kate looked amused. 'Oh, is that what he told you?'

James felt his stomach lurch. Thomas turned and stared at him. Feeling embarrassed, he fiddled with his food.

'Well, that's the wonderful thing about Jimmy,' Kate continued. 'He's always so eager to spare the feelings of others.'

Wendy and Horatio shifted uncomfortably in their seats. James tried to diffuse the situation. 'Look, this is the weekend. Why are we talking about work?' He nudged Thomas's arm. 'Hey, you haven't had any of the dopiaza yet. It's really good.'

Thomas ignored him. Instead he pointed to a small rug on the floor. 'Do you like that?' he asked Wendy.

'Yes, it really suits the room.'

'Doesn't it. Becky had great taste.'

'Becky?'

'Jimmy's previous girlfriend. It's a shame you never met her. You'd have liked her. Everyone liked Becky.'

Kate's colour rose ever so slightly. 'Previous means past,' she told Thomas.

He raised an eyebrow. 'Oh, is that what Jimmy told you? Well, that's the wonderful thing about Jimmy. He's always so eager to spare the feelings of others.'

'A pity that's not true of all of us,' said James sharply. 'Look, why don't we—'

'What's the problem?' demanded Thomas. 'I'm just stating a fact. Kate likes facts.'

'And what facts in particular?' she asked him.

'Do I really need to spell it out?'

'No. I understand what you're saying. Becky was the girl-friend he cared about and I'm the one he doesn't.'

'That's rubbish,' said James forcefully. 'Tom, if you're going to talk shit then you should leave.'

Kate shook her head. 'No, he should stay. I never thought the two of us had anything in common but now it appears that we do.'

'And what is that?' asked Thomas.

'Being unwanted. I'm the girlfriend Jimmy never wanted. You're the son your parents never wanted.'

Thomas swallowed. Kate gave him another of her sweet smiles. James restrained an urge to throttle them both. 'OK, enough. This is getting stupid . . .'

Thomas shook his head. 'No, it's getting good. This way I may still win the magnum of champagne.'

'What magnum?'

'For the sweepstake. You don't know about the sweepstake, do you? All our friends have placed bets on how long you and Kate will last. One month? Two? Six? We offered the one-year mark, only no one would take it. Well, why would they? Who wants to take a bet they've no chance of winning?'

Momentarily, James was lost for words. He saw Wendy shake her head. 'That's horrible,' she said softly.

'No, it's not,' said Kate calmly. 'Anything that makes Tom feel he belongs is to be encouraged. After all, those so-called friends wouldn't give him the time of day if he hadn't shared a womb with Jimmy.' A pause. 'A bit like his parents, really.'

'You know nothing about my parents.'

'Don't I? I know you wouldn't have a job if Daddy hadn't found it for you.'

'That's crap!'

'And how was lunch with Mummy last week? Pity Jimmy couldn't join you, but then again if he'd been free she never would have wasted her time on you. Maybe when Jimmy does dump me you and I should get together, share the magnum and commiserate on our mutual mediocrity.'

Thomas marched out of the room. James glared at Kate. 'What the hell is wrong with you?'

'*Me?*' She looked furious. 'Oh, of course, it has to be my fault, doesn't it? Not his. Not your precious brother. Nothing is ever his fault. Even if he killed you, you'd find a way to blame someone else.'

'I don't have time for this.' Turning, he hurried after Thomas.

He caught up with him five minutes later, flagging down a taxi on Notting Hill Road. 'Wait!' he shouted.

'Piss off!'

'You can't just run away like this.'

'Watch me.' Thomas made to climb into the taxi. Grabbing his brother's arm, James pulled him back.

'Do you want a ride or not?' demanded the taxi driver.

'No, he doesn't,' James told him.

'Yes, I do,' Thomas insisted.

'Well, make your mind up, mate. I don't have all night.'

'He doesn't,' said James, pushing the door shut. 'Sorry for wasting your time.' The driver sped off into the night.

'You promised me you were going to behave!' shouted James.

'Pity you didn't get Kate to do the same. What was all that shit about my job?'

'So that justifies you bringing up Becky? That was vicious.'

'And what about that stuff about Mum and Dad? Now that was *really* vicious. Anyway, why are you shouting at me? She was the one who started it.'

'She said! She started it! It's all her fault! For Christ's sake, Tom, we're not at school any more. Why don't you just bloody grow up?'

He stopped, breathing heavily, aware of passers-by staring at them. He felt drops of water on his face and realised it was starting to rain.

'Yes, we are,' Thomas told him. 'We always will be. Don't you see that?'

James wiped rain from his face. 'What do you mean?'

'Do you have any idea of what school was like for me? Sitting next to you in the classroom, year after year, knowing that however hard I worked you were always going to do better. Knowing that whatever I achieved, Mum and Dad would never care. Knowing that every friend I ever made would end up liking you more. And what made it worse was that you were always so bloody nice about it.' Thomas began to mimic his voice. 'Don't worry, Tom, Mum and Dad are proud of you. They just don't like to show it. Don't worry, Tom, the other kids only laugh at you because they're jealous. Don't worry, Tom, I can't do the homework either. Don't worry, Tom, I have to write the newsletter too. Don't worry, Tom, I'm as big a loser as you, only I'm not and we both know I'm not and never will be.'

James shook his head. 'That's not fair.'

'*Fair?* Don't talk to me about fair. Everything is so easy for you. All our lives you've been the one. The perfect son. The perfect student. The perfect friend. Everybody's sodding golden boy and what was I? The afterbirth. The spare part. The also-ran. The one no one wanted but was stuck with anyway.'

The rain was falling harder now but James no longer felt it. 'I wanted you. I'd have been lost without you.'

'Of course you did. Who doesn't want someone to feel superior to?'

'I don't feel superior. I never have. You're my twin. I love you.'

'Well, I fucking hate you. I wish you'd died in the womb. I wish you'd strangled yourself on your umbilical cord and been a stillborn that Mum and Dad could have cried over then buried, forgotten about and actually had the chance to notice I existed!'

The words were like a blow. For a moment James felt dazed. Then the feeling was gone, replaced by fury that surged out of him like molten lava.

'Then do us both a favour and get the fuck out of my life. All I've ever done is carry you. It's amazing I don't have curvature of the spine I've done it so much. Kate's right. All you've ever done is leech off me and I am sick to death of it. You wish I'd never been born? Well, you've got your wish because as of now I am done with you.'

Then he turned and walked away, leaving his brother behind.

-*

Ten o'clock.

Caroline heard the front door close.

Relief swept through her. She had been calling Robert's mobile all day, only for her calls to go straight to voicemail. Hurrying into the hall, she found him staring at himself in the mirror by the front door.

'Where have you been? You should have been home hours ago.'

'So? What's the problem?' His voice was slurred. She realised he was drunk.

'Did you drive from the station?'

'Of course.'

'Suppose you had an accident.'

'I didn't.'

'But you could have done in your state. You could have been killed.'

'What difference would that have made?'

'What do you mean?'

'I'm dead already.'

She kept her distance, feeling afraid. His body radiated tension like static. 'What's happened today?' she whispered.

'They don't want me any more. I'm surplus to requirements.'

Her heart sank. 'Oh, Bob . . . '

'Don't.'

'Don't what?'

'Tell me it's their loss. That it doesn't matter. Just spare me that crap, all right?'

'But it *is* their loss. You're a brilliant man. You always were.'

He continued to study his reflection. 'But I wasn't always old.'

'You're not old. You have more energy than any man I know. You can do anything you want. This isn't the end, Bob. Really it isn't.'

He began to laugh, the sound shrill and full of bitterness. It frightened her.

'You're right. It's not the end. Instead it's just the beginning. Day after endless day of . . . what?'

Us, she thought but didn't say. In the end she didn't have to.

'I'm surprised you're not breaking out the champagne. This is what you've always wanted. Having me at home all the time to be a supporting player in the sad, pathetic activities you fill your time with and laughingly call a life.'

'I didn't want it like this.'

At last he turned to face her. 'Then I guess the saying is true.'

'What saying?'

'Be careful what you wish for. You might just get it. Well, now you have and I hope you're happy. I hope it feels really good.'

She opened her mouth to protest. He slapped her face, knocking her against the wall, before marching into the living room to pour himself a drink.

Thomas sat in his flat, staring out at the rain bouncing off the pavement below. He had ended up walking home and was soaked to the skin. He kept shivering, but damp clothes were not the cause.

The row with James was playing in his head, over and over on an endless loop. Again he heard himself express the feelings he had kept bottled inside for so many years. He should have felt relieved but he didn't. The only thing he felt was fear.

He didn't mean it. He was just angry. He'd never turn his back on me.

Thomas knew what he should do. Phone and apologise. Say it was just the drink talking. He reached for his mobile and summoned his brother's number, only for his nerve to fail. What if James refused to speak to him? What if their bond really was damaged beyond repair?

And if I don't have him, who do I have?

A chill swept through him. He felt weak and terribly alone. He hated the feeling, but hating it couldn't make it go away.

But there was a way to feel strong again. At least for a night.

He dialled Alice's number. She answered on the third ring, sounding delighted to hear his voice. 'I'm at my dad's,' she told him. 'I've been making him supper. Bangers and mash.' A laugh. 'It's his favourite.' He laughed too while realising he didn't know anything about her father. He didn't know anything about her. Not really. He had never bothered to ask.

'What are you doing?' she asked him.

'I've just been to a dinner party with my brother, his girl-friend and their friends.'

'Sounds fun.'

'Actually, it was boring.'

'I don't believe that.'

'Why? You know their friends?'

'No, but I know you. I can't imagine any dinner being boring with you at it.'

Again he laughed, already knowing what her answer would be when he asked her to come over. As he opened his mouth a warning whispered itself softly in his head:

Don't do this. You're just using her. It isn't fair.

But life wasn't fair. He had learned that long ago. Perhaps she had too.

For her sake he hoped so.

So he asked her anyway.

*

The next morning, Caroline sat in her kitchen, reading the paper.

The left side of her face was sore. She had woken to a bruise around her eye. Fortunately it wasn't too big and she had managed to conceal it with foundation.

There were footsteps in the hall. Robert appeared, looking dishevelled. He had spent the night in the spare bedroom. 'There's coffee made,' she told him. 'I can cook you something if you like.'

He shook his head. 'I don't want to put you to any trouble.'

'It's no trouble.'

'Coffee will be fine.' He poured himself a cup. 'Has the post been?' he asked.

'Yes. We're invited to a drinks party at the Bishops. I'll tell them we're busy.'

'We should go.'

'You hate the Bishops.'

'But you'd enjoy it. We'll go.' He went to stand by the window, staring up at the cloud-filled sky. 'Looks like rain. Goodbye summer.'

'Maybe tomorrow will be better.'

'Yes, maybe it will.'

She sipped her coffee. He came and stood over her, stroking her cheek with his fingers. 'Does it . . . '

'No, it doesn't hurt.'

'You know I love you, don't you?'

She nodded, knowing it was a lie. Once it had been true but not any more. That was what really hurt.

A bitter thought came to her.

Now you know how Thomas feels.

He returned to the window. She continued reading the paper.

SIX

Monday morning.

Seven o'clock. Just out of the shower, a still-yawning Stuart stared at himself in his bathroom mirror.

He looked a wreck: run down, rumpled and overweight. Half-closing his eyes, he allowed the reflection to blur and conjured up the image of a lean, handsome, successful go-getter, raring to face the day. Someone who was in control of his life and didn't spend every waking moment running just to stand still. Someone who didn't have to worry constantly about making ends meet. The Stuart Godwin he longed to be.

Yeah, mate, in your dreams. Get your arse in gear. First viewing's in an hour.

After a breakfast of two doughnuts, consumed while dressing, he drove to Barnet. The route took him through Hadley Wood and the mansions that lined its streets. He stared longingly at them, vowing, as he always did, that one day he would have a mansion of his own. He had told Jennifer this when they had driven the route together and she said that he could live in a cardboard box for all she cared, provided of course that it had a power shower and cable TV. He knew that success didn't matter to her. It was one of the things that made her special.

But still he longed for more.

He reached his first appointment with seconds to spare, only for the prospective tenants not to show up. As the day progressed they weren't the only ones either. It was frustrating but it was part of the job so he just kept on smiling, refusing to allow it to spoil his day.

Besides, there were some consolations. The sense of being followed had gone. He hadn't felt it for over a week now. Occasionally, when he had a quiet moment, he would think about the strange girl from the viewing and wonder what her problem was. But it was *her* problem, and as long as she kept away from him he was happy for it to stay that way.

When the day was over he drove out to Amersham to see his grandmother, a large bunch of lilies on the passenger seat to replace the ones he had taken the previous week. He was tired but happy. Jennifer was meeting him there and he was taking her out after the visit. So far they had kept their relationship a secret but there didn't seem any harm in people knowing. They weren't breaking any rules, after all.

As he headed up the drive he saw Jennifer standing on the steps of the hall. He checked his reflection in the windscreen mirror, vowing that the diet would start the next day. She always looked lovely and deserved better than the burst beach ball who stared back at him.

He climbed out the car and gave her a wave. She didn't wave back. Her expression was anxious. She looked as if she had been crying.

And suddenly he knew why.

For a moment he felt dizzy. His legs seemed made of jelly, unable to support his weight. Briefly he thought he might fall.

Then the feeling was gone, replaced by calm so total that it was as if he was experiencing someone else's tragedy rather than his own.

She hurried towards him. 'You don't have to tell me,' he said.

She hugged him. He hugged her back while trying not to crush the flowers. 'How did it happen?'

'She died in her sleep this afternoon. They wanted to phone you but I asked them not to. I thought you'd want to hear it in person.'

'I would. Thanks.'

He heard her gulp and gave her a squeeze. 'Hey, it's all right. I'm glad she died like that. It's a good way to go.' In the distance he saw two other members of staff watching and realised their relationship certainly wasn't secret any more. The thought struck him as funny and he began to laugh.

'I'm sorry,' he said quickly. 'I don't know why I'm doing this.'

'You're in shock. That's why.' Stepping back, she wiped her eyes and stared into his face. 'But you don't have to go through this alone. You know that, don't you?'

He gestured to the flowers. 'It's a shame to waste these. Perhaps someone else would like them.'

She continued to stare at him, her expression anxious. He kissed her cheek. 'I'm OK, Jen. Don't worry about me. I've had a long time to prepare for this.'

Taking her hand, he led her into the hall.

Tuesday afternoon.
The Mote House was a hotel on the outskirts of Oxford. It was large and impersonal and ideal for those who wanted to keep their rendezvous a secret.

Susan Bishop stood naked in front of the dressing table mirror, turning this way and that, checking herself from every angle and liking what she saw. At forty-two she still had the body of a woman ten years younger.

'The thing I don't understand,' said her companion, 'is how that idiot of a husband could even think of cheating on you.'

Laughing, she returned to the bed. Robert Randall, also naked, lay upon it, his arms behind his head and a contented smile on his face. A half-empty bottle of champagne stood in a cooler on the bedside table. She filled a glass and handed it to him. 'Go on. You deserve it after all your hard work.'

'You sound like a client.'

'And you're always the lawyer. Every time I meet you I know I'll get screwed.'

He downed the glass in a single gulp. Drops of liquid remained on his lips. She wiped them away while he tried to bite her fingers. His mouth felt hot and wet.

'Is Caroline this much fun?' she asked.

He rolled his eyes.

'Didn't think so. God, your wife is such a fool.'

'That's cruel. She feels sorry for you.'

'I rest my case. She's so easy to fool. Self-satisfied people always are. Just let them feel they're better than you and they'll believe anything you tell them.'

He didn't answer. A troubled look came into his face. She stroked his cheek. 'Isn't it a bit late to be developing a conscience? It's been six months now, when you can get it up, that is.'

'I can always get it up.'

'God bless Viagra.'

'I'll never need Viagra.'

'Try saying that when you're eighty.'

'Who says I'll still be seeing you when I'm eighty?'

'I do.' She ran her nails down his chest, tangling them in his chest hair. 'I give you what you need.'

'You think a lot of yourself.'

'So do you. That's what makes this special. We're good together.'

'You think this is special?'

'Don't you?'

He turned and stared at the curtains. She gazed down at him, feeling uneasy. Quickly, she gave herself a metaphorical shake. It was just sex. That was all it had ever been. All she had ever wanted it to be.

Or so she'd thought.

'So why are we here, then?' she asked him.

'Because we're bored. You in particular. You'd split the world in two if you could, just to see what would happen.' He turned back, tugging a lock of her hair. His touch excited her but it was more than desire. He was an unpleasant man. She was an unpleasant woman. But even the most objectionable of people could still have feelings.

'Am I right?' he asked.

She masked her disappointment with a smile. 'Absolutely. Maybe we'll get bored with each other soon.'

'Maybe we will.'

'Maybe I'm bored already. Maybe I've already got my sights on someone else.'

'Like who?'

'Someone younger.'

'If you can find one.' He began to laugh. The sound was hurtful, but she knew how to hurt him back.

'Oh, I can. Don't worry about that. One of your sons, perhaps.'

His eyes widened. The shot had hit its mark. 'Don't be stupid.'

'Who's being stupid? They're good-looking guys. Jimmy, in particular.'

'He's still a boy.'

'Only in your eyes. In everyone else's he's a successful young man who's already making a noise in the world.'

'Is he hell! He's only got where he has because he's my son. It was my reputation that opened all the doors for him.'

'Not according to Caroline.'

'What the fuck does she know about it? Jimmy will never achieve what I have. He doesn't have it in him. If his mother wasn't such a sentimental fool she'd see it too.'

She continued to tug at his chest hair. 'He's still handsome, though.'

He grabbed her wrist, squeezing it hard. 'Don't even think about it.'

'Why not? What does it matter to you?' She gestured to the room they were in. 'As you said yourself, this doesn't mean anything. We're just two people passing some time. How I choose to pass the rest of it is no business of yours.'

His grip grew even tighter. 'Yes, it is.'

Again she laughed. With her free hand she reached for his groin, feeling him respond to her touch.

'Told you this was special,' she said.

Thursday evening.
Kate stood alone in James's flat.

She had her own key now. He'd given it to her at the start of the week. She looked around the room, considering what redesign she wanted before deciding there wasn't much point. She had her own flat in Islington and if they sold both they would have more than enough for a beautiful house in the country. She had always planned that once she was married she would live in the country.

And that was what was going to happen. She would make it happen. Briefly the intensity of her feelings had made her weak but now she had control of herself again. Failure, after all, was not in her genes. She came from a family of achievers and had learned early that when you wanted something you never stopped fighting until it was yours. She wanted James and she was going to have him. No one, not even James himself, was going to stand in her way.

There were still hurdles to overcome. The ghost of Becky needed a proper exorcising. But that was simple enough. It was his friends and family who kept reminding him of Becky and already he was seeing less of his friends. Soon he wouldn't see them at all. They were idiots anyway. Fools who thought they could bet on her future, never suspecting that they were the ones who would soon be history.

And as for his family ...

A photograph of his parents and brother stood on a side table. She studied each face in turn. The father was not a problem; an egotistical narcissist too in love with himself to care whom his son fell in love with. The mother would be harder, but already she was clinging to her son too tightly and weakening her hold as a result. In time he would feel suffocated and make the final pull free.

Which just left Thomas.

Once she had viewed him as her biggest threat, but not any more. After the things he had said to James on Friday night a rift had appeared that, with her help, was only going to widen, eventually becoming an abyss that could never be bridged.

In the photograph Thomas was smiling. She formed her

hand into a gun and pointed it at his head. 'Goodbye, loser,' she whispered, and fired her shot.

Then, smiling, she blew imaginary smoke from her fingers.

Friday afternoon.
Stuart stood beside his grandmother's grave.

She was being buried in Sutton Coldfield, in the plot next to that of his parents and sister. He stared down at the coffin. Jennifer stood beside him, holding his hand. She had insisted on coming, telling him that he shouldn't go alone. He was grateful for her concern even though he didn't need it. He still felt as calm as he had when he heard the news.

The churchyard was on a hill. In the distance he could see rows of houses. Once, one of them had been his home. He squinted, trying to identify it, but was unable to do so. Not that it mattered. The past was the past and he had learned the hard way that there was no point looking back.

The vicar was talking about his grandmother. He tried to pay attention but instead found himself counting the wreaths that lay around the grave. In the build-up to the funeral he had become obsessed with the idea of her not having enough flowers and that it would look as if no one cared. When he phoned her old friends and neighbours to tell them she was dead he had brushed aside their expressions of sympathy, too eager to tell them where to send their floral tributes.

Some of those friends were there now. He noticed them watching him and tried not to feel resentful. He didn't need their sympathy. Loss was a part of life and tears never solved anything.

He turned, staring at the church. His parents had brought him to it every Sunday and he would constantly make faces at his sister during prayers, trying, usually successfully, to make her laugh. Once the service was over they would return home for their Sunday roast and, as they ate, his mother would tell him that he must behave himself at next week's service. He would promise to do so, secretly crossing his fingers under the table, blissfully unaware that soon the day would come when no one would care enough to make him go to the church again.

The vicar finished speaking. For a moment the other mourners bent their heads in silent prayer. Then they gathered round him, offering condolences while he smiled politely and wished they would all just go away.

As Jennifer stood by Stuart, listening to one of his grandmother's old neighbours reminisce, she realised they were being watched. A man stood some distance away, half-hidden behind a tree. Curious, she left Stuart with the others and walked over to him.

He was about sixty, tall and thin with greying hair and a nervous expression. 'Hello,' she said. 'Did you know Edna?'

'Yes.'

'Were you a neighbour?'

He shook his head. 'My name is Gordon. I'm Stuart's uncle.'

'Oh.'

'Are you a friend of Stuart's?'

'I'm his girlfriend.'

'What's your name?'

'Jennifer.'

He offered her his hand. 'Would you like to join us?' she asked.

'I don't think that would be a good idea.'

'You got that right,' said a voice behind her.

She turned to see an angry-looking Stuart. 'What are you doing here?' he demanded of his uncle.

'One of your grandmother's friends told us what had happened.'

'So? This has nothing to do with you. She wasn't your family.'

'No, but you are.'

'Not any more.'

'Stuart, please, can't we just—'

'What? Bury the hatchet? Don't tempt me.'

'Do you think I don't regret what happened? There isn't a day goes by that I don't wish I'd done things differently.'

'Oh, cue the violins.'

'I'm still your uncle. I always will be. If you ever need me . . .'

'Need you? I needed you fourteen years ago and what did you do? Well, I'm not that frightened kid any more and as I told Adam, hell will freeze over before I'll ask you for anything again.'

Stuart walked away. Jennifer remained where she was. Gordon blinked, looking close to tears. She touched his arm. 'He's upset. He doesn't mean that.'

'Yes, he does, and the terrible thing is I don't blame him.'

She didn't answer, unsure of what to say.

'You should go after him. Make sure he's all right.'

'OK. If you're sure.'

'Just promise me something?'

'What?'

'That you'll take care of him. I was watching you. I could tell from the way you look at him how much he means to you. He's not as tough as he makes out and he needs someone like you.'

'I promise.'

'Thank you, Jennifer.'

She hurried after Stuart. He was standing by his car, breathing heavily. 'Don't tell me I was out of order,' he said as she approached.

'I wasn't going to. It's none of my business.'

'That's right. It's not.' He gestured to one of his grandmother's friends. 'She's organised a get-together at her house. A chance to say a final farewell.'

'Do you want to go?'

'I don't have much choice, do I?'

'We don't have to stay long. We can just make an appearance. Nobody will mind. They all know how painful this is for you.'

'I'm fine.'

She nodded, knowing that soon the shock would wear off and the grief would kick in.

He unlocked the car, made as if to climb inside, then stared up at the church. 'They're raising money to rebuild the roof. I'm going to contribute five hundred pounds.'

'That's a lovely thing to do.'

'My mum loved this place.'

'I'd like to give something too.'

'You don't have to. You didn't know my mum.'

'No, but I know you.'

'Thanks.' A pause. 'I'm sorry I snapped at you.'

'You don't need to apologise.'

'We'd better get going. The sooner we get there the sooner we can leave.'

Together they climbed into the car.

Two o'clock in the morning.

Caroline lay in her bed, staring up at the ceiling.

Robert lay on his back beside her, snoring loud enough to

105

wake the dead. Moonlight crept through the curtains, giving the room a faint glow. She turned and gazed at him, her head full of questions she was too afraid to ask.

He had been out all afternoon. Taking a drive, so he had said. She wondered what he had really been doing, and who he had been doing it with.

She knew he had never been faithful. Within a year of their wedding the telltale signs had started to appear. Calls cut short when she entered the room. Discarded receipts from restaurants she had never been to. Business trips that seemed to last just a night longer than was necessary. She had never minded before. Well, not really. It was only a physical betrayal, after all. His only true passion had ever been his career, but now that passion was spent, leaving a dangerously large hole unfilled.

During her years in Fleckney she had seen so many marriages end in divorce. Women she had called her friends, all leading comfortable, secure lives, suddenly finding themselves discarded for younger models. And when the husbands discarded them the village did too. Money was power and in Fleckney it was men who made the rules.

In the past she had always felt immune from the threat of replacement, something she was sure the other women sensed and resented her for. She could already imagine their reactions if her marriage and social standing were to collapse: public expressions of solidarity masking private delight. In her head she could hear their laughter; like the cackle of hyenas, and the most terrible thing of all was there was nothing she could do about it. Robert had always had the power in their relationship and if a suitable substitute appeared he would discard her as casually as if she were a soiled shirt.

And then all she would have were her sons.

She remembered Susan Bishop's words: a son is a son until

he takes a wife. Though marriage was inevitable, she was determined they would remain hers. It would be easy with Thomas. His eagerness for her approval would see to that. The real battle would be for James – but she would win that too, whatever it took and whomever she had to hurt. She had no choice. When you were fighting for survival all rules of fair play went out of the window.

Robert stirred in his sleep. She continued to watch him, remembering her euphoria when this dynamic young man from a wealthy family had asked her to be his wife. Though she dreaded losing him, a part of her had started to fantasise about his death. Under the terms of his will his estate was hers for life, and with that wealth behind her she would always be safe.

He rolled onto his side. The snoring stopped, his breathing now so faint she had to strain to hear it. She imagined it stopping altogether; of touching his body and feeling it grow cold.

She closed her eyes, trying to silence the voices in her head, but minutes grew into hours and sleep remained elusive.

Five o'clock in the morning.
Stuart woke with a start.

He had been dreaming about the funeral. As he stood by his grandmother's grave he heard muffled screams and realised that it was his parents and sister banging on their coffins, trying to escape before the last of the air ran out ...

His heart was pounding. He sat up in bed, wiping his face and finding himself drenched in sweat. Moving softly so as not to wake Jennifer, he went to take a shower.

He stood in the bathtub, letting the hot water blast him, breathing deeply, waiting for his heart to slow. Once it had done so he reached for the shower gel. It stood on the window ledge, next to a plastic model of Nelson's Column that had once been full of bubble bath. He had had it since he was ten and had made his first-ever visit to London with his family. His parents bought it for him and though it was tacky he had always liked it. He picked it up, stroking its surface and remembering the trip.

His mother had left them in the National Gallery and gone to book a table for tea at the Savoy. She had been taken there as a child and had always wanted to take her children too. Though his father and sister loved the gallery, he had become bored and slipped out to Trafalgar Square, marvelling at its size and the mass of people gathered there. Eventually, after asking directions, he walked up the Strand towards the Savoy, only to see his family gathered outside it, all looking distressed. He called out to them and his mother ran towards him and slapped his face. It was the first and only time she had ever hit him and he burst into tears. She wrapped him in her arms, covering his face in kisses, telling him that she was sorry, that she had only done it because she was frightened, and making him promise he would never ever wander off like that again.

He remembered how tightly she held him. She almost crushed the life out of him but he didn't mind. Though he had always known she loved him, it was only at that moment he realised just how intense the feeling was. How precious it was. How warm and safe it made him feel.

And suddenly he longed to feel like that again. Ached for it with every fibre of his being. Just once. Just for a second. To have someone hug him as if their very life depended on it.

As Jennifer's eyes adapted to the darkness she realised that she could hear the sound of running water.

She crossed the hall and entered the bathroom. Stuart was

crouched in the tub, sobbing his heart out while hot water pounded his back, turning the skin red. She turned off the shower, climbed into the tub and wrapped her arms around him, feeling her own skin grow wet. He pressed himself against her as she crooned over him like a mother comforting her child, weaving her magic to keep the monsters at bay.

'It's all right,' she whispered. 'I'm here.'

He tried to speak, his words lost in gulps. She wondered if he had cried like this for his parents and whether he had been alone when he did. She wished she could have been there for him then and let him know that however much he was hurting there was still someone who cared.

They remained like that for some time, saying nothing while he hugged her as if his life depended on it.

Mid-morning.

Stuart and Jennifer lay together in his bed. He had insisted on changing the sheets, even though she told him there was no need. Sweat, like grief, was just a part of life.

'I should be at work,' he said.

She stroked his face. 'Is that where you want to be?'

He pressed himself against her. 'This is where I want to be.'

'Me too.'

'It was peaceful, wasn't it? For her at the end?'

'Yes, it was. And she was happy there. You should be proud of what you did: sacrificing the life you had in Sutton Coldfield to make sure hers was the best it could possibly be.'

'I'd like to show you Sutton properly. The house we lived in. The school I went to. All my old haunts.'

'I'd like that.'

'Though knowing my luck we'd run into my uncle.'

She nodded.

'Do you want to hear about it?'

'Only if you want to tell me.'

'Yes, I do.'

'OK.'

'He was my mother's brother, the only family she had. He was a bank manager. My aunt was very proud of that. Dad was just a car salesman and she always looked down on him because of it.'

'More fool her.'

'Yeah, that's what Mum always said. But in spite of that, she and Uncle Gordon were close. He used to come round all the time and bring my sister Sam and me presents. He was a great uncle.' He sighed. 'That's what made it so hard.'

She squeezed his hand. He squeezed back.

'He and his wife, my Aunty Eileen, were older than my parents. They were desperate for children. They tried for years but Eileen had one miscarriage after another. Then, finally, when they'd almost given up hope she had Adam. He was the apple of their eye and they spoiled him to death. Sam and I tried to make friends with him. He was our cousin after all, but he was like his mother and always thought his family was much better than ours.

'When my parents died, Gordon and Eileen took me in. Eileen wasn't thrilled about it but the one who really hated it was Adam. He couldn't bear the thought of having another child in the house, of not having his parents' undivided attention every second of the day. From the moment I walked through the door he was planning how to drive me out of it again.

'He started telling lies about me. At first he used to break things and said I'd done it. Then, when that didn't work, he started hurting himself. He got hold of some cigarettes once, burned his own arm and said that I'd done it. And then ...'

He stopped, exhaled heavily. 'You don't have to tell me,' she said.

'No, it's OK. After what happened at the funeral you deserve to know.'

'So what did he do?'

'He started stealing things from their friends. Ornaments, jewellery. Stuff like that. He hid them in my room, setting it up so his mother found them and of course she thought I was the one who had taken them.'

She gasped. 'Oh, Stuart ...'

He gave a hollow laugh. 'Yeah, it never rains but it pours. Eileen said I was a delinquent who belonged in a reformatory. Then Gordon told me they'd make sure that no one pressed charges as long as I agreed to go to a foster home.'

'But didn't you tell him it was lies? I mean, what about fingerprinting ...'

'I didn't have to. That was the worst part. I remember looking into his face as he told me and I could see in his eyes that he didn't believe any of it.'

'So why ...'

'Because it was what Adam and Eileen wanted. They were his whole world and if I made them unhappy then I had to go. It was easier that way and Mum always said that Uncle Gordon liked an easy life.' Again Stuart sighed. 'And that's why he's the one I really blame. Adam was a kid, a vicious one I grant you, but just a kid. And Eileen was only my aunt by marriage. But *he* was Mum's brother. He was all the family I had apart from Gran and she was in a home. He knew I needed him but still he did it.'

Fury surged through Jennifer. She tried to control it. This wasn't about her. But when she thought of the anxious-looking man hiding behind a tree her blood boiled.

He stroked her hair. 'So now you know.'

'Thank God you didn't tell me before the funeral. If you had I'd be up on a murder charge right now. You were a kid! You had no one! If my sister's kids were orphaned I'd cut my arm off before I'd treat them like that. I'm glad you told him where to go when we saw him. I just wish you'd flattened him as you did it. I wish I had. I just ...'

She burst into tears.

'Oh, hey, come here.' He hugged her. 'It's done now. It's in the past. I'm an adult. I've got my own life. And everything is going to be OK.'

Monday morning.

Stuart returned to the office.

Pam and Brian offered condolences. He found he didn't mind them any more. 'You don't need to come back yet,' said Brian. 'We can manage without you.'

'Absolutely,' agreed Pam. 'Brian's only lost three sets of keys and dozens of potential tenants.'

'Are you looking to get fired?'

'Are you looking to do your own paperwork?'

'Touché.'

Stuart laughed. 'So how does my diary look?'

'I've put in a few appointments but warned people you might have to cancel.'

'No chance. I'd like to be busy.' He scanned his schedule for the day, pleased to see that it looked satisfyingly full.

Late afternoon.

Stuart arrived at his final viewing, a sizeable semi in a quiet street on the borders of Barnet and Cockfosters. There was no sign of the prospective tenants. He hoped they weren't going

112

to cancel. The commission would be considerable and in the current cut-throat market his was not the only agency with the property on its books.

As he waited outside the house he received a text from Jennifer. **The flowers are beautiful! You shouldn't have done it. Luv u. XXX.** He had sent her a bouquet as a thank you for her support. He knew that he didn't need to, but knowing it only made the desire to send them stronger. Over the weekend they had started planning a holiday and he was looking forward to it already. Just to have a break, to relax, and to have her with him as he did so.

While texting a reply, he heard a man call his name. After pressing SEND and putting on his best smile he looked up . . .

And for a split second he thought he was hallucinating. That he was back in front of his bathroom mirror, blurring his vision to conjure up the Stuart Godwin he had always wanted to be. Because it was that reflection who approached him now. The face was lean, the physique toned and athletic. The hair-cut was fashionable and the tailored suit far more expensive than any he had ever owned.

The shock was so intense it was like an electrical surge. His whole body jolted, the mobile slipping from his hand and falling to the floor.

The man reached him and stopped. Stuart felt an urge to stretch out his arm, half-convinced he would find a plate of glass between them. He opened his mouth to speak but no words came out. His throat was bone dry.

For a time they just stared at each other. Slowly the man looked him up and down. 'Jesus Christ,' he said softly.

Stuart found his voice. 'Who are you?'

The man didn't answer, just shook his head, looking shocked himself.

'Who are you?' Stuart asked again. 'Do I know you?'

'Yes. I think you do. Or at least you did.'

'What are you talking about?'

'I'm sorry. I didn't mean to be cryptic. And I'm sorry if I've freaked you out. I'm going to try and explain but I need you to listen. Is that OK?'

Stuart nodded.

'A few days ago I was looking at some letting websites for my mother. I came across your firm's website and saw your picture. I couldn't believe it. It was like I'd been cloned. At first I thought it was just some weird coincidence but then I remembered other things that have happened recently and began to suspect that it wasn't.'

'What other things?'

'I have a cousin called Vanessa. We're very close. She's more like a sister really. She was working here in Barnet and then one day she just quit her job without telling anyone why and when I tried to contact her she wouldn't return my calls. I assumed she was embarrassed. My mother is always giving her grief about not having a career. And then I remembered that the last time we spoke she told me she was about to go and view a flat with a friend.'

'A flat?'

The man reached into his pocket, pulled out a photograph and showed it to Stuart. 'This is Vanessa. You met her, didn't you?'

'Yes! She's been following me, asking all sorts of questions.'

'Eventually I managed to track her down, and after trying to play ignorant she caved in and told me all about it. She's convinced we're related and that's when I knew I had to come and find you.'

Stuart shook his head. 'We're not related. How can we be?'

'That's what I told myself. It was just a photograph. You

might look completely different in the flesh in spite of what Nessa said. It could just be coincidence. But now here you are and, I mean ... well, God, it's like looking in a mirror.'

Stuart swallowed.

'I know your birthday is New Year's Eve,' the man told him. 'I believe you were born in 1985. Am I right?'

'Yes.'

'In the maternity ward of the Willow Hospital on the outskirts of Birmingham?'

Stuart nodded.

'That's where I was born, on 31 December 1985.'

Another silence. This time Stuart was the one to break it. 'I don't understand this. I'm not a twin. My mother only had one baby that day. I *know* she did.'

'I know it too.'

'So what are you trying to say?'

'I've been doing some research. I've spoken to the hospital and found out the names of all the babies born there on that day. Only three of them were boys. A woman named Mary Godwin gave birth to a boy called Stuart, and my mother, a woman named Caroline Randall, gave birth to a set of twins called James and Thomas. They mixed us up. That's what happened. I managed to track down a retired nurse who worked in the maternity ward when we were born. She told me it was holiday season. They were understaffed, everyone was under terrible pressure and a mistake could have been made. The nurse I spoke to said her friend, another nurse, always had a suspicion something had gone wrong, but it was too late and she was scared for her job so she never said anything. We're twins, Stuart. You're a Randall, and the guy I've always thought of as my twin is the real Stuart Godwin. He's not my twin. He never was. You are.'

Stuart felt dizzy. The man was staring at him, clearly eager to hear his reaction. He knew he should say something but instead his eyes focused on his phone which now lay on the pavement at his feet. He bent down and picked it up, seeking refuge in action while his brain struggled to process all he had heard.

'Say something,' the man pleaded.

The back of the phone had come off. Stuart tried to reattach it but his hands were all thumbs. 'Stupid bloody thing!' he shouted in frustration.

'Let me help.'

'It doesn't matter.'

'But I can do it.' The man took it from him, made the necessary adjustment and handed it back, their hands touching as they did so.

'So you *are* real,' Stuart told him.

'What?'

'You said that when you looked at me it was like looking in a mirror. That's what I thought too. I do that sometimes; look in the mirror and squint and try and imagine that I look like a better version of myself. That I look ... like you.'

'You do look like me, Stuart. *Just* like me. We're identical twins. That's why I said that we once knew each other. Of course we did. We shared a womb for the first nine months of our existence. We share the same DNA. We started life as a single person, only now we're two.'

Yet again Stuart felt dizzy. He took a deep breath, trying to steady himself.

'Are you OK?' the man asked.

He exhaled. 'I don't know.'

'Maybe we should go and have a drink. You look like you could use one and I know I could. Besides, you must have a million questions to ask me.'

116

'But don't you want to see the house first?'

'What house?'

'The one you've booked the appointment for. I've got the keys. I . . .'

He stopped, realising what he was saying. How stupid it must sound. How stupid he was being.

For the first time the tension faded from the man's face, replaced by a smile. Stuart remembered people telling him he had a lovely smile and now, for the first time in his life, he could see exactly why.

And suddenly, in spite of everything, he found himself smiling too.

'I know a good pub nearby,' he said. 'I can drive us.'

'Thanks, Stuart.'

'No problem . . . um . . . this is embarrassing. I can't remember your name.'

'That's hardly surprising, in the circumstances.'

'What is it?'

'Tom.'

PART 2

PART 2

SEVEN

'I feel like I'm dreaming,' said Stuart. 'I keep expecting you'll vanish and I'll wake up.'

'Well, I won't,' Thomas told him. 'This is real.'

He nodded, a part of him still waiting to hear his morning alarm ring.

'Do you wish it wasn't?' Thomas asked.

'No ...' He hesitated. 'I don't know. It's just ...'

'A lot to get your head round?'

'You could say that.'

'It is for me too.'

'I'm sorry.'

'Hey, it's not your fault. You have nothing to be sorry for. Neither of us does.'

It was eight o'clock. They had been talking in the half-empty pub for hours. Stuart sipped his beer. His head ached. Though the initial shock had diminished, he still felt dazed.

'Did you never sense you were a twin?' Thomas asked. 'I've heard that separated twins sometimes sense the existence of the other.'

He shook his head. 'Did your mother never suspect?'

'*Our* mother. No. Why would she? She knew she was having twins but she didn't know what sex we'd be, let alone that we'd be identical. And when we were being born she started haemorrhaging so we were just bundled off while they took care of her.'

'Couldn't the nurses tell we were identical?'

'You were much bigger than me. I was in an incubator for the first few days because I had trouble breathing. You were out in the ward and that's when the mix-up must have happened. Anyway, most newborn babies look the same. In some of the baby photos of Jimmy and me it's impossible to tell us apart. Some people actually thought he and I were identical. How bizarre is that?'

'Why were we born in Birmingham? I thought your parents lived in London.'

'*Our* parents,' Thomas corrected him.

He didn't respond, knowing it was true but still struggling to accept it.

'Dad was on secondment there,' Thomas continued, 'though in fact when we were born he was on a business trip to New York and the weather was so bad he didn't make it back until four days afterwards.'

Stuart thought for a moment. 'And by that time I'd been taken home.'

'Did the Godwins never suspect?'

'No. My parents never suspected anything.'

Thomas opened his mouth to protest.

'I know what you're going to say,' Stuart told him. 'They weren't my real parents. But you have to understand that it was totally real to me. They were Mum and Dad and Sam was my sister. They loved me and I loved them and when I lost them I . . . well . . . ' He stopped, feeling suddenly choked.

Thomas reached out and gave his hand a squeeze. Out of the corner of his eye, Stuart noticed a middle-aged woman sitting nearby register the gesture. For a moment he felt embarrassed.

But the woman was smiling. She looked touched.

She doesn't know we've only just met. All she sees is what is right in front of her eyes. One twin comforting another.

'I'm the one who's sorry,' Thomas told him. 'I shouldn't keep pushing the whole parent thing. Especially after all you went through when you were growing up. I wish I'd been there. I wish we could have gone through it together. It still would have been hell but at least we'd have had each other.'

He swallowed. 'I wish you'd been there too.'

'But I'm here now.'

'Thanks.'

'The really terrible thing is that you shouldn't have had to go through it at all.'

Stuart glanced at the photographs laid out on the table. 'Do you know who Jimmy looks like?'

'You said he looks like your mother.'

'He does, but the person he really looks like is my cousin, Adam. *Really* like him.'

'Is that the cousin who's a prick?'

'Yes.'

'Well, Jimmy's no prick. He's a great guy. You'll like him. Everyone does.'

Stuart didn't answer. At that moment he was thirteen again and standing by the graves of his family, trying to come to terms with the fact that all the structure and security in his life had just been ripped to pieces. The pain had been unbearable, only it shouldn't have been his pain at all. Instead it belonged to the handsome, confident-looking man who smiled back at him from the snapshot on the table.

A voice whispered in his head, soft and bitter.

It's not fair.

'You'll have to meet Jimmy,' Thomas told him. 'And our ... I mean *my* parents. I'll arrange it all, after I've filled them in on the situation of course.'

Stuart didn't respond. Everything was moving so quickly and the prospect of meeting Thomas's family unnerved him. How was he supposed to feel about them? How were they supposed to feel about him?

'Don't you want to meet them? They'll want to meet you.'

'How do you know?'

'Because I know them. They'll feel terrible about what happened and all that you've suffered. They'll welcome you with open arms.'

Stuart felt torn. A part of him was curious about them, yet acknowledging it made him feel guilty, as if he were turning his back on his dead family.

'They'll want to be there for you, Stu. How can that be bad?'

'Look, I'm not sure ...'

He heard Thomas exhale. 'It's OK. I understand. This is a hassle you just don't need.'

Startled, he looked up. 'I didn't say it was a hassle.'

'You didn't need to. Look, I get it, Stu. I really do. I may be your brother biologically but at the end of the day I'm still a stranger. You've made your own life now. You've got a lovely girlfriend. You're doing well in your job. Why would you want me complicating it? It's been great to meet you and I hope you feel the same, but maybe it would be better if we didn't see each other again.'

He was taken aback. 'Is that what you want?'

'No. I thought that was what you wanted.'

124

'Of course it isn't. How could it be? You're my twin!'

The words came instinctively. For a split second he considered taking them back. After all, what Thomas said was true. He *had* made a life for himself, a good life. Inviting Thomas into it would only lead to complications.

Except that life didn't seem quite so good any more. It seemed . . .

Empty.

But that wasn't fair. He had Jennifer. They loved each other. Their bond was special.

Almost as special as the bond between identical twins.

'I do want to see you again, Tom. You're right when you said we started life as one person. You're a part of me, just as I'm a part of you. It's hard to accept that my parents and sister weren't my real family, but not as hard as losing them. Not even close. I've lost enough people already and now we've found each other I don't want to lose you.'

Thomas smiled. 'You won't. I promise. You've been alone in the past but you're not alone any more. You'll never be alone again. Not as long as I'm alive.'

A lump came into Stuart's throat. He swallowed it down. Again Thomas gave his hand a squeeze. This time he covered Thomas's hand with his free one and returned the gesture. The middle-aged woman caught his eye. She smiled at him. He smiled back.

'Do you want another drink?' Thomas asked.

'Yes. It's my round this time.'

He went to order at the bar. 'So did you get the brains?' the barman asked. 'After all, your twin clearly got the fashion sense.'

'I guess so.'

'Are you close?'

He gave a quick laugh. 'Let's just say that in all the time we've known each other we've never had an argument.'

'Lucky you. My sister and I can't go five minutes without a row.' The barman finished pouring the drinks. 'It must be strange, having someone look just like you.'

He looked over to the table where Thomas sat waiting.

'Mate,' he said, 'you have no idea.'

Half past ten.

Helen returned home after an enjoyable three-day excursion to Prague.

The lights were on in the house. Vanessa was staying until the following Monday, doing shifts at the local pub while waiting to start a new temping job. Helen would miss her when she went. Though the house was tiny, it still seemed too big when she was there alone.

She let herself in, called out a cheerful 'hello', and smelled cigarettes. Her good mood vanished. Vanessa had promised not to smoke in the house.

'I thought we had an agreement,' she said as she entered the living room.

Vanessa was sitting on the couch. The television was on. A detective series was playing, one that Helen had been watching avidly for weeks. She realised she had forgotten to set Sky+ and felt her annoyance increase.

'Well? Didn't we?'

'You left your bloody mobile behind. I found it on the hall table. I've been trying to get hold of you but I didn't know where you were staying.'

'But I wrote the details down.' She hesitated. 'I think I did.'

'No, you didn't. Efficient as always. Nice one, Mother.'

'So what's the emergency?'

'Tom *knows*. That's the emergency.'

All thoughts of house rules went out of her head. Helen sank down in a chair. Vanessa began to talk about pictures on a website. She tried to listen but was too shocked to take it in.

'So what's he going to do?' she asked eventually.

'He's done it already. He's met Stuart.'

'Oh, Christ.'

'And it's all my fault. If only I hadn't taken that bloody job none of this would have happened.' Vanessa sighed. 'I'm sorry, Mum . . .'

'How were you to know Stuart existed?'

'I meant about the cigarettes.'

'Oh, bugger the cigarettes! Smoke as many as you want. I need a Scotch.'

'Make mine a double.'

Helen filled two glasses then sat beside her daughter, putting an arm round her. 'This isn't your fault, Nessa. If you hadn't spotted Stuart someone else probably would have. How did their meeting go?'

'They really liked each other.'

'Well, that figures. Tom's lovely and by the sound of it, Stuart is too.'

'And so is Jimmy and where does this leave him?'

Just where he is, Helen wanted to say but didn't.

'That's the hardest part. He's not my cousin. He never was.'

'Nonsense. He'll always be your cousin, just as he'll always be my nephew. You haven't stopped loving him, have you?'

'No, but how's he going to feel when he finds out?'

'How is your aunt going to feel? This will break her heart. Does Tom plan on telling everyone?'

'Not yet. But he says he'll have to soon. Stuart wants to meet his real family.'

127

'I think I should be the one to tell Caroline. I'm her sister. It might be best coming from me.'

'And who's going to tell Jimmy?'

'I don't know. We'll cross that bridge when we come to it. But one thing I do know is that we'll get him through this. We're still his family, no matter what.'

They sipped their drinks. The detective series came to an end. 'I recorded it for you,' said Vanessa. 'I know you like it.'

Helen nodded, while feeling no desire to watch it at all.

Midnight.

Jennifer sat listening to a drunken Stuart talk.

Words erupted out of him like lava. At first all she had felt was shock but now a new emotion was taking over, one that was shameful but which she could not control.

Jealousy.

That morning she had phoned her parents and sister, making plans for them to meet Stuart, knowing they would like him and make him welcome. That was what she wanted, for him to feel a part of her family as he had none of his own to speak of.

Or so they had both thought.

'Tom's dying to meet you,' Stuart told her. 'You'll like him. I know you will.'

'Yes, I'm sure I will.'

'And I want you to come when I meet his parents.'

'Of course.' She risked a joke. 'We'll need to check the diary, though. You've got to meet mine too, remember?'

He wasn't listening. 'I didn't want to meet them at first. It seemed disloyal to Mum and Dad. But Tom said that if they were here now they'd tell me to do it. They wouldn't want me to be alone any more.'

'But you're not alone, Stu. You've got me.'

He continued to babble. 'Tom's going to talk to Vanessa about how best to arrange it.' He started to laugh. 'There was me thinking she was a stalker and it turns out she's my bloody cousin!'

She tried to push her jealousy aside. She was happy for him. She really was.

'It's so strange, sitting there staring at yourself. I can't describe it. I want to but I can't. It's just this really amazing feeling, like ... like you've won the lottery, only it's even better than that ...'

She put her hand on his arm. 'Stu, you need to calm down. You've had a lot to drink.'

'Who cares? I've got a twin!'

'But that's not the whole story, is it?'

'What do you mean?'

'Tom has a twin already.'

'No, he hasn't. I'm his twin. His real one.'

'But does he see it like that? I'm sure he's thrilled about meeting you but what are you expecting him to do? Just forget the last twenty-seven years? I understand why you're excited but you're charging at this like a bull at a gate. You need to slow down and think. This other twin, um ... Johnny?'

'Jimmy.'

'Yes, Jimmy. This affects him just as much as it affects you. The family you always thought was yours is actually his. What if he starts growing close to them?'

'What family? Uncle Gordon and co.? He can be my guest.'

'Then consider this. He's spent his entire life believing he's someone he's not. How is he going to feel? How are his parents going to feel? Imagine if your parents and sister and grandmother were still alive and discovered you weren't their real son or brother or grandson? Do you think they'd just embrace Jimmy with open arms? No way, Stu. They'd be gutted and so would you.'

He shook his head. 'I'd ...'

'What? Cope? How do you know? The fact is you don't have the first idea of how you or your family would react, just as you don't know how Jimmy and his family will.'

He stared reproachfully at her. 'Why are you trying to spoil this? I thought you'd be happy for me.'

'I am.' It was a lie but for now that was her problem.

'When I was sitting in the pub I couldn't wait to share this with you. Who else do I have to tell?'

She began to feel guilty. 'I don't mean to sound negative. It *is* wonderful and I can't wait to meet Tom. All I'm saying is don't start making too many plans. We have to move slowly.'

He nodded, the gesture clearly prompted by courtesy rather than conviction. She knew he wasn't listening.

'I'm only saying this because I love you,' she told him.

'And I love you too but you needn't worry. I know how to look after myself.'

His face was shining, his expression almost manic. Fear filled her mind. Though he believed himself strong, she knew the losses he had suffered had made him weak. Too quick to hope and as vulnerable as a newborn to hurt and pain.

And she wasn't going to let anyone hurt him again.

He continued to tell her about Tom. The jealousy remained, together with self-hatred. If anyone deserved a lucky break then he did and his excitement was totally understandable. After all, she could see what was in it for him: a new brother, a new family, a whole new life.

A thought came to her, unbidden and unsettling.

So what's in it for Tom?

*

Seven o'clock the next morning.

Kate sat in James's flat, drinking coffee and watching the business news.

As James's nearly completed deal was mentioned, the man himself appeared from the bathroom, wearing a dressing gown and looking very sexy. 'Will you be working late?' she asked him. 'Wendy wants us to get together with her and Horatio.'

'Oh. My friend Nick was talking about meeting up.'

'Is it a definite arrangement?'

'Well, no ...'

'Wendy's booked the Ivy.'

'Why? Does she fancy doing some star-spotting?'

'Well, she won't need to look very far if you're on her table.'

He rolled his eyes.

'It's true. You're a star of the legal world, just like me. We're an unbeatable team. The sky's the limit when we're together.'

His expression became thoughtful. She knew what was on his mind. 'You should call Tom,' she said. 'He's probably waiting to hear from you.' A pause. 'I mean, that's how it works, isn't it? You're always the peacemaker.'

'Not always.'

'But maybe you should be this time. You said some mean things.'

He didn't answer.

'Tom must have been really hurt.'

'Yeah ...'

'And it's not like he deserved it.'

His face darkened. 'Didn't he? What about the stuff he said to me? I've spent my whole life looking after him and ...' He exhaled. 'Typical Tom. He can dish it out but he can't take it. Well, fuck him. Let him make the effort for once.'

'I'll tell Wendy we'll meet them.' She kissed his cheek.

Then, feeling quietly triumphant, she headed for the door.

Quarter to nine.

Stuart walked along Barnet High Street towards his office.

He received a text message from Thomas. **Hi. Are you still real? I am. At least I think so!** Feeling absurdly happy, he texted back: **100% real and 200% blubber! How are you?**

He entered the office. Pam was working her way through a pile of papers. She gave him a cheerful 'Good morning', and he responded in kind.

She pushed her papers to one side. 'What's up with you?'

He sat down at his desk. 'What do you mean?'

'You look like the cat that got the cream.'

'Ouch. I've actually lost a couple of pounds.'

'I don't mean that. You seem ... I don't know. Glowing.'

Another text came through. **Can't concentrate to save my life. Seeing Vanessa tomorrow night. Let's meet soon. When's good for you?**

'So, when am I going to meet her?'

He looked up to see Pam smiling at him. 'Sorry?'

'Jen. That text was from her, wasn't it? Nobody else could give you a grin that big.'

He longed to tell her the truth, only he had promised Jennifer that for now he would keep it quiet. As long as he didn't burst in the process.

'I don't know,' he said.

'Well, make it soon. She must be amazing if she has this effect on you.'

He nodded. She was amazing. He was a lucky man to have met someone as special as her.

Even if she did try to spoil his excitement about Thomas.

But she didn't do it deliberately. She was just watching out for him.

Not that she needed to. Everything would be fine.

Noon.

James sat at his desk, staring at his phone.

All morning he had been battling the urge to call his brother. He knew Kate was right. It was always him that made the first move and he was sick to death of it.

But it wasn't that easy. He missed Thomas. Though he had spent his whole life being the responsible one, their bond wasn't all a burden. No one could make him laugh as much as Thomas. No one except Becky and he had lost her.

And he didn't want to lose Thomas too. If, yet again, he had to be the one to put things right then so be it. He was the eldest after all, if only by five minutes.

He dialled Thomas's number. It rang three times before going to message. 'Hi, Tom, it's me. I hope you're OK. I just wanted to say ... well, I'm really sorry about what I said. I didn't mean it. Give me a call, yeah? Let me know how you're doing. I miss you. Life isn't the same without you around.'

He put down the receiver, feeling as if a huge load had been lifted from his shoulders.

Duncan White, the Head of Department, put his head round the door. 'I saw your acquisition on the news. Congratulations. I've just had the clients on the phone raving about you. What sort of champagne did they send?'

'Cristal.'

'Wow! Let me know if you need a hand drinking it. Can I sit down? There are a couple of things I want to talk to you about.'

James gestured to a spare chair.

'Firstly, we've just been instructed on a new acquisition. It

133

should be straightforward but the clients want it to happen in a month and I'd like you to handle it.'

'Sure. Who'll be the partner in charge?'

'Well, nominally it's me but you can run it on your own. That's what you've done on your last few deals.' Duncan handed him a pile of papers. 'The clients want a conference call this evening. Can you manage that?'

He nodded, confident Kate would understand. She took her career seriously and would want him to do the same. Besides, the prospect of Wendy and Horatio was not one to gladden his heart.

'What was the other thing?' he asked.

'The secondment to Ercobank is definitely going to happen.'

An email arrived on his screen. He saw it was from Thomas. Briefly he felt delighted, then, suddenly let down that his brother had not bothered to pick up a phone.

'They'd like you to start in six weeks.'

Again he nodded.

Thanks for your call,

the email began.

It was nice to hear from you.

Nice?

'The secondment will be for six months. I hate to lose you but I've promised them my star player and at least their offices are only down the road so you can pop back whenever we need you.'

He continued to read.

I'm fine. Hope you are too.

'Besides, it'll be great experience and, off the record, with that on your CV it means we can put you forward for partnership next year.'

I'll call you soon. Tom.

'James, did you hear what I said?'
'What?'
'With this secondment your partnership is in the bag.'
'OK.' His eyes drifted back to the email.
'You don't seem very pleased.'
He remembered who he was talking to and put on his brightest smile. 'Sorry – that's fantastic.'
'Well, I'll leave you to it and, once again, congratulations.'
Duncan left the office. James reread the email. Again he felt let down. It just seemed so casual. He had made the big gesture. Couldn't Thomas at least have responded in kind?
He knew he was making too much of it. They were back in contact. That was the important thing.
But still it bothered him.

The following afternoon Stuart showed prospective tenants around a house.

They were brother and sister, both with the same heavy features, pale green eyes and monotonous voices. The resemblance between them was striking.

Though it could not compare to the resemblance between Thomas and himself.

They had been texting all day and had phoned each other at lunchtime. A five-minute chat that had ended up lasting half an hour but still seemed too short. There was so much to say when there were twenty-seven years to make up for.

The sister asked if they could change the curtains. He told her they could while noticing they were the same shade of blue as the ones that had hung in his grandmother's room. The realisation came suddenly, together with another; that he had not thought about her once in the last two days.

He began to feel ashamed. Quickly, he gave himself a metaphorical shake. It didn't mean he didn't care. Given the choice, he would willingly sacrifice his knowledge of Thomas's existence just to have her alive again.

Would you? Would you really?

Another text arrived. The surge of excitement he felt was answer enough.

That evening Vanessa sat with Thomas in his flat.

It was a mess, just as it always was. In spite of her anxiety she couldn't help playing the bossy relative. 'You should tidy up.'

'It's not that bad.'

'It is! A tramp would think he was slumming it. I'll help if you like.'

'Not tonight. We've got more important things to do.'

She nodded. A barely touched Chinese takeaway was spread out on a table. Neither of them had any appetite.

'We have to tell them soon,' he said. 'I can't keep blanking Jimmy. He phoned me yesterday. We'd had a row and he was calling to apologise. I should have called him back but I just couldn't. What was I going to say? Hi, Jimmy. Thanks a lot. I'm sorry too and now things can go back to normal. I don't think so. Things will never be the same again.'

Though she knew he was right, her heart still sank.

'I'm sorry you got caught in the middle. Stuart's sorry too. He asked me to apologise for the way he shouted at you.'

She was touched. 'He didn't need to do that.'

'I told him that but he still wanted me to do it.'

'You really like him, don't you?'

'Like is too weak a word. You know when sometimes you meet someone and you feel this instant connection. Well, with Stuart it was like that, only ten times as powerful. It's like a part of me was missing and I didn't even realise until I found it again.'

'But you still love Jimmy, don't you? This doesn't change how you feel about him?'

'Of course it doesn't. Jimmy will always be my brother. That's why this is so hard. I don't want to hurt him but there's no avoiding it.'

'Your parents will be hurt too.'

He shrugged.

'Don't you care?'

'Not like I care about Jimmy.'

'But they're your parents.'

'So? They've never cared about me the way Jimmy has. Why should I care about their feelings the way I care about his?'

'But, Tom . . .'

'Jimmy's the one who's most affected. Mum and Dad aren't losing their identity the way he is.'

'But they are losing their son.'

'Bollocks! He'll still be their son. They're still going to love him. They're not just going to switch their feelings off, are they?'

She didn't answer. Worry clawed at her. Searching for distraction, her eyes roamed over the room, focusing on a pale pink jacket lying in a corner. 'Whose is that?'

'Alice's.'

'Who's Alice?'

'A girl I've been seeing. She left it last time she was here.'

'Is it serious?'

'Not very.' He waved his hand dismissively. 'So when do we tell them?'

'You make it sound so easy.'

'Well, it has to be done, and I think you and your mother should do it. You're not as close to it as me. You'll be less emotional about it.'

She lit a cigarette. 'You know your parents are in Dorset at the moment. They're back at the weekend.'

'Then that's when you should do it.'

She didn't answer.

'Is that OK?'

'Just promise me something.'

'What?'

'That this eagerness to tell has nothing to do with getting back at them.'

He frowned.

'Look, I'm not having a go. God knows, you have reason to feel resentful . . .'

'This is about Stuart. After all he's been through he has a right to meet his real family and I'm not going to make him wait for ever just because knowing the truth might spoil Mum's picture-perfect view of the world.'

'OK. I'm sorry. I only said that because—'

'I'll tell them myself. It's obvious you don't want to.' He snorted. 'Let's face it, if it had been up to you, I never would have found Stuart at all.'

'That's not fair.'

'But it's true.'

He was glaring at her. For the millionth time she wished she had never taken the job and that none of them were any the wiser.

Some hope.

'Mum and I will tell them, Tom. Like you said, it will probably be better coming from us.'

His expression softened. 'Sorry. I shouldn't have said that. I understand why you did what you did. If I was in your shoes I'd probably have done the same.'

'Thanks.'

'And don't look so worried. It'll all be fine.'

She nodded, raising a silent prayer to every God in creation that he was right.

EIGHT

Six o'clock, Sunday morning.

James sat on a window ledge in his living room, staring down at the street below. The window was half open, allowing the smoke from his cigarette to escape. He had promised Kate he was giving up but had always found the habit soothing and on this particular morning he was in need of as much soothing as possible.

He still hadn't spoken to Thomas; just received a couple more cheerful emails that didn't say anything. He knew something was wrong, and, as if to confirm it, Vanessa was coming over that afternoon to 'talk about something important'. When he had pressed her on what that something was she would only say that there was nothing to worry about and that she loved him very much; two assurances that made him worry all the more.

He lit another cigarette, his sense of foreboding growing stronger with every drag.

Lunchtime.

Caroline and Robert attended John and Susan Bishop's drinks party.

It was a beautiful September day. Some of the guests were in the garden while others stood admiring the redecorated drawing room. 'I love what you've done,' Caroline told Susan when her hostess came to greet her.

'I'm so glad you like it. You have the best taste of anyone I know.' Susan glanced anxiously about her. 'Do you think the party's going well?'

'*Very* well. You're a marvellous hostess.' Caroline noticed John standing across the room, talking to a group of men. 'How are things with you two?'

'No better. Can we meet for lunch this week?'

'Of course. Are you free on Tuesday?'

'No, I'm sorry. I could make Wednesday, though.'

'Then Wednesday it is.'

A waiter appeared, offering top-ups. Though tempted, Caroline declined. Helen was coming over that afternoon to talk to her and Robert about 'something important'. She hoped it wasn't to ask for a loan. Though she would be happy to help out, Robert had strong views on the subject of scrounging relatives.

'How was Dorset?' Susan asked.

'Lovely. We were staying with Alec McKenzie and his wife. Alec was at Oxford with Robert.' Actually it had been a difficult stay. Alec owned a construction company and had been constantly on the phone to contractors, a habit Robert labelled showboating and none too subtly either. The atmosphere was decidedly frosty by the end of their visit and Robert spent the whole of the drive home ranting about 'jumped-up builders' while hooting every driver who dared to cross his path.

Not that anyone would guess it now. He had just joined John's group, shaking hands, slapping backs and radiating bonhomie.

'Bob seems to be enjoying himself,' Susan observed.

'Yes. He enjoys a good party.'

'Unlike John. God, he looks bored. Even though this shindig was his idea, I know I'll get it in the neck this evening for having subjected him to it.' Susan shook her head. 'You're so lucky, having someone like Bob.'

She nodded. Abigail Watson, an attractive woman of about forty, had joined John's group and was laughing at one of Robert's jokes. He was smiling at her, his manner warm and charming. Abigail said something and it was Robert's turn to laugh, giving her a conspiratorial wink as he did so.

Is she the one? Is it someone else here?

Caroline scanned the room, suddenly seeing every woman as a potential threat, while an oblivious Susan kept prattling on about how lucky she was.

Half an hour later, Susan stood in the garden, listening to Abigail Watson praise her hostess skills. 'Harry and I are having a party next month and we'll really need to up our game to match this.' Abigail's tone was smug, suggesting she didn't consider it a challenge at all. Susan smiled politely, wondering if Abigail would be quite so smug if she knew that Susan had slept with her husband.

Abigail began talking about her children. While feigning interest Susan noticed Harry Watson casting wistful glances in her direction. Their affair had only lasted six weeks but he had pestered her for months afterwards, even offering to leave his wife so the two of them 'could be happy together'. She put on a fine display of regret while laughing inwardly at his arrogance in assuming that anyone so dreary could ever be the answer to her prayers.

But there it was. He was a man and all men were fools to be

used and discarded, their only functions to pay the bills, flatter the ego and help keep tedium at bay.

All except one.

The longer the meeting went on, the more Jennifer knew she had made a mistake.

She sat with Stuart and her family in the garden of her parents' pub. Now the lunchtime rush was over they could all relax and get to know each other.

That, at least, had been the plan.

'So how does this part of the world compare to Birmingham?' her mother asked Stuart.

'Very well. I like it here.'

'It must have been a wrench, though,' suggested her father, 'having to leave your life there behind.'

'Not really. There wasn't much to miss.'

'And anyway,' added her sister Debbie with a smile, 'there's one particular advantage to living here.'

Stuart looked blank.

'I mean Jen.' Debbie laughed. 'At least I'm assuming that's a good thing.'

'Oh yeah. Definitely. I'm a lucky guy.' The words were spoken as if they had been learned by rote. Jennifer felt herself blush while Stuart, oblivious, sipped his beer and stared distractedly into space.

Her parents asked him about his job. As he answered he fiddled with a serviette, tearing it into strips, radiating nervous energy like heat. She nudged his hand while noticing her parents exchange the briefest of looks.

They think he doesn't want to be here.

And he didn't. That was the awful thing.

Her father began to talk about football. Her nephews joined

in, listing their favourite players. At last Stuart rose to the occasion, telling them about the players he had idolised as a boy. 'I loved football at school. It was my favourite subject.'

'Football isn't a subject,' announced one of her nephews.

'Isn't it? Well, that explains why I left with no qualifications.'

Everyone laughed. Briefly the mood eased.

'We've got a football,' said her other nephew. 'It's in the car.'

'Which is where it's staying,' said Jennifer's brother-in-law Geoff firmly.

'Dad!'

'We're not here to play. We're here to meet Aunty Jen's boyfriend.'

'But it's boring!'

'Ben!' exclaimed Debbie. 'That's very rude.'

'Why? Stuart's bored too.'

Jennifer's heart sank. Yet again her parents exchanged a look. 'I'm not at all,' said Stuart quickly. 'It's lovely to meet you all and the lunch was delicious.'

'Well, you're very welcome,' said her mother. Jennifer hoped it was true. That Stuart's relationship with her parents wasn't over before it had even begun.

Her nephews, clearly restless, jostled each other. 'I've got an idea,' Stuart told them. 'Let's have a kickaround on the green.'

'Can we, Dad? Can we?'

Geoff groaned. 'Go on,' urged Stuart. 'You and me against Messi and Ronaldo.'

The four of them headed off to the car; her nephews arguing over who was going to be Ronaldo. 'That was nice of Stuart,' said her mother.

'He's a nice bloke.'

'I'm sure he is.'

'He is. He must be if he's willing to put up with me.' She waited in vain for laughter. 'He's just ... not himself right now. His grandmother's death hit him hard.'

One of the barmaids came to report a customer complaint. Her parents went to sort it out. Debbie remained where she was. 'OK, Jen, cut the act. I can see you're in a state. What's going on?'

Though she and Stuart had agreed to keep Thomas a secret for now, the need to unburden herself was too great. Debbie sat in silence, her eyes growing ever wider as the story unfolded.

'I want to be happy for him,' she said eventually, 'but I'm scared. He's so excited and we've no idea what his new family are like. They might not want to know him and he'll be so hurt and I've tried to warn him but he just won't listen.'

'What's Thomas like?'

'I haven't met him. I hate him but I haven't even met him.'

'Why do you hate him?'

'Because he makes me feel like I don't exist. He's all Stu talks about, all he thinks about. God, I must sound like such a cow. I don't want to be but I can't help it. That's why I organised this meeting today. I wanted to remind Stu that we've got something special. And we do. He's the one. He really is. I've only just found him and now it's like he's being taken away from me.'

'Well, he's not.' Debbie rubbed her arm affectionately. 'If anything, you're even more important to him now. He needs someone to keep his feet on the ground.'

'But what if he ends up hating me for doing it?'

'He won't. Not in the long run. If this does go tits up then at least you'll be there to pick up the pieces.'

'I want it to work. He deserves it. He *really* is a great guy. I know I keep saying it but it is the truth.'

145

'You don't need to convince me. The fact you think the world of him tells me all I need to know.'

'Thanks.'

Debbie hugged her. As she hugged back she looked over her sister's shoulder at her nephews bouncing around Stuart like excited rabbits. Both clearly adored him. With the unclouded view of childhood they could see what a wonderful person he was.

Let his new family see it too. Let them welcome him with open arms.

And don't let me be discarded in the process.

'Why are you doing this?' demanded Caroline. 'You're my sister. I thought you loved me.'

'I do,' Helen insisted.

'And this is how you show it? Coming into my home and telling lies?'

'They're not lies.'

'Of course they are. They have to be!'

Helen sat at the kitchen table watching her sister and brother-in-law. Caroline paced up and down the room while a white-faced Robert stood in a corner smoking a cigar and saying nothing.

'So he looks like Thomas,' Caroline continued. 'It doesn't prove anything.'

'Carrie, look at the picture.' Helen gestured to the one photograph Caroline hadn't thrown on the floor. 'This isn't just a passing resemblance. They're identical.'

'How do you know? You haven't even seen him.'

'But Tom and Nessa have. If you don't believe me then speak to them.'

'It's just coincidence.'

'Carrie, only three boys were born in the ward that day. Stuart was one and Tom and Jimmy were the others. This can't be a coincidence. You know it can't.'

'The only thing I know is that Jimmy is my son.'

'He still is! That doesn't have to change. Not if you don't let it.'

'You're not listening! He's mine biologically. Do you think I wouldn't know if he wasn't? What sort of mother do you think I am?'

Not wanting to make the situation worse, Helen chose not to answer.

'He looks just like me. Everyone says so.'

'But that's what you say to parents,' interjected Robert. 'It's like paying a compliment. You don't necessarily mean it. You say it to be nice.'

'He does look like me!'

'Only superficially. I've never really noticed that before but now that Helen . . .'

Caroline stared at her husband. 'How can you believe her? For God's sake, you've never even liked her!'

Helen let the insult go. It wasn't anything she didn't know already. Instead she continued to watch Caroline pace.

'Carrie, come and sit down,' she said eventually.

'Don't tell me what to do! You must be loving this. You've always been jealous of me.'

Again Helen let it go. Bending down, she picked up the other photographs.

'Leave those alone! He's a conman. This is all a con and you're stupid enough to have fallen for it.'

'He's not a conman. He didn't find us. Nessa found him.'

'Well, how convenient. You and she probably planned this to get back at me.'

'Oh, Carrie, come on ...'

'To get back at me because I've got everything you want. A wonderful husband, two successful sons and a beautiful home while all you could manage was a daughter who's grown up to be as big a disappointment as her father was.'

Helen's self-restraint vanished. 'So what are you saying?' she demanded. 'That I've failed as a mother?'

'Well, if the cap fits.'

'Then what does that make you, Carrie? Because at least I managed to recognise my own child, which is more than you did.'

'Jimmy *is* my child!'

'No, he's not. You gave birth to identical twins and took home someone else's baby instead of one of them. That's the truth.'

'It's not true! The DNA test will prove it.'

'*DNA test?* You're not serious?'

'So, you don't want him to take one? I knew it! This is just a scam you and Nessa have cooked up to try and get money out of us. You talk about the truth, well there it is!'

'Very well, Carrie, while we're on the subject of the truth then answer me this. Would you be talking about imposters and DNA tests if Stuart was identical to Jimmy?'

Caroline stared at her. 'What do you mean?'

'You know *exactly* what I mean. Jimmy has always been your favourite. It makes me sick the way you've always favoured him over Tom and the real truth is that if I was sitting here telling you that Tom wasn't your biological son you'd be popping open the champagne and dancing on the table.'

As soon as the words were spoken she would have given ten years of her life to take them back. Caroline looked as if she had been shot while Robert just stared reproachfully at her. 'Below the belt, Helen,' he said softly. 'Well below.'

'I'm sorry. I didn't mean that. Carrie, really I didn't ...'

But Caroline was no longer listening. Instead she just collapsed into a chair, buried her face in her hands and began to sob. Helen tried to put her arms around her but was pushed away. She tried again, this time successfully.

'Carrie, listen to me. This doesn't have to be the end of the world. Jimmy will always be your son. No one can take your place in his life. You're the only mother he's ever known and the woman who gave birth to him died long ago. In fact he's going to need you now more than ever to help him get through this.'

'But he *is* mine.'

'That's right. In every way that counts he still is. You're not losing a son. You're gaining another.'

'I don't want another. I just want ...'

'But you'll like Stuart. I know you will ...' Robert was shaking his head at her. She stopped, knowing he was right. Now was not the time. She wondered if the time would ever come. For Stuart's sake she hoped so.

Caroline continued to sob. Helen stroked her hair, whispering soothing words while across the room Robert smoked his cigar and kept his thoughts to himself.

Early evening.

James sat in his living room, flanked by Vanessa and Kate, staring at the photographs spread out on his coffee table. He kept thinking how much Thomas had let himself go, only it wasn't Thomas he was staring at.

'There's absolutely no doubt,' Vanessa was saying. 'Stuart is Tom's twin.'

He nodded, wanting to speak but unable to do so. His head

was spinning so fast he felt as if he were drugged. Vanessa squeezed his hand. 'But the one thing you must believe is that this doesn't change anything. Not for Mum or me.'

He found his voice. 'What about Tom?'

'You're still his brother.'

'No, I'm not.'

'You may not have shared a womb but anyone can see the bond between you. You're closer than any brothers I know. Think of all you've been through together, like that year at boarding school when Tom was bullied so badly. He told me once he never would have survived there if it hadn't been for you. You're the most important person in his life. You know that, don't you?'

He didn't answer. Instead he found himself thinking back to that year, when he and Thomas had been nine. He had settled in quickly; making friends and enjoying life while Thomas, suffering terribly from homesickness, had clung to him like a shadow. Eventually, in an attempt to help Thomas adapt, the headmaster had separated them, placing them in different classes and dormitories and endeavouring to restrict their interaction as much as possible.

But it hadn't worked. In fact it only made matters worse. Thomas started wetting his bed, becoming the number-one target for every bully in the school. Once James stumbled across a jeering gang who had cornered his brother in one of the changing rooms and flew to his defence, leaping on the ringleader and pounding his face, eventually having to be dragged off by a teacher while the rest of the gang backed warily away and Thomas just stared at him with eyes full of gratitude.

He could smell the room now: the floor polish, dirty clothes and sweat. He could hear the jeers too. Only they weren't jeering at Thomas any more. They were jeering at him for spending his whole life believing he was someone he was not.

Emotion overwhelmed him. He started to cry.

Vanessa put an arm round him. 'Oh, Jimmy ...'

'I'm not Jimmy. I'm Stuart Godwin. That's the name I should have.'

'But you don't have it. You're James Randall, son of Robert and Caroline and twin brother of Thomas. This doesn't change who you are. Nothing can do that.'

'That's right,' agreed Kate. 'You're not defined by your name.'

He shook his head. 'It's more than just a name. It's a whole life. Stuart should have had my mine and I should have had his.'

'You can't look at it like that,' Vanessa told him.

'How else am I supposed to look at it? It's all been a lie. My parents aren't my parents. My twin isn't even my brother.'

'Their love for you isn't a lie.'

'Crap! They only love me because they think I'm someone else. If Stuart had grown up with them they'd have loved him instead.'

'But not like they love you,' said Kate. 'How could they?' She gestured to the photographs. 'He's an overweight estate agent without a single qualification to his name. Not much to write home about, is it?'

Vanessa frowned. 'Be fair, Kate. He hasn't had an easy life.'

'I *am* being fair. Jimmy would have been a success no matter what sort of upbringing he'd had. He's a winner and Stuart's not. It's as simple as that.'

'Don't start kicking Stuart. He's as much a victim as Jimmy.'

'Jimmy's not a victim. Only a weakling allows himself to be that.'

'Stuart's not a weakling.'

151

'Oh, please! And why are you sticking up for him? You told Jimmy this didn't make any difference.'

'It doesn't!'

'You could have fooled me. Well, I suppose Stuart *is* your cousin.'

'Jimmy's my cousin. This is a family matter and you're not family so why not do us all a favour and fuck off.'

'Don't start fighting,' James told them. 'Not now, please.'

'I'm sorry,' said Vanessa, kissing his cheek.

'Apology accepted,' said Kate.

'I'm not apologising to you . . .'

'Enough! Christ Almighty, I really do not need this at the moment.' James exhaled. 'Kate, do me a favour and open a bottle of wine. I could use a drink.'

Kate headed off to the kitchen. Vanessa remained where she was. 'I'm so sorry, Jimmy. I can't imagine how you must be feeling but as I said before, this doesn't make any difference. Not to me.'

'What about Mum and Dad? What difference will it make to them?'

'None. You know it won't.'

'No, I don't. Just like I don't know what difference it will make to Tom. He and Stuart aren't just twins. They're identical. It's the most powerful bond in the world. I heard someone describe it as two bodies with a single soul. What chance do I have against that?'

Vanessa didn't answer. In the distance James heard Kate pouring the wine. He willed her to hurry. He needed a drink more than ever.

The telephone rang. Vanessa told him to ignore it but he couldn't. He knew it would be his mother, or the woman he had always thought was his mother.

She was in tears, telling him that it was all lies, and that even if it wasn't it didn't matter. 'Stuart will never mean anything to me. You're my son and you always will be. Nothing on earth can change that.'

'Yeah, I know.' He swallowed. 'I love you, Mum.'

'I love you too, Jimmy, and do you know why? Because you're mine! We're going to get through this and everything will be fine. You know that, don't you?'

He told her that he did. He told himself that he meant it.

But in his heart he knew that things would never be fine again.

From the kitchen Kate listened to James speaking to his mother.

She filled a wine glass then drained it in a single gulp, a secret toast to the triumph she felt but could never express.

She had had high hopes for this meeting, had prayed that whatever it was that Vanessa had to tell them would help weaken the bond between James and Thomas. But never in her wildest dreams had she imagined a blow as lethal as this.

Vanessa was insisting that nothing would change but Vanessa was wrong. Things had changed already.

James belonged to her now. And she was going to keep him.

She returned to the living room, carrying wine for all of them. Vanessa glared at her. Lowering her eyes, she apologised for her earlier comments, saying she had only been trying to spare James's feelings. She even managed to sound sincere.

James returned to the room. Vanessa went to hug him. She did the same, speaking words of comfort and keeping her triumph hidden.

*

153

Half past ten.

Stuart was talking to Thomas on the telephone.

'So how did they take it?' he asked.

'They were shocked, but that was to be expected.'

'Yes, of course.'

'But you mustn't worry. They'll deal with it. And when they meet you they'll love you. I'll make sure of it.'

'Thanks.'

'No problem. We're twins. That's my job.'

'Thanks,' he said again.

'I feel bad about Jimmy, though. I know it's not my fault but I still do.'

Irritation swept through Stuart. James didn't matter. He was the twin now. 'That's right,' he said quickly. 'It's not your fault.'

'Let's meet one evening this week. Which is good for you?'

'All of them. Take your pick. I'll bring Jen.' As he spoke he smiled at her as she watched him from across the room. She smiled back.

The call ended. 'So, Tuesday it is,' he told her. 'Is that OK for you?'

She nodded. 'Thanks for including me.'

'Of course I'm including you. You've included me with your family.'

Another nod. The look in her eyes spoke volumes. 'I'm sorry about this afternoon,' he said.

'Don't be. The boys adored you.'

'What about everyone else?'

'They did too.' Her tone was neutral. He sensed she was lying.

And realised he didn't care.

But that wasn't true. He did care.

Or at least he wanted to.

'You'll like Tom,' he said. 'I'm sure you will.'

'Yes,' she replied softly. 'I'm sure I will.'

Midnight.

Caroline sat at her kitchen table, staring at a photograph of Stuart. He stared back, a stranger whose face she knew as well as that of her own son.

Robert appeared in the doorway, holding a drink. 'It's not true,' she told him.

'Yes, it is. Lie to yourself if you must but don't lie to me.'

'Jimmy is our son. I know he is.'

'How do you know?'

She didn't answer. There was no point. She wasn't fooling either of them.

'How could you not have realised?' he demanded. 'You were their mother.'

'I could ask you the same question.'

'I didn't give birth to them. I didn't carry them inside me for nine months. Christ, I wasn't even there when they were born.'

She gave a hollow laugh. 'Starting as you meant to go on.'

'I was earning money. I was doing my job. Your job was being a mother. It's the only job you've ever had and you royally fucked it up.'

'You can't blame this on me. I was ill! It was the nurses who mixed them up. How was I to know what had happened?'

'Because you should have done, that's why. From the moment they were born the boys have been your whole life.' A snort. 'Or, at least one of them has. And that's the irony, isn't it? You've spent the last twenty-seven years telling everyone you're the perfect mother while pouring all your love and devotion onto a child who wasn't even yours.' It was his turn to laugh. 'Karma really is a bitch.'

She opened her mouth to protest. He walked away, leaving her alone.

The photograph of Stuart was still in her hand. Robert's lighter lay on the table. She opened it up, summoning its flame. For a moment she just let it flicker.

Then, holding it to the photograph, watched it eat away the face.

NINE

Half past nine, Monday morning.

Duncan White stood in the secretarial bay, firing questions at secretary Donna Clarkson. 'So Jimmy's not coming in?'

'No.'

'This is all I need. Why did he have to pick today?'

'He's not doing it deliberately. People get ill.'

'Jimmy doesn't. He hasn't had a day off sick in ... Christ, I don't know.'

'Then this is the exception that proves the rule.'

'But there's a meeting on the Vicourt deal this afternoon.' Duncan ran a hand through his hair. 'Who's going to take it if he's not there?'

'You, I imagine. You're the partner in charge.'

'But I don't know what's going on!'

'Then maybe you should spend this morning finding out?'

'Are you trying to be funny?'

'No, I'm trying to be helpful.' Donna stared levelly at him. 'Jimmy's got a stomach bug, by the way. He sounded really rough on the phone. I'll be sure to tell him how concerned you are.'

One of the other secretaries giggled. Duncan glared at her

and instantly she focused on her computer screen. 'Shall I bring you the file?' Donna asked.

Duncan restrained an urge to tell Donna where she could shove the file. She continued to stare at him. He knew what she was thinking: that he owed his position as Head of Department to his networking skills rather than his legal ability. The awful thing was that she was right. That was why he depended on James so much.

'Yes, bring it to me. And if you speak to Jimmy then give him my regards and say that if there's any chance he could make it in today ...'

Donna raised an eyebrow.

'Tell him to take as long as he needs.'

'I will,' said Donna sweetly.

A muttering Duncan marched back to his office.

Mid-morning.

Back from an external meeting, Thomas listened to a voice message from his mother demanding that he call her immediately.

She sounded furious. He could guess how their conversation would go. She would tell him that this whole mess was his fault, using him as her whipping boy, just as she had done so many times in the past.

Only this time it wouldn't work. All he was guilty of was acting the way any normal person would.

Whereas she, on the other hand ...

How could she not know?

He wondered if she was asking herself the same question. Only he didn't need to just wonder. He knew it for a fact.

And he was glad. Very glad.

He listened to the message again, then pressed delete. He would call her when he was ready and not before.

Papers covered his desk. There was work to be done.
But before starting there was one call he *had* to make.

James sat in his living room, staring at the wall.

His stomach was rumbling. He knew he should eat but the way he felt he'd only bring it straight back up again.

The flat was silent. Kate had left for work hours ago. She had offered to stay but he did not want company. All he wanted was to be left alone.

That, and the power to turn back time.

His mobile rang. Thomas's name was on the display. He couldn't bring himself to answer. He felt too betrayed. All their lives they had never kept secrets from each other, yet now, when it mattered most, Thomas had gone and found Stuart without even telling him, turning his whole life on its head without a word of warning.

The call went to message. A concerned-sounding Thomas asked if he was all right, assured him that nothing had changed and suggested a meeting as soon as possible. The message went on and on, rambling and disjointed. The only thing missing was an apology.

But why should Thomas apologise? He was a victim too. He had grown up with a brother who had always been the favourite, had constantly outshone him and whom he must, at some level, hate.

And now it turned out that brother was no brother at all ...

The room seemed colder. He curled up on the sofa, hiding from the world in the safety of his own home. The home he loved and owned outright, thanks to the inheritance from his grandparents.

Only they hadn't been his grandparents. They had been Stuart's. *And this isn't your home. It's his ...*

*

159

The following morning Jennifer brushed her teeth in Stuart's bathroom.

It was her first day back at college. For weeks she had been looking forward to catching up with friends, hearing their news and telling them hers. Only none of that seemed important now. All she could think of was her impending meeting with Thomas.

Stuart was confident they would like each other. She hoped he was right. She wanted to like Thomas. Only her reaction wasn't the crucial one. What mattered was whether Thomas liked her.

Because he was Stuart's twin. An interloper who enjoyed a bond far closer than her own with the man she loved. If Thomas didn't like her who could tell what effect such disapproval would have on their relationship.

She continued to brush her teeth, battling her anxieties, while in the corridor outside, a cheerful Stuart whistled as he prepared for another day at work.

That afternoon Caroline visited James.

They sat together on his sofa. 'This doesn't change anything, Jimmy,' she said. 'You'll always be my son.'

'What about Dad? Am I still his son too?'

'Of course you are.'

'Then why isn't he here?'

She didn't answer.

'Thought so.'

'No, that's not fair. He's just . . .' she searched for the right words ' . . . dealing with it in his own way. But he loves you, Jimmy. He's so proud of you and all you've achieved.'

'Is he? When I told him about my latest deal he basically accused me of showing off. But I wasn't. I really wasn't . . .'

'That's just him. You know he's never been good at showing his feelings. He's not going to tell you how proud he is but he did tell me.' It was a lie but that didn't matter. All that mattered was telling James what he needed to hear.

And it worked. Briefly his face lit up, though she could still see the dark shadows under his eyes.

'I'm worried about you,' she told him.

'I'm OK. I'm going back to work tomorrow.'

'Are you sure you're ready?'

'I can't hide here for ever. I have to face the world.' He managed a smile. 'After all, you didn't raise me to be a coward.'

'That's right, I didn't.' She noticed new paintings hanging on the wall. 'When did you buy those?'

'Kate bought them.'

'Is she living here now?'

'Yeah. Well, most of the time, anyway.'

She masked her jealousy with a smile. 'So it's serious, then?'

'I guess. She's been really supportive about all this.'

'Which is more than can be said for your brother. He still hasn't called me back. He's probably too scared of what I'm going to say.'

'You shouldn't be angry with him. It's not his fault.'

'Yes, it is. If only he'd—'

'What? Pretended Stuart didn't exist. How could he? Stuart is his twin.'

'*You're* his twin. Stuart is nothing.'

'Not according to Nessa. She said they really like each other.' He exhaled. 'She said I'd like him too.'

'Well, what would she know? Anyway, it's irrelevant. You're never going to meet him. Neither of us will.'

He stared at her. 'But don't you want to?'

'Do *you* want me to?'

'No, but ... well ... you're his mother.'

'I'm *your* mother. His is dead. It's very sad but there it is. He's not going to become part of our family, Jimmy, and nothing is going to change. That's a promise.'

He didn't answer. His eyes were troubled. She could tell he wasn't convinced but it was the truth.

She heard footsteps in the corridor. Kate appeared in the doorway. James looked surprised. 'You're back early.'

'I was worried about you.'

'He's fine,' Caroline told her. 'He's with me.'

'*Fine?* Well, of course he's going to *say* that. You know Jimmy. He hates to worry people.'

'Yes, I know Jimmy very well.'

And better than you ever will.

'Of course you do. You are his mother, after all ... ' Kate stopped, covering her mouth as if appalled at what she'd just said. The gesture was perfect, like that of an actress well trained in stagecraft, while James, completely taken in, gave her a reassuring look. Caroline's hostility increased.

'Yes,' she said quickly. 'I am.'

'It's lovely to see you again, Mrs Randall. What a shame it has to be in such awful circumstances. I can't imagine how you must be feeling.'

'No, you can't. This is something Jimmy and I need to deal with on our own.' A pause. 'In private.' She waited for James to back her up, only he failed to take the hint.

As did Kate who sat beside him and kissed his cheek. 'Are you really OK?'

'Yes, he is. He's going back to work tomorrow.'

'Well, that's great.' Kate smiled at Caroline. 'I keep telling him he doesn't need to hide away. After all, none of this is *his* fault. How was *he* to know?'

The barbs hit home. Kate continued to smile at her.

She forced herself to smile back.

That evening Jennifer sat in a West End bar, listening to Thomas talk.

He was describing his job, complaining about the endless stupidity of his clients for whom he was expected to perform miracles. To hear him speak one would think he was master of the universe rather than a junior accountant at a mid-ranking firm. Not that it mattered to Stuart, who kept making disparaging comparisons with his own profession. His humility made her feel protective. 'Your job is demanding too,' she told him.

'Not like Tom's is. The mere sight of a balance sheet brings me out in a cold sweat. I've always been hopeless at maths.'

'So are most of the people at my firm,' said Thomas. 'The only reason they can do their jobs is because the good lord gave them calculators.'

Jennifer sipped her wine and tried not to gawp at Thomas. Though she had been prepared for his resemblance to Stuart, the reality was still overwhelming. He had the same voice, the same smile, the same throaty chuckle. The only difference was his physical fitness, his accent and his air of easy confidence. It was as if someone had taken Stuart away, groomed and polished him, and Thomas was the finished product.

Stuart made another self-deprecating remark about his lack of academic prowess. Again Thomas laughed. His girlfriend Alice did likewise. She was a slim, pretty girl who smiled a lot and said very little. Not that she had much chance to speak, even if she wanted to.

'Jen's right,' said Thomas. 'You shouldn't put yourself down. You haven't had the opportunities Jimmy and I had.

Mum and Dad spent a fortune on our education, and another fortune on tutors to help Jimmy get into Oxford. Some of the guys we were at school with were morons but most of them ended up at university. If you fork out enough money you can pretty much guarantee the results.'

'So Jimmy went to Oxford?' asked Jennifer.

Thomas nodded.

'Wow.'

'It's not that big a deal,' said Stuart quickly.

'It is! Only one boy from my school went there and he was a genius.'

'I bet he wasn't.'

'He probably just slogged his guts out,' agreed Thomas. 'That's what Jimmy did. Anyone can get there if they work hard enough.'

'So why didn't you?' she asked before she could stop herself.

He frowned. Not wanting to offend him, she hurried to make amends. 'I mean, obviously you could have gone but why didn't you want to?'

'Our school organised a visit there and all the people we met were toffee-nosed twats. Jimmy was really impressed by it all but I wasn't.'

'I wouldn't have been either,' agreed Stuart. 'I hate stuck-up people.'

'Which university did you go to?' Jennifer asked Thomas.

'Exeter. I had a really good time there.'

'How good?' asked Stuart.

Thomas began to describe his student days; an endless social whirl by the sound of it. As Jennifer listened, she remembered one of her teachers describing Exeter as being full of Oxbridge rejects. She wondered if Thomas had been one of them and if he would admit it if he was. Somehow she doubted it.

Thomas continued to talk, entertaining Stuart with tales of student pranks while Alice stared adoringly at him. Jennifer wondered if Alice was finding this meeting as unsettling as she was. It wasn't just the physical similarity. The attention of each twin was so entirely focused on the other that it made her feel like she wasn't there at all.

But she was, and there were things she needed to know.

'How do your parents feel about all this?' she asked Thomas.

'They're completely stunned. But they'll love Stu when they meet him. How could they not?'

Stuart looked pleased. Jennifer tried to do likewise. 'And they'll love you too,' Thomas told her.

'How could they not?' echoed Stuart, giving her arm an affectionate rub. She knew she should drop this particular line of questioning and allow the conversation to return to safer ground. Only she couldn't.

'And how does Jimmy feel?'

'Shocked, like our parents,' Thomas told her. 'But he'll deal with it.'

The answer was too glib for her liking. 'How can you be sure? This has a massive impact on his life.'

'And on mine and Stu's. We're coping, aren't we?'

'But that's different. You're still the person you've always been and Stuart's gaining a new brother but where does that leave Jimmy?'

'He'll be OK,' Stuart told her.

She stared at him. 'Stu, how can you say that? You don't even know him.'

'But I do,' said Thomas calmly.

Stuart nodded. 'Exactly.'

'But ...'

'But what?' Thomas demanded. 'I know him better than anyone. Why would this mess him up? He's great-looking, got a brilliant career and a lovely home. He's got everything you could ever want.'

And you resent him for it.

She looked at Stuart, who was out of shape, whose career was far from brilliant, whose home was shabby and whose life had been far from good. No one could resent Stuart. He would never be competition.

He was staring reproachfully at her, just as he had when he first told her about Thomas and she had tried to contain his excitement.

Thomas was staring at her too. Only his gaze was not reproachful. It was . . .

Suspicious?

Quickly, she backed down. 'I'm sure you're right.'

His expression softened.

'I need to go out for a minute,' said Alice suddenly. 'I promised my dad I'd call him.' She looked apologetically at Thomas. 'You don't mind, do you?'

'Of course I don't.'

'I'll get another round in,' said Stuart. 'What does everyone want?'

They all made their requests. 'Where do your parents live?' Jennifer asked Alice.

'My dad lives in Rotherhithe.'

'What about your mother?'

'She died when I was nine.'

Jennifer felt embarrassed. 'I'm sorry. Forgive me for asking.'

'It's OK. My dad's the best.' Alice rose to her feet. 'I won't be long.'

She made her way towards the door. Stuart walked with her, heading for the bar. Jennifer remained at the table with Thomas. 'Poor Alice,' she said. 'It's hard losing a parent at that age.'

'Though not as bad as it was for Stuart.'

'No.'

'But at least he's got us now.'

She nodded. 'Look, Tom, I'm sorry about before. I didn't mean to sound negative about all this. It's wonderful but a bit scary too. It's all happening so fast and Stu's so excited and after all he's been through I just don't want him to get hurt.'

'He won't. I'll make sure of it. He's my twin, after all.'

Again his glibness disturbed her. 'But that's the thing. You already have a twin.'

'Well, that's my problem, isn't it?'

'And in the same way, Stu is my problem. You don't know him like I do.'

The look of suspicion was back. Again she hurried to make amends. She didn't want to antagonise him.

'What I mean, Tom, is that I've known him longer than you.'

'Actually, you haven't.'

'But I was his girlfriend before he met you.'

'And how long have you been that?'

'Um ... well, not that long ...'

'That's my point. Stu and I started life as the same person. We shared a womb for nine months and have identical DNA. Call me pedantic but I think that counts for a little more than sharing someone's bed for a couple of weeks.'

The words felt like a slap. He continued to stare at her. 'Wouldn't you agree?'

She didn't answer. She wished she had kept her mouth shut.

She wished this meeting had never taken place. She wished Stuart had never met Thomas.

'Look, Jen, I understand why you're worried. I can see you love Stu and it's only natural. All I'm saying is that you don't need to. I won't let him get hurt.'

'Neither will I.'

'Then we both want the same thing.'

'Yes.'

'So why are we fighting?'

'We're not.'

'Friends, then?'

'Of course.'

'Good.'

They smiled at each other. She knew she had been right to fear him.

And sensed he might be starting to fear her too.

Stuart returned with the drinks. 'So how are you two?'

'Great,' said Thomas. 'Jen and I are really getting to know each other.'

Stuart looked delighted. For his sake she did too.

Half past eight.

Susan Bishop paced up and down her living room.

She was feeling restless. Robert Randall had phoned that morning to cancel their meeting. He had given no explanation, his tone guarded. She wondered if he was losing interest, or if he had started seeing someone else.

'I thought you were going out tonight.'

Her husband stood in the doorway, holding his briefcase. She had been so lost in thought she had not heard him return from work.

'Not any more,' she told him.

'Well, as you're free, perhaps we could go out for a meal? That Greek place in Wallingford is supposed to be good.'

'I don't think so.'

'Why not? It might be fun.'

'An evening listening to you talk about share prices? Where's the fun in that?'

'We don't have to talk about that.'

'What else do you have to talk about?'

She waited for a denial, only none came. He just looked hurt. Contempt filled her. Though his passivity had its uses, there were times when she longed for him to grow something resembling a backbone.

He walked away. She remained where she was, thinking of Robert, longing for him while hating him at the same time.

And hating Caroline even more.

Ten o'clock.

Back from London, Caroline let herself into the house.

Robert was waiting in the hallway. 'How's Jimmy?' he asked.

'Do you care?'

'Of course I do.'

'Then you should have come with me. Show him that nothing's changed.'

'But things *have* changed.'

'Not if we don't let them.'

He gave a snort.

'What's that for?'

'You, acting like an ostrich. Trying to ignore this in the hope it'll just go away.'

'What else am I supposed to do?'

'Face up to it.'

'For the last two days you've been hiding in your study. How is that facing up to anything?'

'I've been thinking about what's best to do.'

'We carry on as before. What else can we do?'

'What indeed,' he said.

TEN

Wednesday morning.

Back in the office, James tried to concentrate on work.

It was proving difficult. A constant stream of people kept coming to see him; secretaries to fill him in on departmental gossip, trainees with questions they were too scared to ask the partners, and Duncan White to give him back the Vicourt file, together with a list of excuses for why the deal hadn't progressed in his absence. 'The bloody clients have been dragging their feet but I'm sure you can pull them back into line.'

James nodded.

'Good to have you back. You've been much missed.' Duncan gave a hearty laugh. 'So no more stomach bugs for the next five years, OK?'

Another nod. His telephone rang. 'Do you need to take that?' Duncan asked.

James recognised the caller's number and felt his stomach lurch. 'Yes, I do.'

Duncan left the room. He picked up the receiver. 'Hello, Tom. Good timing. I was just about to call you.' It was a lie but one that at least gave him a fleeting sense of being in control. 'We need to meet. Can you make lunch?'

One o'clock.
They faced each other in a French restaurant near Tottenham Court Road. A waiter took their order, two small main courses and two very large drinks. 'It's nice here,' said Thomas, his tone one of forced cheeriness. 'I didn't know this place existed. That's the thing about London. There are so many good restaurants, you can't possibly know them all.'

Their drinks arrived. As Thomas continued to babble James downed his, took a deep breath and proceeded to grab the bull by the horns.

'Why didn't you tell me? Why did you just go ahead and meet Stuart?'

Thomas, suddenly silent, fiddled with a fork.

'Well?'

'Why do you think?'

'I don't know. That's why I'm asking.'

'Put yourself in my shoes. Seeing his picture on that website was the biggest shock of my life. I wasn't thinking clearly. I just knew I had to meet him.'

'Without telling me first?'

'What was I going to say? Hi, Jimmy, how's life and by the way I don't think we're related. How would that make you feel?'

'How do you think I feel now?'

'Not great.'

'You always were a master of understatement.'

'But you were going to feel like that regardless of when you found out. If you want to blame someone then blame the nurses at the hospital, or blame Mum ...'

'You can't blame Mum.'

172

'But you can't blame me either.' Thomas sighed. 'Imagine if the situation was reversed and you were the one who discovered he had another twin. Would telling me be your first priority?'

'Yes.'

'Bullshit. You can't make that claim, Jimmy, because you don't know. There's no rulebook for this situation. You just have to deal with it as best you can.'

'That's easy for you to say. You're still Thomas Randall. I'm the one who's now someone else.'

'You're still my twin. That hasn't changed.'

'But things *have* changed. Stuart's arrived on the scene.'

'So? I've got two twins. Big deal.'

'That's the point, Tom. You can't have two.'

'What are you saying? That I have to choose?'

'Yes.' The word was out before he could stop it. Quickly, he shook his head. 'All I'm saying is that you should have told me first.'

Thomas sipped his drink, his expression thoughtful. 'The last time we saw each other you said Mum wanted you to check out some websites and asked if I'd do it instead. What if you hadn't done that? What if you'd been the one to find out about Stuart? Would you have told me about him? Would you have told anyone?'

'Absolutely.' He tried to sound convincing.

'I don't believe you. I think you'd have kept quiet because that would have been best for you. Well, I contacted Stuart because that was best for me. Don't make yourself out to be a saint, Jimmy. If you were me you'd have done what I did.'

Silence. They stared at each other while the waiter brought the food, which lay untouched before them.

'Look, I do feel bad about this,' said Thomas eventually.

'And I didn't contact Stuart to spite you. I did it because I needed to know the truth.'

'And now you do.'

'But it doesn't change how I feel about you.'

'Last time we met you told me you wished I'd never been born. Are those the feelings you're talking about?'

'You told me you no longer had a brother.'

He gave a dry laugh. 'I must be psychic.'

'I didn't mean what I said, Jimmy. I was hurt and wanted to hurt you back. I felt terrible afterwards. I was scared I'd lost you.'

'And would that still be a loss now?'

'Of course it would! You're the best friend I've ever had.'

'But I'm more than a friend. Or at least I was.'

'You still are. Do you think I'm just going to forget the past? Because I'm telling you I won't.'

James didn't answer.

'Do you want me to promise?'

'That's what kids do. We're not kids any more.'

'But we're still twins. And I *will* promise, but only on one condition.'

'Which is?'

'That you promise I'll always have you.'

Again they stared at each other. Thomas looked anxious, upset even. Unbidden, James's ingrained sense of protectiveness rose to the surface. He didn't want Thomas to feel bad. All he wanted was for Thomas still to be his twin.

'I promise,' he said softly.

'So do I.'

'I'm sorry, Tom. I didn't mean to give you a hard time. I do understand why you did it. It's just . . .' He sighed. 'Well, you know . . .'.

'Yeah, I know. And I'm sorry too, Jimmy. I really am.'

'Don't beat yourself up. I'll survive.' He managed a smile. 'Do you remember what Grandpa used to say when we were upset as kids?'

'Chin up, boys. Worse things happen at sea.' Thomas smiled too. 'God, Grandpa was full of shit.'

They both laughed. For a moment it felt like old times. It was a good feeling.

'Tell me about Stuart,' said James.

'He's nice.'

'*Nice?* Is that it?'

'He's friendly. He's cheerful. He wears shiny suits and needs to lose a stone. He's ... I don't know. He's nice. What else can I say?'

That he'll never mean more to you than I do.

'How do you feel when you're with him?'

Thomas looked amused. 'What? Do we have whole conversations without opening our mouths? Do we share dreams and identical scars from childhood biking accidents? Come on, Jimmy, you don't buy that psychobabble crap.'

'It's not crap. There have been studies done on separated twins.'

'And I'm sure they make fascinating reading but it's not like that with Stuart and me. He's a great guy and I feel a bond with him. But it's not even close to the one I have with you. He doesn't have our history. No one ever will.'

A lump rose in his throat. 'No, I guess not.'

'So I'm afraid you're stuck with me. I'm still going to be calling you all the time to complain about work or give you grief about Kate.'

James rolled his eyes.

'Have you dumped her yet?'

'No!'

'Phew. My money's on you making it to nine months so hang on in there until November and we can split the champagne.'

Again he laughed. He knew he shouldn't but it felt right.

'So do you forgive me?' Thomas asked.

He nodded.

'Thanks. Love you, mate.'

'Love you too.'

The waiter brought them more drinks. Thomas poked at his food. 'This is cold.'

'I wouldn't worry. The food here is terrible anyway.'

'Now you tell me.'

More laughter. 'I propose a toast,' said Thomas. 'To you and me.'

They clinked glasses.

'And to this weekend not being a total disaster,' Thomas continued.

'Why? What's happening this weekend?'

'Stuart's meeting Mum and Dad.'

James put down his glass. 'He's *what*?'

'Didn't Mum tell you?'

'What does Mum have to do with this?'

'I got a message from her this morning inviting Stuart to visit on Sunday.'

James couldn't believe what he was hearing. 'But she promised me she wasn't going to meet him.'

'Well, maybe she just said that to spare your feelings.'

'She wasn't just saying it. She meant it,' stressed James.

'Then she must have changed her mind.'

'She wouldn't. Not about this.'

'How do you know?'

'I just do.'

'It's not that simple, though,' said Thomas. 'This is difficult for Mum. She's bound to feel—'

'I don't need a lecture on how Mum feels. I know her better than you do.'

'Thank you for reminding me.'

He realised what he had said. Thomas was staring coolly at him. Briefly, he felt guilty. Then the feeling was gone, replaced by fury at the betrayal.

'Well, it's true! She doesn't want to meet him. Dad's just bullied her into this like he bullies her into everything.'

'Including you always being golden boy? Was that down to Dad's bullying too?'

'Oh grow up, Tom. This has nothing to do with that.'

'You're not denying it, then? That makes a change.'

'So tracking Stuart down was just your way of getting back at me, was it?'

'No. It had nothing to do with that.'

'Pull the other one.'

'They're entitled to meet him. He *is* their son.'

'And I'm not. Thanks for reminding me. Thanks a fucking lot.'

'Keep your voice down. People are staring.'

James looked about the restaurant. Diners on nearby tables were watching him warily. 'Got a problem?' he snapped and all quickly resumed their meals.

'Calm down,' Thomas told him. 'You must have known this would happen. But you don't need to worry. You'll like Stuart. You're invited too.'

'*Invited?* I don't need an invitation to my own home or are you going to tell me it's not my home any more?'

'Why are you being like this?'

'Why do you think? Christ. This is hard enough and now you expect me to just turn up and smile and play happy families with this bloody interloper?'

'But, Jimmy ...'

'I mean it. There's no way I'm going to be there. No way on earth.'

Thomas continued to protest. Ignoring him, a seething James downed his drink and called for another.

As James plied himself with alcohol in the restaurant, Caroline stood in the hallway, watching a muttering Robert hunt for his car keys.

'I think they're in your golf-jacket pocket,' she told him.

'I've already checked there. Have you called Tom?'

'Yes.'

'What did he say?'

'He wasn't there. I left a message. But I'm worried about Jimmy. How is he going to feel?'

'Jimmy, Jimmy, Jimmy. Do you ever think about anyone else? We're all affected by this. Not just him.' He cursed under his breath. 'Where the hell are they?'

'Try under the paper.' A pause. 'Where are you going?'

He didn't answer, just continued searching, eventually finding the keys under a pile of junk mail. She knew she shouldn't detain him but couldn't let the matter drop.

'Bob.'

'What?'

'You're right about Stuart. We should meet him. Only, must it be here?'

'Why shouldn't it be?'

'What if someone finds out?'

He turned towards her, his expression contemptuous. 'Is

that all you're worried about? What the neighbours will think? I might have known. The only two things in this world that really matter to you: Jimmy and keeping up appearances.'

'This is not about appearances!' She tried to sound indignant while in her heart she knew it was, at least partly, true. What *would* people think if they knew she had raised the wrong child? What would it do to her standing in the community? Could it survive something like this?

Only she already knew the answer, could already hear the mocking laughter. And it turned her blood to ice.

'We're not going to hide Stuart away like a dirty secret,' he told her. 'He's our son and we owe him better than that. Besides, this is my house and I make the rules. Stuart will visit us here and you will make him welcome.'

His mouth was a thin line. She knew there was no point arguing. When Robert's mind was made up, God himself couldn't change it.

'Is that understood?'

She nodded. He headed out to the car. She remained where she was while in her head the laughter grew ever louder.

Half past three.
James returned to the office.

A pile of phone messages lay on his desk. One was from his mother. Angrily, he threw it in the bin.

Duncan White charged into the room. 'Where have you been?'

'At lunch.'

'What about the conference call?'

'What conference call?'

'The one with Vicourt an hour ago.'

'I forgot. I'm sorry.'

'*Sorry?* Is that it?'

'It won't happen again.'

'I'll say it won't. You dropped me right in the shit. I was the one who had to take it and try and sound like I knew what I was talking about. Don't you ever bloody do that to me again!'

Duncan's face was red with fury. On a normal day James would have tried to appease him, but then again, on a normal day he would never have forgotten.

And he was not in the mood to be screamed at. Particularly not by someone who had always reminded him of his father.

'And how did I drop you in it exactly? You're the partner in charge. Call me crazy but doesn't that mean you should know exactly what's going on?'

'I beg your pardon.'

'You heard. So you had to take a conference call you weren't expecting. Big deal. I have to do it all the time, usually because you've gone AWOL.'

'How dare you talk to me like that.'

'What are you going to do? Fire me? Go ahead. I can leave now if you want. Only that's going to leave you in the shit too. There's another conference call tomorrow morning. But hey, I'm sure you'll manage to muddle through.'

'You're drunk.'

'Well, what if I am? How many times have you gone for a supposedly quick lunch, only to return at five o'clock pissed as a newt? All I'm doing is following your example. You are Head of Department after all.'

Duncan's eyes looked as if they were about to pop out of his head. James's father always looked the same way when challenged. Hatred burned inside him. He opened his mouth, preparing to vent more spleen.

And remembered that the man who faced him was not his father but his boss, and that he couldn't afford to lose his job.

He softened his tone. 'I've just had lunch with my brother. He told me my aunt's got cancer. That's why I'm late and that's why I'm drunk. It's been a shock and I don't need you having a go. I've never let you down before and I won't do it again.'

Duncan swallowed, his colour starting to fall. 'Well, I'm sorry to hear that.'

'Thanks.' He told himself the lie wouldn't hurt. Duncan was as likely to meet Aunt Helen as he was to do his job properly.

'You should have told me straightaway.'

'You didn't give me the chance . . .' He stopped, not wanting to provoke another argument. 'But yeah, I should. My head's all over the place at the moment but I'll be fine tomorrow.'

'What sort of cancer is it?'

'Um . . . breast.'

'Well, that's something. They can usually treat it, if they catch it in time.'

'Fingers crossed.'

Duncan left. He sat back in his chair, staring up at the ceiling. His secretary Donna crept into the room. 'Did you hear that?' he asked.

'I think the whole department did.'

'Oh, God.'

'You're right, though. He'd never fire you otherwise he might actually have to do some work.' Donna began to look awkward. 'I'm sorry about your aunt. You're very fond of her, aren't you?'

He nodded, hating himself for using a much-loved relative as an alibi.

Only she wasn't a relative. Not any more.

Donna handed him two more phone message slips. He put them on the pile with the others. Then, needing to talk to someone who knew the truth, he called Kate.

'Oh, Jimmy ...'

'I know it was stupid, but he just got me at the wrong moment.'

'I can't believe your mother would do that to you. Not after all she said. At least you've got me. I'll get you through this. That's a promise you can count on. And you're absolutely right. There's no way you should go home this weekend. Let your parents see what a loser Stuart is and they'll be all over you like a rash.'

'But what if they like him?'

'How could they? He's not you. Anyway, forget about that. The important thing is to make peace with your boss. You can't afford to jeopardise your partnership chances. Even with junior equity your earnings will double ...'

Kate prattled on, totally career-focused as always. Though he knew she meant well, he felt frustrated. What he needed was reassurance that he still had a family, not a masterclass in networking his way to the top of the legal tree.

Becky would have understood that. She would have known what to say to make him feel better. In his head he could hear her voice and it made his heart ache.

But she was in the past. He knew that.

Just as he knew that come the weekend, he would be going home.

Quarter to six.

Helen sat in her living room with her sister.

She had returned from work to find Caroline waiting in the

182

drive. The discovery had taken her by surprise. She hadn't expected to see Caroline for weeks. Once she heard the news, however, everything made sense.

'Bob won't change his mind,' said Caroline, 'You know how stubborn he is. And I just can't face it.'

'Why not? You have nothing to be ashamed of. This isn't your fault.'

'Try telling Bob that.'

'I will if you think it will help.'

Caroline shuddered.

'All right, point taken. But you were ill when the twins were born. You couldn't know what had happened. Stuart will understand that.'

'Who cares about Stuart? It's Jimmy I'm worried about. I promised him nothing would change.'

'It doesn't have to. You'll always be his mother. There's no one to take your place. Poor Stuart lost both his parents a long time ago.'

'Thank God. I couldn't bear it if Jimmy started calling someone else Mum.'

Her sister's coldness shocked Helen. She tried to ignore it. When trauma knocked on the door, finer feelings often fled through the window.

'I'm glad you've come,' she told Caroline. 'I was worried you'd never forgive me.'

'Of course I've come. Who else can I talk to? And I'm not angry with you. It's Tom I'm angry with.'

'You can't blame him.'

'Yes, I can. He's so selfish. The only person he ever thinks about is himself.'

Like mother like son.

'If only he'd left well alone we wouldn't be in this mess.'

'Well, what was he supposed to do? If I were him I'd have acted the same way.'

'I wouldn't.'

She knew it was pointless to argue. 'Look, it's only one meeting. That may be all Stuart wants.'

'But what if someone finds out?'

'How? You're not going to tell anyone and neither is Bob. He may blame you but anyone else wanting to cast blame will point the finger at both of you, and he won't want to risk that.'

'What about Tom?'

'He won't tell either. You've always ...' she struggled for the most diplomatic turn of phrase '... had more in common with Jimmy. Now it turns out Jimmy isn't your biological son. Tom's hardly going to brag about that, is he?' Secretly, she wasn't convinced but at that moment convincing Caroline was all that mattered.

Briefly, Caroline seemed to relax. 'No, perhaps not.'

'Exactly.'

'But what if they find out in the future?'

'By then you may not care. You don't know how you'll feel about Stuart when you meet him.'

'I'm never going to feel anything for him.'

'But you still have to give him a chance. Doesn't he deserve one after all he's been through?'

Caroline didn't answer. Her expression became troubled. Helen decided to keep pushing.

'After all, we know what it's like to lose both parents in childhood.'

Silence. Caroline traced a coffee stain with her finger. The table was covered in them. Normally Helen would have been on the receiving end of a lecture on hygiene, but this was not a normal day.

'Don't we?'

'We didn't lose Dad.'

'We might as well have done. He was never the same after Mum died.'

Caroline continued to trace the stain. 'Do you remember the day she died?'

Helen nodded.

'Dad was at the hospital. He left us with that awful woman from next door. What was her name?'

'Mrs Clitheroe.'

'Yes, Mrs Clitheroe. What a bitch she was. When Dad came back and told us Mum was dead we cried and what did Mrs Clitheroe do?'

'She told us we weren't babies and that tears didn't solve anything.'

'And then she said she knew what would make us feel better and gave us each a Coke. She made us drink it too. I can still remember the way it tasted. Even now after all this time I can't touch the stuff.'

'You used to sleep in my bed for weeks afterwards. You used to cry yourself to sleep. You weren't eating. I was so worried about you.'

'You made me eat. You looked after me. I was lucky to have you.' Caroline swallowed. 'I still am.'

Then she started to cry. Helen watched her, no longer seeing a grown woman but the frightened child her sister had once been. It hurt to see Caroline upset. Over the years they had had their quarrels but at the end of the day they would always be sisters.

'I was lucky to have you too,' she said.

Caroline wiped her eyes. 'Mrs Clitheroe was right about one thing, though. All the tears in the world won't make this better.'

'That's why you need to remember how we felt when Mum

died. It was terrible but at least we had each other. Stuart had no one. I don't expect you to love him, Carrie, but I do expect you to be kind.'

'Will you be there on Sunday?'

'Do you want me to be?'

'Yes, please. I could do with the support.'

'Then I will and so will Nessa. We'll be there for you, and for Jimmy. And it will be all right.'

'Do you know what I wish? That Stuart was dead. He's my own son and yet I wish he was dead. Oh, Helen, how can things ever be all right when I feel like this . . . '

'This Sunday?' exclaimed Jennifer.

A beaming Stuart nodded at her. 'Isn't it great?'

'Um . . . it's fantastic.' She tried to sound excited while feeling alarmed.

'I didn't think it would be so soon but Tom says they're dying to meet me. He's suggested travelling down with us. He can direct me.'

'And Alice too?'

'No. She can't make it.'

'That's a shame.'

'But at least you'll have more chance to bond with Tom.'

'Yes. That is a bonus.'

They were standing either side of the entrance to his flat. He had seen her from the window and met her at the door. 'Are you going to let me in?' she asked.

He made space for her to enter. In the flat upstairs the baby wailed while its parents argued. She knew how the baby felt and hoped she and Stuart wouldn't soon be arguing too. Through the open bedroom door she saw clothes laid out on the bed. 'Are you doing a wash?'

'I'm trying to decide what to wear. I want to make a good impression.'

'Then all you need do is be yourself.'

'That's what Tom said. Apparently Jimmy's really pissed off. He's told Tom he won't be there.'

'That's a shame.'

'Why? He's not family. It's my biological parents I want to meet.'

She nodded. He continued to radiate excitement, sporting a grin that would put the Cheshire cat to shame. She didn't want to dampen his mood but unease nipped at her like invisible fingers.

'So how did Tom and Jimmy's meeting go?'

'OK until Jimmy went all prima donna about my visit.'

'This can't be easy for him.'

The grin vanished. 'Here we go.'

'What do you mean?'

'You should have heard yourself last night. Oh, wow, Jimmy's been to Oxford. He must be a genius. Why not form a fan club and have done with it.'

'I just thought it was impressive he'd been there.'

'Well, it isn't. Tom could have gone too. He just didn't want to.'

'Well, that's his story,' she said before she could stop herself.

He frowned. 'What have you got against Tom?'

'Nothing.'

'Well, it doesn't sound that way. When I spoke to him he kept going on about how much he liked you ...'

Yeah, I bet he did.

' ... and now here you are having digs.'

'I'm not. It's only ...' She stopped, not wanting to dig an even deeper hole for herself. 'I just feel sorry for Jimmy, that's all.'

'Why? He didn't lose his whole family when he was a kid.

He didn't get shafted by his uncle and have to go into foster care. It should have been him but instead it was me while he's poncing around Oxford like an extra in *Brideshead Revisited*. Christ, he doesn't know he's born and there you are making him out to be a victim.'

'But he *is* a victim in this situation. Just like you.'

'Rubbish. Being a victim means having to suffer. When has he ever suffered?'

'I'm just saying . . .'

'Well, don't. You're supposed to be on my side.'

'This isn't about taking sides. All I'm saying is—'

'That the Randalls are going to think I'm a loser compared to him. Thanks a lot, Jen. Don't you think I'm nervous enough already?' He exhaled. 'If you're going to be this negative maybe you shouldn't come.'

Quickly, she tried to make amends. There was no way she was letting him enter the lion's den alone. 'Of course I'm on your side. Don't you remember what I promised you after your grandmother's funeral? No one will ever hurt you again. Not with me around.'

'Jimmy's hurt me. He stole what should have been my life and left me to swim through the shit storm that should have been his.'

But he didn't. Not deliberately. And thinking it isn't going to help anyone.

She wanted to say it, but knew her words would be wasted. Instead she put her arms around him and stared into his eyes. 'I just don't want you to hate him. So he went to Oxford? You could have gone too if you'd been in his shoes but as you said yourself you'd probably have loathed it. If you'd had his opportunities you could have achieved everything he has and more besides.'

His expression softened. For the first time he looked anxious. 'I just get scared. I imagine them comparing me to him and being disappointed.'

'They've no right to be. Jimmy's not half the person you are and neither is ...'

Tom.

' ... any other guy I've ever met. I'm proud of you, and if your parents aren't then more fool them.'

ELEVEN

Five o'clock, Sunday morning.

Unable to sleep, Caroline left Robert in bed and went to make some coffee.

The fridge and cupboards were full of food for the impending visit. Though she dreaded it with every fibre of her being, the hostess in her demanded she put on a good show.

As the kettle boiled she stood by the window, staring up at a darkening sky, daring to hope for weather so bad it would force Stuart to cancel his trip.

Only it wouldn't be a cancellation, just a postponement. Their meeting was as inevitable as death.

The coffee made, she walked to the drawing room. From upstairs came the thunder of Robert's snores. She envied him his ability to sleep.

The family photographs stood neatly arranged on the grand piano. Once they had been a source of pleasure. Now every time she looked at James's smiling face she thought of the son who should have been smiling in his place.

It began to rain. She imagined a storm that turned the roads to glass, causing Stuart to crash and break his neck, allowing her to forget him and take back all the certainty he was stealing from her.

She watched raindrops batter the windows while upstairs an oblivious Robert slept on.

'Jesus Christ!' exclaimed Stuart.

It was early afternoon. Squinting into the sun, he guided his car up the drive towards the Randall family home.

'So what do you think?' asked Thomas from the passenger seat.

'It's a mansion. I used to think my Uncle Gordon's house was big but it's a matchbox compared to this.' As he spoke he caught Jennifer's eye in the windscreen mirror. During the journey he and Thomas had been so busy talking he had almost forgotten she was there. But now, as his nerves kicked in, he was glad she was.

The drive was already full of cars. He parked next to a battered Mini Metro. 'I see Jimmy's here,' Thomas observed.

'Is that his car?'

'Are you kidding? Jimmy wouldn't be seen dead in that wreck.' Thomas pointed to a gleaming Porsche. 'That's his.'

'Lucky sod. I'd kill for a set of wheels like that.' He switched off the engine and exhaled. 'Do I look all right?'

'Stop worrying. They're not going to care how you're dressed.'

'That's what I've been trying to tell him,' said Jennifer from the back seat.

People were gathering on the front steps of the house. His stomach filled with butterflies. Again he caught Jennifer's eye in the mirror. She mouthed the words 'I love you'. He mouthed them back then climbed out of the car.

Thomas led the way. Stuart followed, holding Jennifer's

191

hand. His real mother stepped out of the crowd towards him. She was very beautiful. The photographs had not done her justice. He felt intimidated, convinced that in spite of all he knew he was about to be exposed as a fraud.

Then she smiled, the gesture warm and welcoming. Instantly, he began to relax.

'Welcome, Stuart. I'm so glad you could come.' Her voice was warm too. He opened his mouth to speak, then closed it again, unsure of what to call her.

'I'm Caroline,' she said, coming to his rescue. 'Carrie if you'd prefer.'

'Thank you ... um ... Caroline. It's a lovely name.'

'So is Stuart. I hope your journey wasn't too tiring.'

'No, it was fine. I was worried about the weather but fortunately the sun decided to make an appearance.'

'Yes, I was worried too.' Caroline turned to Jennifer. 'And you must be Jen. Or would you prefer Jennifer? I shouldn't shorten your name without permission.'

Jennifer shook her head. 'Jen is fine. I'm pleased to meet you, Mrs ... Caroline. It was very kind of you to invite me too.'

'The pleasure is mine. Won't you both come and meet everyone else?'

She introduced them to her husband, a tall, imposing man with a booming voice and vigorous handshake who told them to call him Robert before grinning at Stuart. 'You can tell we're related. You've inherited my eye for a beautiful lady.'

Jennifer blushed. Stuart squeezed her hand. 'I see you've taken after me in the looks department,' Robert told him. 'Please accept my profuse apologies for that.'

Stuart laughed. Robert did too, giving him a wink.

The introductions continued. He met Aunt Helen and

Vanessa. 'Stuart knows me already,' Vanessa announced. 'I'm the family stalker.'

It was his turn to blush. 'I'm sorry about that.'

'Don't be. I'm the one who should apologise.'

Aunt Helen, following her sister's example, asked about the journey. As he answered he noticed a tall, handsome young man standing behind the others. Raising his voice, he said, 'And you must be Jimmy.'

'Yes, I am. Hello, Stuart.'

They shook hands. 'I've heard a lot about you,' Stuart said politely.

'And me, you.'

'I didn't think you were going to be here.'

'Fortunately my work commitments fell through.'

'Yes, that is good.'

They stared at each other, both clearly struggling for something to say. Thomas came to the rescue. 'Stu likes your car,' he told James.

Stuart nodded. 'I wish I had one like that.'

'You're welcome to drive it,' James offered.

'I wouldn't want to put you out.'

'You wouldn't be. It's a great car. No reason why we can't both enjoy it.'

Again they stared at each other. He knew they were both thinking the same thing; that by rights the car was his already.

'Why don't we all go inside,' said Caroline.

Half an hour later, Jennifer sat with Stuart in a drawing room so immaculate it looked like a cover shot for *Good Housekeeping*. She tried to imagine someone as untidy as Stuart growing up in such a home. Only, if this had been his home perhaps he wouldn't be untidy after all.

Caroline and Robert were asking Stuart questions about his family, all of which he answered with the excessive positivity of someone sitting a job interview. In his jacket pocket was a photograph of his parents and sister. Jennifer wondered if he would decide to show it.

And how James would react if he did.

He was sitting nearby, watching Stuart with eyes that gave nothing away. Noticing her staring, he gazed down at the floor.

Stuart explained that his mother had worked in local government. 'What a coincidence,' remarked Caroline. 'Helen does too.'

Helen nodded. 'Though all I do is filing.'

'That's what Mum did,' Stuart told her. 'And she only worked in term time. She liked being at home in the school holidays.'

Caroline smiled. 'Well, that's understandable. All mothers want to be with their children in the holidays.'

'*Do* they?' asked Thomas.

'Of course,' Caroline told him.

'So why did Jimmy and I spend ours being looked after by the au pair?'

'You didn't, Tom, as you well know. Stuart, your cup is empty. May I get you more tea or would you prefer something stronger?'

'Tea would be lovely, thank you.'

'You have a beautiful home,' Jennifer told Caroline.

'Thank you, Jen.'

'I'll give you both the grand tour later,' said Thomas.

'I'd like that,' said Stuart, before looking apologetically at Caroline. 'If you don't mind, that is?'

'Of course she doesn't,' Thomas told him. 'After all, it's your home too.'

For the briefest of moments Caroline's smile dimmed. Then

it returned to full power. Feeling uneasy, Jennifer turned to Stuart, relieved to see he hadn't noticed.

'You grew up in Sutton Coldfield, didn't you?' Vanessa asked Stuart.

'Yes.'

'A friend of mine lives there. It seems a really nice place.'

'It is,' Jennifer agreed.

Thomas looked surprised. 'Have you been?'

'She came with me to my grandmother's funeral,' Stuart explained.

'We were so sorry to hear about that,' Caroline told Stuart. 'How are you bearing up?'

'OK, thanks. At least her death wasn't unexpected, and I was lucky to have Jen. She's been great.'

'And now you've got us too,' added Thomas. 'Hasn't he, Mum?'

'Of course he does. And what about your father, Stuart? He owned a garage, didn't he?'

Stuart shook his head. 'He was just a car salesman. But he was very good at it. He loved cars. His hobby was doing up old wrecks. Our drive always looked like a scrap yard. It used to drive my mother mad.'

'That must be where you get it from, Jimmy,' Robert observed.

James looked surprised. 'What do you mean?'

'You've always been a car nut. Don't you remember that old Vauxhall I bought you for your seventeenth birthday? You were always making improvements to it. Old Peter Clark at the garage said you were a natural.' Robert gave a hearty laugh. 'And to think of all the money we wasted on tutors for your Oxford entrance exam. We'd have been better off just getting you an apprenticeship with Pete.'

'It wasn't wasted,' said Caroline firmly. 'James did very well at Oxford.'

'Which college were you at?' Jennifer asked James.

'Brasenose.'

'That's my old college,' Robert explained. 'Though in my day there was none of this private tuition rubbish. You just sat the exam and had done with it.'

'Well, maybe it was easier in your day, Uncle Bob,' said Vanessa.

'And what would you know about it?'

'Only that Jimmy got a First and you didn't. But I stand corrected. I'm sure it was much harder in your day than in his.'

Robert's face darkened. Suddenly there was no trace of his previous good humour. Jennifer's sense of unease increased.

'Yes, I'm sure it was,' said Helen quickly. 'Which university did you go to, Stuart?'

'Um ... actually I didn't.'

'Which is hardly surprising,' said Thomas. 'If Jimmy and I had been through what you have, neither of us would have gone either.'

Stuart gave Thomas a grateful smile. Thomas smiled back. Jennifer saw James register the exchange. Fleetingly, he looked hurt. Then his face became a mask.

'Your parents sound like lovely people,' Caroline told Stuart. 'I'm sorry I never had the chance to meet them.'

'I've got a picture if you'd like to see.'

'We'd love to,' said Robert, all affability again.

Stuart handed him the photograph. Robert studied it for some time. 'Good heavens, Jimmy,' he exclaimed. 'You're the image of your mother.'

Jennifer repressed the urge to stare at James. Instead she watched Caroline, yet again noticing her smile falter.

'He looks even more like my cousin,' said Stuart.

'The one you hate?' asked Thomas.

'And how,' said Stuart with a laugh, before becoming self-conscious. 'Well, hate's too strong a word. It's just ... um ...'

Jennifer came to his rescue. 'Stuart has good reason to hate him. I haven't even met him and I hate him too.'

'Why is that?' asked Robert.

Stuart shook his head. 'It's a long story.'

'Well, then, let's leave it for your next visit.' A laugh. 'Assuming we haven't scared you off, that is.'

'Not at all.' Stuart looked delighted. As did Caroline.

So much so that Jennifer knew it was an act.

Robert handed the photograph to Caroline. As she stared at it her smile became brighter. Only this time it wasn't an act.

She doesn't think Stuart's mother is as attractive as her.

Caroline passed the photograph to James. Quickly, he handed it to Helen.

'Don't shove it aside like it's nothing,' said Stuart. 'They were wonderful people. They deserve more respect than that.'

Silence. Everyone looked embarrassed, even Stuart. 'I'm sorry. I only meant ...'

'Don't apologise,' Robert told him. 'You've every right to be angry. Jimmy, that was bloody rude.'

'It isn't easy for him ...' began Caroline.

'It isn't easy for Stuart either but I haven't noticed him behaving like an oaf. Come on, Jimmy, we raised you with better manners than that.'

James took the photograph back from Helen and studied it. Jennifer watched him, feeling a wave of sympathy sweep over her. She pushed it away, not wanting to be disloyal to Stuart.

'You're right,' he said eventually. 'They do look like lovely people. It's a shame I'll never have the chance to meet them.'

'For both of us,' said Stuart quietly.

James passed the photograph to Vanessa. 'I'm sorry,' he said again. Jennifer's sympathy intensified. Again she tried to push it away, only it clung to her like an anxious child.

'Don't be,' she said. 'And for what it's worth, I'm sure they'd have liked you and that you'd have liked them too.'

James nodded, his eyes lowered. But Caroline was watching her. For a moment the smile was gone, replaced by a look of fury.

Vanessa handed the photograph back to Stuart. As she did so she caught Jennifer's eye and mouthed the word 'Thanks'.

Robert began asking Stuart about his job. Caroline listened attentively, her smile as dazzling as ever.

After tea James helped Thomas show Stuart and Jennifer the upstairs of the house. 'It's amazing,' Stuart kept saying. 'You could fit my parents' place into a couple of rooms.'

'I'm glad you like it,' James said politely.

Stuart ignored him, too busy marvelling at the dimensions of the bathroom. Jennifer, however, gave him a smile.

Thomas showed them his bedroom: still laid out as on the day he had left home for college. He nudged Stuart, gesturing to the rock star posters on the wall. 'At least one of us has good taste.'

'There's nothing wrong with my taste.'

'And this from the man who thinks Justin Timberlake is a genius.'

They both laughed, the sound warm and intimate. James forced himself to laugh too. 'It could be worse,' Thomas told Stuart. 'At least you don't like Celine Dion. Kate adores her.'

Again Stuart laughed. 'It's a shame Kate couldn't be here today,' Jennifer told James. 'We would have liked to meet her.'

'Thanks. She would have liked to meet you too.'

'It's a shame Alice couldn't be here either.'

'Who's Alice?'

'Tom's girlfriend.'

'He's got a girlfriend?'

Jennifer began to look uncomfortable. Quickly, James masked his hurt with a grin. 'Typical Tom, he never tells me anything.' A pause. 'So you've met her, then?'

Jennifer nodded. 'She's not really my girlfriend,' Thomas explained. 'It's just a bit of fun.'

'She's nice, though,' said Stuart. 'We really liked her.'

'And I'm sure I will when I meet her,' James told him.

'Assuming you ever do,' Stuart replied.

He was taken aback. 'What do you mean?'

'Tom's just said it's only a bit of fun.'

'Oh. Sure.'

'Do you want to see Jimmy's room?' Thomas asked.

Stuart nodded. 'If Jimmy doesn't mind,' added Jennifer.

He shook his head. 'Be my guest.'

His room was across the hall from Thomas's, with wonderful views of the garden and the river. 'It's bigger than yours,' Stuart told Thomas.

'Jimmy got first choice.'

'That's not true, Tom,' said James quickly. 'We tossed a coin.'

'That's not how I remember it.'

'Well, that's what happened. Anyway, I always said we could swap if you wanted.' He tried not to sound defensive.

'You're lucky,' Stuart told him. 'I'd have killed for a bedroom like this.'

'It's just a room.'

'Try saying that after years in foster care. Every room I had was less than half the size, and there was always two or three of us sharing.'

James didn't respond. Jennifer was studying him closely. Clearly, she understood how he was feeling. Though grateful for her concern, he didn't want it. All he wanted was to be somewhere else.

'I have to make a phone call,' he announced. 'I won't be long.'

'Don't rush on our account,' Stuart told him.

He made for the kitchen. It was directly below his bedroom from which he could hear laughter. Finding an unopened bottle of wine in the fridge, he pulled it out and prepared to open it, just as he had done a million times before.

Only, he couldn't. Something was stopping him. The sense of being a guest in his own family's home.

He heard footsteps. Vanessa appeared behind him. 'Your parents are rowing. Your mum doesn't want Stuart to visit again. She feels bad for you.'

'Then she shouldn't have asked him in the first place.'

'She didn't want to. Your dad made her.'

'She could have said no.'

'She tried. You know what he's like.'

'Don't I just. You heard him earlier with his digs. Why does he have to do that?'

'Because he envies you. You're doing all the things he still wants to do.'

'And do you know why I'm doing them? For him. All my life I've been what he wanted me to be. Star student, star athlete, star lawyer. The sort of son he could boast about to his golfing buddies.' Bitterness consumed him. 'If what he really wanted was a loser it's a pity Stuart didn't turn up years ago.'

'That's not fair,' she said gently.

He knew she was right, but was too worked up to admit it. Instead he put the wine back in the fridge. 'I've had enough of this. I'm going back to London. Tell them I got an emergency call from work.'

'Jimmy . . .'

'Just tell them, OK.'

As he started down the drive he saw his mother at the window, waving frantically at him. Ignoring her, he headed for the road.

As Stuart and Jennifer were given a tour of the garden, Thomas went to fetch more drinks. Using the excuse of helping, Caroline followed him inside.

She cornered him in the kitchen. 'I hope you're pleased with yourself,' she said.

He poured fruit juice into glasses 'What do you mean?'

'What do you *think* I mean?'

'I don't know. That's why I'm asking.'

'Don't try and be clever, Tom. It doesn't suit you.'

He continued pouring drinks.

'How could you be so selfish? Thrusting Stuart into our lives without a word of warning. Didn't you stop to think how your brother might feel?'

'Which one?'

'Don't be flippant.'

'Who's being flippant? Thanks to your incompetence, I now have two.'

His words were like a slap. 'How dare you say that to me?'

'What are you going to do about it? Swap me? A bit late for that now, Mum. You had your chance when I was born.'

'It wasn't my fault. It was an accident!'

'I know. If it had been down to you I'd be the one with the Brummie accent.'

She tried to glare him into submission but his gaze remained steady. Changing tack, she swallowed as if fighting back tears.

201

'Here we go. If in doubt, cue the waterworks and guilt trip me into submission. Sorry, Mum, but that act's got old. It's time to update.'

'Why are you being like this? Can't you see how hard this is for me?'

'For *you*?' He began to laugh.

'Don't you care how I feel?'

'Not as much as you do. A saint couldn't care as much as you do. You talk about having it hard. How hard do you think it was for Stu, losing both his parents and his sister and having to grow up alone?'

'I lost my mother, remember, when I was even younger than he was.'

'And did Jimmy and I ever hear about it when we were kids. All your constant reminders of how lucky we were to have you. Me, especially. And that's the joke, isn't it? Jimmy was the lucky one. All that favouritism and he wasn't even your son.'

'You sound like your father.'

'Well, what do you know? Blood will out. I get my insensitivity from him and my selfishness from you. Maybe that's why you always preferred Jimmy. He's nothing like either of you.'

She swallowed, for real this time. His eyes remained as hard as stone.

'Not everything is about you, Mum. This is about trying to make Stuart feel special. You've always considered yourself the perfect parent. For once in your life why not try acting like it?'

He took the drinks and walked away. She called his name but he kept on going. Once he would have stopped, but not now. A chill swept through her as she realised a power she had always taken for granted was no longer hers to command.

She remained there for some time, breathing deeply, trying to pull herself together, wishing James was there to tell her that

Thomas was wrong. That she was wonderful. That whatever she did was all right with him.

But he wasn't. Instead he had left her to deal with this alone.

And he shouldn't have. Not when she needed him.

A thought echoed in her brain, soft but as unsettling as a scream.

Your real son wouldn't have done that.

As Robert showed the others the new conservatory, Jennifer noticed Vanessa staring at her.

They made eye contact. Vanessa gestured for her to follow.

They went to stand by the riverbank. Vanessa offered her a cigarette. They lit up. Vanessa blew smoke across the water and said, 'Welcome to the family.'

'Thanks.'

'The visit is going well.'

She nodded, brushing away a fly.

'My aunt is lovely, isn't she? She knows how to make people feel welcome.'

'Absolutely.'

'My uncle can overdo the teasing but he's got a heart of gold.'

Another nod. She managed to keep her expression neutral.

'And you don't believe a word I'm saying.'

Jennifer didn't answer, just watched a pair of swans glide past.

'You don't need to tell me. It's written all over your face.'

She turned. Vanessa's own face was open, her gaze direct but also warm. It was the face of someone she decided she could trust.

'Your aunt hates us being here. I can tell. Stu can't but I can.'

'And what about dear, sweet Uncle Bob?'

'He's glad, but only because it's a way to make Jimmy feel bad.' She hesitated. 'Am I right?'

'I'm afraid so. Are you going to tell Stuart?'

'How can I?' She took a drag on her cigarette. 'Even if I did he wouldn't believe me. He wants to see the best in them because he wants them to be his new family. And I want that too. I want him to be happy.'

'Love hurts, eh?'

She gave a hollow laugh.

'Thanks for what you said to Jimmy. I know he appreciated it.'

'He seems like a lovely bloke.'

'And so does Stuart, which just leaves Tom. Do you like him?'

For a moment she was tempted to lie. But Vanessa's eyes were non-judgemental so she decided to be honest. 'I want to.'

'But already you like Jimmy more.' Vanessa sighed. 'The story of Tom's life in a nutshell. He *is* a good guy but it hasn't been easy growing up in Jimmy's shadow. It can make him a bit ... I don't know ... prickly.'

'Has Jimmy always been the favourite?'

'Yes. It's not his fault, you understand. It's just the way things worked out. And he's always stuck up for Tom and taken care of him. Tom really depends on him, though I guess that's not how Tom tells it.'

'Not exactly, no.'

'Tom loves Jimmy. He really does. Only it can't do his ego much good to have a twin who's better than him at everything.'

'So you think that's why he's all over Stuart?'

Silence.

'That makes two of us.'

Vanessa looked thoughtful. 'I don't think it's the whole

story. They are identical. There's definitely a bond forming. But I do think that's part of it, yes.'

Jennifer turned to watch the others. Thomas was talking to Stuart, gesturing with his hands while Stuart mimicked the gestures back. She knew that copying others was often a ploy to seek their approval and wondered if Thomas knew it too.

'I'm sorry,' Vanessa told her.

'Why?'

'I was the one who first found Stuart.'

'Do you wish you hadn't?'

Vanessa nodded, then shook her head. 'No, I don't. If I hadn't met Stuart I wouldn't have met you and I'm glad I have.'

She was touched. 'I'm glad too. It's nice to have someone I can be honest with. I can't be honest with Stu. Not about this.'

'He's lucky to have you.' Reaching into her pocket, Vanessa pulled out a piece of paper. 'That's my mobile number. If ever you need to talk then call me.'

They finished their cigarettes then went to rejoin the others.

Half past six.

After waving goodbye to Thomas, Stuart and Jennifer, Caroline followed Robert back into the house.

'We should probably go too,' said Helen who stood in the hall with Vanessa.

Robert nodded then headed off towards his study.

'Missing you already,' muttered Vanessa.

'Are you sure you don't want me to stay?' Helen asked Caroline.

She did, but knew Robert would hate it. 'Better not.'

'You handled that beautifully. I was proud of you. So what did you think of Stuart?'

'He seemed very nice.'

'I'll say. I thought he was charming. His parents did a wonderful job.'

Unexpectedly, Caroline felt defensive. 'No better than I would have done.'

'Jennifer was lovely too,' Helen continued.

'You thought so? I found her forward. Did you notice the way she kept forcing her way into the conversation?'

'So what is she supposed to do?' asked Vanessa. 'Just sit there in silence? She loves Stuart. It's only natural she'd want to check you out.'

Caroline pretended to dismiss the remark, while realising Vanessa had hit the nail on the head. It was the way Jennifer had looked at her. As if she could see beneath the bright exterior to the darker emotions that lurked beneath.

They said their farewells. After watching them drive away she stood in the hall, thinking about what Helen had said. Stuart *had* been a pleasant surprise. Even though she would happily never see him again, she had to admit that it was true.

But it was over. That was the important thing. She had come through the ordeal and no one outside the family was any the wiser. Now all she had to do was make sure it stayed that way.

She remembered the hurtful things Thomas had said. Again she felt upset. The telephone stood on the hall table. She picked it up, preparing to call James and seek the validation she needed. Have him reassure her as only he could.

Only he wouldn't. He would still be angry with her for inviting Stuart.

And it wasn't fair! She hadn't had any choice. James should realise that. He owed her that much after all she had done for him.

She returned the phone to its holder. Again the voice whispered in her head.

Well, what can you expect? He isn't even yours.

As they drove through the outskirts of London, Jennifer listened to Thomas and Stuart discussing the visit.

'It went very well,' Thomas was saying. 'Mum and Dad really liked you.'

'Did they tell you that?'

Thomas nodded. Stuart smiled. Though she didn't believe it, Jennifer did too.

'Well, I liked them too,' said Stuart as he guided them though a mass of parked cars, constantly glancing into the windscreen mirror as he did so. 'And thanks for coming with me. I couldn't have handled it if you hadn't been there.'

Again she smiled, pleased he had remembered her.

Then realised he was still talking to Thomas.

They stopped at a set of traffic lights. She watched a pair of teenagers kiss in a bus shelter, oblivious to everything except each other. Once she and Stuart had been like that, the two of them united against the world. It had only been a couple of weeks ago but seemed like an eternity.

She realised Thomas was talking to her. 'Pardon?'

'Did you enjoy the visit?'

'Yes. Your family is lovely.'

'With one exception,' observed Stuart. 'All that stuff with the photograph. What was that about?'

She bit her tongue, not wanting to provoke an argument, while waiting in vain for Thomas to rush to James's defence. Perhaps he didn't want to risk hurting Stuart's feelings by doing so. Perhaps.

'Thanks for sticking up for me,' Stuart told Thomas, 'about college.'

'It's my job. We're twins, remember. We support each other.'

'Does Jimmy support you?' Stuart asked.

'Sometimes.'

'But not all the time?'

'No.'

'That's because he's jealous of you. He wants to be the best all the time. I'm not like that. You can be better than me at everything and I won't care.'

They stopped for more traffic lights. The two of them stared at each other. Jennifer watched them, feeling like a ghost. Stuart smiled at Thomas. Thomas smiled back, then, looking embarrassed, gave him a playful punch on the arm.

'I'd better phone Alice,' he said suddenly. 'I promised I'd call to let her know how it went.'

Stuart nodded.

'It's not serious. Her and me, I mean. It's just . . .'

'You don't need to explain. You like her. That's good enough for me.'

Thomas reached for his mobile. Stuart continued to stare, his expression one of tenderness. It was a look Jennifer had seen before. He had worn it when he said he loved her.

Only she didn't remember it being so strong.

A multitude of emotions surged through her; insecurity, fear, jealousy, hate.

The lights changed. Stuart didn't notice. She told him and quickly he steered them away.

TWELVE

'I told you not to go,' said Kate.

It was early the following morning. James sat in his kitchen, drinking coffee and trying to ignore an unwanted lecture.

'I said it would only upset you.'

Hoping to drown her out, he switched on the radio. No such luck. She just raised her voice. 'And I was right, so next time, listen to me, OK?'

He refilled his cup.

'And go easy on the caffeine. You'll be bouncing off the walls at this rate.'

'You sound like my mother.'

'Hardly. Unlike her, I care about your feelings.'

'She cares too.'

'So why hasn't she phoned to check how you're doing?'

He pretended to listen to the business news.

'Well?'

'This isn't easy for her.'

'It's ten times harder for you. She should realise that and so should Tom, or are you going to tell me it's hard for him too?

Acting like he and Stuart are best friends. Talk about rubbing your nose in it.'

'He wasn't doing it deliberately.'

'Oh, please. Anyway, I'm only quoting what you said last night.'

'I didn't mean it. I was just angry.'

'You have every right to be! All Tom's ever done is lean on you. Only he doesn't need you any more now Stuart's there to take your place.'

A chill swept through him. 'That's not true. Tom told me his bond with Stuart will never be the same as his bond with me.'

'That's right. It'll be *better*. Tom is nothing compared to you, but compared to Stuart he's a star. And that's what he's always wanted, Jimmy. To climb out from under your shadow and have a chance to shine.'

He shook his head, while in his heart he knew she was right.

'You've spent your whole life worrying about him and your mother but now, when the chips are down, neither of them can spare a thought for you.'

'Of course I worry about them. They're my family.'

She stared at him. He knew they were both thinking the same thing.

Her expression softened. 'I don't mean to sound cruel. I just hate seeing you hurt.'

'I'm OK.'

'No, you're not, but you will be. I'll get you through this.'

'That's what Mum said.'

'And I'm sure she meant it but that was before she met Stuart. She promised she wouldn't but she did and now she's going to meet him again. Chances are she'll start to like him, just like Tom does. You can't rely on either of them any more, Jimmy. It's not their fault, but now Stuart's on the scene things will never be the same and for your own sake you need to come to terms with that.'

He swallowed, feeling scared and alone. He hated the feeling, but hating it wouldn't make it go away.

'But nothing's changed between us. You're still the guy I fell in love with and you'll always be able to rely on me.'

His mobile rang. It lay on the table between them. She picked it up, staring at the display. 'It's Tom,' she told him. 'He's probably calling to say things are still the same, just like he did over lunch. Only you know better.'

Again they stared at each other.

'Don't you?'

'Yes.'

She disconnected the call, then walked around the table and hugged him. He hugged her back, grateful she was there.

Tom stood in his living room, staring at his mobile display.

He cut me off! The bastard cut me off!

Angrily, he tossed the phone aside. It wasn't fair, not after he had lain awake half the night, feeling guilty. That was why he had been calling, to explain that all he had been trying to do was make Stuart feel comfortable.

After all, Stuart was his responsibility. What else could he have done?

Besides, it was hardly the end of the world. So James had felt unwelcome in his own home. He had felt like that all his life. Over the years the two of them had shared so many experiences. It was only right they should share that one too.

A sleepy looking Alice appeared from the bedroom. 'Who were you calling?'

'No one.'

'Are you coming back to bed?'

He shook his head. The hated alarm would be ringing in less than half an hour.

'Then I'll make you breakfast. Why don't you have your shower and it'll be ready by the time you're done.'

Twenty minutes later he sat in the kitchen, eating bacon and egg. The bacon was crisp and the egg yolk broken just as he liked it. The coffee was just as he liked it too: strong and sweet. 'This is delicious,' he told her.

She looked pleased. 'I could make you toast if you like.'

'No, this is fine.'

'Well, let me know if you change your mind.'

He nodded, wondering why she felt the need to do so much for him. Not that he was complaining. He liked being made to feel special.

He wondered what his parents would think of her. Would they like her or would they think he could do better?

Would they think he could never do better?

Or would they realise he needed her to boost his ego and despise him for it?

Assuming they cared enough to think anything at all.

She sipped her own coffee, wiping a lock of hair from her face. He stared at her, suddenly relieved she had not accompanied him to Oxfordshire that weekend.

Mid-morning.

Caroline opened the door to a man holding a bouquet of flowers and a rectangular box. 'Mrs Randall?' he asked.

'Yes.'

He handed her the bouquet. She noticed it contained her favourite orchids. 'Thank you,' she said. 'Is the box for me too?'

'No. It's for your husband.'

It was a bottle of expensive Scotch. The brand Robert adored. 'Do I need to sign anything?' she asked.

He shook his head. After thanking him again she closed the door then read the card attached to the flowers.

'Dear Caroline and Robert, thank you for your hospitality and for making us feel so welcome. It was wonderful to meet you. Stu and Jen.'

She stared at the gifts. Together they must have cost a fortune. Unexpectedly, she was touched. Stuart didn't earn much. He shouldn't be spending so much on them. She would tell him so the next time she saw him.

Except that she didn't want there to be a next time.

Again she read the card, wondering if Jennifer had insisted on being included in the greeting. It wouldn't surprise her.

Bet she didn't contribute financially. Just wanted to steal some of the credit.

Not that it mattered. The relationship wouldn't last long if she had anything to do with it. Stuart deserved better than that pushy little madam.

Only she didn't care. Stuart could go out with whomever he chose. It was of no interest to her.

Feeling unsettled, she sought refuge in action, searching for a vase big enough to hold the bouquet.

Noon.

James sat in a meeting of the Promotional Committee.

The committee had been set up by the Head of Marketing as a forum for brainstorming ways to raise the firm's profile. That, at least, was the official story. Rumour had it that its real purpose was to help justify the Head's continued presence on the payroll. Duncan White was designated member for the Commercial Department, but as Duncan considered the Head 'a useless cunt who should have been put out to pasture years ago', James generally deputised for him.

The meeting had been running for an hour. Representatives from Property and Litigation argued over which department should host an all-day seminar for potential clients. 'We can't,' announced the woman from Property. 'We've just held one.'

'How many new instructions did you get?' asked the man from Litigation.

'At least a dozen.'

'Not according to the people I've spoken to.'

'I think I know my department's business better than you. Actually it proved a very profitable event.'

'All the more reason for holding another one,' suggested the Head of Marketing.

The woman from Property silenced him with a withering look. 'As I was saying,' she continued, 'it's pointless us doing another. We have all the work we can handle, which is more than can be said for Litigation judging by last month's figures.'

'You can't read anything into that. We didn't send out as many bills as usual.'

'And was that the reason for the previous month too?'

'There's nothing wrong with our turnover. We're the engine of the firm ...'

James rolled his eyes at Kevin Blake who was deputising for the designated member from Banking. Kevin responded with a gagging gesture, forcing James to disguise laughter as a sneezing fit. Kevin grinned at him. He had dark hair and eyes and a mischievous expression and bore a marked resemblance to Thomas.

As the argument continued James found himself remembering Christmas lunches with Thomas and his parents and paternal grandparents. While their grandmother gave their mother unwanted tips on how best to cook vegetables, their retired lawyer grandfather quizzed their father about his work while continually commenting on how much more efficient things had been in his day. He and Thomas had always had a bet on how long their father could go without swearing, and another on which of them could make the other laugh the quickest. Though he sometimes won the first, he could never win the second. That was why he was good at masking laughter now. Growing up with Thomas had taught him all he needed to know.

Suddenly he was ten years old again, gorging himself on turkey, making faces at his brother across the table and begging his parents to let him have some wine.

'You're too young,' his father told him.

'I'm not. French kids drink wine all the time.'

'They do not,' said his mother. 'Anyway, we don't live in France.'

'Bummer,' muttered Thomas, instantly causing James to lose the second bet. Not that he minded. What mattered was being with the people he loved and who loved him back.

Only they wouldn't have done. Not if they had known.

His head began to ache. He felt as if a virus had invaded his brain, searching out his most treasured memories, deleting his own image and inserting Stuart in his place.

Perhaps Stuart was experiencing the same thing. He hoped so.

But at least Stuart could form new memories. After all, his real family was still alive.

He thought of a business trip he had made to Birmingham a couple of years ago. It was the only time since his birth he had ever returned there. Killing time between meetings he had wandered round the city centre, hunting for a birthday present for Becky while looking forward to returning home to her, all the time totally unaware that this was where his home should have been.

What would my life have been like? What job would I be doing?

He tried to imagine himself as a lettings agent, only he couldn't. He knew he would hate it. That it wouldn't suit him at all.

'Jimmy?'

But he hated being a lawyer too. He had only become one to make his father happy. Not that it had worked. The only feeling his success seemed to inspire in his father was envy.

'Jimmy?'

His real father sounded like a very different sort of man. The sort who would never have pushed his son to be something he didn't want to be.

The sort of father he would probably have chosen . . .

'Jimmy!'

He snapped back into the present. Everyone was staring at him. He tried to look alert while wondering how long he had been lost in a world of his own.

'So, do you think it's a good idea?' the Head asked.

'Um . . . it could be . . .'

'It's just that your dad used to run their Commercial Department,' said Kevin, coming to his rescue. 'He could help set up a joint seminar between our two firms, assuming you thought it was a good idea.'

'But he doesn't run it any more. He's retired.'

'You could still ask him,' suggested the Head.

'No, I couldn't.'

The man from Litigation frowned. 'Why not?'

'Because it's a stupid idea,' said the woman from Property forcefully.

'That's a bit harsh ...' began the Head.

'Where's the benefit in running a seminar with another firm? It would just end up as a catfight over who could land the biggest contracts.'

'What does that matter?' demanded the man from Litigation. 'We're the better firm.'

'In Property, yes, but their Litigation Department is very strong.'

'There's nothing wrong with our Litigation Department ...'

The arguing resumed. James mouthed 'Thank you' at Kevin and received a reassuring smile in return. It reminded him of the looks Thomas had given him in the classroom when he needed help answering a difficult question.

Except that was not how it had been. Thomas had always been the one in need.

His head continued to ache, the virus hungrily ripping his memories to shreds.

Lunchtime.
Jennifer was in a pub, having a drink with friends from college.

Stuart phoned. She went outside to take his call. 'I've been thinking about our holiday,' he said.

Her spirits soared. Since Thomas's appearance holiday plans had become a thing of the past. 'You still want to go?'

'Of course. How about next month? We could tie it into half term so you don't have to miss too much college.'

'Don't worry about that. We're about to start on managing guest complaints and I've already had more than enough experience of that working in the pub.'

He laughed. Two friends walked by, both mouthing the word 'Party' at her.

217

'Where do you want to go?' he asked.

'I don't mind. Anywhere.'

'You said you wanted some sun.'

'Well, yes. That would be great.'

'So how does a fortnight in a five-star hotel in Mauritius sound?'

'*Mauritius?* Stu, we can't afford that.'

'Yes, we can. The only real expense will be the flights.'

'What about accommodation?'

'Tom's taken care of that.'

'What does Tom have to do with it?'

'The guy who owns the hotel is a family friend. Tom gets one free holiday a year and can take us too. He says the water sports are amazing. He's going to teach me how to water-ski and scuba dive. Isn't that great?'

She didn't answer, too busy feeling her heart sink through her stomach and down onto the floor.

'The hotel restaurant is amazing. The chef was trained by Raymond Blanc.'

'Right.' She hesitated. 'It's just … well, I'm not that keen on water sports.'

'Neither is Alice, so you two can chill by the pool while Tom and I do our thing and then we can all party in the evening.'

'Right,' she said again.

'Well, try and sound enthusiastic. I'm offering you a dream holiday and you're acting like it's a wet weekend in Wales.'

'That's the point, Stu. I'd be happy with a weekend in Wales as long as it was just you and me. That's what the holiday was supposed to be about, us having time together.'

'But we will be together.'

'Not if he's there.'

'Oh, for God's sake ...'

'You know what I mean.'

'So what do you want me to do? Call him back and say thanks for the freebie but do you mind staying in town as Jen doesn't want you around?'

'Of course not.'

Liar, liar, pants on fire.

'You bloody do! Christ, Jen, what's your problem? I have the chance to spend quality time with my twin for the first time in my life and you want me to blow him off.'

'I'm sorry ...'

'Yeah, so am I. Sorry I asked you to come.'

She felt upset. It wasn't just the words. It was also the tone. There was so much anger in his voice when only moments ago it had been full of warmth.

Just like Robert's had been when Vanessa contradicted him. But that was stupid. Stuart was nothing like Robert.

'Well, if you want to stay here and dodge the rain then be my guest.'

'No, I want to come. You just took me by surprise, that's all.' She risked a joke. 'It's your own fault for being as lovable as a Malteser.'

'Malteser?'

'Don't you remember those adverts that asked if you loved someone enough to give them your last Malteser? Well, that's the problem. You're my last Malteser.'

'Actually, that was for Rolos.'

'Was it? Then I take it back. I don't like Rolos at all.'

He laughed. She felt relieved. 'Tell Tom it sounds fantastic,' she said.

'Look, I've got a viewing. I'll show you the hotel website tonight. It'll blow your mind.'

She disconnected the call then stared out at the car park. Someone was parking a Porsche. It was the same colour as James's.

She wondered if James would feel as sick about the holiday as she did.

Slowly, she made her way back to her friends. 'Did you tell him about the party this Saturday night?' one of them asked.

'I didn't have time. He was in a rush.'

'Well, try and come. It'll be fun.'

She nodded, knowing it would be but also knowing that Stuart wouldn't commit until he knew what Thomas was doing.

Because Thomas came first now: the magical twin who could do no wrong. If she wanted their relationship to last she would just have to learn to live with it.

And she would try. She really would.

But what if I can't?

Late afternoon.

Caroline went to answer the phone.

'Hi, Mum. It's Jimmy.'

Relief swept over her. It was hours since she had left a message to say she was thinking of him. His silence had suggested he was still angry.

'Sorry to be ages calling you back,' he said. 'Things are frantic.'

She went to sit in the living room. 'What are you working on?'

'Nothing you'd be interested in.'

'Try me.'

He laughed. 'I have done in the past. Your eyes just glaze over.'

'That's not true.'

'So you want to hear all about corporate restructuring, then?'

'Oh, yes. More than anything.'

'Well, don't say I didn't warn you.'

It was her turn to laugh. Suddenly she felt absurdly happy. He always had this effect on her. The mere sound of his voice could brighten the dullest of days. As he described his latest deal she feigned interest while knowing she wasn't fooling him in the slightest. Not that it mattered. It was just part of their routine.

'It all sounds fascinating,' she told him.

'But now you're going to tell me you hear someone at the door.'

Again she laughed. 'Am I that obvious?'

'Afraid so. Not that I blame you. It bores me too.'

'Maybe so, but you're a natural at it. Just like your ...'

She stopped, kicking herself.

'Father,' he said, finishing the sentence for her.

'Their visit was his idea. I didn't want them here.'

'You don't need to explain.'

'You're not cross with me?'

'No.'

'Honestly?'

'Honestly.'

She sat back on the sofa, staring out into the hall where Stuart's flowers stood on a table. They were beautiful but they would soon wither and die. They didn't mean anything. Not like speaking to James.

'I'm sorry too,' he said.

'Don't be. I know how you must have felt.' Which she did. Having to sit and watch her welcome another son into the family. It must have seemed such a rejection.

'I knew it would be hard. I just didn't expect it to be as bad as that.'

Guilt consumed her. 'It didn't mean anything,' she said. 'It was just a case of being polite.'

'Yeah, right.'

'You don't believe me?'

He didn't answer. Though his pain distressed her, a tiny part of her was glad of it. There was nothing as reassuring as knowing how intensely one was loved.

'Jimmy?'

'I want to . . .'

'But?'

'You saw what they were like together.'

'*They?*'

'Tom and Stuart.'

She felt as if she had been slapped.

'It's not just them being identical. It's the way they act.'

Tom's the one you're upset about. Not me. Not me at all!

Her sense of guilt vanished, replaced by indignation.

'It's like they've known each other all their lives.'

'I see,' she said coldly.

'When we were little everyone used to refer to us as the twins. It pissed me off sometimes but it was true. We were a unit. Only we're not any more. Now Stuart's here I feel like a bit player in my own brother's life.'

'Well, that's rather between you and him, isn't it?'

'What do you mean?'

'If you've got a problem with Tom then I'm hardly the one to talk to, am I?'

'I'm just saying . . .'

'I know exactly what you're saying. If Tom so much as smiles at Stuart it's a tragedy whereas I could invite him to move in and it wouldn't bother you.' She exhaled. 'Thank you, Jimmy. It's nice to know just how low I rank in your affections.'

'Don't be daft, Mum. I'm not saying that at all.'

'Yes, you are.'

'Why are you being like this?'

'Perhaps because I imagined seeing me with Stuart might have actually bothered you a little.'

'It did. Mum . . .'

'Yet all you can do is talk about Tom. How do you think that makes me feel?'

'You tell me. After all, your feelings are the only ones that matter.'

She was taken aback. 'I beg your pardon . . .'

'Your message said you were worried about me but that was crap. The only thing you were worried about was that I hadn't been sobbing down the phone, asking for reassurance that you still love me. I'm surprised you didn't rig up a boxing ring in the garden so Stuart and I could slug it out to prove which one of us was most deserving of your affection.'

'But I do care about you. You know I do. It's just . . . well, can't you see how difficult this is for me?'

'You've got another son who wants you to love him. How difficult is that?'

'How difficult do you think? I raised the wrong son. Can you imagine how bad that makes me look?'

In the silence that followed she realised how shallow she must have sounded.

How shallow she really was.

Just as Robert had said.

And she couldn't stand it. So she lashed out.

'All I want is a little loyalty. That's not too much to ask for, is it? Not after all I've done for you. I mean, you're not even my child ...'

He slammed down the phone. She remained on the sofa, trying to summon anger but feeling only self-loathing.

Putting down the receiver, she burst into tears.

That evening Stuart showed Jennifer the hotel website.

They sat together in his bedroom, staring at his laptop screen. She kept saying how amazing it looked, how great their holiday would be and how pleased she was that Thomas and Alice would be coming with them.

Saying all the things he wanted to hear.

Only he didn't. Not when he knew she didn't mean a word of it.

He felt frustrated. Why couldn't she be as happy as he was? If their situations were reversed he would be happy for her.

She began to talk about things they would need to buy for the trip. As he listened he found himself wishing she wasn't coming at all.

But he *did* want her to come. He loved her. Since his parents had died he had never loved anyone as much.

Except Thomas.

So who would you choose, if you could only have one of them in your life?

The question flashed in his brain like a neon sign. He tried to ignore it, scared of what the answer might be.

'Are you listening?' she asked.

'Yes. You're asking if we should take Maltesers or Rolos and my view is that there's enough room in my bag for both.'

She laughed. He put his arm around her, kissing her cheek.

While praying there really was enough room.

*

Two in the morning.

Unable to sleep, James sat alone in his living room.

A half-empty bottle of whisky stood on the coffee table. He downed his glass, trying to drown the thoughts that buzzed in his head like hornets. Though the room was in darkness, the curtains were open and the light from the street lamps allowed him to see. He stared at the Klimt prints on the far wall, remembering how his mother had commented on them during her last visit, after promising he would always be her son. It was hard to believe that had only been six days ago.

After all I've done for you. I mean, you're not even my child ...

No doubt she would apologise, claiming she hadn't meant it. He would tell her it was forgotten, playing the role of the perfect son, just as he had done all his life. Only it would be a lie. What was said could never be unsaid and from now on, whenever they spoke, he would always be hearing those words.

He wondered how long it would be before he heard something similar from Thomas.

He refilled his glass, knowing he would hate himself in the morning. But that was hours away and he still had the night to get through first.

He thought of the photograph Stuart had shown him of his real family. At the time he wanted to tear it to shreds but now he wished he could see it again.

Not that it would change anything. They would still be dead.

Perhaps, if he had lived Stuart's life, he would be too. Perhaps he would have been in the car with them. Perhaps his life would have ended fourteen years earlier with nothing but a name on a tombstone to prove he had ever existed.

Or perhaps they wouldn't have made that fateful journey and would still be alive. Perhaps he would be living near them, married with children of his own whom he would bring to visit their grandparents every Sunday, telling his mother all his news, helping his father do up old cars and teasing his sister about her boyfriends just as he teased Vanessa.

It might have been a good life. He might have been happy. Only now he would never know.

Stuart was the one who had known them. Stuart was the one they had loved.

And he envied him that.

But Stuart was also the one who had suffered. Suffering that should by rights have been his. Would he have coped as well? Would he have coped at all?

He didn't want to think about that. The guilt was too much to bear.

Time passed. He continued to drink, trying in vain to silence the thoughts that screamed ever louder to be heard.

THIRTEEN

Next morning Caroline arrived at the village hall for a meeting of her charity committee.

To her surprise she heard voices coming from the meeting room. It sounded like everyone was already there. She checked her watch and saw she wasn't late. Could she have got the time wrong?

She stopped outside the door, checking her make-up in the mirror of her powder compact while half-listening to the conversation.

'I just don't understand it. How can you not know your own baby?'

She closed the compact, her blood running cold.

'When I think of the lectures she's given me on raising children and all the time she was raising someone else's . . . '

Caroline's legs turned to jelly. She fought an urge to run while recognising Susan Bishop's voice. 'You're not being fair. These things happen.'

'Not with identical twins, they don't!'

'Exactly. How can you make a mistake over that?'

'It's possible.' Susan continued to defend her. 'It can take

227

weeks to determine whether twins are identical. Besides, she was ill when they were born ...'

'She still should have known. I would.'

'So would I ...'

'Poor Thomas, having to watch his mother favour someone else's child ...'

'And not just any mother but Mother of the Year ...'

A ripple of laughter, as sharp as a knife.

'Imagine how he must be feeling ...'

'Imagine how the other boy must be feeling, knowing his own mother didn't recognise him ...'

'Apparently she didn't even want to meet him ...'

'Probably too ashamed ...'

'Probably worried his suit wouldn't match the curtains ...'

The laughter grew louder. 'Please stop,' said Susan anxiously. 'She'll be here in a minute ...'

'No doubt eager to disparage all our children ...'

'She does, doesn't she? When my son failed his A levels she was so patronising I could have slapped her ...'

'That's enough!' said Susan forcefully. 'This is a dreadful thing she's going through and she deserves our support.'

'Oh Susan, you're too nice. Imagine if one of us was in her position? She'd be the first to throw stones ...'

The discussion continued. Caroline remained where she was, breathing deeply, trying to gain some degree of composure.

You can't run. You can't show weakness. You have to face them.

Again she opened the compact and stared at her face. It was like that of a frightened child. She hated it. She hated them. She was afraid of them.

But she would never give them the satisfaction of seeing it.

Straightening her back, she entered the lion's den.

Instantly all conversation stopped. She walked briskly to the head of the table through a silence thick with embarrassment and malicious glee.

'I'm sorry to have kept you waiting,' she said crisply

'Not at all,' said Moira Cooper sweetly. The same Moira who had just been condemning her. The same Moira whose son Ryan had failed his A levels.

Was I patronising? I didn't mean to be. I honestly didn't.

But she had been. She knew it. Moira knew it. They all did.

She pulled out the agenda for the meeting and pretended to study it, aware of all them waiting for her to falter.

'Shall we get down to business?' she asked.

'Yes, let's,' said Susan Bishop brightly.

She cleared her throat, ready to begin.

'How are the boys?' asked Abigail Watson.

She managed not to flinch. Abigail was smiling, her expression one of innocent curiosity. The rest followed suit, only most were not as accomplished actresses as Abigail and the spite was clear to see. All except Susan who looked anxious: her one true friend for whom she was sincerely grateful.

No weakness. Ride it out.

'James is unsettled, naturally, but he knows Bob and I love him and that as far as we're concerned he'll always be our son. Thomas is fine and Stuart is a charming young man of whom any mother would be proud.' She paused, exhaling slowly. 'Thank you for asking, Abigail. It was very thoughtful of you.'

Abigail's smile faltered. Others too looked taken aback. Clearly, none of them had expected her to be so honest. Not that it changed anything. The character assassination had already begun.

Again she cleared her throat. 'So, turning our attention to the agenda ...'

The meeting commenced. She chaired it as she had so many times before, her manner calm and confident, giving no hint of the turmoil that raged beneath.

How do they know? Who was it that told?

Who did this to me?

An hour later Susan Bishop walked home with Caroline.

'But how did they find out?' Caroline kept asking.

'You know what village life is like. Nothing stays secret for long.'

'Who told you?'

'No one.'

Caroline looked confused.

'Well, no one directly. It was already being discussed when I arrived.'

'But who heard about it first? Who told them?'

'I don't know. I'm so sorry. I can't imagine how you must be feeling ...'

Caroline wasn't listening, too wrapped up in her own train of thought. 'None of the family would have told. I'm sure of it.'

'Why not?'

'Because that's what we agreed.'

'*Did* you? I mean, did everyone?'

'Yes ...' Caroline hesitated. 'My sister did.'

'But not the others?'

'Well, not expressly. But it goes without saying ...'

'Of course it does. Only, with the best will in the world, the truth does have a way of slipping out. The important thing is to remember that whoever it was didn't do it deliberately because that would mean they were trying to hurt you and no one would want to do that.'

Caroline began to look troubled.

'Bob certainly wouldn't.'

They had reached the drive of Caroline's house. Caroline stared at her. 'Bob?'

'You know what men are like. When things go wrong they always need someone to blame. If I was in your situation John would blame me. He'd say that as a mother I should have realised. He'd probably spread the word himself just to make me suffer.'

Caroline grew pale.

'But Bob's nothing like John. He'd never want to punish you. Not that there's anything to punish you for.'

'I need to go. I'll call you later.' Caroline started up the drive.

'Yes, call whenever you need. I'll always be here for you.'

Caroline turned back. 'Thanks for sticking up for me.'

'You don't need to thank me. What are friends for? Ignore the others. They're just scared, that's all. Let's face it, this could have happened to anyone.'

The two of them hugged each other. Caroline walked towards her house. Susan remained where she was, watching until her friend was out of sight.

And only then did she start to laugh.

Caroline stood in the hallway, Susan's words echoing in her head.

Whoever it was didn't do it deliberately because that would mean they were trying to hurt you and no one would want to do that.

She wanted to believe this. She wanted to more than anything.

Only she didn't.

Robert came down the stairs. 'I was at my committee meeting,' she told him.

Nodding, he made for the front door.

'They know about Stuart.'

He turned back, looking startled. 'You told them?'

'Of course not.'

'Then who did?'

She didn't answer, her suspicions too painful to share.

'Well?'

'I don't know. Susan Bishop couldn't say.'

His eyes widened. 'What does Susan have to do with this?'

'She's on the committee.'

'Oh. Of course.'

'They were talking about it when I arrived. All of them were saying I should have known.'

He winced.

'Don't look so shocked. You said the same yourself.' She noticed he was holding his jacket. 'Are you going out?'

'I could stay if you want.'

She shook her head.

'No, really I could. I mean, if you're upset.'

Touched, she managed a smile. 'I'm OK. But thank you.'

'It was probably Nessa. She can never keep quiet about anything, though I'm sure she didn't do it on purpose.'

'That's what Susan said. That whoever it was hadn't done it on purpose. Dear Susan: the only one of my so-called friends ...'

'I must go,' he said abruptly. 'Call if you need me. I'm on the mobile.'

'Thanks, Bob.'

He stroked her cheek with his finger. The last time he had

done that he had been apologising for hitting her. Again he seemed to be apologising, only this time there was no need. Not when the blow had been struck by another.

He left. She walked into the living room and stared at James's graduation photograph on the grand piano.

How could you have done this to me?

It was a meaningless question. She knew the answer already. But it didn't excuse a betrayal like this. Nothing could.

Not after all she had done for him.

She thought of the happy boy he had once been, the boy who was always cheerful and eager to please.

Doing whatever it took to make himself her favourite.

He had *made* it happen. If she had ignored Thomas it was James's fault, not hers. He had manipulated her. Played her like the piano on which his picture stood.

As if he had known the truth all along.

Her eyes shifted, coming to rest on a picture of Helen and herself. Helen seemed to be shaking her head, as if warning her against listening to the dark thoughts that flooded her brain.

But she wanted to listen to them. Welcomed them in fact.

Welcomed anything that allowed her to blame someone else.

'I know it was you,' Robert told Susan.

They were sitting together on their hotel bed. She frowned at him. 'What are you talking about?'

'Don't play dumb. You know damn well what I'm talking about.'

She lay back on the bed, revealing her naked body in all its glory. Fortunately they had already had sex and he was temporarily immune to its charms.

'Why do you think I did it?' she asked.

'Because I know you.'

'Is that a fact?'

'Absolutely.'

'Then what on *earth* possessed you to tell me?'

Momentarily silenced, he just stared at her.

'Maybe you wanted the truth to get out.'

'And why would I want to do that?'

'To punish Caroline.'

He shook his head. She prodded his groin with her foot. Angrily, he pushed her away.

'You want her punished. Deny it all you want but we both know it's true.'

'No, it's not. Besides, this reflects just as badly on me as it does her.'

'*On you?*' She started to laugh. 'What? You think it casts a shadow over your parenting skills? The only way you could do that is by actually killing one of them.'

'What the hell do you mean?'

'Who's playing dumb now?'

'I'm a good father.'

'And I'm a virgin.'

'I *am* a good father!'

'So why do you never talk about them?'

'I do, constantly.'

'You never talk about Tom and you only ever complain about Jimmy. If both were to die tomorrow I doubt you'd even notice.'

'They're my sons. I love them.'

'Not really. The only person you truly love is yourself. Tom's only ever been a disappointment and Jimmy's only ever been an ego boost. Only now he's gone and spoiled it by eclipsing you in the success stakes.'

'Rubbish. He's not more successful than me.'

Again she laughed. 'I rest my case.'

'You don't know anything.'

'I know you feel threatened by Jimmy. I know the only reason you invited Stuart to your home was to remind Jimmy who was boss.'

'Shut up.'

She moved beside him and began to massage his neck. 'Stop being so defensive. I'm not judging you. When it comes to issues of decency, I'm hardly in a position to throw stones.'

He didn't answer. She nibbled his ear. It tickled. Against his will he smiled.

'That's better,' she whispered.

'You still shouldn't have done it.'

'Who said I did?'

'You did.'

'No, I said you *wanted* me to. That's not the same thing.'

'Who else would have done?'

'You've always said your sister-in-law has a mouth like the Channel Tunnel.'

'It wasn't her.'

'But it wasn't me. Why would I?'

'To hurt Caroline. You hate her enough.'

'Only because she gets in the way of us.'

'There is no us. Not in the way you mean.'

'We're good together. That's what I mean. This is what it is, but it's still good. Better than good, in fact.'

She began to kiss his neck, her breath hot against his skin. Her arms tightened around him like vines. Six months ago he would have found it erotic. Now he just felt smothered. She radiated need while all he wanted was sex. Once that was all she had wanted too but now all she wanted was for him to leave Caroline. She would never admit it but he knew it was true.

A part of him longed to end it yet he kept holding back. The sex was still good and besides, he didn't want her as an enemy. Not when she took such pleasure in inflicting pain.

Just as he had taken pleasure inflicting it on James.

She continued to caress him. He allowed her to do it, waiting for desire to eliminate shame.

That evening he sat in his study, staring at a wooden paperweight on his desk.

It was in the shape of a Rolls Royce. James had made it for him years ago. He picked it up, turning it over in his hands and stroking its grooves with his fingers. It was a beautiful piece of work: remarkably accomplished for such a young boy.

How old was he? Ten? Eleven?

What was it for? Christmas? Birthday?

And why can't I remember? I should be able to remember.

But he had kept it all this time. That counted for something.

He remembered visiting the boys at school. Standing by a sports pitch, watching James score a try or hit a six. Sitting in an assembly hall, watching James receive prizes. Meeting teachers who told him what an exceptional boy James was.

There had been few such occasions. He had usually been too busy working. But when he had accompanied Caroline the boys bounced around him like excited puppies, eager to tell him their news and show him all they had achieved. It had been a good feeling. To know how much they missed him. How much his presence meant.

His gaze fell on a leather chair in the corner of the study. In his mind's eye he saw a teenage James sitting in it, asking him about Oxford and promising to gain admission to his old college. 'I'll study twenty-four hours a day if I have to,' James had vowed. 'I won't let you down, Dad.'

And he never had. Whatever had been asked of him, James had always delivered. He was a fine son, the sort any man would have been proud to father.

Only that man wasn't him.

And it hurt. For the first time he realised how much.

But pain was good. It showed he cared, that he was not the person Susan said he was. That he was capable of loving someone other than himself.

He remained at his desk, turning the car over and over in his hands, searching for answers that continued to elude him.

The following morning James sat at his desk, staring at his computer screen.

Donna entered, carrying a pile of amended documents. 'I think you should check these,' she told him.

'Why? I told you to email them straight to the client.'

'But some of the amendments don't make sense. For starters the purchase price is different in each document. I'm no rocket scientist but even I know that's wrong.'

He checked the pages she had flagged. 'Shit.'

'Good thing one of us was paying attention, eh?'

He gave her a sheepish smile.

'Is this about your aunt?'

'They're just mistakes. Everyone makes them.'

'You don't, but lately you haven't been yourself at all.'

'Ain't that the truth.'

She stared at him.

'It's no big deal,' he said quickly.

'It could be. I'm not the only one who's noticed. Some of the partners have too.'

He felt alarmed. 'Like who?'

'That creepy guy from Litigation who only ever talks to women's tits. I heard him tell Mike Fisher you seemed really out of it in a meeting.'

'That doesn't matter. It was only the Promotional Committee.'

'But then Mike told Creepy Guy that on a conference call yesterday you were all over the place.'

He thought back to the call. His performance hadn't been great but it had been adequate. Or so he had thought.

'Look, Jimmy, I'm not trying to freak you out. I'm on your side. God, you're the best boss I've ever had. I just thought you should know.'

'Thanks.'

'Maybe you should take some time off and clear your head.' She gestured to the agreements. 'Before something really bad happens.'

'It won't. I appreciate the heads-up but everything is under control.'

Ten minutes later he made his way to the toilet on the other side of the floor. Duncan White stood by the photocopier with Mike Fisher. The two of them were talking but fell silent as he approached.

'Are the clients happy with the new agreements?' asked Duncan as he passed.

'They haven't received them yet.'

'Weren't they expecting them last night?'

'This morning.' It was a lie but one that Duncan would never check.

He continued on his way, aware of the conversation resuming behind him.

Once in the toilet he stared at himself in the mirror, alarmed to see just how tired he looked.

But everything would be all right. He had it under control.

After splashing his face with cold water he returned to his desk. Donna gestured that she had a call on hold. He picked up the receiver, assuming it was the client and already rehearsing his excuses.

Only to discover he didn't need them at all.

That evening he sat with his father in the bar of a private members club.

It was in a Georgian house in Mayfair: the sort of place where the rooms were all oak-panelled and the staff wore uniforms and treated members with the excessive deference his father had always enjoyed.

They sat together at a quiet table. On it, covered by a folder, was a pile of papers he had brought from the office to review at home.

Their drinks arrived. 'No chance of an ashtray?' his father asked the waiter.

'I'm sorry, sir.'

'Bloody nanny state. Next thing they'll be banning alcohol.'

The waiter smiled unctuously then slid away. James folded his arms, bracing himself for the usual interrogation about work, together with the inevitable disparaging of his progress compared to that of the great Robert Randall. Instead his father sipped his drink, looking uncomfortable. Feeling the same, he gazed about the bar, saw someone he knew and waved.

'Who's that?' his father asked.

'Some guy who's on the other side of my latest deal.'

'Which firm?'

'Shawcross Oliphant.'

'Do you know what we called them at my place?'

'What?'

'Smarmy Onanists.'

James found himself smiling.

'What do you call them?'

'Shaft Your Orifice.'

'Is he shafting yours on the deal?'

'He's trying to, but with no success.'

'That's my boy.'

'Yeah, that's me.'

Silence. His father began to drum a tune on the table. He sat, watching.

'"The Entertainer",' he said eventually.

'Sorry?'

'You're playing "The Entertainer", the sole piece in your finger-piano repertoire.'

His father nodded. 'Five years of piano lessons and it's the only piece I remember.'

'You're doing better than Tom and me. Ten years of lessons between us and we can barely manage "Chopsticks".'

'And to think of all the money I wasted on lessons.'

'We did tell you we weren't any good.'

'But it made your mother happy. There was nothing she loved more than sitting in the front row at school recitals, listening to the two of you butcher the classics.'

Again James smiled.

'How is your brother?'

'I don't know. We haven't spoken for a while.'

'Normally you two are as thick as thieves.'

'Well, we used to be.'

Another silence. James sipped his Evian, wishing it was something stronger.

'I had to invite Stuart to the house. I couldn't just pretend he doesn't exist. And I had to make him feel welcome. You probably felt I was getting at you but I wasn't. The truth is, Jimmy, I wasn't sure how to play it. There's no rulebook for a situation like this. But one thing I *am* sure of is you mustn't let it affect your relationship with Tom.'

'Unfortunately that's not just up to me.'

'You know Tom. He loves playing the big man. At the moment he's playing it for Stuart but once the novelty wears off he'll come looking for you. People talk about blood ties as if they're sacred but it's shared history that really counts. You'll always be his true brother, just as you'll always be my true son.'

He masked his surprise with nonchalance. 'And where does that leave Stuart?'

'Where indeed.'

'What did you think of him?'

'A nice enough chap but he hardly compares with you.'

'He hasn't had my opportunities.'

'It's not just about opportunities. It's about knowing how to make the most of them.' His father sighed. 'I remember when I was at school. Most of the boys in my class were so complacent. Their parents were wealthy and they expected everything to fall into their laps. My parents were wealthy too but I never expected anything. I knew I didn't need money behind me to get somewhere. Just like you.'

Suddenly embarrassed, he shook his head.

'It's true, Jimmy. You've got my drive. Look at all you've achieved.'

'Having your reputation behind me didn't hurt.'

'Didn't it? You had to prove yourself twice as much as anyone else. But you've done that. And I'm proud of you.'

He looked down at the table, trying to remember when his father had last expressed pride in him. 'Thanks,' he said quietly. 'That means a lot.'

'Why?'

'Because I did it for you.'

'I know you did. That's what I meant when I said you're my true son. Stuart doesn't change anything. Not where you and I are concerned.'

He looked up. His father was smiling. He unfolded his arms, feeling the last drops of animosity drain away. They were still family. That was what mattered.

'Another drink?' his father asked.

'Sure.'

'Make it a strong one this time. The Scotch here is excellent.'

'As excellent as the stuff you used to keep in your study cabinet?'

'And how would you know about that?'

'How do you think?'

'So that's why it always used to taste so watery.'

'We didn't think you'd notice.'

'Of course I noticed. I was a kid once too. By the time I was ten I was already taking swigs from your grandmother's sherry.'

'Sherry?' He grimaced.

'You're telling me! It was your grandfather's fault for being teetotal. Be grateful you had a father with taste.'

The waiter brought more drinks. They clinked glasses. 'I think they water it down here too,' his father remarked.

'Are you going to complain?'

'Am I hell. It's still better than bloody sherry.'

They both laughed. He noticed the man from Shawcross Oliphant was leaving and gave him another wave.

'It's a long time since we did this,' his father observed. 'We should make more of an effort. After all, we never had much time together when you were growing up. That's something I regret.'

Again he felt embarrassed. 'Well, you were busy with work.'

'It wasn't just work. Your mother was always so possessive of her boys. Whenever I'd try to get close to either of you she'd always make me feel like I was trying to steal you away.'

'I never knew you felt like that.'

'Well, I did. Not that I blame her. The home was always her domain. I was never there enough for it to be mine. I'd tell you not to make the same mistake but I'd be wasting my breath. You're my son, after all. You'll do things just as I did.'

He wasn't convinced but nodded anyway.

His father started to laugh.

'What?' he asked.

'I'm trying to imagine you with a Brummie accent.'

He didn't respond. Unexpectedly, the comment made him uncomfortable.

'A lucky escape, eh?' his father suggested.

'It's just an accent.'

'It's a bloody awful one. How is anyone supposed to take you seriously when every time you open your mouth you sound like Ozzy Osbourne?' His father took another sip of his drink. 'You had a very lucky escape.'

He told himself to let it go. Just to enjoy the fact they were getting along. But in his head he saw the photograph of Stuart's parents and knew he couldn't.

'That's a bit harsh, Dad. The Godwins were good people.'

His father snorted.

'They were.'

'Come on, Jimmy. You heard what Stuart said about his father.'

'Yes. He sounded like a good guy.'

'No. He sounded like a loser.'

'He didn't.'

'He spent his life selling second hand motors. What does that tell you?'

'That he enjoyed it. And he was good at it, so Stuart said.'

'It's still a loser job.'

'So you think I'm a loser?'

His father frowned. 'Why do you say that?'

'Because last time we met you told me I'd be a natural at it.'

'I was joking. Come on, Jimmy. You're much better than that.'

'*Better?*'

'You know what I mean.'

'Yes, I do. I'm your true son. Therefore I must be as remarkable as you.'

The frown deepened. 'Why are you being unpleasant?'

'Why are you acting like you're better than Mr Godwin?'

'Oh, for God's sake . . .'

'Well?'

'Do you really need me to answer that?'

'No. I get it. He had a regional accent whereas you speak with a silver spoon in your mouth. So much for not needing family wealth to get on in life.'

'It's not just the accent.'

'Then what is it?'

'Jimmy, drop it.'

'Why? You're the one who brought it up. Why are you better than him?'

'Well, what did he ever achieve?'

'So it's about success. You're better than him because you earn more.'

'It's not quite as simple as that.'

'But that's your basic point.'

'Yes, if you put it like that. Most people just coast through life. It takes balls to actually get somewhere. I have them. He didn't. Anyway, why are you so bothered? He was nothing to you. You didn't even know him.'

'No, I didn't.'

'So be grateful. I tell you, Jimmy, you should thank your lucky stars the hospital fucked up the way it did. You may have it in you to get somewhere in life but you'd have found it a damn sight harder with that loser holding you back.'

He sipped his drink. His father watched him, the benevolent expression replaced by one of anger. There was nothing his father hated more than being challenged. He should have known better. He had had it drummed into him enough times.

'I'm sorry, Dad,' he said softly. 'You're right, of course.'

His father nodded.

'He was a loser, just like you said.'

Another nod.

'Do you think John Bishop says the same about you?'

His father's jaw dropped.

'*Do* you?'

'What the hell are you talking about?'

'John Bishop earns more than you ever did, and his father was only a butcher from Kent. Wow, Dad, while we're on the subject of balls, his must look like melons compared to yours.'

The look of anger became one of fury. 'Don't compare me with him!'

'Why not? You're the one who's so big on comparisons.'

'Only ones that are true.'

'So you're more of a man than John Bishop?'

'I'm ten times the man that henpecked jerk will ever be.'

'Well, you'll certainly never be henpecked. Not when you bullied and belittled all the spirit out of Mum years ago.'

'Don't take that tone with me! Who the hell do you think you're talking to?'

'A better man than Mr Godwin. He never bullied his wife. What a loser he must have been. Thank God I had you to learn from instead.'

'You did learn. You'd be nothing if I hadn't pushed you.'

'That's right. I'm a big important lawyer like my big important father. All I need do is marry Kate, treat her like a doormat and knock her up with a couple of kids I can't be bothered to spend any time with and the wheel really will have turned full circle.'

'That was your mother's fault. Not mine.'

'So you're not denying you bully Mum?'

'I'm a good husband.'

'Yeah, and so was Henry the Eighth. Next thing you'll be claiming you were a good father too.'

'I was!'

'Bullshit. You'd written Tom off by the time he started school. The only time you noticed he existed was when you were shouting at him to get out of your way.'

'That's not true.'

'Of course it is.'

'Tom's only got himself to blame. He should have made me notice him the way you did.'

'I shouldn't have *had* to make you. Neither of us should. If you were any sort of parent you'd have realised that.'

'I provided for you. I gave you everything.'

'*Everything?* All you ever gave Tom was an inferiority

complex and all you ever gave me was stress-related ulcers. Mind you, we should consider ourselves lucky. You probably gave that Swedish au pair the clap.'

His father swallowed.

'I was six years old. Tom and I were playing Cowboys and Indians in the garden with Mum. You couldn't join us. You said you had to work. But I went to look for you and what did I find? You in your study hard at work screwing the au pair on your desk. In my innocence I went and told Mum that neither of you had any clothes on and she told me I'd imagined it and that I was never to talk about it again. Which I didn't. Not to her or Tom or anyone.'

'It never happened. It's all in your head.'

'I can still see it now. You were telling her she was a dirty bitch who couldn't get enough. It's a classy line, Dad. I must remember to use it the first time I cheat on Kate.'

His father's expression was murderous, his hands clenched into fists. 'I'm warning you, boy. You'd better stop this right now.'

'I'm not a boy any more. I'm a man, and a more successful one than you.' He laughed. 'And that absolutely kills you, doesn't it?'

'I'll kill *you* if you don't shut your lying mouth.'

'What are you going to do? Hit me?' He clapped his hands. 'Bravo, Dad. For the first time in your life you're picking on someone your own size.'

'I mean it, Jimmy.'

He leaned across the table, staring into his father's eyes. 'Hit me, then. Only know this: if you do I swear to God I will rip your arm off and shove it down your fucking throat.'

Slowly, the fists unclenched. The murderous expression remained.

'What's the matter, Dad? Not feeling so tough now?'

'Don't call me that. Not any more.'

'What? Are you disowning me? I should be flattered it's taken you twenty-seven years. With Tom it took less than twenty-seven months.'

'You leave Tom out of this. At least he's mine. Not like you. You're a worthless Brummie mongrel and you are nothing to do with me.'

James rose to his feet and stared down at his father, suddenly certain they would never see each other again. He waited to experience a sense of loss but it never came. Perhaps it would in time.

But he wasn't holding his breath.

'That's right,' he said. 'I could never be your son. Not when you're a hundred times the man I'll ever be.'

Then, snatching up his papers, he walked out of the bar.

Robert remained where he was, shaking with fury. He reached for his glass but his grip was so tight it shattered in his hand. The waiter hurried over to clean up the mess. 'Are you hurt, sir?' he asked.

'I'm fine.'

'Are you sure . . .'

'Of course I'm bloody sure! Bring me a refill, will you, and quickly.'

The waiter scurried away. Robert looked about the room, noticing a dozen pair of eyes hastily being averted. In the distance someone was laughing. The sound was soft and high-pitched. It reminded him of Susan. He pictured her face. Her expression was mocking, taunting him with the fact that she had been right about him all along.

The waiter returned with a fresh drink. As he lifted the glass he noticed blood on his finger. He wiped it away with a hand-kerchief, wishing it belonged to James instead.

Midnight.

Caroline sat in bed, waiting for Robert to join her.

He emerged from the bathroom, wrapped in a towel. She pulled back the sheets in readiness but he just paced back and forwards, radiating aggression like a trapped animal. She sat very still, feeling trapped herself.

'Aren't you going to ask?' he said eventually.

'I didn't want to pry.'

'I was in town meeting Jimmy. I wanted to tell him that none of this mess matters. That he's still our son. That we still love him.' He exhaled. 'More fool me.'

'Why? What did he say?'

'You don't want to know.'

'But ...'

He turned towards her. 'Trust me. You *really* do not want to know.'

'You make it sound as if he hates us.'

His silence was more eloquent than any speech. A chill swept through her.

'Does he?' she asked.

'You should have heard him, Carrie. Going on and on about how wonderful his real parents must have been. How much better his life would have been if he'd grown up with them. Listening to him, you'd think all we've ever done is hold him back.'

She swallowed.

'I'm surprised you're not defending him. He can't do any-thing wrong in your eyes.'

She didn't answer, instead remembering her visit to the post office that morning. Two of her so-called friends had been there when she arrived. Both greeted her with over-wide smiles, as did the man behind the counter. Did he know too? Had the three of them been discussing her beforehand, gleefully tearing to shreds the perfect façade she had spent so many years creating?

Just as James had intended when he told people the truth.

'What did he say, Bob? What did he say about me?'

Robert's expression softened. Pity crept into his eyes. It frightened her far more than his aggression had.

'No, don't tell me. I don't want to know.'

Tossing the towel aside, he climbed into bed. 'So there it is,' he said. 'What's done is done and now it's finished.'

'Finished?'

'With Jimmy. We're finished with him. Both of us.'

'No ...'

'Yes. That's how it has to be. You see that, don't you?'

His jaw was set. She felt like crying but didn't dare. Tears would only make him angry and that was the last thing she wanted. Otherwise he might discard her the way he was discarding James and she couldn't risk that. For better or worse her life was with him. She was too old and too scared to try and make another.

'Yes,' she said. 'I see that.'

He kissed her cheek. 'Good.'

Then he switched off the light and lay down to sleep. She lay beside him, staring at the ceiling, trying not to imagine the things James had said, only for ever more savage possibilities to fill her mind.

Time passed. He started snoring.

And only then did she allow her tears to fall.

FOURTEEN

Sunday afternoon.

In Oxfordshire Jennifer stood by the riverbank, staring up at the perfectly blue sky while a breeze from the water cooled her skin.

Her mobile was pressed to her ear. She pretended to talk to her sister, grabbing any excuse to escape from a social gathering in which she knew she was not welcome.

Thomas waved to her from the garden table where he sat with Robert. Smiling, she waved back; both of them feigning friendship that masked ever-increasing hostility. She knew he was using Stuart and he knew that she knew.

He and Robert were deep in conversation. Whatever they were discussing she was sure it wouldn't be James. Whenever she mentioned his name Caroline and Robert raced to change the subject as if embarrassed to acknowledge his existence.

She hadn't been the only one to notice either. Stuart had commented on it the previous night as they lay together in the guest bedroom. His voice had had a gloating quality: the same tone of gleeful satisfaction that Robert had used over dinner to describe a failed business venture of a neighbour. Exactly the same.

You know what they say. Like father, like son.

Though Stuart was nothing like Robert. He was a good person.

But why? Because that's his true nature?

Or because he's never had the chance to be anything else?

She could see him in the distance, standing near the kitchen window, helping Caroline prepare afternoon tea. She considered joining them but decided against it. She knew that in spite of all the gracious charm Caroline was as wary of her as Thomas. Robert was the only one who seemed relaxed with her and only because he was too self-involved to notice anyone else.

The sun was in her eyes. She shielded them with her free hand while staring at the house. It was such a beautiful place. The sort of home Stuart must have dreamed of during those years in foster care. He had been so happy when this second invitation had come, convinced it meant acceptance. For his sake she wanted to believe it, yet every fibre in her body screamed that he was merely a pawn in a game between Thomas and his parents.

And it made her afraid. For Stuart. For both of them.

'You're right,' Robert said. 'The firm is nothing but your stepping stone to better things. The only question is what those things should be.'

'What do you think they should be?' asked Thomas.

Robert began making suggestions. Thomas made enthusiastic noises while relishing the change that was taking place.

Throughout the weekend his father had constantly sought him out, questioning him about what he was doing. As he answered he kept waiting for disapproval but instead, for the first time in his life, received encouragement and support.

And it felt good. Like a drug so powerful it caused addiction with one hit.

'How many new accounts are they giving you?' his father asked.

'Um ... I get my share.'

'But not as many as you'd like?'

'Well, no. But I ask for them, though.'

'It's not enough to just ask, Tom. You have to demand. The trick is to sound as if you expect to get them. That they're a right, not a privilege.'

He nodded.

'Wave my name around if you like. Tell your boss I'm surprised they're not making better use of you. That'll make him sit up and take notice.'

'You wouldn't mind?'

'Of course I wouldn't.' His father smiled. 'Make use of my reputation. That's what it's for. Give it a couple of years and you'll have quite a reputation of your own.'

'You think?'

'I don't think. I *know*. You're my son, aren't you? You could be great at anything you wanted. All you need to do is believe it.'

'I will.'

'Good.' His father looked about him. 'Where's your mother with tea?'

'She won't be long. You know Mum. Wants everything to be perfect.'

His father pulled out a pack of cigars and offered him one. He shook his head.

'Still pretending you've given up?'

'I have.'

His father raised an eyebrow.

'Well, I'm trying.'

His father began to describe ways he had hidden his supply of cigarettes from his parents while a teenager. As Thomas listened he thought of the way his own mother was behaving towards him. Soon after his arrival she had taken him to one side and apologised for their argument the previous weekend. Had admitted, for the first time he could remember, that she had been at fault.

'You did the right thing,' she had told him, 'bringing Stuart into our lives. Last time we spoke I thought you were being cruel but now I see it was no more than I deserved.'

He hadn't answered, half-wanting to deny it yet reluctant to give her an easy ride.

'Stuart thinks the world of you,' she had said. 'Anyone can see it.'

'He thinks the same of you.'

'But Stuart doesn't know me. Not like you do.'

Again he had remained silent.

'I've hardly been a perfect parent, have I?'

Her honesty had made him uncomfortable. 'You've been OK,' he said quickly.

'But I should have been so much more. All your life you've drawn the short straw. I didn't plan it that way. You must believe that. I've always loved you, Tom. It's just that Jimmy kept getting in the way. It's strange. When Helen told me the truth I was shocked, yet deep down I wasn't. I think at some level I've always suspected. From the moment I brought you both home from the hospital I've felt Jimmy needed me more. That I had to ... I don't know ... make up for something. I never knew what that something was until now.'

She was staring at him, her eyes searching. He knew what she wanted. For him to say she was forgiven. That it had all been

James's fault. That they could start over. Again he held back. It wasn't that simple. He was still angry. He always would be.

And yet . . .

When all was said and done she was his mother and he loved her. All he had ever wanted was to be loved back the same way.

All he still wanted, in spite of everything.

And if blaming James allowed it to happen . . .

'I can understand that,' he had said.

His father continued to reminisce. As he listened he imagined James sitting beside him, soaking up their father's attention while he waited on the sidelines, grateful for whatever scraps James managed to deflect his way. Grateful to his brother but hating him too. Needing his protection but also resenting it. Dazzled by his stardom while longing for his own chance to shine.

But James wasn't there. Now he was the star, his only competition a poor imitation of himself towards whom he felt protective. Someone whose dull wattage could never compete with his own brighter glow.

This was his feast now. The one he had waited for all his life.

And no one was going to spoil it.

He watched Jennifer walking by the riverbank talking into her phone. She waved to him. He waved back.

Caroline stood in her kitchen, watching Stuart make tea.

'You shouldn't be doing that,' she told him. 'You're a guest.'

'I like helping.'

'Well, I'm very grateful.' She piled sandwiches onto a plate then checked the contents of the fridge. 'Which do you prefer? Cheesecake or chocolate sponge?'

'Either sounds good to me.'

'Then let's give people the choice, though if you take my advice you'll stick to the cheesecake. I didn't make that one.'

'But the sponge looks lovely.'

She cut it into slices. His expression became wistful. 'My mother made wonderful cakes,' he told her. 'There'd always be a couple sitting in tins in our kitchen. Sometimes my sister and I would creep downstairs at night to steal a slice.'

'And what did your mother say about that?'

'That we appeared to have mice.'

'I used to say that too when my boys did the same.'

He smiled at her. She smiled back.

Then, looking uncomfortable, he turned back to the tea. Feeling the same, she continued cutting the cake.

'They were good to you, weren't they?' she asked. 'Your parents, I mean.'

'Yes. They were the best. Absolutely . . .' He stopped, looking even more awkward.

'It's all right. I understand how strange this must be for you.'

'It must be strange for you too.'

She nodded.

'I'm sorry.'

'Don't be. None of this is your fault. You were only a baby.'

'And you were ill. That's what Tom said. He said they thought you might die.'

Again she nodded. He put the tea cups on a tray. She watched him, thinking about all he had lost and wondering if he did in some way blame her. Whether he felt that her illness was enough of an excuse.

'I'm sorry for what you've been through, Stuart. I wish it hadn't happened. I wish that with all my heart.'

'Do you feel . . .' he began, before leaving the question incomplete.

But she knew what it was. And she wanted to answer.

'Yes,' she said softly. 'I do feel responsible.'

'Please don't. My parents never realised what had happened so why should you? It's ironic, really. If they hadn't died I'd still be in Birmingham and I'd never have met Nessa.'

'I wish you were.' She stopped, shaking her head. 'No, I don't mean ...'

'I know what you mean. I wish it too, but at the same time a part of me doesn't because if they hadn't died I'd never have met Tom or Robert or you and I'm glad that I have.'

They stared at each other. Again he smiled. He had a nice smile. It was different to Thomas's. More open.

And she liked it. She liked him. If he had to be a part of her life then she could deal with it.

Provided certain changes were made.

'Do you think Jennifer is glad?' she asked.

'She's thrilled.' He spoke hastily, confirming her suspicions in two simple words.

'She seems a lovely girl.'

'I'm very lucky.'

'So is she.'

He flushed.

'It's true. I hope she appreciates you, though actually I don't need to. I can see how supportive she's being. It says a lot about her. Some girls would resent the sudden appearance of a new family in their boyfriend's life. They'd feel his attention was being stolen away. Fortunately Jennifer's not like that. She's far too big a person to let jealousy spoil things for you.'

He nodded.

'Why don't you take the tea outside? I'll follow when I've finished.'

He headed towards the garden. She watched him, feeling pleased. The seed of doubt was planted. Now all she had to do was watch it grow.

She finished cutting the chocolate cake. One of the slices crumbled under the knife, leaving her finger covered in cream. She licked it clean. It tasted good. James would have enjoyed it. She had devised the recipe especially for him. In her head she pictured him as a boy, wolfing it down with a big grin on his face while telling her she was the best cook in the world.

Quickly, she banished the image from her mind. She refused to miss him. He didn't deserve it. Not after what he had said. Not after what he had done.

So what do you deserve after last year?

Though it was warm in the kitchen, a chill ran through her. *Because what you did was a thousand times worse.*

She tried to push the thought away but it hung in the air like toxic gas.

And if anyone ever found out ...

But they wouldn't. Not ever. It was her secret and she would take it to the grave.

Putting on her best smile, she went to join the others.

Later Stuart played table tennis with Thomas in the family games room.

A snooker table stood in its centre. It was twice the size of the one his cousin Adam had accused him of wrecking. He wished Adam were there to see it. He wished Adam could see it all.

Thomas served. He returned and they rallied until he hit a shot into the net.

'Eighteen–five,' announced Jennifer, who was keeping score.

He groaned. 'I really suck at this.'

'You're doing well,' Thomas told him. 'After all, you haven't played for years.'

'Neither have you.'

'That's different. Geeks never lose their touch.'

He laughed. The game continued. Two minutes later Thomas hit the winning shot. Stuart clapped his hands and Thomas gave a theatrical bow.

'Well done,' said Jennifer from the sidelines.

Thomas gestured to the table. 'Would you like a game?'

'I'm happy watching,' she replied.

'So you like seeing me getting creamed,' said Stuart. 'Thanks a lot.'

'I didn't mean that.'

'I was only joking.' He restrained an urge to tell her to lighten up.

'We could play something else,' offered Thomas. 'Snooker, perhaps.'

Jennifer looked at her watch. 'Won't that take too long? Stu, you said you didn't want to be driving back too late.'

'No, I didn't.'

She frowned. He realised he *had* said it. But he didn't want to be reminded when he was enjoying himself.

'It doesn't matter,' he said, trying not to sound irritated. 'I'm not tired.'

'But maybe Jen needs to get back,' suggested Thomas.

'No, she doesn't. You don't, do you?'

She shook her head.

Thomas began to arrange the snooker balls. Out of the corner of his eye Stuart noticed Jennifer muffle a sigh. His irritation increased.

Jennifer went to the bathroom. 'Do you think she's OK?' Thomas asked.

'Why? Don't you?'

'She seems a bit fed up. Not that I blame her. All this must be difficult.'

'But she's happy about this.'

'I'd hate to cause problems between you.'

'You're not. Why would you think that?'

'I don't know. Just a feeling.' Thomas sighed. 'Look, maybe we shouldn't see each other for a while. We don't want to risk upsetting her.'

'You won't. She's fine.'

Thomas looked sceptical.

'She is. Honestly.'

'OK, if you say so.' Still looking unconvinced, Thomas chalked his cue.

Jennifer returned. 'Who's winning?' she asked brightly.

'We haven't started yet,' Thomas told her.

She smiled at Stuart. 'Do you want me to keep score again?'

He didn't. At that moment all he wanted was for her to be somewhere else.

'That would be great,' he said.

Monday morning.

Thomas knocked on his boss's door. 'Can I have a word?'

'Of course. What's on your mind?'

'You're planning to give the Fisher account to Maureen, aren't you?'

'Yes.'

He sat down. 'You should give it to me.'

'Unfortunately the decision has already been made.'

'Then it needs to be unmade. They're an internet access company and as I need to gain experience of that industry I should be the one to service them.'

Looking startled, his boss didn't answer.

'You're always telling us juniors we need to broaden our experience. Here's a great opportunity for me to do just that.'

'That's true, Tom, but the thing is . . . '

'Our internet-related business is going through the roof. Think how much more use I'll be if I'm up to speed on it.'

'Yes, but . . . '

'My father certainly thinks so. He was astonished to hear you had me doing the newsletter. He said he thought you'd be making much better use of me than that.'

'Did he?'

'Yes.' Thomas leaned forward. 'So shall I tell Maureen the job's mine? She's already got her hands full with that bank audit so giving the account to me is in both our interests as well as yours.'

His boss exhaled. 'Well, when you put it like that . . . '

'Great.' He rose to his feet. 'I'm glad we've got this sorted out.'

Then, leaving his boss still looking shell-shocked, he marched off to tell Maureen.

She was sitting at her desk, talking hard into the telephone. Noticing him in the doorway, she indicated she'd be some time. Her face had that smug look she always seemed to reserve for him. Little did she know he was about to wipe it away for good.

As he returned to his office he caught his reflection in a pane of glass. Briefly, he stopped to admire it. His chest looked a little bigger, his back a little straighter and his smile was bright enough to blind.

'Looking good,' he whispered. 'Looking very good.'

One of the secretaries overheard and gave him an amused smile. Grinning, he continued on his way.

*

Lunchtime. Needing a sandwich, James reached for his jacket.

His office door flew open. A furious-looking Duncan White burst in. 'I want you in my room immediately.'

'Why? What's happened?'

'Now!'

He followed Duncan down the corridor. Donna caught his eye and made a questioning gesture. Equally baffled, he made the same one back.

They reached Duncan's office. 'Shut the door,' Duncan barked.

'Look, Duncan, what's the problem?'

Duncan threw a document at him. He caught it, studied the front page and saw it was their strategy document for the Vicourt deal. Confusion engulfed him. Though Duncan had told him to put it together, he had never asked to see it.

'I didn't know you had a copy of this,' he said.

'I didn't. Shawcross Oliphant did.'

'*Shawcross?* But they're the other side. How did they get it?'

'You tell me.'

'I didn't send it to them.'

'You might as well have done.'

'What are you talking about? I'd never do that.'

'Not directly. You just leave it lying around for someone else to do it for you.'

'I haven't left it anywhere. I wouldn't!'

'Not even the Apollo Club?'

The words stopped him in his tracks. The Apollo was his father's club, the place where he had taken a pile of documents for review at home.

One of which had been the strategy document.

It hadn't been there when he returned to his flat. He

assumed he had forgotten to print off a copy. He had been in a rush. It was easily done.

Or so he had thought.

He cursed under his breath.

'Oh shit is right. You've dropped us right in it.'

'God, I'm so sorry . . .'

'*Sorry?* Try telling that to the clients.'

His brain was whirring. 'But I don't understand. How did Shawcross get it?'

'How do you think? The bloody club sent it to them. They found it lying on the floor, saw the name Shawcross all over it and assumed it was theirs.'

'But that's not possible.'

'You think I'm making this up? That document looks real enough.'

'But it's on our notepaper. Anyone can see it belongs to us. Why did they send it to them? How stupid is that?'

'Not half as stupid as leaving the fucking thing there in the first place. Nick Hopewell sent it back to me, together with a note saying he'd seen you in the club last week. Thank Christ he did. Knowing what cunts Shawcross are, we're lucky they didn't keep quiet and use it to screw us good and proper.'

He swallowed. 'Well, that's something.'

'Don't be so naive. Do you think they didn't keep a copy? We're fucked on this deal, thanks to you. We'll have to tell the clients. They'll probably pull out, refuse to pay our costs and throw in a negligence suit for good measure.'

James struggled for a positive. 'At least we're insured . . .'

'It's not just the fucking lawsuit. Do you really think they're going to keep this to themselves? No chance. They'll tell everyone and do you know how much damage that will do to our reputation?'

He nodded, feeling sick.

'I should fire you for this. I still might. As it is, you can forget all about the secondment to Ercobank and being made up to partner. After this balls-up you can consider yourself lucky I don't bust you down to paralegal ...'

Duncan continued to rant. James stood perfectly still, no longer listening, trying to work out how the club could have made so terrible a mistake. It didn't make sense. It was so obvious to whom the document belonged. Surely the staff could read?

'And to think you're the great Bob Randall's son. When he finds out what you've done he'll probably disown you ...'

The rant went on. His brain continued to whir, his head filling with questions.

Until suddenly an answer presented itself.

That evening he returned to the club. Though he wasn't a member he told the doorman he was meeting his father and was allowed in.

The bar was almost empty. Monday night was always quiet. He sat at a table, waiting to be served. Soon enough a waiter hurried over, the same one who had served him the last time. 'Can I help you, sir?' he asked, his smile as unctuous as before.

'Do you remember me?'

The smile faltered. At that moment James knew he was right. But he still needed an admission.

'Of course I do, sir. You were here with your father, weren't you?'

'How much did he pay you?'

'I don't know what you mean, sir.'

'You know *exactly* what I mean. My father paid you to send that document to the wrong firm, didn't he?'

'As I said, sir, I don't know what—'

'You can cut the act. He's already admitted it. The only question now is why I shouldn't tell your boss?'

The waiter flinched.

'You'd be out on your ear without a reference.'

'But, sir . . .'

'And it won't just be you who'd suffer. How many members do you think this club will keep once they hear what its staff does for off-the-books cash?'

Faint beads of sweat appeared on the waiter's forehead. 'But your father said it wouldn't matter. That no one would know.'

'He also said he paid you two hundred but I don't believe him. I reckon you held out for more.'

The waiter stared at the ground as if willing it to open and swallow him.

'How much did you get?'

'A thousand.'

'You should have asked for twice that. He'd have paid it. He'd have paid whatever you asked.'

'Well, it's not as if he'd miss it. It's just pocket change to people like you.'

'People like me?'

'Yes, people like you.' Suddenly the waiter looked angry. 'You've had money all your life and you toss it around like confetti. Well, it's not so easy for the rest of us. I have a family. I have responsibilities. How much do you think I make in a month? Less than you'd spend on champagne in an evening. That's how much.'

'Is that what you really think about us?'

'Yes. You all make me sick. Go ahead and get me fired. Leave me and my family on the breadline. Play God with our lives. After all, we're just little people. What do we matter to someone like you?'

'You don't know anything about me.'

The waiter snorted. 'I know plenty.'

'You certainly don't know my father. There's no way in hell he'd ever admit to something like this.'

The comment stopped the waiter in his tracks. 'He didn't?'

'No, so you're in the clear. I couldn't play God even if I wanted to. Which I don't. My father's the one with the God complex and it's my life he's playing with. Not yours.'

The waiter looked confused. 'I don't understand ...'

'You don't need to. All you need know is that your job is safe. I'm not going to say anything. As I said, you really don't know me at all.'

The waiter continued to stare at him. James waited for an apology that never came. He was grateful for that.

'Would you bring me a drink?'

'Of course.' A pause. 'It'll be on the house.'

He smiled, ruefully. 'Why not? You can afford it today.'

The waiter went to the bar. He stared into space, too tired to think. Wanting only to forget.

'You have to tell them,' shouted Kate. 'You have to!'

It was later that evening. She stood in James's living room, staring down at him as he sprawled on the sofa. The look on his face told her to leave it alone but she couldn't. There was too much at stake.

'You can't just let him get away with it. You have to fight back.'

'What's the point? I can't prove it.'

'Then go back to the bar. Talk to the waiter again but this time get it on tape.'

He shook his head.

She felt like screaming. 'Why not?'

'Because he'd lose his job.'

'What about *your* job? You're the one that matters. He's just some lowlife.'

He stared reprovingly at her. She refused to feel ashamed. 'You have to, Jimmy.'

'It won't change anything. I'm the one who left the document in the club.'

'Wrong. You left it in plain sight of your father who should have sent it back to you. Instead he used it to screw you over. You tell them that, they blame your father and you're their shining star again. Because that's what you are. You're going to be the youngest partner they've ever had. You can't let him take that away from you.'

'I don't care about partnership.'

She couldn't believe her ears. 'Then what do you care about? Your father? Why are you protecting him? He tried to stitch you up. You have to expose him.'

'And what would that prove?'

'It would clear your name.'

'No. It would just prove that I'm like him.'

'If only. He may be many things but at least he's not a fool. Christ, Jimmy, I don't understand you sometimes.'

He reached for his cigarettes.

'And please don't light up. You know I hate the smell.'

He blew smoke at her. Angrily, she brushed it away. 'Why are you being so stupid? I'm trying to help you. You've worked hard to get where you are. God, doesn't your career mean anything to you?'

'Not half as much as it means to you.'

'What's that supposed to mean?'

'Why do you love me?'

She was taken aback. 'Why are you asking that?'

'Because I want to know.'

'Oh, this is ridiculous . . .'

'So you can't answer.'

'Of course I can. It's because you're a great guy.'

'No, it's because I'm a great catch. I'm going places, just like you. Together we make the perfect couple. Only now I'm going to mess it up by failing.'

She shook her head. 'This isn't about that.'

'Then tell me the truth. Would you still love me if my career went down the toilet or would you flush me away with it?'

She told herself it wouldn't make any difference. That she would love him no matter what he was.

'What's the matter, Kate? It's a simple question.'

'It wouldn't change anything. I'd still love you.'

'Do you mean that?'

'Yes.'

'Then why are you staring at the floor?'

She looked up. His eyes made her feel guilty even though she had nothing to feel guilty about.

'I'm tired,' he said. 'I don't want to talk about this any more.' Stubbing out his cigarette, he rose to his feet. 'I'm going to bed.'

She remained where she was. The framed photograph of his family stood on a nearby table. The family she thought she had vanquished but whose hold on James remained as vice-like as ever.

She stared at the picture, fighting an urge to smash it to pieces.

*

Nine o'clock the following morning.

James walked through the department towards his office.

It was already busy. People stood in groups, arranging bundles of papers. Two other deals were completing that morning. He smiled at everyone but no one smiled back. A couple of partners glared. Everyone else avoided his gaze. He felt like one of the lepers his history teacher had told him about, forced to carry bells and shout the word 'Unclean' to warn others of their approach.

He reached his office to find it occupied. An anxious-looking junior lawyer called Anthony was watching Duncan White rifle through the filing cabinet.

'What are you looking for?' he asked.

'The Vicourt papers. I'm replacing you with Anthony.'

Anthony mouthed the word 'Sorry' at him. 'It's OK,' he mouthed back.

'Where are they?' Duncan demanded. 'Don't say you've sent them to the other side too.'

'No. They're right in front of you in the file marked "Bull's-eye". That's been the codename for the deal since day one.' He managed not to sound arch.

Duncan pulled them out. 'Is this everything?'

'Yes. Is the deal still going ahead?'

'Probably not, but it might help if we can tell the client you're no longer involved.' Duncan gestured to his desk. 'I've left a franchise agreement on your chair. It needs to be redrafted by close of play. I've skimmed through it and it looks sufficiently straightforward that even you won't fuck it up.'

'Thanks. That means a lot to me.'

'Are you trying to be funny?'

James pushed down his anger. Duncan was glaring at him. Once again he thought how much his boss reminded him of

269

his father. It was ironic really. Each had considered him their golden boy until he made the fateful mistake of speaking his mind.

Duncan marched out of the office. Anthony hesitated, looking apologetic. 'Don't worry about it,' James said kindly. 'And feel free to ask if you've got any questions.'

'You don't ask him anything,' said Duncan, loud enough for the entire department to hear. 'He's done enough damage already.'

Anthony followed Duncan out of the room. James sat at his desk, looking through the franchise agreement, realising it was far more complicated than Duncan had said. Not that he was surprised. When it came to legal knowledge Duncan had never got much beyond ABC, though it didn't stop him acting like the font of all wisdom.

Just like his father.

Suddenly fury consumed him. Kate was right. He had to put the record straight. It was no more than his father deserved.

But unlike his father when he stabbed someone it wasn't in the back.

So he dialled his parents' number.

His mother answered. 'Hi,' he said. 'It's me.'

Silence.

'It's me,' he said again.

'I heard you.' Her tone was glacial. Perhaps she was still angry at him for slamming the phone down on her. He had never done it before.

But he was not going to apologise. He had had good reason.

'Is Dad there? I need to talk to him.'

'Haven't you said enough already?'

'What do you mean?'

'I know all about your last meeting. He told me everything.'

'Oh.'

'Yes. Oh.'

Another silence.

'Aren't you going to say anything?' she asked eventually.

'What do you want me to say?'

'That it isn't true.'

'But it is.'

He heard her exhale.

'And I don't regret it.'

Only as soon as the words were spoken he realised that he did. Not for his father's sake, but for hers. He could imagine what sort of mood his father had been in on returning home. And who had suffered because of it.

The same person who would suffer if he exposed his father now.

And he couldn't do that to her. No matter the consequences of keeping silent. He just couldn't.

'I don't need to speak to Dad. Tell him ... just tell him ... that I've got a problem at work but I can solve it myself. That I don't need to involve him in any way.'

'I will. But I'd prefer it if you didn't call here for a while. I'm sure you can guess why.'

'Yes,' he said softly. 'I can guess why.'

'Goodbye, Jimmy.'

'I love you, Mum. I'm sorry.'

The disconnect tone rang in his ears before the words were spoken.

He remained in his chair, staring into space. Out of the corner of his eye he noticed someone hovering by his doorway. It was one of the trainees, presumably wanting help on some problem.

In the distance Duncan's voice rang out, bellowing a

command. Quickly, the trainee vanished. He looked down at his hands, turning them over as if looking for the telltale signs of leprosy.

Tuesday evening.
After working late Thomas sat in his flat, devouring an Indian takeaway.

His mobile rang. The caller ID read ALICE. Not in the mood to talk, he left it unanswered. Once he would have basked in her devotion. Now he just found it stifling.

Maybe because he didn't need it any more.

He continued eating, and when the phone rang again with her message he left that unanswered too.

Wednesday evening.
Jennifer sat with Stuart on the Tube, racing towards Central London and a meeting with her college friends.

The compartment was crowded. Noticing an elderly couple standing, she caught their eye and indicated they could swap places. They smiled but shook their heads.

'It's very kind of you,' said the old lady, 'but we're getting off at the next stop.'

'It's our pleasure,' she replied while nudging Stuart.

'What?' he asked.

'You could have looked willing.'

'What does it matter? They don't want to sit anyway.'

'They might have done if you weren't scowling.'

'Oh, give it a rest.' Exhaling, he stared at the floor. She watched him, trying to control her temper. She had been looking forward to him meeting her friends. 'He must be amazing,' one had said, 'the way you talk about him.'

And he was. The guy she had fallen for *had* been amazing.

She missed that guy. She missed him a lot.

They reached another station. Yet more people entered the compartment. Not wanting to provoke a row, she refrained from offering up their seats. Instead she checked her watch. 'I hope they hurry up. At this rate we'll be late.'

'So? It's not the end of the world.'

'But it's rude. They've travelled a long way.'

'So have we. Anyway, what's the problem? We're meeting in a bar. Surely they don't need our permission to order drinks.'

'Are you going to be like this all evening?'

He glared at her. She knew he resented her. Thomas had phoned him the previous afternoon, suggesting they meet that evening. Stuart had been all for accepting until she insisted their prior engagement took priority.

'You can see Tom another night,' she told him. 'You can see him every night for the rest of the week if you want.'

'No, I can't. This is the only evening he can do.'

'Funny that.'

'What do you mean?'

'Tom knew tonight was important to me.'

'What are you saying? That he did it on purpose?'

The train stopped at the next station. They exited onto the platform to change lines. Stuart began to stride along it. She followed behind, telling herself not to cause a row. Only it wasn't that easy. Ever since the weekend he had been like a bear with a sore head, jumping down her throat every time she opened her mouth.

And she had had enough of it.

'Yes,' she said. 'I am.'

He turned to face her. 'It's just coincidence. Anyway, it's my fault. I'm the one who should have remembered. Don't start having a go at him.'

'I wouldn't dream of it. We both know Tom can do no wrong. Isn't it interesting, though, that he couldn't be bothered to rearrange any of his plans to meet you.'

'They're important.'

'And yours aren't?'

'His are work-related.'

'Naturally. No doubt he's advising the Chancellor of the Exchequer on how to balance the next budget.'

'When did you become such a bitch?'

'And when did you become such a lapdog?'

He stared at her. 'I'm no one's lapdog.'

'Don't kid yourself, Stu. Tom says jump, you say how high.'

'You don't know anything about our relationship.'

'What relationship? You've only known him five minutes.'

'Which is only about two minutes less than I've known you.'

'That's not the same thing.'

'No, of course it's not. You come first. That's the way it has to be.' He shook his head. 'You've really got Caroline fooled, haven't you? God, if you were any greener you'd need mowing.'

'This isn't about jealousy.'

'You've had it in for Tom from day one.'

'That's not true. I'm just trying to watch out for you.'

'I don't need you to. I'm not a kid.'

'You are when it comes to them.'

'There speaks the green-eyed monster.'

'Yes, well, talking of eyes, maybe it's time you opened yours. Caroline is only putting up with you to keep Robert off her back. Robert is only playing the genial host to hurt Jimmy, and Tom's only using you to feel better about himself.'

He looked shocked. 'Why would you say that?'

'Because it's true. These are not nice people, Stu. They've all got their own agendas. No one I know deserves love more than you but believe me, you are never going to get it from them.'

His eyes narrowed. 'You know what? Fuck this evening. Go see your friends on your own and tell them I'm not there because I can't stand being with a vindictive cow like you.'

He turned and began to walk away.

'I can prove it,' she called after him.

He turned back. 'How?'

'You think Robert's a great guy with a heart as big as the ocean. Well, you're wrong. He's just destroyed Jimmy's career and for what? Because Jimmy had the nerve to tell him a few home truths. His *whole* career, Stu. Years of hard work wiped out in seconds and with no remorse whatsoever. That's how big his heart is. You cut his chest open and you'll find a block of ice where his heart should be.'

'I don't believe you.'

'It's true. Every word.'

'How do you know?'

'Nessa told me.'

'*Nessa?*'

'She's the only person Jimmy's told. He swore her to secrecy but she wanted me to know exactly what you were getting into. I wasn't going to tell you. I didn't want to upset you, assuming you'd even believe me . . . '

'Who said you could talk to Nessa?'

'Who *said*? She's a friend. I don't need permission to speak to a friend. Anyway, what does that matter?'

'Of course it matters! She's my cousin. She's nothing to do with you. Christ, you've got a family of your own. Why are you trying to steal mine?'

'I'm not. Stu, this isn't about Nessa. This is about what Robert did to Jimmy.'

'Who cares what he did to Jimmy? Whatever it was, it will never be enough.'

She stared at him, too appalled to speak.

'Jimmy stole my life! All the shit I've been through is because of him. I'm glad his career is screwed. I hope his life is too. He deserves everything he gets.'

His face was a mask of malevolence. It was like looking at Robert. Exactly like. For weeks she had been trying not to see it. Finally she had no choice.

'And did Adam deserve it too?' she asked.

'Adam?'

'Your cousin who told his parents a bunch of lies about you. Only they weren't lies, were they? You were in pain. You were suffering and you weren't going to do it alone. You had to spread the misery around, just like Robert would have done in your place. You really are his son. There is nothing to choose between you.'

The blood drained from his face, which was suddenly stamped with a hurt so deep she could almost see bone. 'Is that what you think?'

She opened her mouth then closed it again. Suddenly her anger was gone, replaced by the desire to cut out her own tongue.

'Is it?' he whispered.

'No. I don't think that. I was just upset . . .'

'Yes, you do.'

'Stu . . .'

'I never want to see you again.'

Then, yet again, he turned to go.

She grabbed his arm. He pushed her away so hard she

slammed into the wall. She cried out in pain but he just kept going.

A man rushed to help her up. 'Are you OK?'

She nodded then burst into tears.

'Bloody thug. You should have the law on him.' He guided her towards a seat. 'You stay there. I'll get the station authorities.'

'Please, don't.'

'But he assaulted you.'

'No, he didn't. And even if he did I deserved a lot worse. Thank you for your help but I really am all right.'

A train pulled into the platform. After giving her arm a rub, the man climbed aboard and sped away into the night.

Another train came. Then another. For over an hour she sat and watched them, wiping away the tears that refused to slow.

Later that evening Thomas made coffee in his kitchen.

He filled two mugs then hesitated, unsure whether to add milk and sugar. It seemed strange not knowing how his own twin drank his coffee.

But it was early days. Soon they would know all they needed to about each other.

Loading a tray, he returned to the living room. Stuart was sitting on a sofa. He sat beside him, watched Stuart help himself to milk and sugar and made a mental note for next time.

'How are you feeling?' he asked.

'Better, thanks.'

'You don't need to thank me. I haven't done anything.'

'You've listened. That's what I needed.' Stuart sighed. 'How could she say that? How could she even *think* it? Why couldn't she just be happy for me? It's not much to ask, is it?'

'No, it's not.' He hesitated. 'So it's definitely over between you, then?'

Stuart nodded. Thomas felt pleased yet also bad for Stuart. It was an odd combination.

'You know she's wrong about me, don't you, Stu? She's wrong about Mum and Dad too. She's wrong about all of it.'

'Of course. I hate her for saying it. It's almost as bad as . . . well, what else she said.'

Thomas felt relieved. 'How's the coffee?' he asked. 'It's instant, I'm afraid. I know I should grind my own but I'm just too lazy.'

'I prefer instant.'

'Me too. Hey, what do you know? We must be related.'

Stuart smiled, a weak gesture that failed to reach a pair of troubled eyes. 'You don't believe it, do you, Tom? That stuff about my cousin. You don't think . . . '

'Not for a second. I wish I'd been there when she said it. I'd have put her straight. I'd have taken her words and shoved them back down her throat . . . '

He stopped, startled by how angry he had become.

How protective he felt.

Though that was how it should be. He was the strong one now. Stuart needed him, just as once he had needed . . .

But those days are over. I'll never be that person again.

'Why not stay the night?' he suggested. 'We can talk as long as you want.'

'You might not be saying that in a couple of hours.'

'Yes, I will. You're my twin. If I'm going to sit up all night talking then there's no one in the world I'd rather do it with.'

Stuart swallowed, looking close to tears. Tom put an arm around him, squeezing as tight as he could.

*

Friday evening.

James sat in a West End bar, waiting for Thomas.

It was busy, full of people all radiating end-of-week cheer. Most were in their twenties and flirting like it was going out of fashion. An attractive brunette kept trying to catch his eye. He sipped his drink, willing Thomas to hurry.

Ten minutes passed. A text arrived on his mobile. He feared a cancellation but it was only Kate asking when he would be home. After giggling with a friend, the brunette wandered over. 'Hi,' she said. 'I'm Mandy.'

'Hi.'

She raised an eyebrow.

'James,' he added.

'Have you been stood up?'

'I'm waiting for my brother.'

She smiled, showing neat white teeth. Her figure was slim and her features delicate. She looked like Becky, only Becky's eyes had been softer. Her eyes had been her best feature. He could have looked at them all day.

'Do you mind if we join you?' Mandy gestured to her friend. 'It's so crowded here. You just can't get a table.'

'I'm sorry. My brother and I haven't seen each other for a while.'

'Aren't you close?'

'I don't know any more.'

She looked puzzled. Her friend kept staring over. To his relief he saw Thomas, climbed to his feet and waved. Thomas made a questioning gesture, pointing at the bar. Nodding, he held up his pint glass.

'He doesn't look like you,' Mandy observed.

'I look like Mum. He looks like Dad.'

'So your mother's the good-looking parent, then?'

'What's that supposed to mean? Tom's handsome.'

'I'm only joking. There's no need to be rude.'

'We're twins. Feeling protective goes with the territory.'

'My friend's a twin. Only she and her sister are identical. They're really close. Identical twins always are, though, aren't they?'

He thought of Stuart. 'Maybe.'

'I'll leave you to your talk.' She moved away, giving him a provocative smile as she did so. Thomas caught it as he approached. 'You're a fast worker.'

'We were just chatting.'

'Well, I'll believe you. Thousands wouldn't.'

He felt irritated, just as he so often did with Thomas. The sensation was strangely enjoyable. It felt familiar. It felt safe.

'Sorry, I'm late,' said Thomas. 'Things are manic. I've landed a big account.'

'That's great.'

'Yeah, Dad's really pleased. Over the weekend he gave me loads of pointers on how to get what I wanted in the office.'

'Dad did?'

Thomas frowned. 'Well, don't sound so surprised. You're not the only one he's allowed to be proud of.'

'I'm not. I'm glad he's pleased. It's just ... when you spoke, did he say anything about me?'

'No, we talked about me.' Thomas exhaled. 'Or is that not allowed either?'

'Of course it is. Don't be a dope.'

'But I *am* a dope. You're the brilliant one, remember?'

'Why are you being so hostile?'

'Why are you being so superior?'

James took a deep breath. 'Look, the only reason I asked about Dad is because we had a massive row.'

Thomas nodded.

'You know about it?'

'Christ, Jimmy, what were you thinking?'

He felt defensive. 'I was only speaking the truth.'

'Try telling Mum that.'

'I did. She hung up on me.'

'Can you blame her?'

The irritation returned. 'Thanks for the support.'

'What do you expect? They're my parents. I don't like seeing them upset.'

'*Yours?*'

'You know what I mean. Don't make a big deal out of it.'

'And when did you start caring so much about their feelings? Once upon a time Mum being upset would have made your day.'

'That shows how much you know me.'

'Come on, Tom, this is me, remember? I know you better than anyone.'

'No, you just think you do, like you think you know everything. Even when we were kids you were always convinced that every opinion you had was right.'

Silence. He watched Thomas sip his beer, knowing this was his brother yet not quite believing it. There was an assertiveness, a confidence that had never been there before.

And it scared him.

He endeavoured to steer the conversation onto smoother ground. 'Let's not argue. I've missed you. It seems ages since we saw each other.'

'And whose fault is that?'

'You think it's mine?'

'If you'd wanted to meet you could have called days ago.'

'It's not that simple, though.'

'It is for Stuart.'

James forgot about making peace. 'So it's a competition now?'

'I didn't say that.'

'You didn't have to. Let me guess. He's a wonderful listener. Much better than I ever was.'

'Actually I'm the one who does the listening. Stuart has stuff he needs to talk about and I let him. It's only fair. His life hasn't been as easy as yours, has it?'

'Ouch.'

'I'm only speaking the truth.'

'It was still below the belt.'

'I thought you'd approve. You're the one who's so keen on the truth, as Mum and Dad have discovered. It's lucky for them they've got me. At least one of us is grateful.'

'I never told Dad I wasn't grateful, and what I did tell him he totally deserved.'

'And did Mum deserve it? What has she done to make you hate her so much?'

He was taken aback. '*Mum?* I never said anything bad about her.'

'Not even how much better your life would have been if you'd never known her?'

James's jaw dropped.

'So you're not denying it?'

'That's crap. I would never say that about Mum. Dad is *lying* to you, Tom. He's lying to both of you.'

'Well, you would say that ... '

'Do you know what really happened between me and Dad? He started talking about Stuart's parents like they were scum and I wasn't having that so I told him he was the one who was scum. The way he bullies Mum. The way he shags anything that moves. The way he's treated you like an embarrassment since you were a kid.'

Thomas paled. James knew he should stop, but he was too angry.

'For the first time in his life someone faced up to that arsehole and gave it to him straight. And do you know what he did in return? He got a confidential document I'd drafted and sent it to the other side, landing my firm with a probable negligence suit and killing my career stone dead . . .'

'I am not an embarrassment!'

'Of course you're not. That's my point . . .'

'For the first time in our lives Dad is putting me before you and you can't stand it, can you? You can't stand seeing me happy or successful. As far as you're concerned the only job I'm fit for is making you look good.'

'That's not true.'

'Mum and Dad sensed you weren't theirs. Mum told me. That was why they always put you first. It wasn't anything to do with you as a person. They just felt sorry for you. Only they don't any more. They despise you as much as I do. None of us want you around so why not do all of us a favour and go and wreck some other family instead?'

He felt as if he had been punched. Thomas's eyes were dark pools of rage. He stared into them, searching for a drop of remorse but finding none.

'Is that what you really want?' he asked softly.

'Yes. That's what I really want.'

He swallowed. 'So this is the end, then?'

'Absolutely.'

'Jesus, Tom . . .'

'What are you going to do? Cry?'

'I would if I thought it would help.'

'Do you know what Stuart says about you? He says you're a thief who stole his life. But you didn't just steal *his* life. You also stole mine. You stole Mum and Dad. You stole my friends. You stole everyone and everything that ever mattered to me.'

'Stuart's stolen from me too. He's stolen the one thing that matters more to me than anything.'

'And what is that? Your precious sense of superiority?'

'No, Tom. You.'

Silence. They stared at each other. Thomas still looked furious. But there was uncertainty too. Just a flicker, but it was there. And it gave James hope.

'You're right about Mum, Tom. I did upset her. Only not in the way you think. She called me the day after you first brought Stuart to the house. I told her how hard I'd found it. She assumed I was upset about seeing Stuart with her but I wasn't. It was seeing him with you. Seeing you two laugh and joke and act like a team, the way we used to. She wanted to be the most important person in my life but she wasn't. I don't care about losing Dad. I don't want to lose Mum, but I could deal with it. The one thing I really couldn't cope with is losing you. I never realised that before. It took Stuart coming into our lives to make me see it.'

Thomas stared down at the table. James pushed on, trying to make his point.

'I don't blame you for hating me. I *have* stolen from you. All our lives I've done it. But one thing you must believe is that I didn't mean to hurt you. I swear it. You're the last person in the world I'd ever want to hurt.'

'They're just words, Jimmy. They don't mean anything.'

'But actions do. Think about all we've been through together. Like that year at boarding school. Do you remember that? Remember how those guys were bullying you but I made them stop.'

'You didn't have to.'

'It wasn't a question of *having* to. I wanted to! You were my twin. No one was going to hurt you. I wouldn't let them.'

'That wasn't about me. That was about you wanting to play the hero.'

'And what about when they split us up? They put us in separate classes and separate dormitories and told us we shouldn't speak to each other any more. And you hated it. You used to cry yourself to sleep.'

'You hated it too. It wasn't just me.'

'I know. That's what I'm saying. I used to wait until everyone else was asleep and then creep into your bed. The headmaster knew I was doing it. He told me if I didn't stop he'd punish me but I didn't care. I couldn't stand seeing you so miserable. We used to whisper to each other. We got so good at it we barely made a sound. You'd tell me everything that was upsetting you and the next day I'd try and put it right. Don't you remember that, Tom? You must remember.'

Thomas didn't respond.

'Don't you?' James asked.

'You make it sound like all I've ever done is take but I've been there for you too. When Becky left you, you were in bits and I was the one who got you through it. I came over to your flat and you talked all night and I just listened. I've been there for you just as much as you've been there for me. Don't try and guilt trip me, Jimmy. If this is about keeping score then I'd say we were about even.'

James gave a bitter laugh.

'What?'

'Don't kid yourself, Tom. Within ten minutes of getting

through my door you were talking about yourself. About how much you hated Mum and Dad. About how much you hated your job. About how much you hated your life and what could I do to help you change it. We talked about you, Tom. Not me. My heart might have been in bits but it was yours I was trying to put back together again.'

'So what are you saying? That I can't cope without you?'

'No. I'm saying we can't cope without each other.'

Again they stared at each other. James could still see the uncertainty in Thomas's face and made a final push.

'We need each other. We always have. This isn't about keeping scores but if it were then I'd say that on that one we really are even.'

Thomas sighed. 'Maybe that was true once.'

'It still is.'

'No, it's not. Stuart's changed everything.'

'Only if you let him.'

'He needs me, Jimmy. He needs me and I'm going to be there for him.' Suddenly Tom's eyes were pleading. 'I have to be. Can't you understand that?'

James felt a dull ache in his heart, the first rumblings of the pain that was to come.

'Yes,' he said softly. 'I understand everything. You're the dominant twin now. You're Mum and Dad's golden boy, just like I once was. You're me, Stuart is you and I'm ... nothing.'

'You're not nothing. You know who you are.'

'I did three weeks ago. I don't now.'

'You don't need me, Jimmy. You've never needed anyone. If you want to know the truth I've always envied you that.'

'I never wanted you to envy me. That's the truth too.'

Thomas didn't answer.

'Do you believe me?'

'Yes.' It came out as a whisper, as faint as the ones they had used in the dormitory all those years ago.

'But it doesn't change anything, does it? It doesn't change ... this.'

Again Thomas didn't answer.

'Thought not.'

'Jimmy ...'

'You should go. Like I said, I understand. You've got what you've always wanted and I hope it makes you happy. I really do.'

Slowly, Thomas rose to his feet. Leaning across the table, he rubbed James's arm then turned to leave.

'There's just one thing.'

Thomas turned back.

'If it doesn't work out, then don't look to me to pick up the pieces. I won't be there for you. Not any more.'

Thomas walked away. James remained where he was, staring into his drink, fighting an urge to cry.

A minute passed. He heard someone clear their throat. Mandy was smiling at him. Again he noticed her resemblance to Becky. He wished Becky was there. He wished so many things.

'Are you OK, James?' she asked.

He nodded.

'You don't look it.'

'I'm fine, really ... um ...'

'Mandy.'

'Of course. I'm sorry.'

'So you should be. After all, I've remembered your name.'

'No, you haven't.'

She looked confused. 'So what is it, then?'

'My real name?'

'Yes.'

'Stuart.'

PART 3

PART 3

FIFTEEN

October, three weeks later.

While shoppers on Barnet High Street battled to stop their umbrellas blowing away, Pam showed Brian the postcard Stuart had sent.

'Who is this friend he's gone with?' Brian asked.

'I don't know. I did ask, only recently Stu's taken to playing his cards close to his chest. Like about Jen . . . '

'What about her?'

'They've split up.'

'Why? What happened?'

'Stu wouldn't say. I only found out by accident and when I asked him he got defensive. It's strange because Stu used to confide in me but now . . . ' Pam sighed. 'He just seems different somehow.'

A man entered the shop, accompanied by a blast of wind. Brian went to greet him. Pam remained where she was, staring at the card and feeling worried. Though she was only two years older than Stuart, she had always treated him like a little brother and in spite of his expressions of annoyance she knew he enjoyed her bossy concern. Not that she was surprised. In her experience it was always those who claimed self-sufficiency the loudest who were most in need of affection. When Jennifer had appeared on the scene Pam had been happy he had met a girl who seemed to understand that as well as she did.

But Jennifer was gone. Stuart had new friends now.

She hoped they understood it too.

Helen stood in her living room, watching Vanessa inspect the furniture.

'Whatever possessed you to rent an unfurnished flat?' she demanded.

'Because it's in a nice area and I can afford it.' Vanessa gestured to a battered easy chair in the corner of the room. 'Can I take that?'

'Must you? I'm rather fond of it.'

'You're always saying it's a grotty old dust trap.'

'I do *not* say that.'

Vanessa gave her an exasperated look.

'Well, perhaps I do. But your dad liked it.'

'He hated it too. He only sat in it because you were always complaining it never got any use. But if you don't want me to take it then that's OK.'

'It's not that. It's just ...'

'It's all right, Mum. I understand. I miss him too.'

'It's silly. It's only a chair. It can't bring him back.'

Vanessa stroked its faded fabric. 'More's the pity.'

'You take it. I want you to have it and so would Dad.'

'Thanks, Mum.' Vanessa hesitated. 'I think he'd also want me to have the sofa, the dining table, the fridge, the microwave and the TV.'

'Bugger off, you cheeky cow.'

Ten minutes later they sat together on the floor by the

fireplace holding steaming mugs of PG Tips. Wind battered the window but the fire burning in the grate kept the room snug. 'Did you get a postcard from Mauritius?' Helen asked.

Vanessa nodded.

'What did it say?'

'Weather good. Food the same. Nothing really.'

'The same as mine, then. Has Jimmy had one?'

'I doubt it. What could Tom write? Having a lovely time. Wish you were here?'

A log slid forward, nearly knocking over the fire guard. Using a pair of tongs, Helen returned it to its place. 'You're not too hot, are you?' she asked.

'No. I love an open fire. I must get that from you.'

'And I got it from your grandmother. She was the expert. She could have even the dampest of logs blazing in minutes.'

Vanessa began to look wistful.

'What are you thinking about?' Helen asked.

'I'm just remembering what Dad used to say. That the moment we hit October you were hitting the wood pile and the match drawer.'

Helen smiled at the memory.

'Do you think he'd be proud of me if he was here?'

The question surprised her. 'Of course he would.'

'I never gave him much to be proud of. I don't have any goals. I just plod on.'

'You don't plod anywhere. You're living your life the way you want to and he'd be proud of you for that. The only goal he ever had was to earn enough to provide for the people he loved and to spend as much time with them as he could.' She rubbed Vanessa's arm. 'And in my book that's the best goal of all.'

'I should still have some sort of goal. Look at the boys.'

'Yes, look at the boys. The only goal they have is the one

Robert drummed into them when they were barely old enough to stand. Be a success. And look where it's got them. Jimmy's achieving it but only by living a lifestyle he hates. Tom isn't and despises himself as a result. Well, Dad and I didn't want that for you. All we ever wanted was for you to have the confidence to go out into the world and be true to yourself and on that score you've made us both prouder than we could ever say.'

Vanessa nodded. Then started to cry.

'Oh, baby . . .'

'I'm sorry. I'm just really missing Dad at the moment. How stupid is that? It's been five years. I should be over it by now.'

'Why? I'm not. It doesn't hurt as much as it used to but it still hurts.'

Vanessa wiped her eyes. 'It's this Stuart business. It's seeing another family have the rug pulled from under them. It makes me think of what it was like when Dad died. That was like having the rug pulled from under us.'

'I remember when your grandmother died. I thought it would never stop hurting but it did.'

'Do you still miss her?'

'No, though I regret her loss. I regret she never got to meet your father or you. She would have loved you both.' Helen stroked her daughter's hair. 'Especially you.'

'In spite of my lack of goals?'

'Because of it.'

They hugged each other. Helen stared into the flames, watching them dance. Her own mother had told her wonderful stories of the fairies that lived in the fire and would grant her a wish if ever she caught a glimpse of them. She had tried and tried but somehow they had always managed to avoid her gaze.

She still missed those stories. She still missed her mother, in spite of what she had told her daughter.

Vanessa released her grip and sat back. 'You were always closer to her, weren't you? Than to Grandfather, I mean.'

Helen nodded.

'Why?'

'We understood each other. She never cared what people thought about her. She was who she was and if others didn't like it then that was their problem.' Helen tweaked Vanessa's nose. 'A quality she's passed on to you.'

'Pity she wasn't so generous with her beauty.'

'I could say the same. Your Aunt Carrie got all of that.'

'Was she as close to your mum as you?'

'No. Your grandfather was always the special parent to her. I was a tomboy but Carrie was a girly girl. The sort he could spoil. He liked that. And that's why, in a strange way, your grandmother's death was even more of a disaster for her than me. I never expected much of my father. I loved him but I always knew my mother was the strong one. But Carrie thought he was perfect and to watch him crumble when Mum died was something she's never gotten over.'

'At least he was still alive.'

'Not inside. He just gave up. And it wasn't fair. Carrie needed him and he basically abandoned her. That's why she's so terrified of being abandoned now. And why she's never allowed the boys to fully grow up. In her eyes growing up means growing away and she can't let them do that.'

'She can't let Jimmy, you mean.'

'And that's the irony because Tom is the one who's been most affected. He's still searching for her approval, even though he pretends he's not. Since our mother died all Carrie's ever wanted is a man who'll never let her down. She thought she'd found it in Robert but she hadn't. James is a hundred times the man Robert is but even if Stuart hadn't appeared he would eventually have pulled away. It's Tom who really belongs to her. I don't think either of them realise it but it's true.'

'I feel sorry for Stuart. He's so excited about what's happened. He has no idea what a mess his biological family really is.'

'I do too. A less dysfunctional family could probably have coped with his arrival. After the initial shock they'd have pulled together and made it work. But in this case ...' She sighed. 'I used to think of Carrie, Bob and the boys as being like swans. On the surface everything was perfect and all the turbulence was kept safely beneath the surface. But now Stuart's here the façade is cracking wide open.'

They stared at each other. 'I wish I knew what to do,' said Vanessa.

'What do you think your dad would have said if he were here?'

'Just be there for them when they need us. What else can we do?'

The question hung in the air. Helen stared into the flames, as if looking for the fairies to give her the answer she sought.

Early evening, Mauritius.
After their final swim of the day Thomas and Stuart walked along the beach.

Their hotel was on the east coast. 'We have the most beautiful sunrises in the world,' the manager had boasted. Thomas was sure they *were* beautiful but so far neither he nor Stuart had managed to rise early enough to catch one.

They walked past hotel staff clearing loungers from the beach. The heat of the day had eased and the air was fresh and tinged with salt. Water lapped at their toes which kept sinking in the wet sand.

Stuart was limping. He had twisted his ankle taking a tumble from his water-skis. 'Does it hurt?' Thomas asked.

'No.' Stuart attempted to quicken his stride and winced. 'Well, a little, but it was worth it. I haven't had that much fun in ages.'

'You're a natural.'

'Yeah. A natural at falling on my arse.'

'You'll get better.'

'But not as good as you. You look like a pro.' Stuart grinned at him. 'That's what your fan club thinks anyway.'

'What fan club?'

'Those American girls who arrived yesterday. One looks like Angelina Jolie.'

'Yeah, but only if you squint.'

Laughing, they continued along the beach, past the other hotels and on to where groups of locals were gathered enjoying the last of the sun. Some of them waved and asked if they were having a good holiday. Thomas told them that they were.

Eventually they sat together on a rock, staring out to sea. In the distance they could see an island. 'Is that Réunion?' Stuart asked.

'No. Réunion is to the west.'

'I'm glad we're not on the west coast. Apparently it's really humid. This is definitely the best part of the island to be on.'

'So you're enjoying yourself?'

'Do you need to ask?'

'You're not missing Jen too much?'

'No. That's in the past now.'

Thomas nodded, trying not to look pleased.

'Are you missing Alice?'

'No. It was never serious. Anyway, it's more fun just the two of us, isn't it?'

Stuart smiled. 'Definitely.'

A companionable silence. Stuart picked up a stick and drew shapes in the sand. Thomas watched a motorboat riding the waves and thought about Alice. The day after Stuart and Jennifer had broken up he had left her a phone message saying he couldn't see her any more, using pressures of work as an excuse. He had felt guilty as he did it, knowing that James would have expected him to do it face to face.

He hoped she was all right. He hoped James was too. He really did.

An elderly couple approached, carrying souvenirs from the local shops. He saw them registering their twinship in a way people had never done when he was with James. The woman's stare was curious. Perhaps she was wondering which of them was dominant. By way of answer he gave Stuart's hair an affectionate tug.

'A beautiful evening,' the woman remarked.

'Very,' he replied.

'Which hotel are you staying at?' asked the man.

Thomas told him. 'We had cocktails there,' said the man. 'It's a lovely place.'

'It is,' agreed Stuart. 'It's the best hotel I've ever stayed in.'

The woman frowned. 'You have different accents.'

'Our parents divorced when we were kids,' Thomas explained. 'I stayed with Mum. Stu went to live with Dad.' It was a lie he and Stuart had invented on the plane to avoid the barrage of questions the truth would inevitably provoke.

The woman's expression became sympathetic. 'That must have been tough.'

'It was, but we're together now. That's the important thing.'

The couple moved away. Stuart watched them. 'Do you think they bought it?'

'Of course. Look at all that crap they're carrying. If they're dumb enough to buy that they'll buy anything.'

Stuart laughed. He did too. The Randall twins united against the world, just as it was always meant to be.

After dinner Stuart sat in the hotel bar with Thomas and the American girls, watching a dancing display.

The bar was outside, beside a swimming pool. As the display reached its climax the flamboyantly costumed dancers circled the pool, gyrating to the rhythm of pounding drums, while muscular men in thongs breathed fire over their heads, prompting thunderous applause from the audience.

'Was that local dancing?' asked Larissa, the Angelina Jolie-lookalike.

'Only if you live in Las Vegas,' Thomas told her.

Larissa shrieked with laughter. 'Have you been to Vegas?' asked the other girl, Gwen.

Thomas nodded.

'Where did you stay?'

'Caesar's Palace.'

'Was that when Celine Dion was performing?'

'Yes. I got fifty per cent off the bill for damaged hearing.'

Again Larissa laughed. 'So you're not a Celine fan,' Gwen observed.

'I hate her. My brother's girlfriend plays her all the time.'

'I thought you'd split up?' Gwen asked Stuart.

Momentarily, he was confused. Thomas, clearly realising what he'd said, mouthed the word 'Sorry'. Stuart smiled, indicating that it didn't matter. 'Yes, we have,' he said quickly.

'I want to swim in the sea,' Larissa announced.

Gwen frowned. 'Is that a good idea, Rissa? You've had a lot to drink.'

'Don't be boring! We're on holiday.' Larissa tugged on Thomas's arm. 'You'll protect me, won't you?'

'OK, but only against jellyfish. If Jaws turns up you're on your own.' Thomas rose to his feet. 'Are you guys coming?'

Stuart shook his head, feeling woozy from too much wine. 'My ankle's still bad.' He turned to Gwen. 'Though don't let me stop you.'

'I'm happy to stay.' She smiled at him. 'If you don't mind, that is.'

'Of course I don't.'

'Of course he doesn't!' cried Larissa, before dragging Thomas away.

A waiter brought more drinks. 'I'm sorry about Rissa,' said Gwen. 'She can be quite full on.'

'No worries.' Stuart pulled out his cigarettes. 'You don't mind, do you?'

'No. Feel free.'

'Blimey. I thought New Yorkers shot smokers on sight.'

'Luckily for you customs impounded my Uzi.'

He laughed. Gwen looked over her shoulder towards the beach. 'You don't need to worry,' he told her. 'Tom's a great swimmer. He'll look after her.'

She sipped her drink. 'Like he looks after you?'

'I guess.'

'Why do you let him?'

The question took him by surprise. 'I don't. Well, not consciously. It's just that he's the confident one.'

'You seem pretty confident to me.'

He gestured to his glass. 'All guys are lions with alcohol inside them.'

'Why did your parents split you up? It seems hard, you being twins and all.'

'Because neither of them wanted to be without us, I guess. And it wasn't that hard. We used to see each other in the holidays.'

'Tell me about them?'

'They were the best.'

'*Were?*'

'Are. I just meant they were great when we were kids.'

'Why did Tom stay with your mother? Kids generally need their mother more than their father. If you were less confident I'd have thought you'd be the one to stay with her.'

Her questions were making him uncomfortable. 'What is this? Stuart Godwin, this is your life?'

She frowned. 'I thought your surname was Randall.'

'It is. I . . . well, when I was at school there was another boy called Stuart Randall so to avoid confusion I used my mother's maiden name instead.'

'You should keep the name Godwin. It suits you.'

'So does Randall.'

'Not as much.'

'But that's my name. Not that there's anything wrong with the name Godwin. It's just not who I really am.'

She was watching him closely. Her face was thin with angular features and intelligent eyes. He remembered her saying she had studied psychology at college and felt suddenly exposed.

He tried to change the subject. 'How long have you and Rissa been friends?'

'Since birth. Our mothers met in the maternity ward.'

'So you're like twins yourself.'

She rolled her eyes. 'And guess who's the pretty one?'

'You're pretty too.'

'Not like she is.'

'You're different, that's all. Like me and Tom.'

301

'That's hardly a good comparison.'

'He's better looking than me.'

'But you could fix that. All it would take is losing a few pounds. For me it would take thousands of dollars on plastic surgery, though knowing my luck I'd end up looking like the Bride of Wildenstein.'

'You don't need to change anything. You're great as you are.'

'So are you. You've got more about you than your brother, and I don't just mean the extra weight.'

Again he felt uncomfortable. 'That's not true.'

'I think it is.'

'Tom has just as much about him as I do.'

She looked amused. 'You don't have to get so defensive. I'm just stating an opinion. I am allowed to have them, aren't I?'

He nodded.

'I thought you'd be pleased. Aren't twins supposed to be competitive?'

'*We're* not.'

She didn't answer. The look of amusement remained.

'In spite of what you might think.'

She held up her hands in a gesture of submission. 'I'm only teasing. You're easy to tease. Not that that's a bad thing. I only ever tease people I like.'

He sipped his drink, feeling embarrassed. The dancers regrouped around the pool, prompting cheers from the other guests.

'You're right about Rissa and me,' she told him. 'We *are* like twins. I understand her better than anyone. All her confidence is an act. Underneath she's really insecure. She needs everyone to like her. If they don't, she feels diminished. It makes me sad. You can't go through life like that. You're only setting yourself up for a fall if you do.'

'Have you told her that?'

'More times than I can remember. Not that it does any good.'

'Tom likes her. He really does.'

'But this is only a holiday fling.' She smiled. 'It's OK, Stu. I understand that. I'll make sure she does too.'

'She's lucky to have you.'

'We're lucky to have each other. Like you and Tom are.'

Again he nodded.

'I was watching you two earlier when you were playing pool.'

'Why?'

'Why do you think?'

Her gaze was direct. He felt himself blush. A drum began to beat, signalling that a new dance was about to begin.

'Tell me about your ex?' she asked.

'What do you want to know?'

'What she did that hurt you so much.'

'Why do you think she hurt me?'

'I can see it in your eyes.'

Again they stared at each other. Her own eyes were the same colour as Jennifer's but colder, more predatory.

'I'd rather not talk about it,' he said quietly.

'We don't have to talk at all. There are other things we could do.'

He gestured to his glass. 'I think I've drunk enough.'

'I didn't mean that.'

'Then what?'

She stroked his hand. 'Do you need me to spell it out?'

He sought refuge in humour. 'Are all American girls as direct as you?'

'English girls are direct too.'

303

He thought of Jennifer. 'Not all.'

'But your ex isn't here,' she said, as if reading his mind.

'I know . . .'

'I like you, Stu. I'd like to go to bed with you. I know it won't go anywhere but I don't mind. I'm not Rissa. I'm not as weak as her. I don't need you to like me back.'

He shook his head.

'Why not? It could be fun. You find me attractive, don't you?'

Not wanting to hurt her feelings, he nodded.

'So?'

'It's just . . .'

'That you don't want to use me?'

'Yes.'

'Who says I wouldn't be using you too?'

'It's still not right.'

'We all use people.'

'I don't.'

'Sure you do.' Suddenly her tone was harsh. 'Or would you only use me if I looked like Rissa?'

He was taken aback. 'That's not it at all.'

She gave a scornful laugh.

'I don't use people. You may, but I don't.' He rose to leave.

'You're not like your brother, then.'

Her words stopped him in his tracks. 'What do you mean?'

'He's using you.'

'Crap.'

'I watched you playing pool, remember.'

'So?'

'He has this swagger when the two of you are together. You make him feel strong. He likes that, just as he likes the fact you let him win. Because you did, didn't you?' Her eyes narrowed.

'Why is that, Stu? Are you just trying to make him happy, or are you scared he'll stop loving you if you don't?'

'You don't have the first clue about our relationship.'

Again she laughed. 'Poor little Stu. You're the one who doesn't have the slightest clue of how it really works between you and your precious twin.'

'Maybe not, but one thing I do know is that screwing you won't help me figure it out. But for your sake I hope Tom does screw Rissa and then forgets about her. That way you get to feign sympathy while revelling in her pain, because that's how it *really* works between you and your so-called friend.'

She swallowed. He knew he had hit a nerve. And he was glad.

She threw what was left of her drink at him, staining his shirt.

'I rest my case,' he told her.

Then he walked away through the air that was full of the sound of drums and dancers' cries.

Dawn.

Stuart stood in his bathroom, staring at his reflection in the mirror.

Gwen's taunts echoed in his head. He tried to block them out but was unable to do so. A part of him couldn't believe she had said what she had. Everyone knew twins were a unit. If you fought one you fought both. He had seen that enough times in the schoolyard. Trying to turn one against the other was a futile exercise. The bond was just too strong. It was crazy to think otherwise.

Unless that bond seemed artificial . . .

He thought of the mistakes he had made, like referring to himself as Stuart Godwin rather than Stuart Randall, adding fuel to the suspicions that already burned inside her. He had given her ammunition and she had used it.

What was to stop others doing the same? What was to stop them doubting what he and Thomas had was real?

Until eventually Thomas started to doubt it too.

As all the while James waited in the wings to steal Thomas away.

Just as once a car accident had stolen his family and his cousin Adam had stolen his chance of finding another.

But that wasn't going to happen again. He wouldn't let it.

It wasn't enough to call himself Stuart Randall. He had to *become* Stuart Randall. He had to become the person he should have been if he had had the life he was born to. The person who viewed his twinship not as a gift but as a birthright.

And only then would he be safe.

How do I do it? What should I do?

He continued to stare at himself in the mirror, while, on a permanent loop, Gwen's comments kept playing in his head.

Until, suddenly, an answer presented itself.

SIXTEEN

Nine o'clock, Monday morning.

Caroline sat in her kitchen, staring at the postcard Thomas had sent.

It had only just arrived. Helen had received one days ago, as had Vanessa. Helen had mentioned it on the phone, clearly assuming she had received hers too. She had made light of it, joking about the state of the British postal service. For all she knew that actually was the reason rather than being Thomas's way of making a point.

Which was something James would never have allowed him to do.

Only James wasn't on the holiday. Stuart was.

Having a great time! Thomas had written. *Weather hot, girls even hotter and the water-skiing is the best!* His scrawl covered most of the available space, barely allowing Stuart a corner in which to add, *Mauritius is amazing. Hope you are both OK.* She was touched he had asked after them.

She wondered if James had received a card. For his sake she hoped not. It would only be rubbing salt in the wound.

Though after what he had done, it was no more than he deserved.

Or so she tried to tell herself.

But it didn't stop her missing him. However hard she fought against it.

She decided to call him. Just to check he was all right. It wouldn't take long and Robert need never know.

The phone lay on the table beside the card. As she reached for it she heard footsteps overhead and pulled her hand away.

Five minutes passed. Robert appeared, wearing a dressing gown. He had been drinking heavily the previous evening and his eyes were bloodshot. 'Why didn't you wake me?' he asked.

'I didn't want to disturb you.'

'But it's gone nine.'

'What does that matter? You don't have any appointments this morning.'

'Even so. It's a slippery slope. I don't want to end up one of those housebound jerks who only get up to watch talk shows.'

'You'll never be like them.'

'You sound disappointed.'

'Not at all.'

He poured himself a coffee. She showed him the postcard. He read it and laughed. 'Sounds like Tom's enjoying himself. Good lad. And to think there was a time when I thought he might be queer.'

'Why did you think that?'

'You know what they say about boys with clingy mothers.'

'That's not fair and it's not true either.'

'I guess not. If it were, Jimmy would be as bent as a three-bob note.'

She swallowed down her indignation. It was never a good idea to provoke him when he was hungover.

'Not that it matters,' he said eventually. 'Jimmy's not our concern now.'

She didn't answer.

'Is he?'

'No.'

He kissed her cheek. He smelled of sweat and alcohol. It was a smell she loathed.

She wondered if his mistress felt the same.

She wondered if his mistress loved him, and if he loved her back.

She wondered so many things.

'I'm going to watch the business news,' he told her. 'Will you bring me some breakfast?'

'Of course.'

He walked towards the living room. Soon she heard the television. It was on very loud. Again her hand inched towards the phone.

Again she pulled it away.

Two o'clock in the afternoon. James sat in a City pub, sipping a Diet Coke and dreading his return to the office.

His briefcase lay on a chair beside him, full of papers he had been given at the meeting that had taken up his whole morning. The previous evening Duncan White had phoned, asking if he would handle a new deal. He had jumped at the chance, taking the offer as a sign of forgiveness for the Apollo Club debacle. More fool him. The deal was so insignificant any junior could have handled it in their sleep. His assignment to it only acted as a reminder of just how far he had fallen.

He started *The Times* crossword, coming close to completing it before realising he had made a mistake along the way. Taking it as a sign, he made his way back.

His department was quiet. One of the partners stood dictating to an irritated-looking secretary. A couple of trainees prepared bundles of papers. He gave them all a friendly 'hello' and continued on his way.

Then, sensing something, he turned back to find all four watching him.

'What?' he asked.

'Nothing,' said one of the trainees quickly.

'How was your meeting?' asked the partner.

'It was fine.'

Four faces broke into smiles, each one just a little too wide.

Have I made another cock-up? Am I about to get screamed at?

Am I about to get fired?

He racked his brains for possible mistakes but could think of none.

Feeling uncomfortable, he continued towards his office, past the secretarial bay where once again he was greeted by a row of over-wide smiles.

Someone called his name. Duncan White was marching down the corridor towards him. He braced himself for the reprimand.

Only Duncan was smiling too.

'The meeting went well,' he said before he was asked.

'I'm glad to hear it. I'm sure your father will be too. A chip off the old block, eh?'

'Um ... yeah.'

'Well, you know what they say. The apple never falls far from the tree.'

He noticed one of the secretaries watching him. As he turned towards her, she looked away as if embarrassed.

As did the others.

They know. They all know!

A chill swept through him. Unable to mask his discomfort,

he sought sanctuary in his office. Once inside he stood with his hands on the door, feeling dozens of eyes boring into it like lasers.

Someone knocked. 'I'm busy,' he called out.

'Jimmy, it's me. Can I come in?'

He half-opened the door. Donna entered, closing it behind her and switching on the Do Not Disturb light.

They stared at each other. She wasn't smiling. He was grateful for that.

'Your aunt's cancer? Was that just a smokescreen?'

'Yes.'

'Thank God.'

He gave a harsh laugh. 'Because this is so much better, isn't it?'

'It is, actually.'

'Not for me.'

She stared levelly at him. He began to feel ashamed. Ashamed but angry, imagining the news spreading though the firm like a pandemic.

'It's OK,' she said softly. 'I know how much you love your aunt.'

'She's not my aunt.'

'You can't think like that.'

'Who are you to tell me what to think?'

'Someone you could have trusted with the truth. I thought we were friends.'

'And I thought Tom and I were twins. Just goes to show how wrong we can be.'

She looked hurt. Again he felt ashamed. This time the feeling stuck.

'You are a friend, Donna. It's just . . .'

Someone walked past his door, laughing as they did so.

'They're not laughing at you,' she told him. 'You're well liked here. No one's happy about this.'

'Not even Duncan?'

'Forget him. Jealousy makes him vindictive. He'd give anything to be as good as you.'

'How did they find out?'

'Someone from your parents' village is friends with Mike Fisher.'

'And he's been telling everyone?'

'Not everyone. Just a couple of people.'

'Well, that's all it takes. Throw a big enough stone in a pond and the ripples go everywhere.'

His telephone rang. 'Ignore it,' she told him.

'It might be important.'

'The only important thing is what you're going to do.'

'Face it out. Show them I'm still the same person.'

'Prove to everyone you don't need Randall DNA to be a top-class lawyer?'

'Yes.'

'Why bother?'

'What else can I do?'

'Find out who you really are.' She gestured to the office in which they stood. 'You're not this. You never were.'

'Blood will out, eh?'

'It's nothing to do with blood. You're the best lawyer I've ever worked with. If you really wanted to you could run this firm. You could be ten times more successful than your father ever was and have idiots like Duncan kissing your arse. Only it wouldn't make you happy. Instead you'd just be wasting your life.'

'So what should I do?'

'Whatever you want. That's the wonderful thing about you, Jimmy. You could be great at anything you put your mind to.

This world was your father's dream. A part of me is glad about what's happened. Now you can live your own dream rather than someone else's.'

Silence. They stared at each other. Again his phone rang. Again he left it unanswered.

'Take the afternoon off, Jimmy. Go home. Get drunk. Do whatever you want but think about what I've said. I'll be here tomorrow to talk some more. You will be coming in tomorrow, won't you? Bright and early as always.'

He didn't answer.

'Don't,' she told him.

They hugged each other. He smelled her perfume: Eternity by Calvin Klein. He always bought it for her at Christmas, while she always bought him a Gary Larson calendar and a dumbbell made of chocolate.

He would miss her presents. He would miss her jokes and subversive attitude.

He would miss her.

But would he really miss the rest of it?

'Keep in touch,' she whispered. 'And be happy. Whatever you do, do it for you. Not for someone else.'

He walked back down the corridor, once again being met by a row of over-wide smiles.

'Do you think I should go back?' he asked.

It was early evening. He had taken the Tube to Islington where Vanessa was temping. The two of them sat in a pub garden, trying to light cigarettes in a strong wind.

She didn't answer, too busy cursing her lighter as it once again blew out.

'Well?'

'No. If I were you I'd have trashed your boss's office on the way out.' She managed to light her cigarette and passed him the burning end to ignite his own. 'The only question is what you do now.'

'Find another job, I guess.'

'You don't need to do that yet. You've got money saved and there's still some left from your grandparents' legacy.'

'Try telling that to Kate.'

'Sod Kate.' A strong gust of wind blew her cigarette out of her hand. 'Bugger!'

'We could go inside,' he suggested.

'And miss all this fresh air? Not on your life.' She smiled at him. 'I'm glad you're here. I was worried you wouldn't want to see me any more.'

'Why wouldn't I? We're still cousins, aren't we?'

'Of course. We always will be.'

They sat listening to the raindrops bombard the umbrella they were huddled beneath. 'How are they?' he asked eventually.

'Your dad's fine. Your mum isn't but acts like she is.'

'And Tom?'

'In Mauritius with Stuart.'

'Oh.'

'You haven't lost him, Jimmy. He still needs you.'

'I don't care anyway.'

'Yes, you do. You can't fool me any more than he can. Do you know what I keep thinking about? That day when the three of us took your rowboat down the river and were attacked by swans. How old were we? Nine? Ten?'

'Tom and I were nine. You were eight.'

'Your mum made us a picnic.'

'She also made us promise we wouldn't row out of sight of the house.'

'So naturally we rowed as far away as we could.'

'We had your dog, Paddy, with us. It was his fault the swans attacked. He kept barking at them.'

She started to laugh. 'Well, that's what dogs do.'

'Not when you're in an exposed rowboat and there's a least a dozen of them.'

'You and Tom kept trying to push them away with the oars.'

'Which we then dropped.'

'And Paddy jumped in the river.'

'And then that narrowboat appeared with a crew of drunken tourists.'

'Which made straight for us 'cause they couldn't work the controls.'

'And we all had to jump into the river too.'

'And they rammed our boat full on!'

He started laughing too. 'And you pretended you'd drowned and Tom and I dragged you to the riverbank screaming, "You've killed her! You've killed her!" and that tourist woman started wailing that she was a murderer.'

'And you and Tom said you'd keep quiet if they gave you fifty quid.'

'And the woman's husband was about to pay up when you forgot you were dead and started moving!'

'Well, it was Paddy's fault. He kept licking my face.'

'And then Tom said, "You have to pay us anyway as we've all caught cholera!"'

'And then some bystander went and called the police.'

He wiped his eyes. 'And then they took us down to the local police station and gave us a lecture on reckless behaviour.'

'And our mothers came to fetch us. Mine was shouting she was never going to let me out of the house again and yours was shouting the same at the two of you.'

He nodded, giving his eyes another wipe.

And remembered how it had really been.

'Not at me. It was Tom she screamed at. She said she knew it was all his idea, that I could have been killed because of him. I kept telling her it was mine but she wouldn't believe me.'

She stopped laughing. 'But it *was* Tom's idea.'

'What did that matter? I remember the look on his face as she shouted at him: like he wanted to curl up and die. And I had to do something. Christ, he's my brother.'

'And you say you don't care,' she said quietly.

'Well, that was a long time ago.'

'But I still remember it like it was yesterday. It's one of my happiest childhood memories, only now it's spoiled because every time I remember it I keep thinking Stuart should have been there instead of you. And I hate that because I still want it to be you.'

'Well, you know what they say. What can't be cured must be endured.'

'Who says that?'

'My grandfather used to. He had all these bloody sayings he used to parrot to Tom and me when we were kids. It drove us crazy.' He smiled at the memory.

Then found himself wondering whether either of his biological grandfathers had ever said the same thing.

The wind eased. Pulling out his cigarettes, he offered them to Vanessa, only to find her staring solemnly at him.

'I know what you're thinking,' she told him.

'Do you?'

'Your paternal grandfather was called John. Your father was named after him and Stuart's middle name is John in his honour. He was a mechanic. He loved cars too. He also loved jazz music. He played in a jazz band when he was a teenager.'

'How do you know that?'

'I asked Jennifer to tell me everything she knows about Stuart's family.'

'Why?'

'Because I guessed that one day soon you'd want to know it too. Was I right?'

No, he wanted to say.

Only he couldn't.

'What do you know about my maternal grandfather?'

'His name was Eric. He died before Stuart was born.'

'That's it?'

'No, that's not it. That's not it at all.'

'But that's all you know?'

'Yes, Jimmy. That's all *I* know.'

She continued to stare at him. He stared back, realising he was now the one who knew what the other was thinking.

The following day Caroline had lunch with Susan Bishop.

They sat together in a bistro in Oxford, picking at salads and sipping glasses of wine. Their table was by the window. As she ate, Caroline watched irritated shoppers push past tourists studying guides to the colleges.

'How are things with you and John?' she asked Susan.

'Wouldn't you rather talk about what's happened? It might help. I know how hard it must be.'

'I'm coping.'

'Well, if you're sure.'

'I am.'

Susan nodded, looking suddenly hurt. 'I understand. Why would you want to tell me anything? I wouldn't be much use, would I? When we're together all I do is whine.'

'That's not true ...'

'It's just that you've been such a wonderful friend to me. I don't know what I'd do without you to confide in.'

'Susan, it's not that I don't trust you ...'

'It's all right. Like I said, I understand.' Still looking hurt, Susan sipped her wine. Caroline watched her, realising just how badly she needed to open up to someone. The only person she could really talk to was her sister, Helen, and even then she often had the feeling she was being judged.

Which was something Susan would never do.

'It *is* hard,' she said quietly. 'It's hell in fact. I spend all my time just wishing I could turn the clock back.'

For a split second Susan looked thrilled at being trusted. Then the look was gone, replaced by one of intense sympathy. 'Do you feel guilty?'

'Yes. I was Stuart's mother. How could I not know?'

'You were ill. It wasn't your fault.'

'Try telling that to people like Abigail Watson.'

'Forget her. Her own life's so empty she has to fill it with spiteful gossip.' Susan touched her hand. 'Your real friends know the truth.'

'Thank you.'

'As does Bob.'

She didn't answer.

'He *does*, doesn't he?'

'No. He blames me too.'

'How could he?'

'Because when things go wrong men always look for someone to blame. You were the one who told me that.'

'But I was talking about John. Bob is nothing like him.'

'Actually there's very little to choose between them. You probably think Bob is upset about all this but he's not. He's jealous of Jimmy. His career has ended just as Jimmy's is taking off. A part of him is pleased this has happened. It allows him to punish Jimmy for being too successful.'

Susan looked shocked. 'I can't believe Bob would think like that.'

'But he does. The only person he cares about is himself, and the only reason he's upset about this whole ghastly mess is because it might make him look bad.'

Susan shook her head.

'It's true, Susan. Really . . .'

'No, I believe you. I just feel such a fool. For months I've been telling you how lucky you are to have a husband like him. Do you forgive me?'

'You don't need to ask that.'

'Thank you.' Susan sipped her wine. 'How is Jimmy?'

'Bob won't let me speak to him. He's too angry. The last time they met Jimmy told him he was glad we weren't his real parents. That he hated us both. That his life was better without either of us in it.'

'But he didn't mean it. Not when it comes to you. We all lash out when we're hurt. Bob is the one to blame for all this. Who wants a father who's consumed with jealousy? If you've lost Jimmy then it's Bob's fault.'

Caroline didn't answer.

'You could leave him.'

'Leave Bob? I can't do that. He's no angel but he is my husband.'

'But he doesn't love you.'

'I never said that . . .'

'As good as. How can you stay with someone like that?'

'How can you stay with John?'

'Because he's all I've got. You still have Thomas and Stuart and it's not too late to put things right with Jimmy.

319

You deserve better than this, Carrie. You just have to fight for it.'

'How?'

Susan searched through her handbag, eventually pulling out a business card. 'Here's how. This divorce lawyer is the best in the business. My cousin recommended him to me. She's been telling me to leave John for years. I can't, of course. I'm stuck where I am. But you don't have to be.'

She shook her head.

'You shouldn't worry about your settlement. If Bob's as worried about looking bad as you say then he'll more than take care of you.'

'No ...'

'And you could get Jimmy back. He may hate you at the moment but if he sees you're leaving Bob he'll forgive you. I'm sure he will.' Susan paused. 'Not that's there's anything to forgive.'

Caroline tried to imagine a life without Robert but couldn't. He was her husband. Everything she valued in her life was because of him.

Except Jimmy.

'Call the lawyer. Find out where you stand. Bob need never know.' Susan rose to her feet. 'I'm going to the ladies. Just think about it, OK?'

Caroline remained where she was, staring at the card, her throat as dry as bone.

Ten minutes later Susan returned to her friend.

A waiter was collecting their largely untouched meals. 'Was everything all right with the food, madam?' he was asking Caroline.

'It was lovely. I just didn't have as much appetite as I thought.'

Susan sat down, noticing the card was gone.

'And you, madam?' the waiter asked. 'Have you enjoyed your meal?'

'Oh, yes,' she told him. 'It's been wonderful ...'

Early that evening Kate entered James's flat to be greeted by the sound of music. Though she had vowed not to become angry, she still felt her temper rise.

James was in the kitchen, putting a casserole dish into the oven. 'I thought we agreed you were going into the office,' she said.

'No. You *told* me I was going in. That's not the same thing.'

She put down her bag. 'You can't hide for the rest of your life.'

'Who says I'm hiding?'

'What else do you call it?'

A half-empty bottle of wine stood on the table. He poured a glass and offered it to her. Angrily, she waved it away. 'So they know the truth,' she told him. 'It's not the end of the world. You're still the same person and you still deserve partnership.'

He exhaled.

'What?' she demanded.

'Don't you ever think about anything else?'

'One of us has to. Anyway, I have good news. Do you remember Ellen Young?'

'Wasn't she your mentor during articles?'

'That's right. I had lunch with her today. She's now second-in-command of the Commercial Department at Moreshead Thompson. It's a really good firm. I told Ellen confidentially that you were fed up at your place and she said that if you were to apply to them they'd bite your hand off and you could be sure of partnership within a year.'

Silence. She waited in vain for a reaction.

'Well, say something,' she cried eventually.

'Which restaurant did you go to?'

'Oh, for God's sake ...'

He turned away, checking the dials on the cooker. She took a deep breath, struggling to keep her voice calm. 'Look, Jimmy, if you want to leave your firm then fine but don't do it until you've got something else lined up. Go back tomorrow, grin and bear it, but call Ellen. You can be out of there in three months without losing any career momentum. I know you're upset about your family but you have to forget about them. This is about us now. We're so close to where we want to be. Don't blow it, OK?'

'OK.'

His agreement took her by surprise. 'Do you mean it?'

He turned back. 'Yes.'

Relief flooded her. She hugged him. 'I knew you'd see things my way.'

'I do. I see everything clearly now.'

Feeling triumphant, she tightened her hold.

Early next morning she woke to find the bed empty.

The alarm clock on the bedside table read 6.15. James had always been an early riser and was doubtless preparing for the day ahead. Shrugging off sleepiness, she climbed out of bed, hoping to catch him in the shower. He was never sexier than when covered in lather.

She entered the en suite, only to find it empty.

Perhaps he was getting dressed. He kept his clothes in one of the spare bedrooms and would often change there if he had an early start to avoid disturbing her.

It was at the end of the corridor, just by the front door. She walked towards it, while becoming aware that the flat was eerily quiet.

'Jimmy?'

No answer. She entered the bedroom, only to find it empty too. But he had certainly been there. The wardrobe and a couple of drawers were open.

And the travelling bag he kept by the window was gone.

She walked back down the corridor and into the living room. It looked exactly as it had the night before, except for the note that lay on the centre of the coffee table.

Snatching it up, she read the brief lines he had left her:

I have to get away for a while. There are so many things I need to figure out. No doubt you feel I'm letting you down but please try and understand. I'm grateful for your help but so much has changed in my life that I can't just carry on as if everything is normal. I wish I could but I can't.

I'll call you tonight. I'm sorry.

Love, Jimmy.

Unable to contain her frustration, she let out a scream.

SEVENTEEN

The holiday over, Thomas returned to work.

Secretaries crowded into his office to admire his tan. 'It looks like you had a wonderful time,' one of them remarked. 'Got any photos?'

He pulled out his mobile, flicking through the menu to call up the images.

And came across one of him with Stuart.

He stopped, already hearing in his head the barrage of questions he didn't want to answer. Things were changing for him at work. People were taking him seriously and he didn't want the revelation of Stuart's existence to detract from that.

'I don't have any,' he said casually. 'I must have deleted them.'

The secretaries left his office. He checked his diary, pleased to see it was full of meetings.

Feeling enjoyably important, he began to read his emails.

'I love it.'

Back at work himself, Stuart smiled as Pam admired her present: a framed print of a Mauritian sunrise. 'I'm going to hang it in my living room,' she announced. 'It's just the thing to help me get through another dreary winter.'

'And I'm going to open this now,' said Brian, holding the bottle of expensive malt Stuart had bought him in duty-free. 'It's just the thing to get me through another dreary day.' He went to fetch a glass.

'So how have things been here?' Stuart asked Pam.

'Who cares? I want to hear about Mauritius.'

'What can I say? It's paradise.'

'A health club in the sun, eh?'

'Health club?'

'You look fantastic. How much weight have you lost?'

He felt quietly smug. 'A couple of pounds.'

'More like half a stone. Didn't you eat when you were there?'

'Yes, but the heat killed my appetite. And I did loads of exercise. Swimming, water-skiing, jogging ...'

Pam's eyes widened. 'You went jogging?'

'I used to run on the beach in the evening when it was cooler.'

Brian returned. 'Sorry to start talking shop, Stu, but there's an early evening viewing booked in the diary. It's in Enfield. Can you do it?'

His heart sank. 'Oh ...'

'Is that a problem?'

'I've joined a gym and there's an induction this evening.' He sighed. 'But I guess I could rearrange it.'

'No, you couldn't,' said Pam forcefully.

Brian looked surprised. 'But he's just said ...'

'I don't care. He's getting healthy and that takes priority. You can do the viewing, Brian. It's on your way home anyway.'

'But maybe I want to go to the gym too?'

'Oh please. The day you jog anywhere other than the local cake shop is the day I give up breathing.'

They all laughed. Pam gave Stuart a conspiratorial wink. Feeling grateful, he winked back.

On Thursday afternoon he showed a property in Barnet.

It was a five-bedroom house: the most expensive residence on the company's books. The prospective tenants, a professional couple with four small children, seemed very impressed with it.

'So you grew up in Oxfordshire?' asked the husband as they descended the stairs.

'Yes. In Fleckney. It's a village by the river.'

'My mother grew up in Oxfordshire,' the wife told him. 'She had a very happy childhood there.'

'My brother and I did too.'

They reached the ground floor. 'I want to have another look at the living room,' announced the husband. 'You two stay here. I won't be a minute.'

He moved away. 'Are you close to your brother?' asked the wife.

Stuart nodded. 'We're twins.'

Her face lit up. 'How wonderful. Are you identical?'

'Yes.'

'Do people confuse you with each other?'

'All the time. Only our parents can tell us apart.'

'You're lucky. Our youngest two are twins. They're not identical. They're boy and girl, but they're really close. There's a definite bond there.' She laughed. 'Not like their elder sisters who fight like cat and dog. They're with my parents at the moment and I keep expecting a phone call saying they've tried to kill each other.'

He laughed too.

'Is your twin also an estate agent?' she asked.

'No. Tom's an accountant. He's working for a private

company at the moment but he's about to move into industry.' He spoke slowly, replicating Thomas's accent as best he could. He had always had a gift for mimicry and in the final days of their holiday he had listened intently to Thomas's tone and voice patterns, even practising it when alone in his room, to ensure that he could replicate it perfectly.

And it seemed to be working. He kept waiting for the wife to register the deception but she seemed as oblivious as her husband had been.

'You didn't fancy accountancy yourself?' she enquired.

'No. I never had a head for figures. When we were at school I'd spend all my time copying Tom's answers in maths tests.'

She reached into her handbag, pulled out her purse and searched through it, eventually pulling out a small snapshot. 'These are my twins.'

He stared at the picture. Two curly haired toddlers beamed back at him. 'What are their names?'

'Lily and Archie. Lily's the boss. From the moment they were born she's ruled the roost. But she's very protective of him. If any of the other children at their playgroup try and push him around she always sorts them out.'

He thought of all the years he had missed with Thomas; of all the experiences James had enjoyed that should have been his. 'Archie is a lucky boy,' he said quietly.

'Which one of you is the boss? You or your brother?'

'I am, though I let Tom think he is.'

She looked amused. He wondered why he had said that.

Who would have been boss if we'd grown up together? Would it have been him? Would it have been me?

And would it have mattered?

He gave her back the picture. 'They're lovely kids. You must be very proud of them.'

Her eyes widened slightly. He realised his accent had slipped. 'God, I sounded quite Brummie then, didn't I? I worked there for a couple of years and picked up a bit of a twang. I've pretty much lost it now but occasionally it slips out.' He rolled his eyes. 'I often use it when I'm with my parents. It drives them mad.'

She laughed. He sensed the crisis had been averted.

The husband returned. 'This place looks perfect,' he said cheerfully.

They spent a couple of minutes discussing practicalities. All the time he kept his accent firmly under control.

The viewing ended. The couple walked towards their car. Feeling pleased with himself, he prepared to follow them.

Then caught a glimpse of himself in the hallway mirror.

His face was thinner now, his jaw line tighter and his skin clearer. He looked better but there was a still a lot of work left to be done.

And for that, he would need help.

Friday morning.

Once Robert had left for his golf game, Caroline called Kate.

She dreaded making the call. Kate was the last person she wanted to speak to. But she had no choice. She had phoned James at work the previous day, only to be told that he had walked out of the office and nobody knew when he would be back. She had tried his flat and his mobile but to no avail. Thomas and Vanessa might know where he was but by questioning them she ran the risk of Robert finding out.

So that just left Kate.

The secretary she spoke to said Kate was busy. She explained it was an emergency and after thirty seconds a clearly irritated Kate came onto the line.

'Kate, it's Caroline Randall. I'm phoning about Jimmy.'

'What about him?'

'I need to speak to him ...'

'That makes two of us.'

'You don't know where he is?'

'Oh yes. I know *exactly* where he is.'

Her heart lifted. Soon she would be speaking to her son.

But when she heard what Kate had to say the desire vanished completely.

Friday afternoon.

Gordon Taylor stood in a church car park in Sutton Coldfield, doing up his jacket and gazing at the sky. The wind was high and dark clouds were gathering. Rain was coming but there was still time to pay his respects before it arrived.

A bunch of flowers lay on the passenger seat. He took them out, locked the car and walked into the church grounds, staring at the church as he did so. He had known it all his life. Throughout his childhood his parents had brought his sister and himself here every Sunday. His son Adam had been christened here, as had his nephew and niece. His niece's christening seemed like yesterday. It had been such a happy occasion. His sister had been so proud of her firstborn child. He had taken dozens of photographs of mother, father and baby while never guessing that fifteen years later he would be attending their joint funeral.

As he walked towards their grave he saw someone was already there. His heart lifted as he recognised his son. Since Adam had moved to London they had hardly heard from him. Just the occasional phone call, usually when he needed something. Though he had made noises about visiting them that weekend, prompting his mother to restock the fridge, there had as yet been no confirmation.

'Adam?'

No answer. Adam continued staring at the stone.

'It's me, Dad. Why aren't you still at work? Did you take the afternoon off?'

Adam turned to face him.

Only it wasn't Adam. Instead it was someone who could have been his brother.

The resemblance was astonishing. Though the man looked slightly older, the similarity in features, height, build and colouring was remarkable. Gordon found himself remembering the hard years before Adam's birth when his wife had had one miscarriage after another. For a moment he wondered if she had somehow born a son in secret who had now tracked them down.

Shock turned his hands to jelly and he dropped the flowers. Quickly, he bent down to pick them up.

'Who are you?' asked the man. The voice was different to Adam's: stronger, deeper and with the perfect enunciation that suggested privilege and an expensive private school education. It was the sort of accent he always encouraged Adam to try and use in interviews.

He stood up again. 'I could ask you the same question.'

The man gestured to the headstone. 'Did you know them?'

'They were my sister, my brother-in-law and my niece.'

The man's eyes widened. 'So you must be Gordon.'

'Yes, I'm Gordon. Who are you?'

'You're not going to believe me, but I can prove it.'

'Prove what?'

'That I'm Stuart. I'm your nephew. The real one ...'

EIGHTEEN

Two hours later, James sat in his uncle's living room, drinking coffee.

Gordon and his wife lived in a quiet cul-de-sac. All the houses were detached, had single garages, well-tended front gardens and were just different enough to be identical. Through the window James watched two teenage boys stopping to admire his Porsche that was now parked in the drive outside.

'I don't believe it,' his aunt Eileen kept saying. She was a small, plump woman who gazed in wonder at the photographs he had brought of Thomas and himself as boys.

'I didn't either, at first,' he told her. 'When my cousin showed me pictures of Stuart I thought she and Tom were playing a trick on me.'

'It must have been a terrible shock,' said Gordon.

He nodded, then felt embarrassed. 'I'm sorry. I didn't mean it to sound like that.'

'It's all right. We understand.' Gordon smiled at him. Like his wife, he was about sixty, but tall and gaunt with thinning grey hair.

'Did your parents never suspect?' asked Eileen.

'No. There was no reason to do so. I have the same colouring as my mother. People always said Tom looked like Dad and I looked like her.'

'You *do* look like your mother,' Gordon told him with a wistful look in his eyes. 'There's no doubting whose son you are.'

'Or whose cousin,' Eileen added. 'In fact, you could be Adam's brother.'

He sipped his coffee, careful not to spill a drop. Eileen had insisted on using the best china, despite his pleas that she not go to any trouble. She reminded him of his mother who would always put her best food forward when entertaining guests.

Only he wasn't their guest. He was their nephew.

'Did my real parents ever suspect Stuart wasn't their child?'

Gordon shook his head. 'Stuart's grandmother, your father's mother, always said Stuart looked like her brother who was killed in World War Two.'

'Did he?'

'I don't know. It wasn't important. No one ever questioned his identity.'

'Just as no one ever questioned mine.'

A photograph album lay on his lap. He turned the pages, looking at snapshots of his real parents and sister. He studied his mother's face, recognising his own features.

Stuart was in the pictures too; all four of them smiling together. They looked like a happy unit. It might have been an act, of course. If someone were to study his own family album they would conclude the Randall family was a happy one too.

But he sensed it wasn't.

Would they have been as happy if I'd been there instead? Would they have loved me as much as they loved him?

He hoped so.

'It's such a tragedy your mother never got to meet you,' said Eileen. 'She would have been so proud of your achievements.'

'They're not that great. Dad helped open the right doors. If Stuart had grown up in my place Dad would have done the same for him.'

'How do your parents feel about this?' asked Gordon.

'They're coping. They seem to like Stuart. He and Tom have become very close. I guess it's to be expected. They are identical, after all.'

'That must be hard on you,' Eileen suggested.

He felt a dull ache in his heart. 'You could say that.'

Both she and Gordon were watching him, their expressions curious but also sympathetic. He realised that he liked them: these strangers who were his uncle and aunt.

'Stuart lived with us for a time after his parents died,' said Gordon eventually. 'Did he tell you that?'

'Yes.'

'I imagine he also told you it ended badly.'

Yes, he wanted to say. Only he didn't want to make them feel bad. Not when they were all that remained of his biological family.

'We talked about it once,' he replied. 'Stuart told me that what happened is in the past. He's happy. He has a new family now, and if he ever caused trouble in yours then he's sorry for it.'

James saw Eileen's face relax. He saw gratitude in Gordon's. And he was glad.

'You have a new family too,' Gordon told him.

'You don't have to say that. You don't know me.'

'But we want to,' said Eileen. 'And so will Adam. He's coming to stay this weekend.'

'And you must stay too,' added Gordon.

Again both smiled at him. He thought of how they had treated Stuart: casting him aside when he had needed them most.

But Stuart hadn't been their nephew. Perhaps, at some level, they had always known that.

Perhaps it would have different if he had been there in Stuart's place.

'I'd like that,' he said.

The next morning he woke late.

He was sleeping in the spare bedroom. It was small and cosy with pictures of hot air balloons on the walls. From the window he watched Gordon push an antiquated mower over the back lawn before shooing away a cat that was sharpening its claws on a tree by the far hedge.

There was a knock on the door. Eileen entered, carrying a tray with a pot of tea, milk and sugar. 'I thought you might fancy this,' she said, putting it on the bedside table. 'I'll make breakfast when you're dressed.'

'You're very kind.'

'And you're very welcome.'

'This is a lovely room. It's like my bedroom at my parents'. That has a view of the garden too.'

'Are your parents keen gardeners?'

'Not exactly. My mother's very keen on telling the gardener what to do and my father's very keen on complaining about the cost.'

She laughed. 'We could afford a gardener, only Gordon loves doing it himself. He's never happier than when he's making things grow.'

'Did Stuart sleep here when he lived with you?'

She nodded, her eyes suddenly anxious.

'Lucky him. Like I said, it's a lovely room.'

'Well, I'll leave you to it. Call me if there's anything you need.'

He remained at the window, staring up at the sky, realising it was going to be a beautiful day.

An hour later he sat at the kitchen table, devouring a plate of bacon, sausages and egg while watching his recently arrived cousin Adam doing the same. The kitchen was small: less than half the size of his mother's and less neat too. But it was cheerful and cosy and he liked it.

Gordon sat with them, eating toast while Eileen stood by the counter preparing coffee. 'Are you sure you wouldn't rather eat in the dining room, James?' she asked.

'No. This is great.'

'I'd hate for you to think we always eat in the kitchen. This is very untypical.'

Adam swallowed a piece of bacon. 'That's Mum's way of saying we only ever eat here unless we're entertaining royalty.'

'Adam! That's not true.'

'Yes, it is. You're such a snob, Mum.'

'My mother's the same,' said James, before realising the implications of what he'd said. 'But she's not a snob and I can see Eileen isn't either.'

'You're too nice,' observed Adam.

'He *is* nice,' Eileen agreed. 'You should take a leaf out of his book, Adam.'

Adam rolled his eyes at James. 'Parents. Can't live with them. Can't kill them.'

He thought of his father. 'That's very true.'

'It's so weird meeting you. I can't get over the way you look. It's like meeting an even hotter version of me! I tell you now I'm not introducing you to my girlfriend. Once she claps eyes on you I'll be history.'

Eileen frowned. 'I didn't know you had a girlfriend.'

'It's not serious, Mum. She's just someone at work.'

'You work in PR, don't you?' James asked Adam.

'Yes. We act for commercial clients. Some of them are law firms actually.'

'Which ones?'

Adam reeled off a couple of names. 'They're good firms,' James told him. 'I have friends at both.'

'I know about *your* firm. It's one of the best in London. My boss would *kill* to have you on his client list.'

Gordon frowned at Adam. 'I'm sure James doesn't want to talk shop.'

'I'm not, Dad. I'm just saying it's impressive. James must be a brilliant lawyer. No one survives in that environment unless they're bloody good. One of my friends from uni got articles at a big City firm and even though he got great assessments they didn't keep him on because the competition was too fierce.'

'Which uni did you go to?' James asked.

'Kent. You went to Oxford, didn't you? I wanted to go there but I failed the exam.'

'Only just,' said Eileen firmly.

'Yeah, Mum, if "only just" means a million miles.' Adam finished his plate and reached for a piece of toast. 'So what was Oxford like?'

'It was fantastic. But Kent's great too. One of my friends did his Ph.D. there.'

'Who was that? Maybe I've met them . . .'

As they swapped university stories, Eileen started washing dishes. 'Can I help?' James asked.

'Certainly not. You're a guest. So, Adam, tell us about your girlfriend. What's her name?'

'Mai Ling.'

'So she's Chinese?'

'No, she's Welsh. She just calls herself Mai Ling to fool people.'

James laughed. 'Do you have a girlfriend?' Adam asked him

He thought of how he had left things with Kate. 'I'm not sure. Things are a bit ... well ...'

'Don't worry. I'll fix you up with one of my female friends. They're really attractive. Not a dog among them.'

Eileen looked appalled. 'Adam!'

'I'm only joking, Mum. But seriously, James, you must meet my friends. I'm sure you'll like them. It's great you're based in London. That means we can see a lot of each other. You live in Notting Hill, don't you? I'm in Fulham so it's not far away.'

'James may well be busy,' Gordon told him.

Adam looked apologetic. 'Yeah, I shouldn't start assuming. I'm just really excited about meeting you. I always wanted a brother, and a cousin is almost as good.'

James nodded. Adam was beaming at him, looking like an excited puppy. Unexpectedly, he found himself feeling protective towards this young man who seemed so naive and unworldly compared to himself.

Before remembering what Adam had done to Stuart.

But had he? Had any of them? He only had Stuart's version of events.

And now he had met them, he was finding that version ever harder to believe.

'Yes,' he said. 'It *is* almost as good.'

That afternoon he went with Adam to see Stuart's family home.

It was in a nondescript street of terraced houses: one of many branching off from a main road. As it was full of cars, he had to park some distance away. When he switched off the engine Adam's mobile began to ring. 'It's Mai Ling,' Adam told him. 'I'd better take it. I'll be as quick as I can.'

'Take your time. I can go on my own.' He said it to be polite, then realised it was what he wanted.

Leaving Adam in the car, he walked towards the street: two identical rows of houses that seemed to go on for ever. There was a newsagents on the corner. He went inside to buy some cigarettes. The shop was small and gloomy and seemed to stock everything from crisps to kitchen appliances. A group of pre-teen boys stood by a magazine rack, pouring over a copy of *Soccer Monthly* while arguing about which foreign player in the Premier League was the best. He wondered how many times Stuart had come here to spend his pocket money and have similar debates with friends.

After making his purchase he stood outside, lighting up. On a nearby wall someone had scratched the words 'Mandy Yates is a slag'. They were faded and must have been there for years. He wondered if Stuart had known Mandy and considered her a slag too.

He walked up the road, staring through the windows of the houses he passed. In one living room a man sat drinking beer and staring at a giant TV screen. In another a woman vacuumed the carpet while screaming at an excited Labrador to get out of her way. His family had lived at number eighty-six. He stood outside it, staring at its red-brick exterior, feeling a strange sense of anti-climax. A part of him had expected it to stand out from the rest but it didn't. It just blended in.

An upstairs window was open. Rock music blared out, loud enough to disturb the neighbours. He wondered if it had been Stuart's bedroom, and whether Stuart had ever played his music loud enough to prompt complaints.

As he finished his cigarette he noticing a dark mark on the drive. Perhaps it was an oil stain. Something his father had left. A mark to prove they had really existed.

Bending down he traced its shape with his fingers.

'James?'

Adam was walking towards him. Quickly, he rose to his feet.

'Is it what you expected?' Adam asked.

'I don't know what I expected.'

'It's much tidier now. When your parents lived here the drive always looked like a garage.'

'Stuart said my father was always doing up old cars.'

'He used to do repairs on my dad's car when it went wrong. He wouldn't take payment either. My dad always tried to pay but yours always refused. He was a good bloke, your dad. I miss him.'

'So do I.'

The words hung in the air. He realised how odd they must have sounded. How could he miss someone he had never known?

'It's stupid,' he said eventually. 'I thought I'd feel more.'

'Like what?'

Them. Their presence.

Some sense that they're pleased I'm here.

'I don't know.' He sighed. 'More than this.'

An angry male face appeared at the window from which the music pounded. 'Hey! What are you two doing?'

'My family used to live here,' James explained.

'Well, they don't any more so fuck off!'

'Charming,' exclaimed Adam. 'This neighbourhood's really gone to the dogs.'

'Do you want a smack in the mouth?' asked the man.

'Do you want to kiss my arse?' Adam retorted.

The face vanished. They heard a door slam then footsteps thundering towards the front door. James grabbed Adam's arm. 'Come on. Let's get out of here. If you reach my car before me I'll let you drive it.'

'Seriously?'

'Seriously. Now let's go.'

The door flew open. Laughing like idiots they ran off down the street.

That evening they ate dinner in a crowded Chinese restaurant in Birmingham city centre.

Their table was near the door but sheltered from draughts by a row of shrubs at least six foot high. 'Is that what you use as seaweed?' Adam asked one of the waiters.

The waiter looked blank. 'Ignore him,' said Eileen. 'He thinks he's funny.'

'Are you sure I can't pay for the meal?' James asked his uncle.

'Absolutely not. You're our guest.'

'This is very kind of you.' He finished his sweet and sour. 'And the food is wonderful.'

Eileen beamed. 'We've been coming here ever since Adam was tiny. At one point the only food he'd eat was Peking Duck.'

Adam looked embarrassed. 'I didn't eat that much of it.'

'You did! We kept expecting you to grow feathers and a beak.'

'Tom and I were the same about spaghetti with meatballs,' James told them. 'There was this Italian restaurant our parents used to take us to where the staff never bothered taking our order. They knew what to serve the moment we walked through the door.'

The meal continued. He studied the pictures on the wall. One was of a couple on a rowboat in the middle of a lake. It reminded him of a time he and some student friends had rented a holiday cottage on a fjord in Norway. The cottage had come with a motor boat which they had been assured had a full tank of fuel. They had taken it out onto the water, only for the tank to run dry when they were far from shore, necessitating a three-hour paddle home with a single oar. He told them the story, making them laugh, and prompting Adam to describe a near drowning experience while white water rafting in the Rockies. 'Bet you wished you'd had feathers and beak then,' remarked Gordon, prompting yet more laughter around the table.

They finished their meal. While waiting for coffee, James felt the need for a cigarette. 'Do you mind if I go and have one?' he asked.

'Not at all,' said Gordon.

'It's a dangerous habit,' commented Eileen.

'Don't nag, Mum,' Adam told her. 'He's not a kid.'

'Maybe not, but he's still my nephew so I'm allowed to be concerned.'

Adam rolled his eyes at James. 'Bad luck, mate. Bet you wish you'd stayed in London now?'

He shook his head, thinking how pleased he was that he had come.

'I won't be long,' he said.

Within seconds of James's leaving, Gordon saw Adam's smile fade.

'Christ, Dad, how much longer do I have to keep up this sodding façade?'

'All weekend,' said Eileen firmly. 'As we agreed.'

'I don't see why.'

341

'His connections are ten times better than your father's. He can open doors for you your father never could.'

Gordon winced. 'I'm not sure that's true.'

'Of course it's true,' Eileen snapped. 'With so much family money behind him, he must know everyone. Didn't you hear what he said about having contacts at all the big law firms? He could double Adam's client list without breaking sweat.'

'Even so, it just seems . . .'

'What?'

'A bit cold-blooded.'

'It's called being a realist. Something you've never been very good at.'

Adam sniggered. Gordon glared at him, receiving a scornful smirk in response.

'I just feel sorry for him. The poor chap is obviously cut up about what's happened and all you're worried about is how we can use him.'

'Yes, it's very sad,' said Eileen dismissively, 'but it's not our concern. Our only concern is doing what's best for Adam. He *is* our son.'

'And James is our nephew.'

'That's hardly a recommendation. Stuart was our nephew and look how he treated Adam.'

'You know that's not true. We all do.'

Eileen stared levelly at him. He knew there was no point arguing. When it came to Adam the rose-tinted spectacles never left her face.

He looked at Adam, searching for any trace of remorse, but finding none. It made him feel ashamed. For his son. For his wife.

And most of all for himself.

But hating himself wouldn't change anything. His curse was that he could never say no to either of them.

'You want Adam to be successful, don't you?' demanded Eileen.

'Of course.'

'Then we continue making James feel part of the family.'

'I just wish you hadn't invited him for the whole weekend,' complained Adam. 'There's a party tonight. I could have been having fun rather than playing happy families with this boring twat.'

Eileen looked hurt. 'So a party's more important than visiting us?'

'Oh, Mum, don't start . . . '

'I'm just saying . . . '

'Yawn, yawn . . . '

The coffees arrived. James returned to the table. Instantly, all three put on their best smiles. 'Had your nicotine fix,' joked Adam.

'At a price.' James sat down, brushing raindrops from his hair. 'By the way, Adam, while I was outside I was thinking about your job. A lawyer friend of mine was telling me recently that the PR firm they're using is rubbish. Maybe, when we're back in town, I could arrange an introduction.'

Adam's face lit up. So did Eileen's. 'Do you think they'd be interested in my firm?' Adam asked.

'They will if I have anything to do with it. We're family now and family sticks together.'

'I'll drink to that,' said Eileen, her smile so broad it almost cracked her face.

James raised his glass. 'I propose a toast. To new beginnings.'

They all clinked glasses. James grinned at Gordon. Still hating himself, Gordon grinned back.

As James finished his meal, Jennifer stood in a living room in Watford, watching her college friends party around her.

Her hostess Chloe approached. 'Having fun?'

'Yes.'

'Then maybe you should let your face know.'

'Sorry. I *am* having fun. It's just ...'

'You could call him. So you had an argument? My boyfriend and I have them all the time. It doesn't have to mean the end.'

She thought back to their last conversation and shook her head. He would never forgive her. Not after what she had said.

Chloe gave her a sympathetic look. It made her feel guilty. 'Look, Chlo, I should leave. It's a great party and I'm only casting a downer on it.'

'No, you're not. I'm glad you're here.' Chloe's expression became mischievous. 'And so is Barry.'

'Who?'

Chloe gestured to a man standing in the corner of the room. He looked older than the other guests. 'Who's he?' she asked. 'I don't recognise him from college.'

'That's because he doesn't go. He's Amy's brother. He's a builder. He's really nice and he's been staring at you all evening.'

He looked familiar. Jennifer tried to place him but was unable to do so.

Chloe moved away. Barry approached. 'We've met before,' he told her. 'It was on a Sunday a couple of months ago. I was at your parents' pub for lunch. You'd just been on a date. Your sister was teasing you about it.'

She nodded, remembering.

'Are you here on your own?' he asked.

'Yes.'

He gestured to the empty beer bottle in her hand. 'Can I get you another?'

She was about to decline when she noticed Chloe watching them anxiously. 'That would be lovely,' she said.

Barry headed towards the makeshift bar. She watched him go. He was tall, well-built and had a definite look of George Clooney. Just the sort of man she had always gone for until Stuart had burst into her life and thrown all that out of the window.

Oh God, keep him safe. Don't let him be hurt. Please don't let him be hurt.

A grinning Chloe gave her a thumbs up. Forcing on a smile, she gave one back.

Later that evening Adam sat with James in a Birmingham nightclub.

It was crowded. Adam watched a couple of pretty blondes standing together, clearly longing to be chatted up. Normally he would have been first in line, confident Mai Ling would never find out. Only he couldn't. There was still more family bonding to be done.

James looked morose. He had been drinking heavily since they arrived. Not that Adam was complaining. James insisted on paying and he had never been averse to getting hammered on someone else's money.

'So what's your girlfriend like?' he asked James.

'Uptight.'

'Really?'

'Yes. She hated Tom.'

'Why?'

'Because he hated her. They were like kids. Always having digs at each other.'

'That must have made things difficult for you.'

'It did, but not any more. Tom is Stuart's problem now.'

Adam nodded.

James stared into space, cradling his drink in his hands. He muttered something under his breath. It sounded like 'wanker'.

'Who's a wanker?' asked Adam. 'Tom?'

'Stuart. The way he acts. Making me feel like an imposter in my own home.' James downed the rest of his drink and wiped his mouth. 'He's got everything now, and what have I got?'

'You've got us,' Adam told him. 'We're family now.'

James grunted.

'Well, don't sound too pleased.'

'No, I am. It's just ... oh, I don't know. I just fucking hate that bastard.'

Suddenly Adam sensed a new bonding opportunity, one he would genuinely relish.

'And you want him to suffer?' he asked.

'Damn right.'

'But he has. He suffered after his parents died. I made sure of it.'

James's face lit up. 'Yeah?'

'Yeah. You'd have loved it. I made him suffer like you wouldn't believe.'

James raised his glass, only to find it empty. 'I'm going to get some more drinks but when I come back I want to hear all about it.'

He staggered off to the bar. Adam watched him go, no longer wishing he was somewhere else.

The following evening Gordon stood in front of his house, saying goodbye to Adam and James. Eileen stood beside him, looking forlorn, just as she always did when parting with her son. Adam on the other hand looked excited as James had promised to let him drive the first part of the journey.

'You will drive safely, won't you?' Eileen asked him.

'No, Mum. I'm going to wrap the car around the first tree I see.'

'You'd better not,' said James, 'or cousin or not, I'll kick your arse.'

They all laughed. 'It was lovely to meet you both,' James told Gordon and Eileen. 'And thank you for your hospitality. I've had a wonderful time.' He tossed his car keys to Adam who climbed into the driver's seat and started up the engine. Eileen hurried after him, uttering more pleas for him to take care.

Gordon remained where he was. 'Well, this is it, then,' he said.

Smiling, James held out his hand. 'There's just one thing.'

'What's that?' he asked, holding out his own.

Then winced as James gripped it as tight as a vice.

'I lied to you, Uncle Gordon. Stuart hasn't forgiven you for what you did to him. He'll never forgive you, even if he lives to be a hundred. And neither will I.'

His hand was released. He rubbed it, feeling suddenly afraid, while watching James climb into the car which pulled quickly away.

Two hours later, Adam, now in the passenger seat, let out a groan. 'If I don't have a pee soon my bladder's going to burst.'

'You shouldn't have drunk that bottle of water,' James told him.

'I thought we'd have stopped by now.'

'Just hang on. The next services are only a mile away. They're good, actually. I stopped at them on the way up.'

Adam, who would happily have stopped in a war zone as long as it had a functioning toilet, just nodded.

The services were off the motorway. James steered the car down a side road, eventually reaching a garage with no Travelodge or shops attached. In spite of the pain in his bladder, Adam felt surprised. 'I thought you said these services were good.'

'I must have got the wrong one.' James gestured to a sign. 'At least they've got a toilet so every cloud and all that.'

'Yeah. Hallelujah.'

James parked the car in a bay away from the petrol pumps. There were no other cars and the garage appeared deserted. Adam charged into the toilet. It was dingy and reeked of excrement. There were just two urinals and a single stall. Rushing to one of the urinals, he began to relieve himself, sighing with pleasure as he did so.

He heard footsteps behind him. Half-turning, he saw James. 'I didn't realise you needed a slash too,' he said.

James didn't answer. He seemed to be pacing. 'Are you all right?' Adam asked.

'I'm fine, now,' James told him.

Before seizing him by the scruff of the neck and dragging him across the room.

'Are you crazy? What the hell . . .' He fought to control his bladder which was still half full.

James pulled him into the stall and began forcing his head towards the bowl.

'Stop it! James! Please!'

His head entered the bowl, sustaining a hard knock on the enamel as it did so. It was half full of used toilet roll and the smell was revolting. He heard a chain being pulled then water filled his eyes and ears. He tried to keep his mouth closed while feeling pieces of wet paper pushing against it.

The water subsided. James kept holding him down. Again water flooded the bowl. Again paper tried to force its way into his mouth. He began to gag, losing control of his bladder and feeling hot urine soak his trousers.

Then it was over. James pulled him to his feet, thrust him against the stall wall and stared into his eyes. Terrified, he tried to back away. 'Why are you doing this to me? We're family!'

'*Family?*' James stared to laugh. 'That's not how I remember it. Didn't you refer to me as a boring twat? That's hardly sticking together now, is it?'

He swallowed, suddenly understanding.

'When I saw how hard it was raining I decided to give my cigarette a miss. And I'm so glad I did. What an interesting conversation I overheard.'

'That was my mother's fault! She's the one who doesn't like you. I was just saying that stuff to make her happy. You don't know what she's like. She's vicious. If you don't do what she says ...'

'She'll drive you out of the house?' James shook his head. 'I don't think so, Adam. I think that's more your speciality.'

He shook his head, realising he was trembling while feeling urine seep through his clothes and grow cold against his skin. There was something on his face. He wiped it away, then shuddered as he realised it was faeces.

'And stop shaking,' James told him. 'I'm no bigger than you. Grow a pair and stand up for yourself.'

'I don't want to hit you ...'

'Yes, you do. Only you won't because you know I'll hit you back. And that's not your speciality at all, is it? Like when you beat up on Stuart when you were kids. Talk about an unfair fight. You had Mummy and Daddy to hide behind. You knew they'd swallow all the lies you told about him. You knew they'd happily flush him down the toilet just to keep a smile on your smug little face.'

'No! I'm not like that!'

'Yes, you are.' James sighed. 'And do you know what's

really sad, Adam? I could have forgiven you for that stuff in the restaurant. I'm a stranger. You don't know me and suddenly you're expected to act like my new best friend. And I could also have forgiven you for what you did to Stuart. You were only a kid after all. We all do things as kids that we feel ashamed of when we look back as adults.'

Suddenly James leaned forward so their faces were almost touching.

'But you're not ashamed, are you? You're still proud of it. I gave you the chance to gloat in the club and you grabbed it with both hands. You were revelling in the misery you caused Stuart. And you make me sick.'

'But I thought you'd be pleased! You hate Stuart. You said so.'

'Maybe I do, but he didn't deserve what you did to him. Or should I say what you did to me. Because the thing you need to remember, Adam, is that I'm the *real* Stuart Godwin. I'm the one it should have happened to. And you should thank your lucky stars that it wasn't because if it had been I wouldn't just be shoving your head down the shitter. I'd be putting you in a fucking wheelchair.'

They continued to stare at each other. 'And for Christ's sake fasten your trousers,' said James eventually. 'You look ridiculous.'

He began to do so. After giving a contemptuous snort James walked out of the stall towards the door.

Adam hobbled after him. 'You're not going to just leave me here?'

'Looks that way, doesn't it?'

Finally he found some courage. 'You'll be sorry for this.'

James turned back. Adam's courage suffered a heart attack and died.

'Are you threatening me, Adam?'

'No.'

'I hope not. It wouldn't be a very smart move. Believe me when I say you couldn't hurt my career in the slightest, and believe me even more when I say I could kill yours as easily as breathing. As your lovely mother kept saying, I have all the connections. What's more I know all the tricks too. I learned them from the master; Robert Randall himself, and when it comes to being a vicious bastard he's forgotten more than you will ever know.'

James left the toilet. As Adam fastened his belt he remembered his bag was still in James's car.

He ran out onto the still deserted concourse. James was already at the car, lifting his bag out of the boot, opening it and pulling out a small, shiny object.

'Hey, that's my phone!'

'You can use it to call a taxi,' James told him, before throwing it against a wall, smashing it to pieces. 'Oops. Butterfingers.'

'You can't just leave me here. Please!'

'You'll be fine. Hang around here for a few hours and I'm sure someone will give you a lift. For your sake I hope they've got no sense of smell.' James opened his car door and climbed in. 'Bye, Adam,' he called out through the window. 'I'm glad I met you. Have a wonderful life.'

Then he drove away into the night.

NINETEEN

Monday morning.

Susan Bishop sat in her bed, talking to divorce lawyer Giles Murdoch at his Mayfair office.

'Well?' she asked. 'Have you heard from Caroline yet?'

'You know I can't answer that.'

'Oh, I think you can, Giles.'

'This is blackmail.'

'That's such an ugly word. Almost as ugly as the word adultery, especially when it involves a middle-aged married man and rent boys younger than his own son. What would your family say if they knew just what you do for recreation?'

Silence.

'So, I'll ask again. Have you heard from her yet?'

'No.'

She cursed under her breath.

'Perhaps she won't call,' he suggested.

'Of course she will. I'll make sure of it.'

'Well, even if she does, I can't tell her husband.'

'You don't need to. All you need do is persuade her to come and see you at your office. I'll take care of the rest.'

'And if I do, will we be quits?'

'Goodbye, Giles. I know you won't let me down.'

She put down the phone and lay back in bed, imagining Robert's reaction when he realised his wife's visit to a divorce lawyer was common knowledge. His pride would never be able to stand it. He would be forced to start divorce proceedings himself, if only to crush the suggestion that any woman might want to leave the great Robert Randall.

And then he would be hers. It was as simple as that.

The house was quiet. John had left at dawn. With any luck he would work late. But even if he didn't, it wasn't important.

She wouldn't have to put up with him for much longer.

Tuesday evening.

Thomas heard the buzzer in his flat and picked up the intercom.

'It's me,' shouted Stuart.

'Come on up.' He pressed the entry button, smiling as he did so. He was in a good mood. Work was proving enjoyable and he had just been assigned another new client. The evening promised to be enjoyable too. He hadn't seen Stuart since Mauritius and the two of them were going to have an evening out in Chelsea.

He went to stand at his door. From it he could see the lift, which was still on the ground floor. He tapped his foot impatiently.

And heard someone rushing up the stairs.

Stuart appeared at the top of them. 'Hi! How are you?'

He opened his mouth to reply. Then he just stared.

'Are you OK?' Stuart asked.

'What's happened to you?'

'Do you mean the haircut? I got tired of the dragged-though-a-hedge-backwards look.'

'It's the same as mine.'

'If only. It doesn't look half as good on me.'

'It looks fine,' he said.

But he was lying. It didn't look fine. It looked wonderful.

Startled, he turned and walked back into his flat. Stuart followed, talking nineteen to the dozen. 'Sorry I'm late. I went to the gym after work and it was so crowded I had to wait for most of the machines ...'

'You went to the gym?'

'I've joined one near me. Seeing you do your stuff in Mauritius made me realise how chronically unfit I am. I'm enjoying it actually. A trainer's been showing me loads of exercises.'

They reached the living room. Thomas stared at Stuart's face. It looked leaner, more sculpted. For the first time he noticed cheekbones.

And he noticed something else.

'You've got a new suit.'

'I'm smartening up my image. I don't want to keep showing you up.'

'You're not. You were perfect as you were.' Thomas stared at the suit. It was an excellent fit: elegant and chic. At least as good as any he possessed.

'That's not just off the shelf, is it?'

'It would have been if it was just up to me.' Stuart grinned. 'Fortunately, I had expert help.'

'From whom? The guys in Moss Bros?'

'No. Dad.'

'But your dad's dead.'

Stuart's grin faded. Thomas realised what Stuart had meant. It left him feeling both embarrassed and uneasy.

'I'm sorry, Stu,' he said quickly. 'I'm used to hearing you refer to Mr Godwin as Dad.'

The grin returned. 'That's OK. Do you like the suit?'

He nodded. 'So you met up with Dad?'

'That's right. I knew I needed help. I'm rubbish when it comes to clothes. I would have asked you but you kept saying how busy you were.'

'I wasn't *that* busy.'

'Hey, it's not a problem. Dad said I should feel free to call him any time.'

'When did he say that?'

'The last time I saw them. Don't you remember? I'm sure you were there when he said it.'

'No, I wasn't.'

'Oh. Well, anyway, he was brilliant. He even insisted on paying for it. He paid for lunch too. Wasn't that nice of him?'

'You had *lunch* together?'

'Yes. It was last Friday. I took the day off work so after we'd got the suit we went to the Ivy. I've always wanted to go there ...'

'But the Ivy is near my office. Why didn't you call me?'

Stuart looked surprised. 'Why would I? You had an all-day meeting.'

He thought back to Friday. He *had* had a meeting. That was true.

'So what did you talk about over lunch?' he asked.

'We didn't. I was too busy star-spotting. You'll never guess who was there ...'

'But you must have talked about something.'

'Dad wanted to know all about Mauritius.'

'What did you tell him?'

'How beautiful it was. And what a star athlete you were. Dad loved the card, by the way. He wanted to know all about the girls so I told him about your exploits. He was really impressed.'

355

Thomas's unease vanished, replaced by delight. 'Was he?'

'Absolutely. He said you were a real chip off the old block. Anyway, enough about that. It's great to see you. It seems like ages and I've got so much to tell you.'

Stuart hugged him. As he hugged back he caught a glimpse of the two of them in the mirror on the wall. Quickly, he checked their profiles, relieved to see that his was still the leaner of the two.

Later they sat together in a restaurant on the Kings Road.

Thomas cut into his salmon fillet while watching Stuart devour a plate of pasta. 'Someone's hungry,' he observed.

'It's all this exercise. My appetite's gone into overdrive.'

'Don't overdo it at the gym. Unlike me, you're not used to it.'

'But I'm getting there. I managed four K on the running machine yesterday.'

'That's my point. I normally run at least twice that.'

Stuart looked impressed. Thomas felt pleased.

'I wouldn't go more than a couple of times a week,' he advised.

'I won't be able to go at all this weekend.'

'Why?'

'We're going to see Mum and Dad.'

He was taken aback. 'Since when?'

'Dad invited us on Friday. Didn't he tell you?' Stuart thought for a moment. 'Or was I supposed to do that? God, I think I was. Sorry, Tom. Work's been busy for me too and I must have forgotten.'

'Yes, you must have done.'

'You can make it, can't you?'

'I'm not in the mood for Mum and Dad this weekend.'

'But I've already told Dad I'll go.'

Thomas picked at his food, feeling anxious. He didn't want to let Stuart go on his own. It just didn't feel . . .

Safe

. . . right.

Only he could never admit that.

But there was another way.

'Well, it's up to you,' he said nonchalantly. 'I'm sure you'll have a great time.'

'I don't want to go without you.'

'I don't mind. Maybe it's a good thing. After all the time we spent together in Mauritius we don't want to risk getting on each other's nerves.'

Stuart looked alarmed. 'Am I getting on yours?'

He didn't answer, pretending to be focused on his food.

The alarm intensified. 'Am I?'

Slowly he swallowed his mouthful. 'No.'

'So maybe you and I could do something over the weekend?'

He continued eating.

'If you want, that is?'

He waited a moment before nodding. Stuart's face lit up. The sight made him feel strong and in control. Just like the dominant twin he was.

And suddenly the prospect of a weekend with his parents didn't seem so bad.

'You know what,' he said. 'If Mum and Dad are expecting us then maybe we should go . . .'

Thursday morning.

Caroline returned home from the shops.

Robert emerged from the living room. She gestured to the bags she was carrying. 'I've been getting in food for when the boys come.'

He nodded.

'They are both coming, aren't they? Tom has confirmed, hasn't he?'

Another nod. He seemed to be studying her. It made her feel uncomfortable.

'I'll put this stuff away,' she told him, then headed off to the kitchen, searching through the bags for the frozen stuff to put in the freezer. It was crowded already. She moved its contents around, trying to make some room.

'I heard something interesting this morning.'

She jumped. He was standing right behind her, his gaze as intense as before.

'What was that?' she asked, while trying to focus on what she was doing.

'I had a phone call from a guy I used to work with. No one you'd know. He's been married for twenty-five years. He's got three children. He thought his marriage was rock solid. Only now his wife has told him she wants a divorce.'

'That's sad.'

'It will be for her if she thinks she's going to take him for half his assets and the marital home. After all, he's the lawyer. He's the one with connections. By the time he's through with her she'll be lucky if she's left with the clothes on her back.'

She felt a chill run through her.

'Not that it will come to that. He's going to have a little chat with her. Make sure she understands the situation. There won't be any divorce unless he decides that *he* wants one.' He paused. 'Do you think she'll understand?'

She didn't answer.

'Do you?'

'Yes. I'm sure she will.'

'Good. That's what I told him. I can see you're busy. I'll leave you to it.'

He walked away. She remained where she was.

Does he know? Oh God, does he know?

But he couldn't. There was no way. Susan would never betray her. She would trust Susan with her life.

Did he sense her resentment? Was that it?

Or was it just coincidence?

Later, when he was watching television, she retrieved the business card Susan had given her. It was hidden somewhere Robert would never dream of looking, even if he knew there was anything to look for.

But she couldn't take any chances.

So she ripped it to shreds.

Friday afternoon.

In their usual hotel room Susan Bishop handed Robert a glass of champagne. 'Go on,' she told him. 'You've earned it.'

He downed it, watching her as he did so, his eyes cold. He had seemed tense since his arrival. At first she had put it down to sexual frustration. Now she knew better.

'What is it?' she asked.

'Have you heard of Megan Fox?'

The name rang a bell. 'Is she a model?'

'She's a Hollywood actress. Someone was talking about her at the golf club. Apparently she's a real stunner, like Monica Bellucci's younger, sluttier sister.'

'And what? You're going to fly to LA and make a move on her? I hate to burst your bubble, Bob, but even for someone with your limitless confidence I think that's aiming a little high.'

'No, I'm not planning anything. But I was curious to see what she looked like. I would have gone online but the guy at the club said there were some great pictures in one of those gossip rags Carrie loves. She keeps a whole pile in her bedside table.'

'So, did you whack off to her photograph?'

'I would have done,' he told her.

She stroked his chest. 'What was the problem? Didn't she match up to me?'

'No. The problem was that inside the magazine I found Giles Murdoch's card.'

Somehow she managed to keep her expression neutral. 'Who's he? An interior decorator?'

His eyes narrowed. He grabbed her wrist. 'Don't fuck with me. You know damn well who he is.'

'Stop it!'

'Giles is a friend of yours. John's mentioned him in the past. A fucking shark of a divorce lawyer by all accounts. What were you thinking, Susan? Get Carrie to divorce me and make a space for yourself in the marital bed?'

She pulled her arm free. 'Are you crazy? Why would I want to do that?'

'Because you want me to leave her. Don't insult me by denying it.'

She rubbed her wrist. 'I'm the one who's being insulted.'

'And I'm the one who's being fucked with. And I don't like it.'

He continued to stare at her. She stared back, trying to look scornful while her sense of being thwarted grew so powerful it made her want to scream.

'You can't prove it was me,' she told him.

'Oh, for God's sake ...'

'You can't! You don't know it. And you don't know Carrie either. You should hear the things she says about you when we're together.'

She waited in vain for a reaction. Instead he just sighed.

'She hates you. She wants to leave you.'

'Carrie would never say that.'

'She says you're selfish, that the only person you care about is yourself.'

'I seem to remember you were the one who said that.'

'I'm not lying.'

'It doesn't matter anyway. Carrie isn't going to leave me. We had a little chat and she understands the situation. So much so that when I checked the magazine a few hours later the card had already gone. You can try and manipulate her as much as you want but it won't work. I'm the one pulling her strings, not you.'

She shook her head, wanting to slap him. Wanting to slap herself.

He gestured to the room they were in. 'I've told you time and time again, this is what it is. This is all it is. This is *all* it will *ever* be. I don't want to leave Carrie, but even if I did you're the last woman in the world I'd leave her for. Who wants to marry someone who doesn't have a heart?'

She snorted. 'That makes two of us.'

'Exactly, so I know what a toxic combination we'd be. You're better off than you know, Susan. John is a good man. He puts up with whatever shit you throw at him, just like Carrie does with me. That's why things have to stay as they are. They may not be perfect but believe me, outside the bedroom, you and I could never make each other happy. When it comes to warmth and tenderness we just don't have it in us.'

Suddenly his expression softened, became almost pitying.

And she couldn't stand it. Rising to her feet, she reached for her clothes.

'Is this the end?' he asked.

'You wish!'

'What are you going to do? Go public with our affair? It won't hurt me. Not any more. My career's over, boys will be boys and Carrie will stay with me no matter what. But it could hurt you. Most of your so-called friends would cut you dead. And what about John? Maybe he won't be able to handle it. Maybe he'll decide he's had enough. Do you really want to risk that?'

She picked up her wig. It was long and black and a million miles from her neat blonde cut. Whenever she met him she wore it and a pair of huge dark glasses. She parked some distance from the hotel too.

Because she didn't want anyone to know about them.

And she still didn't. He was right. The risk was just too great.

She turned back. He was still on the bed. She swallowed, tasting hate but finding it still flavoured with desire. In spite of everything she still wanted him in a way that was more than physical. In a way that he would never want her.

He made her weak. He made her needy. He made her everything she despised in other people.

And he had to suffer. She needed him to suffer.

But for that to happen she would also need to stay friends.

Casting the wig aside, she rejoined him on the bed. 'I'm not going to tell anyone,' she said. 'You're right. We wouldn't make each other happy. Except in bed, and we can't live our lives there, can we? I do need John. I may despise him but he has his uses.'

He nodded, looking relieved: totally unaware that they were now at war.

'As do you,' she told him, moving in for a kiss.

*

Sunday afternoon.

Thomas stood by the window in his parents' kitchen, watching his father and Stuart in the garden.

It was a lovely late autumn afternoon. Cool, but sunny. The two of them stood by the riverbank. His father said something and Stuart gave a hearty laugh. Thomas wondered whether the joke was really as funny as Stuart was making out. He knew he should have gone outside with them but after eating a huge lunch he felt lazy. Besides, his father had said they would only be a few minutes.

But that was half an hour ago.

'Why not join them?' his mother suggested.

'I'm still too bloated.'

'You certainly seemed to enjoy your meal.'

He nodded, watching Stuart decline his father's offer of a cigar, no doubt trying to flaunt his new healthy lifestyle. Their mother had been most complimentary about Stuart's more streamlined appearance.

Not that it mattered. Imitation was the most obvious form of flattery.

'Well, you've always loved pheasant,' his mother continued. She was looking pleased with herself. It angered him. It was just a meal. It didn't make up for the past.

'Actually, Jimmy was the one who loved it.'

'But you do too. You always said so.'

'It's too salty. I prefer beef. I just didn't want to hurt your feelings.'

Her face fell. 'I'll make beef next time,' she told him.

He nodded.

'It sounds like work is going well. I'm so pleased. Dad is too. He was saying as much before you arrived.'

'Well, I want to make my mark.'

'You'll certainly do that.' She smiled at him. 'Your firm is lucky to have you. You could be running the place in a few years.'

'That's what you always used to say to Jimmy.'

Her smile faltered. 'I said it to you too.'

'Clearly your memory is better than mine.'

Sunday papers covered the kitchen table. He flicked through a colour supplement, looking at displays of designer cufflinks, admiring a pair shaped like diamonds while sensing her eyes upon him. 'The prices they charge are ridiculous. They're beautiful, but even so.'

She didn't answer. He wondered if she had taken the hint.

Just as she would have done had he been James.

'I think I will go and join the others,' he told her.

'I'm sorry about the meal, Tom.'

'It's OK, Mum. It's just a meal. Forget it.'

Knowing that she wouldn't, he left the room

An hour later Caroline was still in the kitchen, now making coffee.

Stuart appeared in the doorway. 'Do you mind if I join you? Tom's talking to Dad about work and I'd only be in the way.'

'I'm sure you wouldn't.'

'I would. Trust me. They're talking about stock options and I still think stock is something you use to flavour food.'

She laughed. 'You shouldn't put yourself down. Even in fun.'

'I'm sorry. Force of habit.'

'Well, it's a bad one.' She stopped. 'No, not bad. Just unnecessary. You have much more going for you than you realise.'

'You don't have to say that.'

'Yes, I do. I'm your mother. But even if I wasn't it would still be true.'

'Thanks.'

'Do you mind me calling myself that?'

'No. I like it.' He hesitated. 'How old were you when your mother died?'

'Eight.'

'That's young.'

'So is thirteen. That's how old you were.'

'How did you feel when it happened?'

'Like my world had collapsed.'

He nodded. Without having to ask she knew he had felt the same. It was something the others could never truly understand. Not Robert, James or Thomas.

But he could.

'What was she like?' he asked.

'She was lovely; strong but gentle. She made me feel safe, though the tragedy is I only realised that once she was gone.'

'I used to take my family for granted. They were always going to be there, only suddenly they weren't.'

She touched his arm. 'That's not true. They're still inside you. They'll always be a part of who you are.'

He nodded. Again she knew exactly what he was feeling.

'I'm sorry, Stuart. People used to say the same to me. It's rubbish, isn't it?'

His face broke into a smile. She felt glad.

'Do you mind me talking about this?' he asked.

'No. I'm pleased you feel you can. You can talk to me about it whenever you want. I mean that, sweetheart. Any time, OK?'

He continued to smile. She realised she had called him sweetheart. It was a name she never called anyone.

Except James.

She stared at his face, noticing for the second time the loss of weight. It was more like Thomas's than ever, yet all she could see were the differences. It wasn't quite as handsome, yet it had far more strength: greater character and infinitely more warmth.

And I could love you. In fact I think I'm starting to already.

He hugged her. As she hugged him back she thought of all he had been through, expecting to feel guilty but not doing so.

Thomas was the one who made her feel guilty, just as Robert was the one who made her feel vulnerable.

And now, unexpectedly, Stuart was the one who made her feel safe.

Robert lit another cigar while listening to Thomas talk.

'So I think I should hold out for the bigger account. That's what I think, but what do you think? What would you do if you were me?'

He gave his opinion, speaking slowly while Thomas nodded, appearing to absorb every word as if he were the Oracle at Delphi. Earlier that afternoon he had given career advice to Stuart where yet again his guidance had been received as if it were something special. He had enjoyed Stuart's reaction, just as he now enjoyed Thomas's. It was always enjoyable to have one's approval so highly valued.

Yet there was a difference.

Stuart had wanted his approval. Thomas needed it.

Quite desperately.

And it made him uncomfortable. Need was a weakness, one that he despised. Especially in his own son.

He took a drag on his cigar. Suddenly James's voice echoed in his head.

All you ever gave Thomas was an inferiority complex.

Thomas continued to fire questions at him. He stared at his son, feeling guilty, while resenting the person who made him feel that way.

'Maybe we could meet for lunch next week,' Thomas suggested. 'We could go to the Ivy. I know you like it there.'

He took a deep drag on his cigar, as if trying to suck down his contempt.

'Yes,' he said. 'I'd enjoy that.'

That evening Stuart drove Thomas and himself back to London.

They were stuck in traffic. A row of immobile car lights stretched as far as the eye could see. As they waited for movement he talked about the weekend, still full of the high spirits the visit had engendered. 'I had a really good talk with Mum this afternoon. She was telling me about our grandmother . . . '

'There's something I need to tell you,' said Thomas suddenly.

'What?'

'Jen's got a new boyfriend. It's quite serious, apparently.'

'How do you know?'

'Nessa told me. She and Jen are still in contact. His name is Barry.'

Stuart swallowed, his high spirits evaporating like mist on a warm day.

'It's her life,' he said quickly. 'She can do what she wants.'

'You don't have to put on a brave face for me. I know you cared about her. It's got to hurt. After all, it hasn't taken her long to forget you, has it?'

He told himself he didn't care. That he wasn't hurt. That he wasn't jealous.

'Nessa was going to tell you,' Tom continued, 'but I said it should be me. I'm your twin. If someone's going to be there for you then I want it to be me.'

'I don't need anyone to be there for me.' His tone was sharp.

Thomas looked surprised.

'I'm sorry, Tom. That came out wrong. I'm glad it was you.'

'Well, you'd want to be there for me, wouldn't you?'

'Of course,' he said, while wondering why Thomas couldn't have picked a better moment to break the news. Five minutes ago he had been feeling on top of the world. Now he just felt depressed.

But then, there was never a good time for news such as this.

The ash on Thomas's cigarette had grown so long it suddenly collapsed onto his shirt. 'Shit! This is brand new!' Thomas exclaimed, while frantically brushing it away. Stuart watched him, feeling the familiar rush of love sweep over him.

Only this time it was laced with two other emotions, both as unexpected as they were new.

The first was protectiveness.

The second, exasperation.

Later that evening Thomas stood at the door of his flat, watching the number on the lift display climb ever higher.

He was feeling unsettled, just as he had been throughout the weekend. It wasn't that his parents liked Stuart. He could deal with that.

It was the fact that they appeared to like him so much.

It doesn't mean anything. They're just trying to make him feel welcome.

He kept telling himself that, but the feeling persisted. It

made him feel weak. It made him feel like the person he had believed he would never be again.

But it wouldn't last much longer. Reassurance was only a few floors away.

The lift door opened. A pretty face broke into a smile.

'Hi, Alice,' he said.

TWENTY

The following morning Thomas woke with a start.

He lay in bed, his heart racing, unable to remember his dream but still glad to have escaped it. Outside it was still dark. He had been sleeping in a strange position and his leg began to cramp. He sat up in bed, stretching it out. His skin was cold and damp with sweat.

Alice lay beside him. He stared down at her, grateful for her presence. After the way he had behaved, most girls would have stayed away.

Lying back down, he wrapped himself around her, using the heat of her skin to warm his own.

Noon.
Kate sat in a taxi, returning to the office from an external meeting.

She switched on her mobile to check for messages and found one from James.

'I'm in London. I got back last night. I'm sorry I haven't called for so long. Things have been difficult. A lot has happened. I'd like to tell you about it but I'm not sure you'd want to listen. I wouldn't blame you if you didn't. But I hope you do.'

She switched off the phone, experiencing an uncomfortable mixture of relief and anger. Part of her wanted to ignore the call but she had to give him one final chance to see things her way.

Her way or the highway. It was as simple as that.

Lunchtime.
Stuart sat at his desk, describing flats to a potential client.

He was feeling restless. Though his job had often proved vexing, he had never found it dull.

But he did now.

Over the weekend Robert had talked to him about broadening his horizons. 'You can't stay a lettings agent all your life. I'm sure it's rewarding work but it won't make your fortune. Property development on the other hand could be a goldmine.'

'I don't have the funds for that,' he had pointed out. 'Besides, in the current market, isn't that too risky?'

'I could help. I *am* your father.'

While continuing to describe flats, he turned the idea over in his head, picturing himself as a financial high flyer with an expensive West End flat and a luxury car, enjoying all the perks of success that were James's but should by right have been his.

He wondered whether Thomas could be persuaded to come into business with him. Perhaps they could go into partnership. He couldn't think of anything that would make him happier. He could take care of the building side while Thomas managed the finances. They could scale the heights together.

And rub James's nose in it in the process.

The conversation ended. He put down the phone.

'Why are you talking like that?'

Pam was staring at him. 'Like what?' he asked.

'You were using a really posh accent.'

He felt startled. He hadn't realised he was doing it.

'I didn't sound that posh,' he said defensively.

She raised an eyebrow.

'Well, what does it matter? Clients like it.'

'And do they also like being made to feel like time-wasters?'

'Eh?'

'You were really abrupt with that guy. I'd be amazed if he calls back. He's probably on the phone to a rival agency as we speak. What's up with you, Stu? Do you think this job is beneath you all of a sudden?'

He wasn't in the mood for a lecture. 'I've got viewings. I'll see you later.'

She gave him a quizzical look. Ignoring it, he made for the door.

Mid-afternoon.

Thomas was reviewing papers in preparation for a meeting the following day.

He heard footsteps. Maureen Wells stood in the doorway, staring at him through horn-rimmed glasses that made her look like an officious owl. 'Are you working on the Dunstable account?' she asked.

He nodded, wondering if she was still bitter. The account had been as good as hers until he had stolen it from her.

'I've got a meeting tomorrow,' he told her.

'It must be hard to concentrate in the circumstances.'

'What circumstances?'

'This business with your brother.'

'You *know* about that?'

'Everyone does. The secretaries can't talk about anything

else. They keep saying what a terrible shock it must have been.'

He tried to mask his own shock with insouciance. 'Well, I'm coping.'

She laughed. 'Aren't you just?'

'What do you mean?'

'That you've spent the last few weeks acting like the cat that got the cream.'

He felt a lurch in his stomach.

'That's what people don't understand. We always thought you and James were close, yet here you are acting like this discovery is the best thing that's ever happened to you. It seems very cold blooded, though I guess you're just putting on a brave face.'

'I am.'

'It's just that one of my friends is a lawyer. She's worked with James. She says he's a total star. It can't have been easy living in his shadow.'

The words stung. 'I've never been in his shadow. I'm just as good as he is.'

She smiled. He realised he had just proved her point.

'I just thought you should know what people are saying,' she told him.

'I don't care. They can say what they like.'

'I wouldn't let it bother you. I'm sure they all think just as highly of you as they ever did.' Her smile grew ever brighter. 'Good luck with the meeting, by the way.'

Then she walked away.

For the rest of the afternoon he remained in his office, trying to concentrate while imagining the dozens of whispered conversations taking place outside.

*

That evening he told Alice what had happened.

They sat together in his flat. She listened in silence, a sympathetic look on her face. 'I'm sure people don't think badly of you,' she said eventually. 'You're not happy about losing Jimmy. You're happy about finding Stuart.'

'Exactly.'

'What do they expect you to do? Sit in a heap and cry? You have to get on with your life.'

He nodded, grateful for her support.

'Who do you think told them?' she asked.

'I don't know.'

'At least we know it wasn't Stuart.'

'*Stuart*? Why would he tell?'

'He wouldn't. That's my point.'

'So why mention him?'

'If I hadn't met him I might have thought it was him.'

Thomas was confused. 'What do you mean?'

'Well, to be honest, when you first told me about him I was worried. You're identical twins but your life has been so much better than his. I thought he might really resent you. But when we met him and Jen in the pub I stopped worrying.' She smiled at him. 'He obviously thinks the world of you.'

'Yes, he does.'

'That's why he's copying you. Changing his hair and losing weight. Buying new clothes.' She gave a little giggle. 'Soon your parents won't be able to tell you apart.'

'Yes, they will,' he said quickly.

'It's nice that he gets on well with them. You did the right thing introducing him to them. He must be so grateful to you.'

He didn't answer. His mind was starting to race.

Does he resent me? Does he deep down?

Just like he resents Jimmy.

'Maybe, next time he has lunch with your father, you could go too . . .'

Is that the real reason he's copying me?

'I'm sure you'd all really enjoy that . . .'

Why did he have lunch with Dad on the one day I couldn't make it? Was that deliberate?

Did he want me to feel excluded?

'Your father certainly would . . .'

Is he trying to replace me?

'He must be so proud of both of you . . .'

After all, how well do I really know him?

Worries flooded his brain while Alice prattled on, oblivious.

Mid-morning.

Caroline heard the front door bell.

She felt excited, hoping it would be a delivery of flowers from Stuart. Instead it was somebody asking if she wanted to change her electricity supplier.

She stood in her hallway, feeling disappointed. After both of his first two visits, Stuart had sent a thank you gift and a part of her had hoped he would repeat the gesture.

She knew she was being silly. He was her son. He didn't need to reward her for her hospitality. It was reward enough to see him.

Perhaps he had realised that. Perhaps that was the reason.

The idea made her feel warm inside.

Until another possibility occurred to her.

Did Tom talk him out of it? Is he jealous?

Does he think Stuart and I are getting too close?

Is he trying to make trouble between us?

She tried to push the thought from her mind.

But it remained firmly in place.

That afternoon Thomas stood in his boss's office, listening to a lecture.

'The Dunstable account is an important one. We need to impress the clients but you were all over the place in the meeting. Everyone could see it. If I hadn't stepped in God knows what would have happened.'

He breathed deeply, trying to keep his composure while spotting Maureen talking to someone outside the office door. Was she trying to eavesdrop?

'It won't happen again,' he said.

'It had better not. You were the one who told me you were ready for more responsibility. Don't make me regret giving it to you.'

'I won't.'

His boss stared at him, while in the corridor someone was laughing.

'I won't,' he said again.

'Look, I know what's happened with your brother. It must be difficult and—'

'How did you find out?'

'A friend told me. He knows someone in Fleckney.'

He felt relieved. So it hadn't been Stuart after all. 'And you told everyone else?'

'I haven't told anyone. Actually, Walter Phelps told *me*.'

The relief vanished. 'How did he find out?'

'I don't know. You'd have to ask him. Anyway, my point is that what with all of this maybe you're not the best person to be handling the Dunstable account.'

'You're taking it off me?' He felt sick, imagining what his father would think of him if that were to happen.

'Not necessarily. I just thought ...'

'I'm fine about what's happened with my brother. It's no big deal.'

His boss's eyes widened.

'Look, of course I'm upset, but I'm a professional. It won't affect my work. I'm sorry about this morning but I promise it won't happen again.'

'Very well, Tom. But remember what I've said. If you're struggling to cope then tell me and I'll find you something else to do.'

Like what? The newsletter? Some other crap job that no one else will touch?

'You don't need to worry. I'm fine.'

On his way back to his office he saw Walter talking with a couple of secretaries. For a moment he considered challenging Walter as to his source. Only he couldn't. Now was not the time to appear weak.

Back at his desk he checked his emails. One was from Stuart, asking him to call. The tone was warm and chatty, just like his messages always were.

Just like James's messages had always been.

Their writing styles were remarkably similar. He had never noticed it before.

But Stuart wasn't James. He would never be any competition.

Does he know that? Does it make him angry?

Is that why he told everyone?

He deleted the message, slamming his finger down on the key as if killing a bug.

*

That evening Kate went to see James.

As he let her into his flat she noticed his changed appearance. His skin was pale and he had put on weight. 'You look a mess,' she told him.

'Thanks. I've been depressed all day but now I feel so much better.'

'Well, what do you expect? I haven't heard from you for days. You could have been lying in a ditch for all I knew.'

'Yeah, I'm sorry.' He led her into the living room. It smelled of stale smoke. She went to open a window.

'Do you want a drink?' he asked.

'No. I want an explanation. What the hell happened to you? The last thing I heard you'd just met your uncle. Did something go wrong?'

'You could say that.'

She sat down. 'What happened?'

He told her. When she heard about the incident in the toilet she was horrified. 'Are you crazy? He could press charges.'

'He won't.'

'If someone did that to me my first stop would be the nearest police station.'

'Not if you knew you'd deserved it. And he did.'

'Why? Because he gave poor little Stuart a hard time years ago? Boo hoo!'

'You make it sound like nothing. You just don't get it, do you?'

'It *is* nothing to you! You could have got a criminal record. How many law firms will touch you with one of those?'

'Is that all you care about?'

'Yes! At this point in time it is. I go to the trouble of fixing you up with a potential job and then you decide to swan off to the Midlands in search of your inner child. I had to lie to Ellen and say you hadn't called her because you were ill.'

He looked blank. 'Ellen?'

'Ellen Young. The woman who's going to make sure you get partnership. Christ, Jimmy, I don't know why I bother sometimes.'

Silence. She waited in vain for an apology.

'So where were you for the rest of the time?' she demanded.

'Whitby. I was staying in a guest house. It was by the sea.'

'And what were you doing there?'

'Just trying to clear my head.'

'Time-wasting, in other words.' She exhaled. 'Well, that's got to stop. Firstly, you have to smarten yourself up as I refuse to be seen with you looking like that. Secondly, you're to phone Ellen and arrange to meet with her.'

'So that's what I'm to do, is it?'

'Yes.'

'And if I don't?'

'Then we're through. I can't be with you, Jimmy. Not like this.'

He started to laugh.

'What's so funny?'

'You're being honest for once. It's refreshing.'

'What are you talking about?'

'I'm talking about when you said you'd still love me if my career went down the toilet. What a joke that was. In your eyes I *am* my career. It's all I've ever been.'

The words stung. 'That's not true.'

'Of course it's true. Tom was right about you. He always said I was nothing but another designer accessory to go with your designer handbags and designer suits, and that if I ever dared stop being a corporate powerhouse you'd trade me in for another model. You've probably already got one on standby. Let me guess. It's one of your clients. You're always telling me how rich and successful they are. I used to think you were trying to make me jealous but you were probably just sizing them up as potential replacements if I ever failed to deliver.'

She didn't answer. The barb had hit home.

'I'm right, aren't I? What's his name, Kate? Or, more importantly, what does he do and how much does he earn?'

His eyes sliced through her like X-rays. They made her feel guilty. They made her feel ashamed of who she really was.

And she couldn't stand it.

'And who are you to lecture me about love?' she demanded. 'You can't even inspire it in your own family! Where's your precious Tom now? Where are your precious parents? Nowhere, that's where. They all ditched you the moment Stuart walked through the door. That's how little they thought of you. You think I'm cold but I'm an amateur compared to them. And I'm an amateur compared to your uncle and his family too. The moment they met you they realised you were only good for being used.'

He swallowed. She sensed she had hurt him. And she was glad.

'Not so judgemental now?' she taunted. 'Who knows? Maybe that's why Becky dumped you too. Maybe she woke up one morning and realised that what she thought was love was only pity.'

Again he swallowed. 'Maybe she did.'

'Tom *was* right, Jimmy. I never loved you. I only loved what you represented. When you were successful you were just about tolerable and now you're not you're nothing.'

'Then why are you still here?'

'I won't be in a minute. This really is it.'

'Goodbye, then.'

His tone was casual, as if he didn't care. But she needed him to care. It wasn't enough to leave him. He had to regret her doing so.

'You don't want me to go. I'm all you've got.'

'Then I'd rather have nothing.'

'You *do* have nothing! Even this flat isn't yours. Everything you own belongs to Stuart. All you've ever been is his stand-in.'

'And he's welcome to all of it. I don't need it. I used to think I did but I was wrong.'

'And what's prompted this sudden revelation? Seeing what failures your real parents were and deciding that if they can make do with crap then you can too?'

He shook his head.

'Then what?'

'It's the time I've spent with you.'

It was her turn to swallow.

'It's being with someone who can't make a purchase without checking whether the product has a suitably exclusive label. It's being with someone who can't enter into a friendship or start a relationship without checking the other person's income and prospects. It's being with someone so obsessed with the trappings of success they've lost the gift of spontaneity. That's who you are, Kate. And I pity you for it.'

She couldn't take his condemnation any more. 'Fuck you!'

He smiled. 'I take it back. Now that *was* spontaneous.'

'Don't you ever pity me, and don't presume to know me either. You know nothing about me at all.' She turned to go.

'Aren't you going to tell me?'

'What?'

'My replacement's name.'

'It's Brad.'

'I hope it works out. I hope he makes you happy. I really do.'

'Oh, he will. You can be sure of that. He's not a loser like you.'

She left the flat and summoned the lift. When it came she pressed the ground floor button and watched the doors close.

And only then did she burst into tears.

Wednesday morning.

Robert sat in his study, looking at his watch. He was meeting Thomas for lunch in London and would need to leave in a few minutes.

He knew what it would be like: an hour listening to Thomas alternately boast and beg for approval. An hour of hearing mediocre achievements described as if they were remarkable while constantly being asked to agree that they were indeed so. It was that combination of narcissism and neediness that seemed to define Thomas. One that he had never really noticed before, but now he had he couldn't stand.

Not that it was entirely Thomas's fault. Caroline was needy too. He had inherited that from her. And as for the narcissism ...

He caught his reflection in a windowpane.

Blood will out.

No, it wasn't Thomas's fault. He was not the one to blame.

But knowing that didn't make the prospect of lunch any more appetising.

Five minutes passed. Ten. Twenty.

And still he remained at his desk.

'So you really can't make it?' Tom asked.

'No. I'm sorry. My old firm have asked me to prepare some advice for them. They need it urgently. I have to work on it now.'

'I understand, Dad.' He struggled to keep the reproach out of his voice.

And the suspicions out of his head.

'Thanks, Tom. We'll have lunch next week.'

'I'd like that.' He reached for his diary. 'What day is good for you? At the moment I'm free on all of them.'

'Let me check and call you back. How's work by the way? Still showing them what a star you are?'

He thought of his disastrous meeting the previous day: of how he had almost lost an important account.

'Of course,' he said quickly.

'Jolly good. Well, I won't disturb you any more. Bye, Tom.'

The line went dead. The suspicions grew ever more alive.

Is he trying to avoid me? Is he even at home?

Is he meeting Stuart instead?

Are they sitting together in a restaurant?

And are they laughing at me?

He tried to ignore them but they continued to flood his mind like an incoming tide drowning a beach.

Later that afternoon Stuart walked back to his office after a viewing.

He was feeling irritated. He had just phoned Thomas to describe his idea of the two of them working together, only for Thomas to cut him off mid-sentence.

He told himself it was nothing. Thomas was just busy. Now he thought about it, there had been times when Jennifer had called him at work and he had been forced to end the call abruptly.

But he had never hung up on her.

Perhaps it was a mistake. Thomas had hit the disconnect key by accident.

So why hasn't he called me back to say that?

His irritation increased. Since having the idea he had been able to think of nothing else. The Randall twins in business together. He got a buzz just imagining it.

And now Thomas couldn't even be bothered to hear him out.

Does he think it's stupid? Is that what it is?

Or is he getting bored with me?

Jennifer had said that Thomas was just using him. Had she been right?

And had he now served his purpose?

He shuddered, as if someone had walked on his grave.

That evening Thomas talked things over with Alice, eager for her opinion.

'Stuart wants us to go into business together. Can you believe that? Why would I want to go into business with him?'

'It might be fun.'

'It's not as if I'm not doing well where I am. Or at least I was until he started causing trouble. That's probably why he did it. If he makes things difficult then I won't have any choice but to leave and work with him.'

'*With* him.'

'That's what I said.'

'I thought you said *for* him. I'm sorry.'

'I wouldn't be working for him.'

'Of course you wouldn't. You'd be equals. It could be good. People can make a fortune in property, and Stuart knows the market so well already. He'd know when to buy and when to sell. You wouldn't really have to do anything. You could leave it all to him.' She smiled. 'I wouldn't mind a job like that.'

He didn't answer. In his head was an image of Stuart telling their parents how well they were doing, basking in their approval and soaking up all their praise.

Just as James had.

While he skulked in the background, as unwelcome as a bad smell.

'It may not come to anything, though,' she told him. 'It's just an idea.'

'Do you think he told Dad about it at lunch?'

She looked confused. 'They didn't have lunch today. How could they? Your father was busy.'

He didn't answer.

'Your father wouldn't cancel you and then meet Stuart. That would be a horrible thing to do. And even if they had met, Stuart would tell you about it. He'd never keep secrets from you. He idolises you. Of course he does.'

Still he remained silent.

'You're everything he wants to be ...'

Friday evening.

James stood under an umbrella in a West End street, sheltering from the rain while watching employees stream out of a publishing house.

One of whom was a slim, pretty girl in her mid-twenties with dark hair cut in a stylish bob and a smile that could still unleash a million butterflies in his stomach.

'Becky!'

She stopped, staring at him as he made his way over while the girl who she had been talking to waited a few feet away.

'Hello, Jimmy,' she said. The smile had faded. She looked cornered. When he remembered what they had once been to each other, the realisation broke his heart.

'Can I talk to you?' he asked.

'Why? It's over. I'm sorry, Jimmy, but it is.'

'Please. I just need to talk to somebody.'

'You have lots of people you can talk to. What about Tom? He only works round the corner?'

He couldn't help himself. He started to laugh.

'What's so funny?'

'So you don't know?'

'Know what?'

The friend moved away. He waited for Becky to follow. Instead she remained where she was.

'Know what?' she asked again.

Thomas left his office, carrying a briefcase full of papers. After yet another unproductive afternoon he would have to work all weekend.

A group was waiting for the lift, Maureen among them. Not wanting to have to face their questions he made a detour towards the stairs, descending them two at a time and hurrying out onto the rain-soaked street.

'Tom!'

Turning, he saw Stuart.

He tried to mask his shock. 'What are you doing here?'

'I've come to see you.'

'You should have called first.'

'I have been! I've left loads of messages. Why haven't you answered them?'

The front door opened. Maureen and her group appeared. He felt trapped. 'I've been busy,' he said, wiping raindrops from his face.

'You still could have called. What's going on?'

'Nothing.'

'If there's a problem then tell me and we can talk about it.'

'There isn't a problem.'

'Then why are you acting like there is?'

'I'm not acting like anything.' He exhaled. 'You shouldn't have just turned up like this.'

'Why not? It's what brothers do. We are still brothers, aren't we?'

'Of course we are.'

'Then why are you acting as if you're ashamed of me?'

'I'm not! It's . . . well, it's complicated.'

'How is it complicated? We're twins. We're a team. That's what you said in Mauritius.' Stuart glared at him. 'Or was that just the drink talking?'

He shook his head. Out of the corner of his eye he saw Maureen approaching. His sense of being trapped increased.

'I'm not a toy you can discard. A twin is for life, not just for Christmas.'

'Am I interrupting something?' asked Maureen chirpily.

'Actually, we were just leaving.' Thomas turned to go.

Stuart grabbed his arm. 'Aren't you going to introduce me?'

Reluctantly, he did so. Maureen stared at Stuart. 'Wow. You really are identical.'

Stuart beamed. He forced himself to do likewise.

'We're going for a drink,' Maureen told them. 'Would you like to join us?'

He opened his mouth to refuse.

Only for Stuart to beat him to it.

'We'd love to,' he said firmly. 'Wouldn't we, Tom?'

TWENTY-ONE

'I can't believe it,' said Becky eventually.

They stood together in a crowded wine bar. As he had told her about Stuart her eyes kept darting over his shoulder. At first he thought she was looking for an escape route. Only now did he realise she was checking for a table.

'We've got one,' she said suddenly. 'Let's grab it before someone else does.'

It was in the corner. As they hurried towards it he noticed another couple with the same idea winning the race. Quickly, he hurled his coat over their heads to land on one of the available chairs. Scowling, the other couple backed away.

They sat down. 'I want to say I'm sorry,' she told him, 'but it sounds so trite.'

'You don't have to say anything. I just wanted you to know.'

'Tom must be devastated.'

'You'd think so, wouldn't you?'

Her eyes widened. 'He can't be pleased. You were his life-support system. He depended on you.'

'And he hated me because of it. I always knew that, but never in my wildest dreams did I guess how much. All I ever was to him was unwanted competition. With Stuart in the picture he had the chance to eliminate me and he took it.'

'What do your parents say about it?'

'They don't say anything to me. Not any more.'

She looked confused. He told her how things had ended. His hand rested on the table between them. As he finished speaking she reached out and covered it with her own. An electric charge ran through him. He watched her, sensing her feel it too.

Quickly, she pulled her hand away.

'Why?' he asked.

'Hospitals make mistakes. It happens.'

'That's not what I'm talking about.'

He saw her swallow. 'I know.'

'So?'

'Don't . . .'

'But I want to know. I *need* to know. We had something amazing. You said so yourself just before I went to New York on that business trip and when I come back a week later I find a note telling me it's over and you won't even take my calls. One minute I'm your soulmate and the next you're running from me like I've got the plague. What did I do wrong?'

She didn't answer.

'Why won't you tell me?'

'What good would it do? It's in the past, Jimmy. Can't we just leave it there?'

'I have a right to know.'

'I can't.'

'Why not?'

'Because I still care about you!'

Her words took him by surprise. 'What do you mean?'

Looking flustered, she rose to her feet.

'Yes, run away. Ditch me like the rest of them.' Anger

consumed him. 'I'd have done anything to make you happy. You're the one person outside my family I've ever truly loved. I did everything I could to make them happy too and what do I get in return? The one time I really need them they all kick me into touch. Why should I expect anything better from you?'

Her lip was trembling. She seemed close to tears.

'Just go,' he told her.

She remained where she was. He noticed the other couple eyeing the table. 'We're leaving,' he told them. 'It's all yours.'

'No, it's not,' said Becky suddenly.

Then she sat down again.

They stared at each other. He drummed his fingers on the table, longing for a cigarette.

'I want one too,' she said as if reading his mind.

'I thought you'd given up.'

'I will if you will.'

'We could be each other's sponsor at Nicotine Anonymous.'

She smiled. Reluctantly, he found himself smiling too.

'Do you remember the last time we came here?' she asked.

He nodded. 'It was the night before I went to New York.'

'It was crowded then too. You did the same trick with your coat to get us a table. You hit the chair from twenty feet. I was really impressed.'

'All those years playing cricket at school finally paid off.'

'I was really down that night. Do you remember that?'

'Yes. It was just after your stepfather died.'

'You never got to meet him. I wish you had. He was a wonderful man, a million times more of a father than my own ever was.' She sighed. 'I just need you to understand how I was feeling back then.'

He realised she was going to tell him. A multitude of emotions swept through him; relief, expectation. And suddenly, fear.

Again he saw her swallow. 'Try not to hate me too much ...'

Thomas stood at the bar of an Irish-themed pub, trying to make himself heard over the noise of a band playing off-key covers of the Cranberries.

Stuart appeared. 'We need another pint. Maureen's boyfriend has arrived.' He pulled out his wallet. 'Let's go halves.'

'I can afford it. I don't need your help.'

'Why are you being so grouchy?'

'Why did you have to drag me here?'

'Because I wanted to meet the people you work with. Is that a problem?'

He shook his head.

'Are you worried I'm going to show you up?'

'No, but ...'

'I may not have an Oxford degree like Saint Jimmy but I'm more than capable of holding a decent conversation.'

'It's nothing to do with that.'

Stuart looked sceptical.

'Maureen's a bitch. She's always trying to undermine me. She's somebody I don't want to be around any more than I have to be.'

The scepticism became sheepishness. 'I'm sorry. You should have said.'

'You didn't give me much chance.'

'She's probably jealous because she's not as good as you.' Suddenly Stuart grinned. 'Well, sod her. Nobody puts my brother down when I'm around.'

He forced himself to grin back while realising it was exactly the sort of thing James would have said.

The barman finished serving their order. Stuart continued to talk, most of his words lost in the thud of music. As Thomas paid for the drinks he noticed a girl at the other end of the bar watching the two of them. He smiled at her. She smiled back. He felt his self-assurance start to return.

They returned to their table. The band took a break, making conversation much easier. Maureen introduced her boyfriend: a self-satisfied City trader called Paul who began bragging about the likely size of his annual bonus. Thomas's other colleagues excused themselves. He watched them go, wishing he and Stuart could follow suit.

'What will you spend your bonus on?' Stuart asked Paul.

'Rent, probably. I'm buying a flat in a new development in Canary Wharf but it's not ready for another six months and my lease is about to run out.'

'Maybe Stuart could help,' suggested Maureen. 'He works in lettings.'

'What area?' Paul asked.

'Barnet, Southgate and Enfield,' Stuart told him.

Paul looked disdainful. 'I wouldn't want to live anywhere like that.'

Stuart looked amused. 'Well, that's me told.'

'That was rude,' Maureen told Paul.

'I'm just being honest.'

'Well, I think it was rude.' Maureen turned to Thomas. 'Don't you agree?'

'I don't know.'

'He's insulting your brother. Doesn't that bother you?'

'No.' He felt embarrassed. 'I mean ...'

'It doesn't bother me,' said Stuart quickly. 'So why should it bother Tom?'

'I'm glad to hear it,' Maureen told Stuart. 'I really like your suit, by the way.'

'Thanks.'

'You have much better taste than Tom.'

'Actually our father chose it,' Thomas informed her.

'Well, it was nice of him to help you,' Maureen said to Stuart. 'But then it's only fair. After all, he helped Thomas get his job.'

Again Thomas felt embarrassed. 'He didn't help me get my job.'

'That's not what I heard.'

'Well, you heard wrong.'

'Everyone in the firm's heard it.'

'Why would Tom need help?' demanded Stuart. 'He could land any job he wanted.'

Maureen didn't answer. She just looked amused.

'You're lucky,' Paul told Thomas. 'We don't all have well-connected parents to open doors for us.'

'Or help us get into Oxford,' added Maureen. 'Actually no, I'm wrong there. You didn't go to Oxford, did you, Tom?'

'He never applied,' Stuart told her.

Again Maureen looked amused. Thomas's embarrassment increased. He tried not to squirm in his seat.

'In spite of what you might think,' Stuart continued.

'I stand corrected. After all, you've known Tom so much longer than I have.'

'No, I haven't,' said Stuart calmly. 'And that was my loss. But one thing's for sure; I know him a lot better than you do. He didn't want to go to Oxford.'

Paul snorted. 'Everyone wants to go to Oxford or Cambridge. Anyone who says they don't is just trying to save face.'

It was Stuart's turn to look amused. 'I can't see why. Everyone I've ever met who went to either place has been a self-satisfied jerk.'

'Actually, Paul went to Cambridge,' Maureen told him.

'I rest my case.'

Paul's jaw dropped. Even Maureen looked startled. Stuart took a mouthful of beer, wiped his mouth and rose to his feet. 'Well, it's been fun meeting you both. Paul, try not to go too crazy with your bonus. Mind you, how crazy can you go on fifty quid?'

Thomas followed Stuart to another table. 'You shouldn't have said that to Paul.'

'He asked for it. Anyway, what do you expect me to do? Just sit there while they take shots at you? I see what you mean about Maureen, by the way. She probably failed to get into Oxford herself and is still sore about it. That's why she's digging at you. She can't stand the fact that you would have walked in but just couldn't be bothered to do so.'

He nodded. Stuart gave his arm an affectionate punch.

And suddenly he understood what was going on.

You know I failed the exam. You know I wanted to go there more than anything.

Just like you know I wouldn't have my job if it wasn't for Dad.

You're trying to protect me.

Just like Jimmy did.

He felt nauseous.

'Your glass is empty,' said Stuart. 'I'll get us some refills.'

'I don't want to stay here.'

'We have to. Don't give them the satisfaction of thinking they've got to you. Anyway, forget them. I'll get the drinks and then I'll tell you my business idea. I think you're going to like it.'

Stuart headed off to the door. Thomas remained where he was.

The feeling of nausea remained too.

*

'I could never hate you,' James told Becky.

'It's easy to say that.'

'Only when it's true.'

She fiddled with a lock of hair. It was something she always did when she was nervous. He fought an urge to reach out and stop her. He didn't want her to be anxious. Suddenly he wasn't frightened any more. He just wanted to know.

Because when he did he could forgive her.

And then, just maybe, they could get back together.

She sipped her drink. 'I wasn't just upset about my stepfather that night. I'd been going for a promotion at work and I hadn't got it. I was really disappointed.'

'I remember. I told you it was their mistake.'

'You were really sweet about it. You said all the right things.'

'I meant every word.'

'But I still felt bad. You were doing so well. I felt like I was letting you down.'

'You weren't. How could you ever think that?'

'Because my head was a mess, Jimmy. I need you to understand that.'

'I do.'

'My stepfather's funeral was two days after you flew to New York. I'd had to organise everything. My mother couldn't. She'd just taken his death as another excuse to fall apart. In her eyes my stepfather's death was her tragedy, not mine. I used to envy you your relationship with your mother. You could tell her things. She'd listen to you. To my mother I was only ever someone who threatened to steal her spotlight.'

He remembered the last time he and his mother had spoken. A terrible sense of loss swept over him. He missed her presence in his life. Not as much as he missed Thomas's, but it was close.

Becky was watching him anxiously. Clearly, she could sense what he was thinking. Her concern gave him a warm feeling inside, together with the belief that once the truth was out in the open they really could start again.

'I'm fine,' he told her. 'This isn't about me.'

'Are you sure?'

He smiled. 'Yes.'

She smiled back, only the gesture missed her eyes. Her nervousness remained.

But soon he would banish it for ever.

'I was dreading the funeral. I wanted you to be there but you couldn't.'

'I wanted to be.'

'I'm not blaming you. I was the one who insisted you didn't cancel your trip. I knew it was important. And I knew you wouldn't be gone that long.

'The day before the funeral your mother called. You'd told her about my stepfather and she wanted to check I was all right. I was touched. I'd never felt comfortable with her before. She'd always been friendly but I sensed she resented me. But on the phone she was so sweet. She talked about how upset she'd been when her own father died. And she also said she knew you couldn't come to the funeral and that she hated to think of me going alone. So she offered to come in your place.'

He was taken aback. 'She never told me that. So did she go with you?'

'Yes. I was driving up to Shropshire so your mother suggested I stop by your parents' house so I could pick her up and we could go together.'

'And was she OK with you?'

'She was lovely. She sat next to me in the church and stood beside me by the graveside. She even held my hand. My mother was being unbearable while yours was totally supportive.'

He nodded, masking his surprise so as not to disturb her flow.

'The funeral was in the morning. We had a wake in the early afternoon and then I drove your mother home. We stopped for coffee at a service station on the way. I'd held it together all day but while we were sitting there I started to cry. Your mother gave me a hug. She let me talk. She did all the things my mother would never have done. I was so grateful. I can't tell you how much.

'She said she didn't want me to drive back to London on my own. I should spend the night at your parents' house and then drive back the following morning. I was feeling wiped out so I agreed.'

'Your dad wasn't there when we got back. He was spending the day in London. It was just after he retired and he was doing freelance work for his old firm. Your mum said that after what I'd been through I needed a drink and opened a bottle of wine. She didn't have any herself. She said she was battling a cold and was on antibiotics. But she made me drink. She said it would do me good. And it did. At first, anyway.'

'At first?'

'Are you sure you want to hear this?'

'Yes.'

Again she touched his hand. This time he felt no spark. A sudden sense of alarm dulled his senses to anything else.

'Your dad came back. I was pleased to see him. He'd always been nice to me. Whenever we visited your parents he used to go out of his way to make me feel welcome. He'd ask about work and how I was getting on. He always seemed interested. I liked that.

'He came and sat with us. At first we talked about my step-father but then your mother started talking about you. She was saying how well you were doing. How important the New York trip was. How it was just the start of even bigger things and that the sky was the limit where your career was concerned. She was so proud of you. I wanted to be proud too but instead I felt scared. You seemed so out of my league and if we stayed together I'd just be holding you back.'

He felt indignant. 'But that's rubbish. You know it is.'

'I do now. But at the time ...' She sighed. 'I was tired and vulnerable, and I'd had a bit to drink.'

'And?'

'Your aunt phoned. Apparently your mother had arranged to spend the evening at hers. They were going to watch some DVD. What with the funeral your mother had forgotten. She wanted to cancel but your father said your aunt was looking forward to it and that he could keep me company while she was gone. So off she went.

'Your dad and I shared another bottle of wine. He was being so kind. He said he could tell that your mother's comments about you had bothered me and that I was wrong to feel that way.' She swallowed. 'He said that if you didn't realise how lucky you were then you were the biggest fool in the world.'

James's heart had started to race. He took a deep breath, trying to slow it while telling himself that he could cope with whatever she had to tell him.

'We were sitting together on the sofa. He put his arm around me. He made me feel safe, just like my stepfather had. He kept saying how lucky you were, how lucky any guy would be who was with me. He asked if I wanted to know a secret and when I said yes he told me that secretly he envied you. That when he was your age no girl as attractive as me would have looked at him twice. I told him that was nonsense. That he was a very handsome man. He said I was just being kind and I told him I wasn't. And then he kissed me.'

James's stomach turned over.

'At first it didn't feel wrong. I was very drunk by then and it all seemed . . . ' She shook her head. 'I don't know. It didn't seem sexual. That was the thing. It was just his way of being kind. And then I realised he was undoing my blouse.'

She stopped.

'Go on,' he demanded.

'I didn't try to stop him. I was too shocked. But then he tried to put his hand up my skirt. I said no but he said it was OK. We weren't hurting anyone. It could be our secret. Again I said no but he ignored me. He pushed me down and moved on top of me and suddenly all the warmth had gone out of his face. His eyes were bestial. It was as if I'd stopped being a person and was just an object he was going to use. I kept telling myself to fight but I couldn't. I was so frightened. And then . . . '

'He *raped* you?'

'Yes. Only I don't think he saw it like that. That's the terrible thing. All the time he kept telling me how much I was enjoying it. I think he genuinely believed I was. He was drunk too, remember. And when it was over he climbed off the sofa, looked down at me and do you know what he said?'

'What?'

'Now tell me I wasn't better than my son.'

He opened his mouth but no words came out.

'I didn't answer, so he asked me again. He kept asking. He

had this edge to his voice. He kept on and on until I said yes and when I did he looked triumphant.

'I said I wanted to leave. He told me I couldn't drive in the state I was in. Instead he suggested I go and have a bath. That's what I did. I was too scared not to. When I came out of the bathroom he was waiting on the landing with a cup of coffee. He told me to drink it, and as I did he said that what had happened was our secret. That he wasn't going to tell anyone and that I wasn't to either. I promised I wouldn't. Then he kissed me on the cheek and told me to go to bed.

'I didn't sleep a wink that night. At one point I heard your mother return. I was terrified she was going to come and say goodnight so I locked my door. But she didn't. I guess your dad had told her I was asleep.

'The next morning I got up really early. I wanted to sneak away but I bumped into your mother who said she was making breakfast and that I couldn't leave without some food inside me. She was so sweet to me, just like she'd been at the funeral.' Again Becky stopped, looking suddenly close to tears. 'And I felt so ashamed.'

He wanted to tell her it was all right. That she had nothing to feel ashamed of. He wanted to hold her.

Except that he didn't. Not any more.

'Your father joined us. He started chatting to your mother about some drinks party they were going to that evening. He was acting so normal yet when your mother was busy he kept giving me this meaningful look, like he was warning me to keep my mouth shut. At one point I nodded and he smiled.

'And then I left. I had to stop twice on the motorway to be sick. When I got home I just went to bed and stayed there for the rest of the day.'

She had started to shake. Again he wanted to hold her. Again he found he couldn't. In his head was an image of his father expressing sympathy over Becky breaking up with him. For the first time in his life he knew what it was to truly wish someone dead.

'I'm so sorry,' he managed to say. 'I am *so* sorry . . .'

'That's not the worst part,' she told him.

'Jesus Christ, what could be worse than that?'

'What happened next.'

He had to know, yet couldn't bring himself to ask. In the end he didn't have to.

'Two days later your mother came to see me. I was at work. She just turned up, saying she was passing and asking if we could have lunch. I wanted to say no but it would have looked strange so I had to say yes.

'We went to a bistro. The waiter took our order. Your mother was being just as lovely as she'd been on the day of the funeral.

'And then, when the waiter had gone, she leaned forward and said, "I know you slept with my husband."

'At first I was so shocked I couldn't speak. Then she said that your dad had told her all about it as soon as I left the house, and I blurted out, "But he said he wouldn't tell anyone." Then she reached inside her handbag. She'd kept it open on top of the table. I thought it was strange, but then she pulled out her mobile and switched off the record function . . .

'And that's when I knew she'd planned the whole thing: coming to the funeral, taking me back to the house, talking about you in a way that was going to make both your dad and me feel insecure, plying us both with alcohol and then leaving us alone together.

401

'I told her that he'd forced me. She just laughed. "Who's going to believe that?" she asked. "I've seen the way you flirt with him." I told her that was a lie but she said it didn't matter. That's what she'd tell the police. That it would be my word against theirs and that I wouldn't have a leg to stand on in court.

'I started to cry. I asked her why she was doing this to me. She said she knew I wanted to take you away from her and told me I had to break up with you. That way you'd never need to know what had happened. And if I didn't she'd tell you herself and play you the recording. "Maybe he'll believe it was rape," she told me, "but it won't change anything. Once he knows he'll never want to touch you again."'

James felt a chill run through him.

'I said I'd tell you she'd orchestrated it and again she laughed and said that she knew you far better than I did. That you might believe the worst about your father but you'd never believe it about her. How could you? She said that the mother–son bond was the most powerful bond in the world; that you loved her more than anyone and no one, least of all me, was ever going to take you away from her.

'I never would have told you but now I have to. You're breaking your heart over losing your parents when you're lucky to be free of them. I'm sorry you've lost Tom. That *is* a tragedy. But losing your parents is a blessing.'

His vision blurred. He could feel his brain bulging inside his head, trying to absorb what she was telling him.

But it couldn't. There just wasn't room.

'I don't believe you,' he said.

'But it's true. Your dad . . .'

'I don't mean about my dad. I can believe he's capable of what you say. But my mother isn't. She wouldn't do that to me. She knew how much I loved you. She just wouldn't.'

'I'm not lying . . .'

'You bloody are.' He began to shout. 'You're sick! You have to be to make something like this up.'

She burst into tears, trying to reach for his hand. He pulled away.

'You see?' she cried. 'Your mother was right. You can't bear to touch me.'

'I wish I'd never met you. To think of all the months I spent dreaming about you, wishing we were still together. Well, not any more!'

Rising to his feet, he marched out of the bar.

Tom sipped his drink and listened to Stuart talk.

'You and I in business together could be great. Dad said he's got loads of contacts, I know my way around the property market and you know your way around finance. We'd be a great team, Tom. Don't you think so?'

He didn't answer. He had noticed something.

'Don't you?' Stuart asked again.

'Why are you talking with that accent? Why are you trying to sound like me?'

'Because it's easier if we sound the same.'

'*Easier?*'

'We don't have to make up stories about our parents splitting us up as kids. People aren't going to question us being twins. They'll just accept it.'

'Is that why you're dressing like me too? Is that why you're doing all this exercise?'

'Well, yes. It makes sense, doesn't it? Anyway, back to my idea . . .'

'But you can't. This is my identity we're talking about.'

Stuart looked amused. 'Tom, don't be daft. This isn't

Invasion of the Body Snatchers. I'm not trying to be you. I'm just trying to be *like* you.'

'Yes, but ...'

'I don't see what the problem is. It's only superficial appearance stuff. I don't mean it as a threat. I could never threaten you. You're much brighter than me. I could never do your job but you could do mine standing on your head.'

He told himself Stuart was right. That he was just being paranoid.

Then he noticed something else.

The sleeves of Stuart's jacket had slid up, revealing his shirt cuffs.

And a pair of diamond-shaped cufflinks.

Just like the ones he had seen in the catalogue the previous weekend.

'Where did you get those?'

'Mum gave them to me. We had lunch yesterday.'

'Why?'

'Because she knew I was trying to smarten up my image and wanted to help.'

'No. Why did you have lunch?'

'She wanted to see where I work.'

'So she actually came and saw your office?'

'Well, of course.' Stuart laughed. 'Not that there's much to see: three desks, a couple of computers and a coffee machine.'

'Why didn't you tell me you'd had lunch with her?'

'I would have done if you'd taken my calls. By the way, I had to bite the bullet and tell my colleagues about our situation. They're all dying to meet you ...'

'What did you talk about?'

Stuart stopped laughing. 'Not this again.'

'What?'

'You asked me this when I told you I'd had lunch with Dad.'

'So?'

'So what does it matter? God, Tom, it was only lunch. You must have had lunch with her dozens of times.'

Not me. Jimmy. Always Jimmy. I was just the afterthought. Just like I would have been if you'd cancelled at the last minute.

'I need the gents,' he said quickly.

Stuart began to look concerned. 'Tom, what are you worried about? Do you think I spent the meal bad-mouthing you? Because I wouldn't. Not to anyone.'

Just as Jimmy wouldn't. Whatever Mum and Dad said about me he'd always fight my corner.

Is that what you did too? Tried to convince them I was worth noticing?

Stuart continued to speak. He turned and walked away.

The toilets were near the entrance. On his way there he passed the bar. The girl who had stared at him earlier was there again. Their eyes locked. Desperate for anything that would make him feel better he stopped to speak to her, flirting for all he was worth.

She flirted back. Only her heart wasn't in it. Ever so often she would cast longing glances over his shoulder at the table where Stuart still sat.

'What's the problem?' he demanded. 'Aren't I good enough for you?'

'No, it's not that . . .'

'But you'd rather be with my brother. That's the story of my fucking life. People would always rather be with my brother.'

She opened her mouth to protest. Shaking his head, he walked away.

Paul and Maureen stood near the toilets. Maureen was

saying something to Paul, who started laughing. Though neither appeared to have spotted him he knew he was the butt of their joke.

He marched up to them. 'What's so funny?'

Both looked startled. 'Nothing,' said Paul.

'If you've got something to say then say it to my face.'

Maureen looked exasperated. 'Sod off, Tom. You're drunk.'

'And you're a bitch.'

Paul's face darkened. 'You've got two seconds to apologise.'

'Really? One. Two. Screw you.'

Paul grabbed him round the neck. He was built like a rugby player and his arm was like a vice. He began to bang on Thomas's head with his knuckles. 'So you think you're a hard man, do you? Maureen's right about you. You really are a total loser.'

He struggled, his head aching, while hearing sniggering all around him.

'Leave him alone!'

He looked up. A furious-looking Stuart stood in front of them.

'Your arsehole brother just called my girlfriend a bitch.'

'Well, that's Tom's problem. He's always been truthful. And while we're on the subject of arseholes, there's only one here and I'm staring straight at him.'

Thomas felt the banging on his head stop. 'Are you trying to mess with me?' demanded Paul.

'Looks that way, doesn't it? What are you going to do? Start talking about your bonus in the hope I'll drown in your endless stream of macho bullshit?'

The sniggering continued. Only now Paul was the object of derision. Thomas felt the grip release. He stood up, backing away from Paul while seeing Stuart immediately position himself between them.

Just like James when he had got into a confrontation with someone at the gym.

Coming to his rescue, just as James had done.

Drawing admiring glances, just as James had done.

And he couldn't stand it. Pushing past people, he hurried out into the street.

Stuart ran after him, calling his name and eventually grabbing his arm. He tried to pull away. 'Let me go! It was my fight. Why did you have to get involved?'

'Because you were in trouble. He was going to hurt you.'

'You should have let him.'

'Are you crazy? I'd never let anyone hurt you. You're my twin. I love you.'

'And so did Jimmy.'

Stuart stared at him. 'What does Jimmy have to do with it? He's gone.'

'No, he's not! Don't you see? I thought he was but I was wrong. He's like some sort of Hydra. I cut his head off and now yours has grown back in its place.'

'Tom, I don't understand . . .'

'This wasn't supposed to happen! I didn't bring you into my life for you to do this to me! This was going to be *my* time. I was going to be the star. I was going to be the one that mattered to Mum and Dad.'

'But you do matter.'

'But not as much as you! You've only been on the scene five minutes and already it's like living with Jimmy all over again. You're the one they want to be with. I'm the one they want to avoid.'

'This is stupid. I'm not Jimmy. I'm nothing like him.'

'And that's the point. Jimmy was a star. I could never compete with him. But I could compete with you. You were just a poor imitation of me. That's the only reason I got in contact with you. That's why I brought you into the family. Christ, why couldn't you have just stayed that?'

He saw Stuart grow pale. For a moment Tom's self-hatred was so intense he wanted the ground to open and swallow him. But he couldn't give in to it. To do so would be only to admit what a colossal failure he really was.

'Well?' he demanded. 'Aren't you going to say something?'

'Jen was right. She said you were using me. I should have believed her but I believed you instead. I'd have believed anything you told me.' Stuart shook his head, looking dazed. 'God, I was so happy we'd found each other. I had a twin. It's the ultimate bond. Two halves of the same whole. I drove her away because I was scared she was going to spoil it.'

'More fool you.'

'So what do you want, Tom? For me to disappear like Jimmy did?'

'Yes. That's exactly what I want.'

'Well, fuck you!'

Suddenly Stuart grabbed him by the shoulders and stared into his face.

'I'm James Randall. The *real* one. Your parents are *my* parents and I'm not going anywhere. You're stuck with me, brother, only I'm in the driving seat now. You really want to know what Mum said about you over lunch? She said you were a joke. She said she was embarrassed by you. I stuck up for you, of course. I told her she was wrong. Only next time, and believe me there *will* be a next time, I'm going to tell her she's right. I'm going to do the same with Dad too.'

'You can't do that to me!'

'Watch me. You thought you could play God with my life. Now I'm going to do it with yours. I'm going to drive you out of the family, Tom, just like you did to Jimmy, and there is *nothing* you can do about it.'

Tom couldn't control himself. He swung at Stuart.

Only for Stuart to block the blow then swing back, punching him hard in the mouth, causing him to lose his balance and fall.

Stuart marched away. Tom sat sprawled on the ground, wiping his mouth and watching drops of blood mingle with the rain.

James stormed out of the wine bar and down the street.

As he turned the corner he collided with another man. The man cursed, calling him a moron. He opened his mouth to say the same.

And saw it was Stuart.

They stared at each other. Again he felt the urge to kill.

And as he stared into Stuart's eyes he knew the feeling was mutual.

For a moment they remained like that.

Then, turning, both hurried away.

TWENTY-TWO

An hour later Stuart returned home.

He opened his door to be greeted by the sound of music pounding overhead. He felt the familiar rush of irritation before telling himself it didn't matter. His father had already offered to help him buy somewhere better. At the time he had declined the offer but now he was going to take it. His father had also offered to help him find a better job and he was going to take that too.

Perhaps he could find a flat in Thomas's street. Perhaps he could even find one in Thomas's building. That would be perfect. That way Thomas would be forced every day to watch the twin he had tried to discard outshine him at every turn.

Because that was what Thomas deserved. After such a betrayal there could be no forgiveness. When his uncle had forced him into foster care he had thought he understood what betrayal really meant. Now he knew he had been mistaken.

As he pushed his door shut he noticed an envelope lying on the floor. It looked official. Though it could wait until the morning, his curiosity was piqued.

So he opened it.

It was a letter from the lawyers handling his grandmother's estate. Not that there was any estate to speak of. Just the odds and ends she had had with her at the home and which were now stored in his living room.

Or so he had thought.

But the letter mentioned another, written by his grandmother a few years earlier before her memory started to fade, which she had instructed them to forward only after she was dead.

He reached inside the envelope and found a smaller one with his name upon it. He recognised his grandmother's writing. Sitting down on the sofa in the living room, he tore it open and began to read:

Dear Stuart,

This isn't an easy letter for me to write. A part of me doesn't want to write it at all. It's true what they say; what we don't know can't hurt us. But sometimes, in spite of the pain, we can feel grateful for having been told.

Do you remember when you were ten years old and your parents took you and your sister to London? It was the first time you'd ever been there. Your father took the two of you to the National Gallery. You bought me back a beautiful print of Gainsborough's The Morning Walk as a present. Gainsborough has always been my favourite painter. You and your father hung it in my living room for me. Do you remember that?

Your mother wasn't with you at the gallery. She wanted to take you and your sister for tea at the Savoy just as her parents had taken her when she was a girl. She had gone on ahead to reserve a table ...

The tea room wasn't as crowded as Mary Godwin had feared. As the waiter showed her to her seat she counted nearly half a dozen empty tables. She smiled to herself, remembering how her husband John teased her for being a worrier. As always he was right.

The waiter offered her a menu. She explained that her family would be joining her shortly. To pass the time she looked about her, thinking how much smaller it was than she remembered, before recalling that she had only been eight years old at the time.

An elderly couple sat at the next table, both expensively dressed. The woman smiled and asked if she was from London. She explained that she was from Sutton Coldfield. 'My family and I are just visiting for the day.'

'So are we,' the woman told her. 'We're from Oxfordshire.'

'That's a lovely part of the world. Are you here sightseeing?'

'If only,' said the man ruefully.

'It's a half-term treat for our grandsons,' the woman explained. 'We were planning to take them to a museum but all they want is to go to Leicester Square and see some action film.' Again the woman smiled. 'They're a pair of Philistines.'

'My son is the same. He's at the National Gallery with my husband and daughter but I'm sure he'd rather be at the cinema too.'

'How old is your son?' asked the man.

'He's ten.'

The woman beamed. 'The same age as our grandsons.'

'They're *both* ten?'

Noticing something, the woman began to wave. Following her gaze Mary saw a handsome blond boy stride across the room towards them. For a moment she was sure she knew him before realising he bore a striking resemblance to her nephew, Adam, except older, better looking and with a much warmer expression. As he approached she gave him a smile and received a lovely one in return.

'This is Jimmy,' said the woman. 'Jimmy, this is ... I'm sorry, dear, I don't know your name.'

'It's Mary. Mary Godwin.'

Jimmy offered her his hand. 'Hello, Mrs Godwin.'

'Hello, Jimmy. I'm pleased to meet you.'

'Where's Tom?' asked the man.

'Still in the cloakroom,' Jimmy told him. 'He's being a real tart. He's trying on all the aftershaves.'

The man laughed. 'Jimmy, don't call your brother a tart,' said the woman.

'Well, he is! He's going to stink.'

'He's not the only one.' The woman grimaced. 'Oh, Jimmy, how much of that stuff are you wearing?'

'Loads. They were giving it out free.' Jimmy grinned at Mary.

'I gather you and your brother are both ten,' she said.

He nodded. 'We're twins.'

'How wonderful. My son Stuart is ten too. When is your birthday?'

'New Year's Eve.'

'Good heavens! That's Stuart's birthday too.'

'Well, what a coincidence,' the woman exclaimed. 'Funnily enough, the boys were born in your neck of the woods. In Birmingham, actually.'

'Really? Which hospital?'

'The Willows. I think that's what it was called.' The woman thought for a moment. 'Yes, I'm sure it was.'

Mary was about to tell her that Stuart had been born there

413

too when the very person entered the room. She opened her mouth to call out a greeting.

And saw that he wasn't wearing the same clothes as he had been an hour ago.

And that his hair was shorter.

And that he was waving not at her but at the elderly couple.

'There's Tom now,' said the woman.

She blinked, as if trying to correct her vision.

But when she opened her eyes it was still Stuart that she saw.

Suddenly she was back in the maternity ward, waiting for Stuart to be born. Her labour had started prematurely and she had been frightened for his safety. She remembered a nurse telling her there was nothing to be worried about, that her new baby would be fine. 'There's a woman down the corridor having twins,' she had been told. 'Now that's where the problems can lie. They'll be the first set of twins born here in months so it's a red letter day for us.'

Her heart stopped. For a moment she couldn't breathe. The boy Tom was talking about the film he had just seen. He had Stuart's voice, but not his accent. He had some of Stuart's gestures yet did them differently. Momentarily, he turned and stared at her. His eyes were blank, as if looking at a stranger.

Which of course he was.

The air came rushing back. She gave a gasp. Tom and his grandparents didn't notice. But Jimmy did. He gave her an anxious look. This handsome stranger who looked like her nephew's older brother.

She turned back to Tom, desperate to believe this was just some chance resemblance but unable to do so. He and Stuart were clones of each other. They were identical.

Identical twins.

The hospital must have mixed them up. That was the only possible explanation. And that meant . . .

That Jimmy could be hers.

Was hers.

The shock was too great. She couldn't take it in.

All she could do was leave.

As she crossed the room she heard the woman call out but just kept going.

She reached the entrance of the hotel and rested her head against the door. Through it she could see men in uniform helping people in and out of taxis. It all looked so normal. Only it wasn't. For her nothing would ever be normal again.

'Excuse me, Mrs Godwin.'

Jimmy stood in front of her, holding her handbag. 'You forgot this,' he told her.

She took it from him. He turned to leave. She told herself to let him go. If she couldn't see him she could try and pretend he didn't exist.

But she couldn't. Not like that. Not without knowing . . .

'Jimmy.'

He turned back.

'What's your name? Your surname, I mean?'

'Randall.'

'It's a nice name.'

'Thanks. Godwin's nice too.'

'Do you really think so?'

'Yes.'

'I'm glad. Is it nice being a twin?'

He rolled his eyes.

She felt alarmed. 'You don't like it?'

'No, it's fun. You've always got someone to play with.'

'Like a best friend?'

'Yeah.'

'What are you parents like? Are they nice?'

'Yes. Well, Mum is. Dad is too but he's always working. He's a lawyer.'

'Do you want to be a lawyer when you grow up?'

'Dad wants me to.'

'But what about you? What do you want?'

'I dunno.' He glanced towards the tea room. 'I'd better go.'

Again she told herself to let him go. Again she found she couldn't.

'Do you like your life, Jimmy? Are you happy being you?'

He laughed.

'Are you?'

'Yes I am.'

'I'm glad. Goodbye, Jimmy. It's been a privilege to meet you. It really has.'

For a moment he just stared at her.

Then, suddenly, he leaned forward and kissed her on the cheek.

'Goodbye,' he said, then ran back to the tea room.

She walked out into the concourse, heading towards the street. She kept waiting for the tears but they didn't come. Instead she just felt numb.

As she reached the street she saw her husband standing on the corner. Her legs threatened to collapse beneath her. She couldn't bear to see Stuart. Not after what she now knew.

Her husband ran towards her. He looked upset. She tried to pull herself together. She couldn't have him asking questions. He adored Stuart, just as she did. The truth would kill him, just as it was killing her.

'Stuart's gone missing,' he told her.

She nodded, telling herself that she was going to be strong. That she was not going to fall to pieces ...

And then reality kicked in.

'He's *what*?'

'He was with us in the gallery and then he just disappeared. We looked all over for him.'

Again her heart stopped. Again she felt as if she couldn't breathe.

'We looked everywhere,' her daughter Samantha told her, on the point of tears. 'Mum, I'm scared.'

'It's all right, darling. It's going to be all right. It's going ...' A series of horrific images flooded her brain. Stuart in the back of a car screaming for her. Stuart being molested. Stuart being dead ...

'He just disappeared,' her husband told her again.

'He can't have just disappeared, you stupid man! Someone's taken him.' She turned on her husband, pounding his chest with her fists. 'God, what were you thinking? How could you let him out of your sight? How could you let this happen?'

'Mum!' It was Samantha again. 'There he is!'

Stuart was marching up the street towards them, eating a hot dog and with his trademark impish grin plastered across his face. Letting out a cry of relief, she ran towards him.

'Hi, Mum. I've been in Trafalgar Square. One of the pigeons pooed on a Japanese tourist. They nearly pooed on me ...'

'How could you just wander off like that?' she screamed. 'Do you know how frightened we've been? Do you?'

He opened his mouth to speak. She slapped his face. He dropped his hot dog and burst into tears.

And suddenly she felt it. The most powerful emotion known to man: the all-consuming rush of maternal love.

Wrapping her arms around him, she covered his face in

kisses, telling him she was sorry, that she had only hit him because she had been frightened, making him promise that he would never ever wander off again, while raising a silent prayer of thanks to every God in creation.

Because she had him back. Her Stuart. Her baby. The son she would gladly die for.

The only son she would ever want . . .

. . . at first your mother vowed she would never tell anyone. But eventually she realised that your father had a right to know. She told him six months later, when you and Samantha were on a school camping trip. She wanted him to have time to come to terms with the news. Which he did. It didn't change anything for him. You must believe that. He loved you just as much as he ever did. You were always his son, just as you were always hers. And just as you were always my grandson too.

I know I should have told you when they died. I want to say I didn't because I was frightened the truth would confuse you, only I'd be lying. I kept silent because I was weak and selfish. You were the only family I had left and I couldn't bear the thought of losing you too.

Your real family are called Randall. They live in Oxfordshire. Your twin is called Tom and the boy they took instead of you is called Jimmy which I imagine is short for James. I know it's not much but it's enough. You could find them if you wanted. I'm sure you could.

If you're reading this then I'm now dead. I want to thank you for being the best grandson any woman could ever have. When your family died I thought I'd never get over it but I did and it was all down to you. You gave me the strength to keep on going. That's something your mother always said about you. That you had far more strength inside you than you ever realised. I think you're going to need it more than ever to cope with this, but I know you'll find it, just as you always do.

Be happy my darling. God bless you. Try not to judge me too harshly.

All my love for ever.

Gran.

For a long time after he had finished reading, Stuart just stared at the letter, watching the words blur in front of his eyes.

She knew. All this time she knew!

He couldn't control it. Hatred for his grandmother surged through him. How could she have kept the truth from him for so many years? If she'd only had the courage to be honest he could have avoided foster care. He could have reclaimed his identity while still in his early teens. He could have finished growing up in a luxurious home. He could have had a first-class education. The world could have been his oyster. He could have been anything he wanted.

She had stolen all that from him.

And he would never forgive her.

On the table beside him was a framed photograph of his family, taken when he was only three. He was sitting on his mother's knee while his sister sat on her father's, and his grandmother stood behind them. She was smiling at the camera. The hate became unbearable. Picking up the picture, he prepared to hurl it against the wall.

And saw his face reflected in the glass.

Only it wasn't his face. It belonged to someone else, someone no one in the photograph would have recognised.

Someone who had revelled in watching James being expelled from a family he had always believed was his. Someone who was planning to rule the world and enjoy watching Thomas suffer as he did it.

His parents and sister were smiling too. He could feel the love coming out of the frame. Had the mix-up at the hospital not happened he would never have known them. They would have been strangers he might pass in the street without a second look. It was hard to imagine, but it wouldn't have been hard to live with.

After all, how could he miss people he had never known?

Except that he would have missed them.

They had been his life. They still were. They knew the truth but it didn't change how they felt about him. How much they loved him.

Just as it didn't change how much he still loved them back. Even his grandmother.

Suddenly the hatred was gone. In its place was understanding.

Forgiveness.

Peace.

I am Stuart Godwin. That's not who I was born but that is who I am.

And I am grateful for that.

When he thought of what he was turning into he felt ashamed. Had his mother been there, she would have been ashamed too. The realisation hurt. Even though she was dead, her good opinion still mattered. The fact that she had not given birth to him did not change the fact that she would always be his mother.

And no one could ever take her place.

His knuckles were sore from when he had punched

Thomas. Again he felt ashamed, remembering the things he had said and wishing with all his heart that he could take them back. He didn't want to hurt Thomas. He didn't want to hurt anyone. All he wanted was to put things right.

With understanding came clarity.

And the knowledge of what he had to do.

TWENTY-THREE

Early the next morning James sat staring at a snapshot of Becky.

He had a whole pile of them. They had been hidden in the back of a drawer so Kate would never find them. He didn't want her to know they existed. It would have only caused her pain.

But now she was gone and he could look at them as much as he liked.

In the snapshot Becky was sitting in a café in Paris, frowning as he photographed her eating a croissant. 'You always take my picture when I'm eating,' she had said reprovingly. 'People will think I'm a complete hog.' He had laughed and told her that she looked beautiful, before promising not to show them to anyone.

And he was keeping his word. No one would ever see them.

He ripped the snapshot into pieces, adding it to the pile of ruined images that lay spread across his living room floor.

'Do you think he meant it?' Thomas asked Alice.

They were lying together in his bed, staring up at the ceiling. 'It sounds as if he did,' she told him.

'But he was angry. He may regret it now. It's possible, isn't it?'

She touched the bruise on his face. He winced.

'He shouldn't have done that,' she said.

'Perhaps he wishes he hadn't. Perhaps if I call him ...'

'You mustn't. If you do it's like saying you deserved it.'

'I did. I said some terrible things. He was just reacting to them.'

'You didn't deserve to be humiliated like that, especially not in front of someone you work with.'

'But Maureen wasn't there.'

'You said she was standing by the entrance of the bar.'

His heart sank.

'Besides,' she continued, 'if you call him you'll just be confirming what he already believes.'

'What do you mean?'

'He called you a joke. If you phone and apologise he'll think he was right.'

He shook his head. 'He never called me that. My mother did.'

'Why would your mother say that to him? She hardly knows him. I think he's only using her as a cover to express what he feels about you himself.'

He felt confused. 'I don't know ...'

'I'm sorry. It's none of my business. It's just that I care about you and hate seeing you feeling guilty over something that isn't your fault.'

'But it is my fault ...'

'And I don't want you to do anything that might make things worse.'

'I won't call him. You're right. I'll let him call me.'

She kissed his cheek. 'It'll be all right. You'll see. I'm here for you.'

He hugged her, grateful she was there.

*

Lunchtime.

Stuart ate a pub lunch with Pam.

He told her about the previous night. She listened in silence, just picking at her food. 'So what are you going to do?' she asked eventually.

'Stop trying to be a Randall. Gran's letter made me realise I'll always be a Godwin. And I'm fine with that.'

'So I'm never going to meet Tom, then?'

'I doubt it. All morning I've been hoping he'd phone and say he didn't mean any of that stuff about using me.' He sighed. 'But it looks as if he did.'

'You must hate him.'

He shook his head. 'I feel sorry for him, if you want to know the truth. It must be awful going through life feeling so unwanted. I was supposed to make things better for him but instead I just made them worse. And I don't want that. I want him to be happy. If my bowing out is what it takes then that's what I'm going to do.'

'How do you think Mr and Mrs Randall will take the news?'

'I'm sure they'll cope. Jen was right about Tom using me. She was probably right about them too.'

'I'm sorry.'

'So am I. About Tom, most of all. I've had parents before but I've never had a twin. In spite of everything if he was in trouble I'd still want to be there for him. The real tragedy is that I'm the last person he'd ever want.'

'Give it time,' she told him. 'Feelings aren't set in stone. His may change.'

'I hope so,' he said quietly.

'For what it's worth you've still got me.'

'I thought you were supposed to cheering me up.'

She threw a chip. It hit him on the nose.

'Ouch.'

'You deserve it.' Her tone became serious. 'Maybe you could have Jen too.'

'She's with someone else now.'

'You could call her. It's worth a try. She was special.'

'How do you know? You never met her.'

'I didn't need to. Seeing your face when you talked about her told me more than a dozen meetings ever could. Do it. Make the call.'

He didn't answer. In his head he was planning the other call he had to make.

Half an hour later a distraught Caroline argued with Stuart on the telephone.

'I don't want to hurt you,' he told her. 'It's just what I have to do. Reading the letter made me realise I'll always be a Godwin and that it's wrong for me to try and pretend to be someone else.'

'But you're not pretending!' she cried. 'You're my son. I'm your mother!'

'You're Jimmy's mother. He's your real son. My mother died when I was thirteen. I loved her and it's wrong to try and replace her, just as it's wrong to try and replace my father and sister.'

'But Jimmy isn't my son. Not any more. He's turned his back on me.'

'But Tom hasn't. He still loves you. He's a much better son to you than I could ever be.'

Her throat went dry. At that moment she knew.

This is Tom's fault. He's the one responsible. He's the one to blame.

'I'm sorry,' he was saying. 'And I'm really grateful for all you've done ...'

Unable to listen any more, she slammed down the receiver.

Then, desperate for someone to talk to, she reached for her car keys.

Helen stood in her driveway, helping Vanessa load a chair into the back of a van.

She heard the screeching of tyres. Peering round the van, she saw Caroline climbing out of her car.

'Carrie! What are you doing here?'

By way of answer Caroline burst into tears.

Ten minutes later the three of them sat at Helen's kitchen table. 'He can't just cut me out of his life,' Caroline was saying. 'I'm his mother.'

'I know you are,' said Helen soothingly, 'but you have to try and understand—'

'Tom's making him do this.'

'You don't know that.'

'Stuart as good as said so.'

'He said nothing of the sort,' said Vanessa sharply. 'You've just put two and two together and made fifty.'

Helen frowned at her daughter who responded with a dismissive shrug.

'Stuart can't do this to me,' Caroline continued. 'I love him!'

Vanessa snorted. Again Helen frowned at her daughter. As did Caroline. 'What's that supposed to mean?'

'You've only known him ten minutes and for the first nine you were trying to pretend he didn't exist. Now suddenly he's your own flesh and blood and losing him is the biggest tragedy since 9/11. Give me a break.'

'Nessa!' snapped Helen. 'That's enough.'

'Is it hell! Talk about hypocrisy. Stuart's only doing to Aunt Carrie what she did to Jimmy and I don't remember her beating herself up about that.'

'That was completely different,' Caroline told Vanessa.

'How? He *was* your real son. Stuart was right about that. In fact that's probably why Stuart's blowing you out now. Given your track record for maternal loyalty, he's probably decided to jump before he's pushed.'

A furious Caroline rose to her feet. 'How dare you say that to me? You don't have a clue about what happened between me and Jimmy.'

'Trust me, you're the one who doesn't have a clue.'

'You don't know the things Jimmy said about me. They were unforgivable.'

'You don't know them either. All you know is what Uncle Bob told you and if you're dumb enough to believe him then God help you.'

Caroline's eyes widened. 'What do you mean?'

'What do you think I bloody mean? Just how thick are you?'

'Vanessa!' exclaimed Helen. 'Don't talk to your aunt like that.'

'Oh shut up, Mum! Stop being so wet. I'm only saying what we both think.'

'Tell me what you mean,' demanded Caroline.

'Do you want to know what *really* happened the last time dear sweet Uncle Bob met big bad Jimmy? Uncle Bob started saying the Godwins were a bunch of losers who weren't fit to eat his shit and Jimmy pointed out that Uncle Bob was hardly one to cast judgement on others after the way he's constantly bullied and cheated on you. Big bad Jimmy was sticking up for you and dear sweet Uncle Bob got pissed and decided to teach him a lesson, so he got hold of a confidential document Jimmy had drafted and sent it to the other side's lawyers, basically killing Jimmy's career stone dead. And how did big bad Jimmy react? Rather than telling his bosses the truth, he took the blame because he was scared that if he didn't then dear sweet Uncle Bob would take it out on you.'

Caroline swallowed.

'Not once, in all this business with Stuart, has Jimmy ever said anything bad to me about you. All he's done is try to protect you, and how do you repay him? By turning your back on him and treating Stuart like the lost prodigal. Now that Stuart's seen sense and kicked you into touch, you come running round here expecting us to tell you what a poor victim you are. Well, dream on, Aunt Carrie. You're a stupid, selfish bitch and you deserve everything you get.'

Caroline slapped Vanessa's face.

Vanessa slapped back, twice as hard. Gasping, Caroline collapsed back into her seat.

'Jimmy still loves you!' Vanessa shouted. 'And so does Tom. Christ knows why after the way you've treated them both but they still do. You should consider yourself blessed that you've got two sons like that, just as I consider myself blessed that I didn't get stuck with a mother like you.'

'She didn't mean that,' Helen told Caroline.

'I bloody well did,' snapped Vanessa.

'Is it true?' Caroline asked.

'No,' Helen insisted. 'You're a good mother . . .'

'I mean about Jimmy and Bob.'

Vanessa raised her eyes to heaven.

'Is it?'

'You know them both. Which one would you believe?'

Again Caroline rose to her feet. 'I must go.'

'No, Carrie, stay . . .' began Helen.

Ignoring her, Caroline made for the door.

'Let her go, Mum,' said Vanessa.

'But you can see the state she's in. What is she going to do?'

'I'll give you three guesses.'

They stared at each other. Helen thought for a moment.

'I only need one,' she said.

Jennifer stood in a giant IKEA store, trying to dodge trolleys pushed by harassed shoppers while listening to Barry quiz a salesman about bathroom tiles. He was redecorating his bathroom and had asked her to come and give her advice on a suitable colour scheme. It was hardly the most romantic location for a date, but then, as she kept trying to tell him, it wasn't really a date at all.

'These ones are popular,' said the salesman, pointing to a particularly garish design.

'Do you like them?' Barry asked Jennifer.

'I would if I were wearing shades.'

'They're not that bad.'

'Are you kidding? It would be like having an acid trip every time you went to the loo. Mind you, that could be a blessing. Think of all the money you'd save.'

'Jen's only joking,' said Barry to the salesman.

'I think that's fairly obvious,' she told him.

He started asking her opinion on other designs. Her mobile rang. She struggled to mask her shock when she saw the caller ID.

'It's my mother,' she told Barry. 'I'd better take it.'

After moving out of earshot she pressed answer. 'Hello, Stuart.'

'Is this a bad time?'

'No.'

'You sound like you're standing in the middle of a motorway.'

'Well, the bathroom department at IKEA, so same difference.'

'Hardly. The motorway has a speed limit.'

She felt her lip twitch. Quickly, she bit down on it.

'What are you doing there?' he asked.

'Looking at bathroom tiles.'

'So your new man's into DIY?'

She was taken aback. 'My new man?'

'Tom told me. Nessa told him.'

She felt indignant. All she had told Nessa was that she had agreed to have a friendly drink with Barry. Trust Tom to turn it into some huge romance.

And trust Stuart to believe him. To think that she could just forget about him so quickly and move on to someone else.

Or was he just projecting his own feelings onto her.

She felt hurt. And angry. Too angry to explain. 'Well, what did you expect? Life goes on. Or was I supposed to just sit around and pine for you?'

'No.' A pause. 'Is he nice?'

'Yes. I'm very lucky.'

'I'm glad. Look, I won't disturb you any more. Take care of yourself . . .'

'Is that it?'

'What?'

'You called me. There must have been a reason.'

'No. No reason at all.'

The line went dead. Her anger faded. The hurt remained.

James sat with his mother in his living room, listening to her talk about his father.

'I didn't know what he'd done to you at work,' she was saying. 'I didn't know any of it until Nessa told me. You must think I'm a fool but your father was so convincing. He can make you believe anything.'

'You don't need to explain, Mum. I understand.'

'Do you really?'

'Yes.'

'Does that mean you forgive me?'

'There's nothing to forgive.'

She hugged him. He hugged back, squeezing as hard as he could.

'I was scared I'd lost you,' she told him.

'You'll have to try a lot harder to do that.'

'Has he really ruined things for you at work?'

'No.'

'But when I called they said you'd left.'

'I have.'

She looked confused.

'It was my choice. I only became a lawyer to make Dad happy. It was never what I wanted. Now it's time to find out what that is.'

'And do you know yet?'

'No, but when I do you'll be the first to know.'

'Thank you. And what does Kate say about this career change?'

'We broke up.'

'I'm sorry.'

He smiled. 'Liar. You couldn't stand her.'

'No. I just didn't think she was good enough for you. She told me you were meeting your biological family.' A pause. 'Are they nice?'

'Nice isn't exactly the word I'd use to describe them.'

'Why not?'

He told her what had happened. She looked appalled. 'How could they treat you like that? What sort of people are they?'

'I'm glad you can see it like that. Kate couldn't. When I told

431

her, all she could do was freak out about the possibility of an assault charge.'

'Well, even if Adam brought one you could plead justification.'

'I don't think the law works quite like that, Mum.'

'Well, it should. What a nasty piece of work. He and Stuart deserve each other.'

He was taken aback. 'Why? What has Stuart done?'

'I invited him into our home. I went out of my way to make him feel welcome and then this afternoon he phones to say he's decided he's a Godwin after all and that I won't be seeing him any more.'

James's jaw dropped. 'You're kidding?'

'No. That's exactly what he did.'

He felt smug. Hearing Stuart badmouthed was music to his ears.

Until he realised the implications of what his mother was saying.

'Stuart told you this afternoon?'

'Let's not waste time talking about him. I'm so happy to see you, Jimmy ...'

'And you saw Aunty Helen and Nessa after you'd spoken to him.'

'Yes.'

'So the only reason you're here now is because of what Stuart did.'

She began to look flustered. 'The reason isn't important. The only thing that matters is that we're close again.'

'But it *does* matter. You could have spoken to Nessa any time. You could have asked her what she knew. But you didn't.'

'That was your father's fault. You know what he's like. You know how persuasive he can be.'

'But you know me too. Didn't it even cross your mind he might be lying?'

'Why are you being like this? You said there was nothing to forgive.'

'Yes, but that was before I realised the only reason you could be bothered to find out the truth is because Stuart's blown you out. If he hadn't you'd still be happily thinking the worst of me.'

'I wasn't happy. I've been miserable.'

'Then why didn't you tell me?'

'I tried to. I left a message on your mobile.'

'One message! And even that didn't say anything. Christ, Mum, couldn't you have tried a bit bloody harder than that?'

She swallowed, looking close to tears. He knew she was trying to make him feel guilty and it was working. In spite of everything he hated seeing her upset. Needing distraction, he looked about the room, his eyes coming to rest on a Christmas card that had arrived in the post that morning. It was the first such card he had received that year. Hardly surprising, as it was still November. The previous Christmas his first card hadn't arrived until 1 December at the earliest . . .

Last Christmas.

Something stirred in his brain. A memory he had long forgotten, an incident that had seemed so unimportant that it wasn't worth remembering.

Until now.

She continued to look upset. He forced on an apologetic smile. Only if she were relaxed would she tell him what he needed to know.

'I'm sorry, Mum. I didn't mean to have a go. This whole Stuart business has really got to me. Just hearing his name brings me out in hives.'

'I did try to contact you,' she told him.

'I know how hard it's been for you. I'm just being a jerk. Do you forgive me?'

'There's nothing to forgive.'

'Hey, that's my line.'

Her face relaxed. His plan was working. A part of him didn't want it to, but he had to discover the truth.

'Dad's got a lot to answer for,' he said. 'After all the lies he's told.'

She nodded.

'Though compared to Becky's, his are small-time.'

'Becky?'

'I saw her last week. I wanted to tell her what had happened with Stuart.'

'And what did she say about it?'

'Not much. She was too busy giving me some cock and bull story about why she broke up with me.'

'What story?'

He told her. She looked shocked. 'I can't believe she said that.'

'Do you know the terrible thing? I actually believed her until she brought you into it. All that stuff about you setting it up and recording your conversation with her. That's when I knew she was lying.' He shook his head. 'And to think I was heartbroken when she ended the relationship.'

'You're well rid of her.'

'You said it. Good riddance to bad rubbish.' He gave a dismissive wave of the hand. 'And while we're on the subject of rubbish, what do you want for your Christmas present?'

'Your presents are never rubbish.'

'So why do you always ask me to keep the receipt?'

'I don't!'

'I'm looking forward to Christmas. At least I won't have to work through it like last year. Do you remember?'

She nodded.

'You were really sweet about it. Dad and Tom weren't. They both said I was trying to look important. You were the one who understood.'

'Of course I did. I'm your mum.'

'You even sat with me sometimes to keep me company. I really appreciated that.' He laughed. 'Even though we'd end up chatting and I'd get nothing done.'

She laughed too. 'Was I a nuisance?'

'No. I enjoyed it. Particularly the time I spent teaching you how to record things on your mobile.'

She stopped laughing. For the briefest of moments a look of alarm flashed across her face. Then it was gone, replaced by a smile that could blind at twenty paces.

And that was when he knew.

'I was getting ready for my New York trip. I left the day after New Year. And then, when I was away . . .' He exhaled. 'I think we both know what happened next.'

'What are you saying?'

'That Becky was telling the truth.'

'No. She's a liar. You said so yourself.'

'Only to catch the real one out.'

They stared at each other.

'I told you how upset Becky was about her stepfather, and how bad I felt about not going to the funeral and that's when you started planning.'

Again she looked like she was going to cry. This time it wasn't an act but it still left him cold.

'How could you, Mum?'

He saw her swallow.

'Tell me why.'

'Because she was no good.'

'So you got her *raped*?'

'She wasn't raped! She wanted it to happen. You never saw the way she used to look at your father. You never knew the real her but I did.'

'You're the one I don't know.' He ran a hand through his hair. 'Do you know what the worst thing is? It's just about conceivable I could forgive Dad. Becky said he genuinely seemed to believe their sex was consensual. But as for you ...' He shook his head, momentarily too disgusted to speak.

'I did it for you. I was trying to protect you.'

'From what? A sweet, wonderful girl who loved me? A girl I wanted to spend the rest of my life with?'

'And that's why! I was scared. She was coming between us and I couldn't stand it. You're the one person in the world that really matters to me.'

'And you're the one person in the world who makes me physically sick. You say I matter to you but you don't know me at all. What did you think I was going to do? Cut you out of my life the moment I had a wedding ring on my finger? I would *never* have done that. Not in a million years. You couldn't bear the thought of not coming first any more, just like you couldn't bear it when I told you I was more upset about seeing Stuart with Tom than seeing him with you. Everything is about you! You don't love me. You're not capable of it. All you're capable of is wrecking a young girl's life because she had the audacity to fall in love with your favourite piece of human jewellery.'

She started to cry. He watched her, expecting to feel loathing but feeling something much more final.

'It's funny,' he said. 'I never thought Stuart and I had

anything in common but we do. His mother died when he was thirteen and so did mine. You're not my mother. You never will be again. Not after this.'

A look of real horror spread across her face.

'And now I want you out of my house. You've got ten seconds. Otherwise I'll throw you out.'

'You wouldn't.'

'Try me.'

She rose to her feet. He pointed to the door. 'Go.'

'You can't treat me like this!'

'You probably said that to Stuart this afternoon. What are you going to do, Mum? Arrange for Dad to rape Jennifer?'

'Jimmy, please!'

'I think the reason Stuart's backed away from you is because Tom is jealous. Because Stuart mattered to you, didn't he, just like I did? We both mattered in a way that Tom never has. Well, now Tom's all you've got left. You've still got time to put things right with him. You've still got one son. Your tragedy is that you could have had three, and the tragedy for the three of us is that you don't deserve any.'

She opened her mouth to protest.

'Get out!'

She rushed for the door. He followed, barely waiting until she was through it before slamming it shut and turning the lock.

Ten to eleven. Susan Bishop walked across Piccadilly Circus, enjoying the noise, the bright lights and the bustle of the crowd.

Her husband John was away that weekend on a business trip. She had come to London to have dinner with friends and had booked herself into a hotel to avoid having to travel back home the same night.

Her hotel was in a square off Oxford Street. Pulling up the

collar of her coat against the wind, she headed into Soho, staring into the windows of crowded bars. One looked particularly fun and she was about to enter until she saw two of the largely male clientele kissing and realised it was not the sort of place she would enjoy.

Feeling frustrated, she continued on her way.

And saw James standing on a street corner, trying to light a cigarette.

She approached him. 'Hello, Jimmy. What are you doing here?'

He stared bleary eyed at her. Clearly, he was blind drunk. 'Don't you remember me?' she asked. 'I'm Susan Bishop, your mother's friend.'

'My mother.' He gave a derisive laugh.

'Are you all right?'

'No. I'm not drunk enough yet.' He continued trying to light his cigarette. She cupped her hands around his, helping shelter the flame from the wind. His skin felt warm. He looked a mess but he still looked good, and she had always found him the more attractive of Robert's sons.

An idea came to her. One that made her feel warm too.

Twenty minutes later they entered her hotel room.

He sat down on the bed. She searched through the bar, looking for spirits and finding two small bottles of whisky. After filling two glasses she handed him one then sat down beside him. 'So what's the problem?'

'You wouldn't believe me if I told you.'

'How do you know until you do?'

He didn't answer.

'Is this about Stuart?'

He shook his head. She remembered the way he had

laughed when she had mentioned his mother and decided to play her hunch.

'Your mother would hate to see you so upset.'

'She's not my mother.'

'Well, not biologically, but she still loves you.'

He sipped his drink, saying nothing.

'You're lucky to have her. She's a good woman.'

'No, she's not. You have no idea what she's capable of.'

She watched him drink, biding her time, knowing that with every drop consumed the looser his tongue would become. When his glass was empty she gave him the other one, then sat beside him on the bed and stroked his arm.

'Now,' she said softly, 'why don't you tell me what's been going on ...'

Sunday morning.

Caroline lay in bed, trying to concentrate on the morning paper.

Robert was already up. He was playing golf and would soon be leaving. She longed for him to go, wishing he would stay away for ever. That way he would never find out about Stuart.

Because when he did she was the one he would blame.

Unable to focus, she decided to get up. Heading for the bathroom, she stepped into the shower, turning up the temperature gauge to its full strength as if punishing her skin. She deserved to be punished, after what she had done.

Then she turned it down again.

After all, she had already been punished more than enough.

When she re-entered the bedroom Robert was there. She felt alarmed. When she had returned home the previous evening he had been waiting to quiz her on her whereabouts. She had made up a story about meeting a friend for a meal. Better that than tell him she had disobeyed his instructions and seen James.

'Your son's just called,' he told her.

She tried to control her panic. Was it James? Did Robert know what she had done? Was it Stuart?

'Which one?' she asked.

'Tom.'

She tried not to show her relief.

'He wants to come down this afternoon.'

'But he can't. You won't be here. Didn't you tell him?'

'No. I said it was all right. When he arrives tell him I've been called away. He'll understand. Besides, you'll be here. That'll make him happy enough.'

She felt sick. Thomas was the last person in the world she wanted to see.

But to refuse would only make Robert angry.

'Of course,' she said.

Early that afternoon Thomas arrived at his parents' home.

He had taken a taxi from the station. Not having a car himself, he had always relied on James or Stuart for a lift. As he paid the driver he realised that this was the first time in years that he had come home alone.

His mother waited at the door. Trying to mask his nervousness, he gave her a smile. He had heard from Vanessa what had happened with Stuart and how his mother was trying to blame him. He had come to try and repair the damage.

She smiled back. He felt himself relax.

Then, as the taxi pulled away and her face hardened, he realised it had just been an act.

'Hi, Mum.'

Turning, she walked back into the house.

He followed her inside. 'Where's Dad?'

'He's out.'

'When will he be back?'

'He won't.'

'Why not?'

She turned to face him. 'Because it's only *you* that's come.'

He swallowed.

'Why did you do it, Tom? You were the one who thrust Stuart into our lives. You were the one who made us care about him and then you take him away from us.'

He remained silent.

'You can't even answer me, can you? All you can do is stand there.' She stared at him, her expression one of utter contempt. It made him feel ashamed. She seemed to sense it. Shaking her head, she made as if to turn away.

Suddenly the shame vanished, replaced by a tidal wave of suppressed resentment and rage.

'Don't turn your back on me!'

She stopped, the scorn in her face replaced by shock.

'Don't turn your back on me! It's all you've ever done and I am sick to death of it! You want to know why I did it? Because it was the best way I could think of for getting back at you. All my life you and Dad have treated me like I'm invisible. Everything has always been about Jimmy. Every fucking thing. I thought it would be different with Stuart but it's just the same. He's the one that matters. I'm the one who might as well not exist.'

'That's not true.'

'Yes, it is. For once in your life have the decency to admit it.'

'What about boarding school? Don't you remember how

unhappy you were? You were desperate to leave but your father wouldn't hear of it. So I worked and worked on him and eventually made him change his mind. I hated thinking of you being unhappy. Why would I do that if I didn't care?'

He started to laugh. 'Is that the best you can do?'

'It shows that you matter.'

'All it shows is that you're still lying. The only reason you fought so hard for us to come home was because you were missing Jimmy. I heard you tell Aunt Helen. I was the one supposed to be grateful but he was the one it was all about. I went and told Jimmy and he said you'd told him you were only doing it for me. He was trying to protect me, just like he always did. He was the best brother anyone could ever have and I drove him out of the family and made him hate me because of you.'

'You can't blame me for that. You lost him yourself. It's your fault.'

'It's all our faults; you, me and Dad. Jimmy was the best thing that ever happened to any of us and we crapped all over him. Not that he cares. He's probably grateful. His real parents sounded like decent people. He's probably thanking his lucky stars that it's their blood that flows in his veins and not yours and Dad's.'

Her colour rose. He knew the barb had hit home.

'I think you should leave,' she told him.

'Do you know what Stuart told me the last time we met? He said that out of the two of you, it was you he despised the most. He said that though Dad's a vicious bastard at least he's honest about it. He doesn't con people the way you do. And he was right. You con everyone.'

'And do you know what your father told me?' she asked suddenly. 'Just before he left the house today?'

442

'What?'

'That he wished the Godwins had taken you instead of Stuart.'

'And is that what you wish too?'

'Oh, no. Not at all.'

'You're lying again.'

'Only because you haven't let me finish.'

He stopped. Her eyes had become slits.

'I'd wish that you'd been in the car with them when it crashed so there was no possibility of you ever tracing me. That way I'd still be left with two sons I cared about rather than one I wish I'd never conceived.'

He tried to look as if he didn't care. As if it didn't break his heart.

'Goodbye, Tom. I'd ask you to give Jimmy and Stuart my love but I'd only be wasting my breath. Neither of them will ever speak to you again, and in spite of what you say, that really is your fault, not mine.'

He turned to go, while behind him she started to laugh.

Early evening.

Caroline was preparing supper in the kitchen when Robert appeared, carrying his golf bag. 'How was your game?' she asked.

He threw his bag across the floor.

She risked a joke. 'As bad as that?'

'Why didn't you tell me about Stuart?'

Her stomach turned over.

'I called him on the way home. I had a lead I thought he could use. Only I gather we won't be seeing him any more.'

'I didn't want to upset you. I thought I could persuade him to change his mind.'

443

'*You?* He's doing this because of you. It's you being so clingy that's scared him off.'

'You can't blame this on me. Tom's responsible. He admitted it this afternoon. He did it because he was jealous.'

'And whose fault is that? From the moment you met Stuart you've been all over him like a rash, just like you were with Jimmy. How do you expect Tom to feel?'

She knew it was madness to argue with him. But after the trauma of the last two days her emotions were in shreds and she just couldn't take being his punch bag.

'About as bad,' she replied, 'as he did when he arrived here, only to discover that his own father had taken to the hills rather than stay around to say hello.'

'Don't try and put this on me. You're like a creeper. You choke the life out of everyone you get close to.'

'And you're a saint in comparison, aren't you? You just choke the career of anyone who dares tell you anything you don't want to hear.'

He stared at her. 'What are you talking about?'

'Jimmy told me what you did to him.'

'I told you to stay away from him.'

'And I disobeyed you. I wanted to see him because he *really* was a son we could both be proud of. And you couldn't stand that, could you? You went and sliced his legs off because he'd committed the unpardonable sin of becoming a bigger success and a better man than you could ever dream of being.'

'You hold your tongue.'

'Why? He *is* a better man. Your own father thought so.'

'Leave my father out of this.'

'Like you did, you mean? How many times did you visit him when he was in the home? Twice in three years? He kept asking for you and you kept making excuses. It was the boys and I who went to see him. And he was so happy to see us. Particularly Jimmy.' She started to laugh. 'Your father thought the world of Jimmy. He told me once how proud he was to have a grandson like that. "He's twice the man his father is," he told me, "and he'll be twice the success too." And what do you know, he was absolutely right.'

He pointed a finger at her. 'That's enough.'

'Your father would also have been proud of Stuart. He's twice the man you are too. Don't act like his loss is a tragedy, Bob. For you it's a blessing. If he'd stayed around he'd only have ended up outshining you just like Jimmy did.'

He grabbed her round the throat, slamming her against the fridge. She cried out in pain as he leaned forward, staring into her eyes.

'You don't talk to me like that,' he told her. 'This is my house. All of this is mine. Everything you have is because of me. I make the rules here and if you disobey them I will take it all away and leave you with nothing. Do you understand?'

She tried to pull his hand away.

'Do you?'

She nodded. He released his grip. 'Now get me some supper,' he told her. 'I'm hungry.'

Then he walked away.

She watched him go, wanting to run but knowing there was nowhere she could go, rubbing her throat and remembering the countless nights when she had lain awake watching him sleep and willing him to die.

A knife lay on the kitchen table. She picked it up, turning it over in her hands, imagining they were in bed now and she was pulling it out from beneath the pillow, ready to plunge it into his heart.

*

445

Thomas returned to his apartment building.

The porter sat at his desk, reading the paper. 'Hello, Mr Randall,' he said cheerfully, then frowned. 'Are you OK?'

'Sure.' In fact he had spent most of the return journey in tears and realised his eyes must be red. Feeling ashamed, he hurried towards the lift, longing to see Alice. He had phoned and told her what had happened. She had said she would be waiting for him. That he wasn't alone. That he still had her.

The lift arrived at his floor. He let himself into the flat and found it in darkness. Surprised, he called out a greeting.

For a moment he heard nothing.

Then came sounds from his bedroom.

He walked down the corridor, threw open the door and switched on the light.

Alice was lying on the bed, a sheet barely covering her nakedness. A stocky man of about thirty lay beside her.

He gasped. The air in the room was stale and full of the smell of sex.

'Who the hell are you?' the man demanded.

'This is my boyfriend,' Alice told him. 'And this is his flat.'

'Your *boyfriend*?' The man looked horrified. 'You said this was your place.'

She giggled. 'Oops.'

The man reached for his clothes. 'Look, mate, I'm really sorry. I didn't know, honestly I didn't.'

Thomas tried to speak but shock paralysed his throat.

The man pulled on his trousers, reached for his shirt and jacket and hurried past Thomas towards the door. Alice remained lying on the bed. 'Bye, Ricky,' she called out. 'Be sure to call me.'

The door opened and shut. Thomas stared at Alice. She stared back.

'Boo!' she cried suddenly.

He jumped. She started to laugh.

'You remind me of my dad,' she told him. 'When I was sixteen he caught me in bed with a boy and he looked just as shocked as you do.'

He found his voice. 'How could you do this to me?'

'You don't get it, do you?'

'Get what?'

'How it works between us.'

'I don't understand . . . '

'You've never got it. Not once. From the moment we met you were playing the big man. You thought I was attracted to your confidence. But you were wrong, I knew it was just an act. What attracted me was that underneath all that posturing you really needed me.'

He shook his head.

'It's true, Tom. You needed me to admire you. It made you feel special. Not that I minded. I like being needed. It makes me feel special too. Everything was great until Stuart came along and messed it up. Once he was on the scene you didn't need me any more so you tossed me aside like a used rag. You didn't even have the courage to break up with me face to face. You did it by voicemail. And I hated you for that. I *really* fucking hated you.'

Suddenly she sat up in bed, her eyes boring into his.

'It was so easy turning you against Stuart. I couldn't believe how easy it was. I hardly had to do anything; just make a couple of ditzy remarks and let your insecurity do the rest.'

'You're twisted.'

'And you're a fool.'

'I want you out of here.'

'Oh, I'm leaving. There's nothing here worth staying for.'

She climbed off the bed and reached for her clothes. 'You'll need to change the sheets, by the way. Ricky's only a little guy but when he comes it's like Krakatoa.'

Ten minutes later she was gone. He sat in his living room with the lights off, staring into the shadows and listening to the silence that surrounded him.

TWENTY-FOUR

Monday began just like any other November day.

That was what Vanessa thought as she stood by the window in her new flat, staring up at the dull, grey sky and wondering whether she would need an umbrella on her journey to work. A wind was blowing, but not harshly. The temperature was cold but not bitter. The radio had announced that there were delays on the Tube but only minor. It was all so typical, so predictable and so totally safe.

She had no way of knowing this was a day that would haunt her for the rest of her life.

Thomas stared at the note that had been waiting for him when he arrived at his desk. In it his boss told him that he was being taken off the Dunstable account and a couple of others besides. Maureen would handle them in his place.

But in the meantime the latest newsletter had to be written. As he had done such a good job with the last one, he could fill his time preparing the new one too.

He turned the piece of paper over in his hands, imagining

his father's scorn. Once the prospect would have upset him but now it just made him smile. It didn't matter. None of it mattered any more.

His boss appeared in the doorway. 'I'm sorry, Tom. I just think it's for the best.'

'So do I. If I were you I'd have done the same.'

'You don't mind?'

'No. I don't mind at all.'

An hour later Maureen saw Thomas walk towards the lift. He was wearing his coat and carrying his briefcase. She felt cross. The files she had taken from his office were incomplete and she had several important phone calls to make.

She hurried after him. 'Wait a minute ...'

He pressed the lift button. 'They're on my desk.'

'What are?'

'The papers you're missing. Everything you need is there.'

'It had better be.' She turned to go.

'I'm sorry we've never got on. It's my fault. I've always felt threatened by you. You're much better at this job than I'll ever be. I've phoned the clients and told them you're taking over. I also told them how lucky they are.'

There was no trace of sarcasm in his tone. She realised he was being sincere.

'Thank you,' she said. 'I appreciate that.'

The lift arrived. He prepared to step into it.

'Tom, where are you going?'

'There are things I need to do.'

'But you are coming back, aren't you?'

'Of course.'

He stepped into the lift. She remained where she was.

Though the lobby was well heated, a shiver ran through her, as if she had just met a ghost.

Early afternoon.
Susan Bishop sat in her car in a quiet side street, adjusting her wig and putting on her shades, just as she always did before she met Robert.

As she checked her appearance in the windscreen mirror, she pictured him waiting for her in their usual room, sipping champagne, wearing nothing but a towel and a self-satisfied grin. When she thought of the bombshell she was about to drop, she found herself grinning too.

Switching off the engine, she climbed out of the car.

'You're having a busy afternoon,' observed Antonio the porter as he watched Thomas Randall walk past his desk.

'Yes. I've had a lot to sort out. Fortunately, I'm nearly done now,' Thomas held up a letter. 'I've just got to post this.'

'I can post it for you. I get my break in twenty minutes.'

'No. I should do it. But I appreciate the offer.'

Thomas left the building. Antonio returned to his paper.

Susan straddled Robert, feeling him thrust inside her.

He reached his climax, letting out a loud grunt as he did so. 'Oh Christ,' he groaned. 'I needed that.'

She started to laugh.

He wiped sweat from his forehead. 'What's so funny?'

'I was just wondering.'

He reached for the champagne bottle on the bedside table. 'Wondering what?'

'How I compare with Becky.'

His hand froze in mid-air.

'I want to know. How do I compare with your son's girl-friend?'

'I don't know what you're talking about.'

'It's OK. You don't have to tell me. I can guess. On a scale of one to ten, Becky must have scored at least fifteen. What is it they say about rape? It's the ultimate expression of man's power over woman.' She stroked his chest. 'And when it comes to dominating women, I've never met a man whose need is greater than yours.'

'I didn't rape her.'

'That's not how she tells it.'

'Then she's a bloody liar. She wanted it as much as I did.'

Again Susan laughed. He grimaced, clearly realising what he had said.

'Oh, Bob, you really must learn to control your emotions. Heaven help you if the police start asking questions.'

His eyes widened. 'Is she going to press charges?'

'I couldn't say. You'd have to ask her.'

'What did she say to you?'

'She didn't say anything. Jimmy told me. I bumped into him in the West End on Saturday night. The poor boy was drunk and in a terrible state. Mind you, who can blame him after the story he'd just heard.'

'It was consensual. If she says different she's a liar.'

She covered his mouth with her fingers. 'There's no need to get so excited. When she told Jimmy she didn't say anything about going to the police. And even if she did she couldn't prove anything. It would be your word against hers and after all this time it doesn't make for a strong case, particularly when you can rely on Carrie to tell everyone you're the gent-lest of men.'

He watched her warily. 'What are you up to?'

'I'm only making conversation.'

'Are you going to tell Carrie?'

'Why tell her something she already knows?'

His jaw dropped.

She feigned surprise. 'Oh, Bob, did you think Jimmy heard the story from Becky? Well, he didn't. Or at least he didn't believe it. Not until Carrie confirmed all the juicy details.'

'What are you telling me?'

'That Carrie set the whole thing up. She played you like a virtuoso. Who would have thought it? Your pathetic little wife isn't the victim she seems. In fact I'd go as far to say that even I couldn't stoop as low as she did.'

'I don't believe you.'

'It's true. She was jealous of Becky's hold over Jimmy and wanted her out of the way. Why do you think she suddenly decided to become Becky's new best friend at the very moment when Becky was at her most vulnerable and Jimmy was so far away? Why do you think she invited Becky to stay the night? Why do you think she plied you both with alcohol while talking about Jimmy's triumphs in a way that was going to intensify your feelings of competiveness? And why do you think, with her perfect memory, she just happened to forget she was supposed to be spending the evening with her sister? She planned it all, Bob. You and Becky were her puppets. She even went to see Becky afterwards, got her to admit the sex, recorded the conversation and told Becky that she'd play it to Jimmy if Becky didn't end the relationship there and then.'

The blood had drained from his face. Clearly, he believed her now. Triumph flooded through her. It was better than a hundred orgasms. His emasculation was almost achieved. Now all that was needed was the killer blow.

'I don't blame you for wanting Becky. From what I hear

453

she's very attractive. Jimmy certainly thought so, and unlike you he never had to force her.'

'That's enough,' he told her.

'Jimmy's attractive too. At least I've always found him so. I never thought the feeling was mutual but on Saturday night I discovered just how wrong I was.'

He looked as if he were about to have a stroke.

'It was wonderful. Three times in an hour and each one better than the last. How many decades ago was it that you could manage that? I thought alcohol was supposed to reduce a man's ability to perform but that's certainly not true of your son. I'm surprised the guests in the adjacent rooms didn't complain about the noise.'

He tried to push her off him. She dug in her knees. 'Now now,' she said teasingly. 'You mustn't get so upset. Jimmy's only done to you what you did to him, and at least he didn't have to resort to rape to achieve it. Perhaps the hospital didn't get it wrong all those years ago. You're a lot more alike than you think.'

The struggling stopped. He lay still, looking suddenly old and very tired. She smiled down at him, her victory complete.

'Jimmy wasn't better than me,' he said weakly.

'Oh, but he was.'

'His body isn't better. He's got that bloody appendix scar and that stupid birthmark around his nipple.'

'Haven't you heard? Scars are sexy. He looked magnificent to me.'

'Did he?'

Something in his tone stopped her in her tracks.

'I'd imagine so,' he continued. 'After all, he's never had his appendix out and his birthmark is behind his left ear.'

She felt her smile fade while watching his blaze across his face.

'He turned you down, didn't he? You came on to him like a bitch in heat and he turned you down.' It was his turn to laugh. 'Oh, this is priceless. You lure him to your hotel room, ply him with compliments and alcohol and he still refuses to screw you.'

'Don't laugh at me!'

'I can't help it. This is too good. Susan Bishop: the self-appointed love goddess of Oxfordshire can't even get a vulnerable drunk to service her.' His laughter intensified. 'Oh, the humanity!'

'Shut up!'

'You were right about Becky. On a scale of one to ten she really was a fifteen. She was young, sweet and tender and everything you'll never be again or ever were to start with.'

'Don't compare me with her.'

'Why not? I do it all the time. Every time we've ever screwed I've fantasised you were her. Even today I was doing it. I need to. How else could I get it up for a shop-soiled slut like you?'

Her vision blurred, a red mist forming behind the eyes. Her longed-for triumph had turned to ashes and the realisation was driving her insane.

'I lied when I told you I'd never leave Carrie. I'd leave her for Becky. I'd leave her today if Becky would have me. I'd even be faithful. Only she wouldn't touch me with a ten-foot pole, just as Jimmy wouldn't touch you, so I guess I'm doomed to spend the rest of my life servicing desperate housewives in tacky hotel rooms just to pass the time.'

He was still laughing. She couldn't bear to look at his face. Rising from the bed, she walked away towards the table by the far wall. A mirror hung above it. The one before which she had often pranced, admiring the splendours of her own body.

Only she didn't admire them now. For the first time she saw the skin that was starting to sag and the wrinkles that were forming. For the first time she saw that she was growing old and that the power she had always taken for granted was beginning to slip away from her.

He remained where he was, rocking back and forth with mirth as if it were the best joke he'd ever heard.

And the red mist took control.

A metal statue stood on the table. Picking it up, she crossed the room and slammed it down on his head, silencing him for good.

After reading the sports page, Antonio began to play Angry Birds on his phone. He had only downloaded the app a few days ago but was already hooked.

Thomas returned. 'You were a while,' Antonio told him. 'Did they move the post box?'

'No. I just fancied a walk.' Thomas wiped raindrops from his hair. 'Guess I should have taken an umbrella.'

'I guess you should.' Antonio smiled. 'How is your brother, by the way?'

'Which one?'

'I still can't get my head around that.'

'Imagine how I feel.' Thomas turned to go.

Then turned back, his eyes suddenly thoughtful.

'How is your wife doing? Is there any more news?'

Antonio shook his head. Two months earlier his wife had started having fainting fits. They had seen several doctors but so far none of them could identify the cause.

'I'm sorry to hear that. I can imagine how stressful it must be for both of you. I pray it's nothing serious. I really do.'

He was touched. 'Thanks, Mr Randall. I appreciate that.'

'Goodbye, Antonio.'

'Goodbye, Mr Randall.'

Thomas walked away. Antonio returned to his game.

Susan stood, staring down at Robert. She was still holding the statue. It seemed frozen in her hand just as shock at what she had done kept her frozen to the spot.

He was still lying on the bed; one of his eyes, open but sightless, stared up at the ceiling. The other no longer existed, buried in the wreckage of the left side of his head.

She heard a pounding. Panic-stricken, she turned towards the door, expecting the police to burst through and dropping the statue, which landed on her toe. With the pain came the realisation that what she heard was simply the hammering of her own heart.

No one's coming. For God's sake calm down and think.

Their room was on the top floor. In all the time they had been coming here she had rarely seen other guests in the corridor. Chances were they were the only ones currently in occupation. Who else would be in residence in the middle of the afternoon?

Leave now. Go home and stay there. No one knows about the affair. Why would anyone suspect you?

It was a good plan. It could work. But first she had to take care of business.

After putting on her gloves she fetched a towel from the bathroom and began to wipe any surface she might have touched. When she had finished she searched Robert's jacket, removing the pre-paid mobile he always used to call her. She was grateful for his caution. Pre-paid calls could not be traced.

She also took his Rolex and the cash and credit cards from his wallet, making it appear that robbery had been the motive.

457

When she was finished she wrapped the statue and other objects in the towel and placed it in the bag she always brought to make her appear like a regular guest.

Finally she showered, dressed and reapplied her disguise, checking her appearance in the mirror and seeing a woman in a shapeless dark coat with an ocean of thick black hair and shades big enough to cover much of her face. She wasn't sure what security cameras the hotel had but as long as she kept her head down and spoke to no one it would be all right. It was a large hotel. Dozens of people came and went all the time. Why would anyone pay any attention to her?

As she shut the door she hung the Do Not Disturb sign on the handle. Robert always booked the room for the night. No one would discover his body until the following morning.

She wasn't sure if there were cameras in the lift. Not wanting to take any chances, she descended by stair. As she entered the lobby her heart was pounding but the man on reception was too busy greeting a large party of tourists to give her a second glance. Another party was opening umbrellas, preparing to step out into the wet street. Keeping her head lowered, she slotted in beside them and left the hotel.

Five minutes later she sat in her car, removing the wig and glasses. She had done it. Now all she had to do was drive home safely and stay there . . .

What if you missed something? We had sex. What if the police can make a DNA match? You have to go back and get the sheets.

Only she couldn't. She didn't have a key and would only be exposing herself by asking for one.

Her stomach heaved. Opening up her bag, she vomited into it, amazed at how much waste her body could hold.

And with the cleansing came clarity.

Even if the police find something they can't trace it back to you. No one knows about you and Robert. Why would anyone ever suspect you?

For a moment she felt herself relax.

What about Giles Murdoch? He knew you wanted Caroline to divorce Robert. What about Jimmy? After what happened on Saturday night could he put two and two together?

She told herself to calm down. Giles would never expose her. To do so would be to expose his own sordid intrigues and she knew he would never risk that. As for James, he had been so drunk that when he had rebuffed her advances she had managed to convince him he had misread the signs and offended her deeply. He actually apologised before he left. He would never suspect her, assuming he even remembered their meeting at all.

No, it would be all right. As long as she kept her head and her composure, all would be well.

Taking a deep breath, she started the engine.

Tuesday morning, half past nine.

Rosita Lopez, Thomas's cleaner, let herself into his flat.

Her money lay on the table by the door. As she hung up her coat she noticed Thomas had left five times the usual sum. Startled, she picked up the accompanying note.

Dear Rosita,

The money is all for you. It's a thank-you gift as I won't need your services any more. I'm very grateful for your hard work and sorry I can't say goodbye in person.

There's one thing I'd like you to do. Please ask Antonio to call the police. Perhaps you could leave your set of keys with him. Tell him the police should check my bathroom. Under no circumstances should you go in there.

Thanks again, Rosita. Take care of yourself.
Thomas.

She let it fall onto the floor, feeling herself grow cold all over.

The bathroom was halfway down the corridor. Though every instinct told her to leave well alone, still she had to know.

As she reached the door she told herself it was only a joke.

But when she opened it she saw it was all too true.

Bursting into tears, she went to carry out his request.

Half past eleven.

Chambermaid Molly Clark stood on the top floor of the Mote House Hotel, vacuuming the carpet and listening to her co-worker Agnes complain.

'The Do Not Disturb sign is still on 719. I can't get in there to change the bed.'

Molly looked at her watch. 'They should have checked out half an hour ago.'

'Do you think they've overslept?'

'Only one way to find out. Try knocking and if they don't answer just go on in. What's the worst that can happen?'

Agnes headed off down the corridor. Molly continued pushing the vacuum cleaner over the carpet.

Then dropped it when she heard Agnes scream.

An hour later a group of people stood outside the hotel, speculating as to what had prompted the sudden arrival of two police cars.

Ed Morris, reporter for a local paper, was among them. His girlfriend worked at the hotel and had tipped him off.

She appeared from the lobby. He waved to her, backing away from the crowd for the sake of privacy.

'It's definitely murder,' she told him. 'The poor guy's head had been bashed to a pulp. That's what Agnes said.'

'Bloody hell! What's the stiff's name?'

'The register says Daniel Drake but it's an alias. Apparently he always paid in cash so whoever he was he was probably doing the dirty on his wife.'

'So was his bit on the side the one that killed him?'

'I don't know. I heard one of the police say that he'd been robbed but they've managed to ID him from an old receipt in his wallet. His surname is Randall. I don't know his first name but he's from a place called Fleckney. Do you know where that is?'

'No, but I'll find out.'

'There's one other thing. The policeman was saying they've contacted his wife to come and ID the body and her sister's coming instead. The wife is too distraught.'

'Well, that's hardly surprising.'

'No, that's the point. She's in bits because her son's just killed himself.'

'Shit! Murder and suicide in the same family on the same day.' He kissed her cheek. 'I think I smell a scoop.'

One o'clock.

James stood in his kitchen, ignoring the telephone that was ringing off the hook. There was no need to answer it. He already knew.

He had gone out early for a long walk. The post had arrived in his absence. Among the pile of circulars had been a letter from Thomas.

Dear Jimmy,
   I hate putting this in writing. I know I should tell you to

461

your face but you'd only talk me out of it and I can't let you because I know I'm doing the right thing.

. I've made such a mess of things. I've been such a fool. You were right. I only brought Stuart into the family to get back at you. I just couldn't go on feeling like I didn't exist. I wanted to make Mum and Dad notice me the way they always did you. The irony is that within a month of Stuart walking through their door he was the only one they noticed and I was back to being the shadow they looked straight through. Ironic, isn't it? By rights you should be gloating but you won't. You're too big a person. I always envied you that, just as I envied you so many things.

The last time I saw Mum she told me she wished I'd been the one the Godwins had taken instead of Stuart. She also said she wished I'd died in the car crash with them so I could never have grown up to trace her. It killed me to hear her say that and what made it even worse was that she had a point. You and Stuart are much more alike than you realise. You're both strong, you're both decent and you both have giant hearts. I know you hate each other and I understand why but the tragedy is that in different circumstances the two of you could have been friends. You'd have made a winning team and you'd never have had to carry each other the way you've both had to carry me.

This afternoon I saw my solicitor and made a new will. I've left everything to Stuart. Please don't be hurt by that. He should have had all the things I did and it's the only way I can think of to try and put things right.

I want to thank you, Jimmy, for being the best brother anyone could ever have. When I think back to the happy times in my life there isn't a single one that wasn't made better because of your presence. Your companionship has always been my greatest blessing and though I've never

462

achieved much in my life the one thing I'm truly proud of is
that I was able to call you my twin.

I love you. I'm sorry.

Tom.

His phone kept ringing. Sinking to the floor, he began to sob.

Thursday. Vanessa sat with James in his flat, reading Thomas's letter.

She wiped her eyes. 'I should have been there for him.'

'You didn't know how he was feeling,' James told her. 'Neither did I, and I'm the one who really should have done.'

'You mustn't blame yourself. We both know whose fault it is.' She gestured to the letter. 'How could your mother have said that to him? She might as well have wielded the razor blade herself.'

He winced.

'I'm sorry. I'm just so angry. How could she do that? And how could she have done that to Becky and to you? She's an evil bitch.'

'Not in the eyes of the world.'

A local Oxfordshire paper lay on the coffee table. Robert and Thomas stared out of the front page, beneath the headline 'Double Tragedy for Local Family'. The two-page story inside had a picture of a devastated-looking Caroline leaving the local police station. 'Robert was a wonderful husband and Thomas was a wonderful son,' she was quoted as saying. 'I can't imagine life without either of them but I know they'd want me to be strong and that's what I'm trying to be.' The article referred to the 'unbearable loss no loving mother should ever have to face', before complimenting her on her dignity and courage in the face of overwhelming pain. A couple of national papers had also covered the story. Though neither had put it on their front page, the tone of the articles had been much the same.

Vanessa put the note to one side. 'Mum says flowers and cards keep arriving at your house. People are sending them from all over the place, telling her to keep strong. God, if they only knew.'

James gave a hollow laugh.

'Is there any more news on your dad?'

'No. The police couldn't find anything in the bedroom. They hoped the security tapes might give some clues but apparently the hotel had some technical problems and the system wasn't running. As he was robbed, they think it might have been a call girl. They've been checking his phone records but so far nothing.'

'How do you feel about it?'

'I don't think about it much to be honest. All I can think about is Tom. I'm sorry Dad died the way he did but I'm not going to be a hypocrite and say I'll miss him now he's dead.' He sighed. 'That probably sounds terrible.'

She rubbed his arm. 'No, it doesn't. I knew him too, remember.'

'They're releasing his body. There's a joint funeral next Tuesday.' Again he sighed. 'I'm dreading it.'

'I'll be there. I'll help you through it.'

'Thanks.'

'Your mother will be too, acting the grief-stricken widow and broken-hearted mother.'

'Well, that's what she is. Who's going to say anything else? Victims are always untouchable.'

'She's no victim. She hated your dad and as for Tom... '
Vanessa exhaled.

He put his arm around her. They sat together in silence. His
eyes had a faraway look. She guessed he was reliving childhood incidents with Thomas, just as she was.

'I'll make some coffee,' he said eventually.

'Do you want help?'

'No. You stay put.'

He walked away. She opened the newspaper, staring down
at her aunt's face. The face of tragedy and loss with whom
countless readers could identify. It made her sick but there was
nothing she could do. People were more likely to piss on the
tomb of the unknown soldier than blame a mother for the suicide of her son.

If they only knew. Christ, if they only knew ...

Tuesday afternoon.

The day of the funeral.

The car park of Fleckney Church was full of reporters, all
eager to witness the main event in the hottest news story of the
week.

It was the suicide note that had done it. A tabloid had
printed a copy it had received from an anonymous source and
suddenly a straightforward family tragedy had become something else entirely.

As journalists began to dig deeper the story of the separated
identical twins had been revealed, provoking widespread panic
about monitoring procedures in maternity wards. One paper
reported that dozens of parents of newborn babies were
demanding DNA tests to confirm they had the right child.

And now that Caroline Randall's mask of saintliness had
slipped, many of her so-called friends had volunteered their

opinions as to just what sort of mother she had really been. 'She didn't care about Tom at all,' one had revealed. 'He might as well not have existed for all the attention she ever paid him. From the time they were babies, Jimmy was the only one that mattered to her.' Though all such quotes were given anonymously, the content of the note gave them the glow of sacred truth.

And just when people might have thought that James was the lucky one, another titbit emerged: details of the roles both his parents had played in ending his relationship with the girl he loved. The papers were careful to present it as simply a rumour and those involved all denied its truth, but in a matter of days public opinion had become so heated that it was widely accepted as fact.

'Both parents make me sick,' announced one comment on an internet forum that expressed the views of many. 'How could they have treated their sons like that? What's even worse is that they didn't even realise one of their children wasn't theirs at all. Though I would never condone murder, the father's death is no loss to anyone. As for the mother, if anything she's even worse!'

And so the press waited, cameras at the ready, to capture whatever further drama there might be.

James stood by the graveside, feeling the wind blast his face while watching his father's coffin being lowered into the ground.

His mother stood between him and Stuart, clutching tightly to their arms as if frightened she would collapse without their support. Five days earlier he would have thought it an act but after the battering the media was giving her he could tell her need was real. He tried to summon sympathy but felt only hate.

There were dozens of mourners. It seemed all Fleckney had

come to pay their respects. Only that *was* an act. If the papers were anything to go by, few of them had a good word for either of his parents. Most just wanted to enjoy the spectacle.

Vanessa stood to his right. She was the one who had sent Tom's suicide note to the press. Though he understood her motivation, he was still furious with her. It was because of her that the whole Becky saga had come to light. Vanessa swore she had not been the one to tell and he believed her. What puzzled him was the identity of the source. Becky herself would never have done it. So who had?

Susan and John Bishop stood whispering to each other near the back. He tried to recall the details of his meeting with Susan. Had he told her? What exactly had he said? He struggled to remember but as was so often the case when a sea of alcohol was involved the whole encounter remained a blur.

The pallbearers lowered Thomas's coffin into the ground. Stuart and Vanessa both started to cry. He noticed Aunt Helen watching his mother, her expression a mixture of concern and quiet contempt. Unlike others in the village, she would know for certain the Becky story was true. Though his aunt would always defend her sister against the world, he sensed their relationship would never be quite the same again.

The ceremony drew to its close. People began to move away. His mother kept hold of his arm. 'Will you come back to the house?' she asked.

'No.'

'Please.'

He shook his head. He couldn't face being near her. He couldn't face the prurient curiosity of their so-called friends. He couldn't face any of it.

'You owe it to your brother,' she told him.

'Who are you to tell me what I owe Tom?'

He tried to pull away. She kept hold.

'Let go,' he said forcefully.

'Don't,' Stuart hissed at him. 'You're just giving everyone a show.'

'It *is* a show. Don't you understand that? This is Tom's funeral but we're the main event. In death as in life he might as well not be here.'

'They might be here for us but we're here for Tom. That's what matters.'

'Don't tell me what matters. Not when you helped put him in the ground.'

Helen appeared beside him. 'Jimmy, now is not the time.'

Stuart's face had darkened. 'Yes, it is. If he has something to say, let's hear it.'

He realised his aunt was right. Shaking his head, he turned to go.

This time it was Stuart who grabbed his arm. 'Well?'

He turned back. 'Who's making a show now?'

'This is my twin's funeral. If you're going to make accusations about me then have the guts to do it to my face!'

He stared at Stuart, feeling all the old resentment surging through him. '*Your* twin? You hardly knew him. I was the one who was there for him. I was the one that took care of him. Why couldn't you have just stayed away? If you hadn't come crashing into our lives none of this would have happened and Tom would still be alive!'

His mother started to cry. Vanessa joined Aunt Helen. 'Jimmy, leave it!'

'And where were you,' Stuart demanded, 'while he was bleeding to death in the tub? He said in his note that he didn't call you because he was worried you'd talk him out of it but that was a lie. The real reason is he knew you'd just use it as another excuse to remind him of what a tragic failure he was compared to the all-perfect all-conquering Saint Jimmy!'

James punched Stuart in the face, knocking him to the ground. A gasp went up from the spectators while behind him he heard cameras flash.

'That's for Tom!' he shouted. 'That's for *my* brother!'

Then he turned and walked away, ignoring his mother's cries for him to stay. The journalists gathered round him, taking more pictures. Ignoring them too, he climbed into his car and drove away.

Three hours later an exhausted Stuart arrived home.

He parked his car and walked towards the flat.

And found Jennifer waiting on the doorstep.

He couldn't help it. He burst into tears. She came and hugged him, holding him tight, saying nothing.

They stayed like that for several minutes. Eventually his tears began to slow. 'Why have you come?' he asked.

'I wanted to be here for you.'

'But what about . . .'

'What?'

'Him.'

'There is no him. There never was. There's only ever been you.'

He swallowed.

'The last time we saw each other I said some terrible things,' she said. 'I know you can never forgive me. I can go now if you want. I just wanted you to know that you're not alone.'

'I can forgive you.'

'Do you mean that?'

He didn't answer, just tightened his hold on her.

Late Wednesday evening.

Susan Bishop stood by the window in the living room, sipping a glass of wine, smoking a cigarette and staring out at the dark night.

The day's papers lay on a table beside her. Two front pages showed James punching Stuart while a distraught Caroline wept in the background. Though she had dreaded the funeral, she had forced herself to attend. Failure to do so would have attracted comment and at this moment in time appearances were everything.

She took a drag on her cigarette, amazed at how calm she felt. She had already disposed of the clothes she had worn and all the other objects she had taken from the hotel room, and from what she had read and heard the investigation into Robert's murder was quickly grinding to a halt. The press had speculated that the culprit was 'a high-class call girl'. It was a title she found perversely amusing, just as she had found it perversely amusing to spread the story about Robert and Becky. She had been very careful, just telling one friend that she had heard it from another and then standing back and watching the rumour fly.

Two circular lights illuminated the darkness. John was back from the office. She turned to greet him. 'How was your day?' she asked.

'Rather sad. Giles Murdoch is dead. The poor bloke was just leaving his office for a meeting when he suddenly dropped dead of a heart attack.'

She managed not to show her delight. With Giles gone the last risk of detection had vanished. 'That's awful,' she said.

'At least it was peaceful.' He gestured to the papers. 'Not like poor Bob. It's hard to believe I was only playing golf with him a few days ago. What a terrible business.'

'It certainly is.' She took another drag on her cigarette. 'Are you ready for supper?'

'No. I ate at work.'

She exhaled. 'You might have told me before I defrosted pork chops.'

'I'm sorry.'

She felt the familiar contempt rise up in her. 'As always,' she said archly.

'There's something else I should tell you.'

She sipped her wine. 'What?'

'I want a divorce.'

She nearly choked on her drink. 'Are you mad? You can't divorce me!'

'People divorce all the time.'

'Not people like us.'

'I'm in love with Frances. I want to marry her.'

'Who the hell is Frances?'

'My secretary.'

She remembered all the times she had regaled Caroline with her imaginary fears about him and his secretary. For a moment she thought she might faint.

And then suddenly she saw the funny side.

'You've been having an affair? I mean ... *you*?'

He nodded.

'How long has this been going on?'

'Six months.'

She started to laugh. 'I'm sorry. I can't help it. It's like discovering Mother Teresa was a coke fiend.'

'It wasn't serious at first,' he said calmly. 'She was just

471

someone I enjoyed talking to. She listens to me, which is something you never do.'

'Well, I'm all ears now. This is the funniest thing I've heard in ages.'

He didn't react. 'It was only recently that I realised I loved her. It was the same time I realised you and I couldn't go on like this.'

'Well, that's where you're wrong. That's *exactly* how we're going to go on. You really don't want to take me on in the divorce court, John. Believe me when I say you won't have a penny to your name by the time I've finished with you.'

'Actually, you'll never get another penny from me ever again.'

His calmness was unsettling. 'What are you talking about?'

He opened his briefcase and pulled out a paper file. 'I knew you'd fight dirty and that I'd need some ammunition of my own so I took the precaution of having you followed by a private detective.'

Her heart stopped.

He held out a photograph of James and her stepping into a hotel lift. 'Isn't he a little young for you?'

'Nothing happened. We just had a drink together.'

'Hmm.'

'You can't prove otherwise.'

'Then what about this?'

He held out two more photographs. The first showed her sitting in her car putting on her disguise to meet Robert. The second showed her entering the Mote House Hotel.

'So I was there. It doesn't prove I was sleeping with Robert.'

'No, but your telephone conversations do. I found one of your pre-paid mobiles. You shouldn't have been so explicit when talking on it, but then how were you to know that it was bugged?'

'Well, what if I was? So we had sex. It doesn't prove I killed him.'

'No, it doesn't.' He paused. 'But this does.'

He produced a final photograph: a shot of the window of their hotel room. In it she could be seen slamming the statue down on Robert's head.

'You really should have drawn the curtains. But then, why would you? You were on the top floor. You weren't overlooked. How were you to know that my detective had booked the next-door room, climbed from one balcony to another before either of you arrived and set up a camera? It's amazing how small they make cameras these days. Some are so tiny you'd never notice them at all.'

She dropped her wine glass. Her legs had begun to shake.

'Oh, and if you're wondering, that last photograph isn't a photograph at all. It's just one shot from a film. We have the whole thing recorded.'

She collapsed into a chair. He put the photographs back into his briefcase and locked it shut.

Then he sat down and stared at her.

'Throughout our marriage all I've ever done is try and make you happy. In return all you've done is belittle, humiliate and betray me and that's how we've ended up here.'

'So what are you going to do?'

'Do?'

'Are you going to show the film to the police?'

He shook his head. Relief flooded her, so intense she started to cry.

Then she heard the sound of cars pulling up in the drive.

'I don't need to,' he said. 'They've seen it already.'

She began to scream. He continued to stare at her while in the distance the doorbell rang.

Thursday.

The house was silent. All the noise came from outside. They waited at the end of the drive with their cameras, their microphones and their endless questions, like vampires ready to suck out her last drop of life.

Caroline stood in the living room, watching them through a crack in the curtains she never opened any more. The weather was dry and mild for the time of year. It was the sort of morning she would once have spent in her garden, planting and weeding, making her home as beautiful without as it was within. Keeping up appearances, only there wasn't any point any more. Not now everyone knew.

She told herself to stay strong. That it would soon be over. That her story was just one in an endless procession of nine-day wonders for the media to chew over then spit out, leaving her to try and rebuild her life from the scraps that remained.

The morning post lay on a side table, as substantial as the previous day's had been. She flicked through the envelopes. Most were handwritten. She knew what they would say. The same messages of hate she had received yesterday and would receive tomorrow too.

She focused on one that had been typed. It looked official, a circular or notice of some sort. She tore it open, grateful for anything that reminded her of normality.

But it wasn't a circular. Just a single sheet of paper, covered in angry scrawl:

This is all your fault. You make me sick. How can you call yourself a mother after what you've done? You're an insult to

all the millions of women out there who can't have children
of their own. I don't know how you can look at yourself in
the mirror. I really don't.

How could you not know? That's what I don't under-
stand. You MUST have known. They were your children. You
carried them inside you. What sort of woman are you? How
could you possibly not know ...

She didn't read any more. Just threw it and all the others
into the bin.

The piano was covered in framed photographs. One in particular held her gaze, taken at a charity lunch back in August. She
and Robert stood together outside the village hall, bathed in sunshine and with James and Thomas on either side. It hurt to look
at it now. To remember the last time they had all been together.

Before the sky collapsed on top of them.

June, six months later

James sat at his kitchen table, staring at the boxes that surrounded him.

He had sold his flat and the new owners would be moving
in the following day. All his furniture had been included in the
purchase price. The men from the storage company would
soon be arriving to take his personal possessions away.

A rucksack lay on the floor beside him. His passport and a
one-way ticket were on top of it. That evening he was catching a flight to Mumbai. He intended to spend a couple of
months in India before travelling on to the Far East. It was the
sort of trip he had always wanted to take but had never had
the time; too busy trying to climb another rung of the career
ladder and make his father proud.

Two Bon Voyage cards stood on the table. One was from Vanessa, telling him not to smuggle any drugs and to check that any girls he met in Thailand were not men in drag. He had laughed as he read it. The anger he had felt towards her at the funeral had faded long ago. She had only been doing what she thought was right.

And, in a strange way, it had worked out for the best.

The other card was from Becky. He had contacted her after the funeral, wanting her to know that he now believed her story, that he had not been the one to make it public and that he was sincerely sorry for the unwanted attention she was now receiving. At first she had refused to take his calls. But later, once the media storm passed, she called him back and they had started to see each other. It was only as friends. That was all it could ever be now. It was something he regretted but could accept. The fact that she was back in his life was enough.

In her card she said that if he got as far as Fiji she might come and join him. It was a place she had always wanted to see. Though it had not been one of his intended destinations, he had gone out that morning and bought a guide book.

He checked his watch. The storage company would be arriving in half an hour so there was just enough time to do one final thing.

A notepad lay in front of him. Picking up his pen, he began to write.

Caroline sat in her garden with Helen, staring out at the river.

'It looks very high today,' Helen observed.

'Apparently they've had floods in Oakley. Fortunately, the banks here are high.' She sipped her tea. 'How is Nessa?'

Helen began to describe her daughter's latest temping job. Caroline looked at her roses, remembering the countless times

Susan Bishop had sat where Helen did now, complimenting her on the beauty of her garden. Susan Bishop. The woman to whom she had given her friendship and who had repaid her by sleeping with her husband and taking his life. The woman to whom, in a bizarre way, she owed a huge debt of thanks.

Once news of the arrest became public, Susan had become the new focus of media attention. Caroline's own alleged wrongdoings had suddenly seemed insignificant compared to the enormity of Susan's crime. In the build-up to the trial, as details of Susan's other affairs had emerged, leading to the break-up of at least one marriage, people in Fleckney could talk of little else. But once it was over and Susan had begun a life sentence it was as if she had never existed. At the parties Caroline still attended no one mentioned Susan any more, just as no one mentioned the damning comments about Caroline so many of them had given to the press. Life in the village went on as usual. People made polite small talk, attended each other's social functions and tried to act as if none of it had ever happened.

But it had. And things were very different now.

Caroline turned, shielding her eyes against the sun and looked up at the house. It was hers for life now, as was everything else Robert had owned. She was a wealthy woman, and as such her place in village life was always assured. At last she had the security she had spent so many nights longing for.

And yet she would willingly sacrifice it all for what she had lost along the way.

'Has Nessa seen Jimmy?' she asked.

Helen told her what she knew about both James and Stuart. She listened, soaking up the information like a sponge just as she had so many times over the last six months.

'Thank you,' she said eventually.

'You don't need to thank me.'

'Yes, I do. How else would I hear about them?'

'Give it time. Things can change.'

'You don't believe that any more than I do.'

Helen didn't answer. Caroline felt an ache in her heart as she remembered a time when she had taken having two sons for granted.

James's voice whispered in her head.

Your tragedy is that you could have had three.

They continued drinking tea, and talked of other things.

Stuart stood in the hallway of his flat, staring down at the handwritten letter that had just arrived.

Dear Stuart,

This is a letter I never thought I'd write. I'm sure it's one you never thought you'd receive. You can tear it up unread if you want. I wouldn't blame you. But I hope you don't.

It's funny. When I started this my purpose was to apologise for the things I said at the funeral. But already I realise that I want to apologise for so much more.

When Vanessa first told me about you she referred to us both as victims. But she was wrong. Victims suffer and you were the only one of us who did any of that. I never had to cope with the losses you did. I had a comfortable, privileged life and countless opportunities others could only dream of. Best of all I grew up with a twin brother whom I often wanted to throttle but who still meant more to me than anyone else. You were the one who was born James Randall but I was the one who stopped you living his life. I didn't do it deliberately but I did do it, and for that I am sincerely sorry.

I want to thank you for doing such a wonderful job of

being Stuart Godwin. I'm not sure I could have done so well and I know I could never have done better.

I hated you for coming between Tom and me but I don't any more. It's taken me all this time to realise that you were the one person in this world who loved him as much as I did.

Take care of yourself.

Jimmy

A lump came into his throat. He tried to swallow it down.

Jennifer appeared beside him, resting her head on his shoulder while reading the letter herself.

'Do you still hate him?' she asked when she had finished.

He didn't answer.

'Do you?'

'No.'

She took his free hand and kissed it. 'I'm glad.'

They remained like that for some time, his hand in hers and her head still resting upon his shoulder.

EPILOGUE

Devon, July 2018

Rampleton was a pretty town built around a central square. On this particular Saturday afternoon it was hosting a market and dozens of people wandered the rows of stalls, examining the items on sale and enjoying the summer sun.

'What do you think?' asked James, holding up a map of Europe just before the French Revolution.

Becky grimaced.

'I like it,' he told her. 'It'll look great in the living room.'

'I was thinking more of the toilet.'

'There won't be room. Your kabuki masks are going in there.'

She punched his arm. 'Where are you guys from?' the stall-holder asked.

'We're from Exeter,' James told him.

'So you're English? I just wondered. It's your accents ...'

'We've been living abroad,' Becky explained.

'Where?'

'We were in Japan for the last two years, teaching English as a foreign language. Before that ...'

481

As Becky gave the stallholder their itinerary James watched her, marvelling at how things had worked out.

She had joined him in Shanghai three months into his trip and long before he was scheduled to reach Fiji. 'I've always wanted to see China,' she had told him. 'Perhaps we could travel together, just for a week or two.'

But that had been four years ago.

They had returned to England in March and settled in Devon. Both were now working freelance: he for a succession of local solicitors while planning to retrain as a lecturer, she as an illustrator of children's books. They had bought a beautiful old cottage and used the second bedroom as a shared study. Only they wouldn't be able to do so for much longer. Not now she was ten weeks pregnant.

'Are you getting it?' she asked, gesturing to the print.

'Of course.'

'I despair of you.'

'Shut your face, Kabuki Queen.'

Laughing, she went to look at another stall. He paid for the print. 'You're a lucky man,' the stallholder told him.

He nodded, knowing it was true. His life was good. It was complete. There was nothing missing.

Except . . .

He still thought about Thomas constantly. It was rare that a day passed when he wouldn't feel a sudden impulse to phone his brother and share some funny incident, only to remember they would never share anything again. Over time the intense pain had eased but a profound sense of loss still remained.

'How long are you guys staying here?' the stallholder asked.

'We'll probably head home in about an hour.'

'If you decide to stay for the evening there's a good

restaurant just opened.' The stallholder searched through a pile of papers and handed James a flyer. 'The food is delicious and I'm not just saying that because the owners are friends of mine. There's one of them now actually.'

For the sake of politeness James looked.

And saw Stuart buying two ice cream cones from a stall at the end of the row, one of which he passed to a boy of about three who looked exactly like him and sat perched upon his shoulders.

Then they disappeared from view.

Without knowing why he was doing it, James hurried after them. In the background he could hear the stallholder calling but he just kept going.

He reached the end of the row and looked about him. The area was thick with people. For a moment he feared he had lost them. Then he saw them standing with Jennifer who was holding a buggy in which a red-haired girl of about two lay sleeping.

Quickly, he moved closer.

'Why did you have to get him that?' Jennifer was demanding. 'He won't eat his tea now.'

'It's only a cone.'

'Try telling my mother that when he won't touch her casserole.'

'What was I supposed to do? He kept asking for one.'

'You could try saying no. Honestly, Stu, you're such a pushover.'

The little boy started to laugh. Stuart did the same. Jennifer's face broke into a smile. 'I don't know which one of you is the bigger kid.'

James cleared his throat. They turned towards him. Stuart and Jennifer looked startled. The little boy smiled.

'Hi,' James said.

'Hi,' they replied.

He held up the flyer. 'I've been hearing great things about your restaurant.'

'Well, we haven't poisoned anyone yet,' Jennifer told him.

'Give it time,' Stuart added.

James laughed. It sounded forced. They did the same. It sounded forced too.

'What are you doing here?' Jennifer asked.

'We're shopping.'

'We?'

'Becky and me. She's my partner. We live in Exeter. You live here, don't you?'

Stuart nodded.

'My parents retired here two years ago,' Jennifer explained. 'We started coming for holidays and really liked it. There's so much space. It's great for the kids.'

The little boy was staring at him. 'Who are you?'

'My name is James. What's yours?'

'Tommy.'

'*Tommy?*'

'Yes.'

'Well, that's a good name. You ... well, you look like a Tommy.'

Jennifer pointed to the little girl in the pushchair. 'And this is Meghan.'

'She's asleep,' Tommy told him.

'Do you need to get her home?' James asked.

'She's fine,' said Jennifer quickly. 'Why? Do you need to go?'

He thought of Becky. 'Well, I probably should ...'

'Thanks for your letter,' said Stuart suddenly. 'It meant a

great deal to me. I wrote back but my letter was returned. On the envelope it said you'd moved.'

'I did. I went abroad.'

Silence. He told himself he should leave while realising he wanted to stay.

'I heard what you did to Adam,' Stuart continued. 'I'd wish I'd seen it.'

'So do I,' added Jennifer.

Stuart smiled at him. 'Thanks.'

'My pleasure,' he replied.

Then, suddenly, he started to laugh. Yet again Stuart and Jennifer followed suit.

Only this time it felt natural. Good, in fact.

Meghan woke up, saw Tommy's ice cream and screamed for one of her own. Stuart gave her the remains of his cone which she promptly dropped down her dress. Groaning, Jennifer pulled out a tissue and began to clean her up.

'The joys of parenthood,' Stuart said with a grin. 'Do yourself a favour and book your vasectomy today.'

'It's too late for that. Becky's due in seven months.'

Stuart looked delighted. 'What date? It's not too near Christmas, is it?'

'No, thank God. It's late January.'

Again Stuart grinned. 'Phew!'

'Tell me about it. I remember all the people who used to give Tom and me a combined birthday and Christmas present. They'd always say it was an extra-special gift but it never was.'

'They'd always try and make it look special by wrapping it in expensive paper but I was never fooled.'

'Neither were we. In fact they just went straight to the top of our hate list.'

'Mine too. By the time I was ten that list went on for ever.'

Again they both laughed.

Tommy tugged Stuart's ear. 'Daddy, when are we going?'

'Soon, kiddo,' Stuart told him.

'I mustn't keep you,' said James quickly. 'It's not fair on the kids.'

'But we'll see you tonight,' said Jennifer, pointing to the flyer.

'I don't know. We were going to head back soon . . .'

'You must come,' Stuart told him. 'Bring Becky. We'd love to meet her.'

'Yes, you must,' said Jennifer firmly. 'And just so you know, Tommy likes toy cars and Meghan likes anything cuddly that looks like a cat.'

Stuart looked embarrassed. 'Jen, he doesn't have to bring presents.'

'Yes, he does.' Jennifer turned to James. 'That's what uncles do, isn't it?'

He didn't answer. In his head was an image of a nine-year-old Thomas sitting in a rowboat on the river, laughing uproariously as a flock of swans attacked. For a moment he felt the familiar sense of loss.

Then suddenly it was gone, replaced by the sense of something precious having been found.

Ten minutes later Becky stood holding the print and apologising to the stall holder. 'I don't know where he's gone. I'm really sorry.'

'No need to apologise, love. He's already paid.'

She saw James approaching. She prepared to quiz him on his whereabouts. Then she just stared.

'What's happened to you?' she asked.

'What do you mean?'

'Your face. It's ... I don't know. Glowing.'

He didn't answer, just gazed at her, looking almost as happy as he had when she told him they were going to have a baby.

'Tell me!'

'You'll find out this evening,' he said and kissed her.

ACKNOWLEDGEMENTS

Firstly I would like to thank my mother, Mary Redmond, and my friends; Graham Watts, Paula Hardgrave, Gillian Sproul and Russell Vallance for reading this book as a work in progress and giving me their invaluable feedback.

Secondly I would like to thank my agent, Lisa Moylett, for her constant encouragement and support, as well as for all her tireless work on my behalf.

Thirdly I would like to thank my editor, Hannah Green, for making this final version of the book so much better than the one I first gave her.